Lost Children

Ophelia Finsen

The Yorkshire Saga
Hob Hurst's House
Hob Hurst's Daughter
Hob Hurst's Legacy

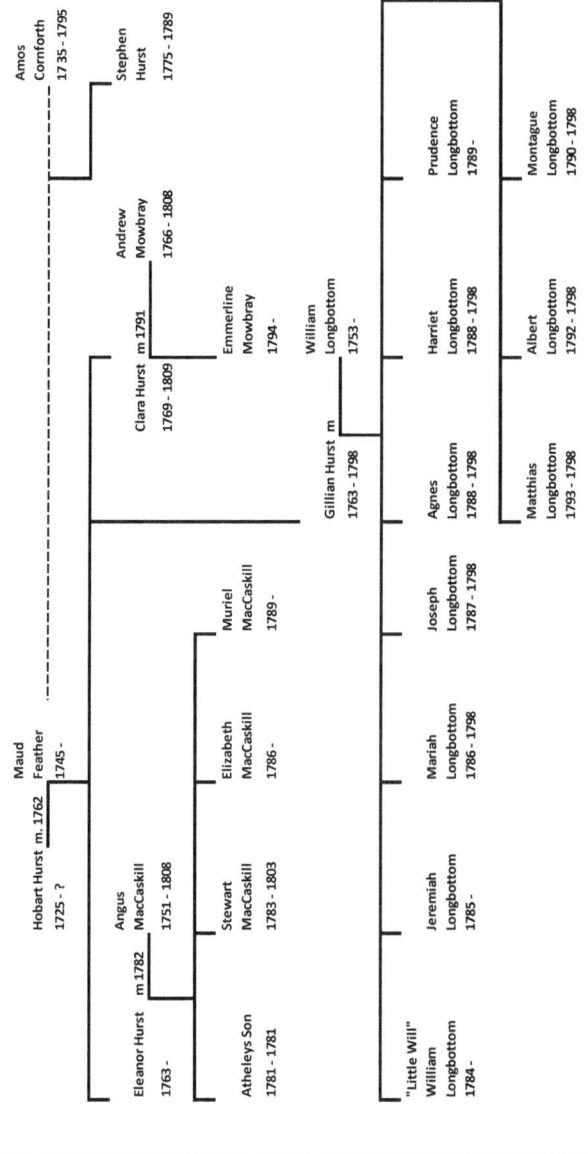

Amos
Comforth
1735 - 1795

Stephen
Hurst
1775 - 1789

Hobart Hurst m. 1762

Maud
Feather
1745 -

Andrew
Mowbray
1766 - 1808

Clara Hurst   m 1791
1769 - 1809

Emmerline
Mowbray
1794 -

William
Longbottom
1753 -

Eleanor Hurst   m 1782
1763 -

Angus
MacCaskill
1751 - 1808

Stewart
MacCaskill
1783 - 1803

Elizabeth
MacCaskill
1786 -

Muriel
MacCaskill
1789 -

Gillian Hurst   m
1763 - 1798

Atheleys Son
1781 - 1781

Prudence
Longbottom
1789 -

Montague
Longbottom
1790 - 1798

Harriet
Longbottom
1788 - 1798

Albert
Longbottom
1792 - 1798

Agnes
Longbottom
1788 - 1798

Matthias
Longbottom
1793 - 1798

Joseph
Longbottom
1787 - 1798

Mariah
Longbottom
1786 - 1798

Jeremiah
Longbottom
1785 -

"Little Will"
William
Longbottom
1784 -

1814

Prudence

Prudence Longbottom sat on her mother's grave and looked towards the coming evening. The sun was bright and unblemished. It would be a cold night. She ought to be getting back, for her Aunt would worry. She lingered regardless.

Prudence had taken to sitting here perhaps two months ago. Aunt Gilly thought it was strange considering Prudence had never been particularly close to her mother. She did not remember her that well, given how young she had been when her mother had passed. Reality and need did not always match where history was concerned. The intensities of a girl becoming a woman had glorified vague memories of a harassed, sad and waifish woman into a martyr who 'would have understood'. It was now ten years since the woman had died, and only now had Prudence's father and step mother agreed to a memorial stone.

People had said that it was a bigger, grander stone than the wife of a blacksmith warranted, and looked knowingly at one another. Prudence was too giddy from idolatry of a woman she barely remembered and never knew to question what the silence said. Aunt Gilly folded her arms and tutted, remembering with swifter scandal than at the time, of all the trouble that had surrounded Gillian Longbottom and her tragic brood of children.

Prudence pulled off her bonnet and lent back against the memorial stone. Her blonde hair was like a thick hatch of straw insulating her head, and she overheated easily. The headgear of the age was nothing but an irritation. She gazed across St Hilda's Churchyard and her eye settled on the small gravestone to the twins. Jemima and Mariah. Aunt Gilly said it had been asking for trouble, Will naming one of the girls after a dead young sister. She forgot that the twins had only been named after they had expired, but that didn't make for such a good story when she was in that mood. The one when she grumbled about dead and lost children, how it was a part of every woman's life. On some days she said women ought not to be so precious and accept the loss. That was when she was irritated by Magdalene. Other days she had endless empathy, for Gilly had lost four of her own children. She would say that no one knew the pain of life as a woman did. Prudence heard all these contradictions with a smile, but she knew better than to point out the truth to her aunt. As Gilly said, Prudence was still an unmarried maid and had no idea about a woman's real life.

For now at least.

Prudence shifted to look at the engraving on the memorial. "I will be married in a month, mother."

There was no response. She was sure her mother would be pleased. Her eyes wandered over the inscription, something she knew by heart. She was lucky she could read, for there were many girls her age who did not know their letters. Prudence, not married early in life, had time on her hands and had set to improving her mind so that she might be able to read. Might be able to write letters. Not that she had many people to write to. She had tried writing to her cousin Muriel, but the exchange had died out quickly. They had barely met with one another in person, and although they spoke the same language they seemed to live in different worlds. Muriel was baffled by tales of farming and housekeeping, just as Prudence did not understand when Muriel rattled on about the textbooks and lectures that filled her life. That was probably city living. Prudence had never been out of the Esk Valley and could hardly imagine the wider world.

Her eyes returned to the stone.

In Memorium of Gillian Longbottom,
relict of William Longbottom of Commondale.
Daughter of Hobart Hurst.
Born 1763. Passed out of this life in 1798.
Mother to William, Jeremiah and Prudence Longbottom.

Also in memory of her children: Mariah 1786 – 1798, Joseph 1787 – 1798, Agnes 1788 – 1798, Harriet 1788 – 1798, Montague, 1790 – 1798, Albert 1792 – 1798, Mattias 1793 – 1798.

The death toll was followed by some scripture Prudence's father had picked. Although Prudence had listened to the entire bible over the years, for her father was a devout Christian man, she did not worry too much about the details and let the words and sayings wash over her whilst her mind wandered. She knew she was a good person. She also knew she was no scholar.

She ran her fingers lightly over the list of dead siblings. She hardly remembered them. Just snippets of memories, with neither anchor of time nor moment before that bad winter when the fever had taken so many. It was no wonder her mother had lost heart and passed away only a few months later.

"I shall take my leave of you." Prudence abruptly stood up, begrudgingly taking the bonnet but neglecting to put it on. It was a warm late spring and her hair seemed to soak up the heat. "I will see you soon again, mother dearest."

With that, she was scampering with the joy of a nine-year-old, the age she had been when she had lost her mother, rushing across the graveyard with a quick wave to the poor dead twins, and out onto the dirt cart track across the undulations of land back to Ainthorpe. She danced her way through the early evening sunshine with the merry exuberance of a soul who rarely questioned and always presumed the best in folk. Wasn't it just grand to be alive? She headed up Longlands Lane, waving to labourers in the fields who were packing up from a day's work. One of the farmers was herding a small group of milk cows out to a different pasture. Prudence went past the parsonage, and further along the track before cutting off at Toad Beck to run across fields that made up part of her uncle's farm. Whooping as she disturbed a gathering of starlings that had been coursing through resting grassland, looking for bugs and worms. Through a copse of trees and up towards the hardened stone building of Strait Farm.

Aunt Gilly was standing outside, shaking a mat into the sunshine. "Neil!" she scolded the youth lounging on the stonewall edging the cottage garden. "Will you not go fetch your mother a pail of water as she asked?"

"That's women's work," he muttered as he picked at his nails. "I've had a hard day labouring. You should ask Prudence."

"Prudence isn't here just now."

"She ought to be."

"She is our guest come to stay."

"Aye, you say that now whilst you wish to vex me. Other times you say she should be earning her keep."

Prudence ducked back down into the copse of trees. She had said she would fetch the water when she'd set off wandering, but had grown distracted by the thought of the graveyard and telling her mother all about her fiancé. She found the pail where she had left it, hooked on a stunted tree branch, and hurried back down to the beck to fill the pail with water.

Neil spotted her first, and sat up on the wall, breaking out into a grin. "Your ears have been burning, eh?"

Gilly turned around. "Ah, Prudence, what a thoughtful girl you are. A pail of water. At least someone is prepared to help me."

Neil unrolled his lanky frame onto the ground, languidly sauntering down the slope to meet his cousin. "You've been a while fetching that water."

"Neil Beecroft, you ought to respect your elders," Prudence laughed. "I am almost ten years your senior."

"Aye, but a lass."

"Neil, do get out of the way whilst she's about her work."

"Working now!" Neil laughed.

Prudence passed Gilly the bucket. "I have been working most of the day. Cleaning, scrubbing, helping with the bread."

"Indeed she has. If Prudence has time, it is because she is so quick and efficient. It comes of working at Danby Grange, it does," Gilly continued as she carried the pail inside.

"At least you can say you were paid for your time then."

"You have your home and your keep here," Gilly reappeared out of the door. "And we pay you what we can."

Prudence set herself down on the little bench in the garden. Danby Grange felt like a lifetime ago, although in truth the employment had only ceased last year. She had been a maid in the house, a servant of many trades as she had shown aptitude and willingness to take on more work. Any type of work. She was incapable of saying no. Sometimes to her own detriment. Her mind wandered to the eldest son of the household and she scolded herself and blocked him from her thoughts. She had left on her own accord and with a glowing reference. Magdalene, Will's wife, had been in the second half of her pregnancy, and of such a size with it that she was struggling. Prudence had gone to her elder brother's little cottage to help until the baby was born and Magdalene was herself again. It had not happened quite so, for the baby turned into twins at the birth, then a day later the tiny girls expired. Prudence had stayed for a time, for at first Magdalene had been inconsolable. Then it had all become too much and she had come across the valley to stay with her aunt and uncle.

"Ah, here comes the top boy of the household," Neil burst out as he saw his elder brother, Kenneth, coming down the track to the farm. "You been reaping the harvest of your inheritance? Oh look now," he changed tactic when he saw what his brother was carrying. "That fresh honey comb there? Give us a bit."

"You leave that be," Gilly shrieked. "That's for sale; we'll be needing the money. Rent'll be due soon."

"Thought that was why we had taken on the honourable lodger."

Gilly swatted Neil with a cloth. "I have two sons to support here. Your father works this farm as best he can, but it is not big enough for the pair of you."

"Yes, yes, so you tell me every day," Neil muttered. As the second son it was expected he would leave and form his own life. Kenneth had everything ready for him without asking for it. Simply down to an accident of birth, the order of arrival. "I shall go in and rest my feet," he said, hunching his head down to get under the low door lintel.

"Will we be eating soon, Mother?" Kenneth asked.

"You ask me the same thing every day, and I tell you the same, when your father is in."

"Is Curnow back?" Prudence asked.

"I saw him sitting on hill yonder," Kenneth gestured behind him.

"That lodger of ours," Gilly muttered. "Still, his money has helped, I won't deny it and we won't have it for all that much longer. Prudence, go fetch him. We're all hungry and it is supper time."

Prudence hopped back to her feet. "We will be back anon."

"Anon," Gilly rolled her eyes. "What nonsense you all do speak."

"*Hy lodrow, hy lodrow o gwynn,*
Hy lodrow, hy lodrow o gwynn,
Hy lodrow o gwynn a-ugh hy dewlin,
Owth yskynna Bre Gammbronn war-nans."

"I can't say I understand it, but it does sound awfully beautiful. Might you teach it to me one day?"

The lean, muscular man perched on the brow of the hill stopped singing rather abruptly. He had only just realised he had an audience. The approach was coming, but he did not move to signal a welcome or even an acknowledgement of presence. He continued to gaze out to the skyline as if he could almost catch sight of his homeland, if only if it were not for the sunlight haze.

A little terrier sat obediently by his feet. The dog lacked the self control of the master and looked back to see Prudence come huffing up the incline with a silly smile on her face. The dog returned her joy with like and trotted down to her, wagging his tail. He was always sure of a fuss and some titbits from the kitchen when this woman was about.

"Ki," the man said, his voice low and steady but with a threat only audible to canines that he was to mind himself. The dog hurried back to his master.

"Ki was only saying hello," Prudence reached Curnow and set herself down on the grass beside him without invitation. "It does sound beautiful when you sing. Such strange words. Won't you teach me it?"

The man turned his head to regard her for the first time. Curnow Pengelly did not carry an excess of flesh, and had a much sculpted, angular face fitting to a well-formed skull. He might have been considered handsome if it weren't for the permanently low-browed scowl he wore. "It's the language of my land. You're not from there."

Prudence tittered. "I know that, Curnow. I'm just from up the moors. But it doesn't mean I can't be interested. Isn't it worth people being interested in? Why, people who have never been to France like to learn themselves some French."

Curnow merely sniffed.

"Well, can you tell me what it's all about?"

He was silent for a moment, giving the proposal some serious consideration. "It's called *Bre Gammbronn*," he said. "Camborne Hill."

"Those words were about a hill? Like I was just walking up now?"

"Those words were about white stockings."

Prudence burst into laughter. "Oh Curnow," she said, giving his shoulder a push. "You do say the funniest things."

"Woman, you talk rubbish," Curnow said very gravely. "What brings you here?"

"Supper's ready. Aunt sent me."

"Away then, let us be gone."

He was on his feet and walking back to the farm before he had finished speaking. Prudence scrambled around inelegantly and hurried after Curnow. Ki ran between the two in delight. They veered down a steep flank in the field and through a little gate onto a track that ran up towards Strait Farm. Prudence soon caught up with and fell in to step with Curnow. They were almost exactly the same height, something that irritated him, she knew, for he was a little short compared to the local men. She knew the local farm workers sometimes laughed about it over at the Fox and Hounds, about how they grew the men short down south. Sun was close to the earth, they said, folk didn't need to reach up very high. Prudence found it difficult to imagine Cornwall, what with it being so far away and her never having been outside of Eskdale. She'd asked Curnow about it, but he'd just given her one of his curt replies. Not that he was always so short on his words, indeed when the mood took him he could give very elegant monologues on his home country, and he had such a voice when he sang in his native tongue. Even when he spoke the English of Cornwall, it felt like a foreign language, and it took a little while to get one's ear in. Most of the time he spoke an odd accented version of the Yorkshire the locals spoke, and got by. Besides, he'd been here so long now that most folk just shrugged their shoulders and said that was just Curnow Pengally's way. *Nowt to get excited about,* as her uncle would grumble many a time.

Coming down the track in the opposite direction they met the local gamekeeper. It was the time of day when everyone was making their way home. In the crook of his arm there was a shotgun, and he carried a number of dead birds, tied together by their legs and hanging upside down like war trophies. As they neared, Prudence let out a little gasp as she saw the chestnut and black speckled plumage, and recognised the birds as kestrels. There was congealed blood on the feathers. Closed eyes, tiny black orbs that had once sparkled with life.

"Mr Hart."

"Mr Pengelly."

The two men greeted one another as the parties met in the track.

"Been doing some hunting," Curnow observed.

"Aye, these hawks are a pest on his lordship's hunting stock."

"Why, you must be wrong," Prudence blurted out even though she had not been greeted. His lordship's hunting stock was the birds bred for the local aristocracy to go out shooting. "Those are kestrels you have there, hover hawks. They only take things like little mice. They would never..."

"Miss Longbottom, are you trying to tell me about my business?" John Hart's face had turned an unpleasant ruddy colour.

"Only that you've made a mistake and shot some beautiful birds that had done nothing wrong."

Hart laughed coldly, without humour. "A maid telling a gamekeeper about his business, that'll be the day," he scoffed, giving Curnow a knowing look. "All birds are sport and as we find ourselves on his lordship's lands, which I am employed to care for, I would suppose I know best."

"But I've watched these birds on many an afternoon..."

"Sounds like you're in want of work," Hart interrupted her, unintentionally shaking the brace of dead birds at her in his irritation. "The sooner you're married with a house to mind and a little'un to watch the better, wouldn't you say, Mr Pengelly?"

"If it stops the prattle."

"Indeed, Mr Pengelly, indeed," Hart grinned in appreciation. "Good evening to you."

Prudence slapped Curnow's shoulder as Hart marched off down the track, whistling a victory tune to himself. "Ought you not to show some loyalty to me? It's not Mr Hart's roof you lodge under."

"Neither is it yours," Curnow pointed out. "And you do prattle. Let's away now. I've a hunger on me."

Prudence was upstairs brushing her hair when the bidder came to the cottage. She put her brush down on her lap and was still. Her aunt's voice was quite loud and came up through the floorboards.

"Why, Seth Knaggs what are doing turning up at this time of day? I hope you're not here in professional circumstances."

There was some mutterings, probably Seth fussing with his hat and making a long apology. Seth never did like to use one word where ten would fit. Prudence got down onto the floor and pressed her ear to a gap in the floorboards – it was a good thing they slept above the kitchen – so that she could hear what was being said.

"...and you know there is no time to be wasted, for there are people to be told. Old Abraham Pudsey has passed away..."

"Abraham Pudsey," Aunt Gilly interrupted.

"By..." her uncle drew breath.

"Died at the dinner table, just as you will. Face splashed the broth up and down. Tis a terrible tragedy."

A chair scraped across the floor and Aunt Gilly sat down. "I can't quite believe it. And so sudden like that. I wonder what the widow and the girl will do."

"I doubt they've had chance to think," Uncle Benjamin said.

"But why would you come here so soon?" Aunt Gilly asked, looking back to Seth Knaggs. "It is late in the day and we weren't kin. Surely we would be one of the last to be invited to the funeral. Heaven knows you can talk, and I can't imagine as bidder you've gotten around all the necessary already."

"No indeed, it has been said that I can talk when I wish. But the widow asked me to come here promptly, so that Mr Beecroft might be ready. Abraham kept bees, as well you know, and the hive is at the bottom of the garden. She wishes to be rid of it, and wanted you to take it. You must talk to the bees tomorrow at the funeral meal, then take the hive back home with you."

Aunt Gilly shook her head. "She moves fast."

"Bees must be told," Seth Knaggs said rather primly.

"Aye, they must," Benjamin sighed. "I'll see to it tomorrow. But he's to be buried tomorrow? You're to bid everyone for tomorrow?"

"He will be buried tomorrow afternoon at two. At St Hilda's. Then we are to return to the Pudsey cottage to take the food, and Mr Beecroft may talk to the bees."

"You'd best get on, if you're to tell everyone where they need to be for two, in time." Aunt Gilly said.

"Aye, I shall not linger this night."

"What are you spying on?"

Prudence yelped as Neil nipped her at the waist. In scrambling up she hit her knee on the side of the bed and doubled forward in pain as the thump vibrated through her knee cap at a particularly painful angle. She swung around and dropped into the narrow little bed in the corner. "What are you doing up here? You're sleeping down in the kitchen."

"Yes, since you got me kicked out."

"Stop your grumbling, it's only for a few more weeks. And the kitchen is ever so comfortable."

"I suppose." Neil slumped down on the floor. They were in the main bedroom, although that was a rather grand title given that the attic space of the cottage was one room. The 'main bedroom' was a small annex at one end separated off by a rough wood panel rather like what one would see in the stable stalls up at the properties of rich folks. The little side annex at the end was where the lodgers or any employed farm workers would sleep, the rest of the family either in the main section or down in the kitchen. Her aunt, uncle and Kenneth slept up here as well, with Neil relegated to maid's sleeping position for now. And it was as good, if not better than a lot of families round these parts had for living accommodation. Indeed, when Prudence had been living with her father and step mother, she had slept in a little bench in the kitchen, and at Danby Grange in servants' quarters in the attic. It all meant privacy was a treasured thing hard to come by, which was why Prudence was already early, in bed before anyone else would come up. When she had been working as a servant she was often last to bed, and an easy target for interception whilst on her way up through the quiet house. At the Grange it was a different world to the living circumstances of the people she considered her peers. Although her father had once mentioned her mother and the very well-to-do circumstances she had come from. Gillian had grown up with a proper bedroom, not just a partition in the attic with the good luck of being over the kitchen rather than the cow shed. An actual bedroom that she had shared with her twin sister. No setting off to work as a domestic as soon as she had reached womanhood. The children had even had a tutor for some time. Their father had been a rich merchant, although a rum sort, she occasionally heard from local gossip when the older folks had time to down tools and reminisce.

"It'll make a bit of a change."

Prudence glanced over at her cousin. "What will? Sleeping in the kitchen?"

"No, you daft ha-pence. Tomorrow, Pudsey's funeral. And the food after."

"You'll be helping to shift the bee hive."

"I expect Kenneth and father can manage it, after father's spoken to the bees. He's good with them, like."

Prudence couldn't remember her own mother's funeral, she reflected the following day as she watched the six white-gloved farmers carry Abraham Pudsey's coffin into the church. Had there been many people there? Had she cried? Had anyone cried? Had she even been there? Perhaps they had kept the children away. It was always hard to know how people would react. She'd been to a lot of funerary meals and a few services since, no one very close to her, but there was always some distant relative or old farmer up the valley who had passed on, and these things were always a chance for folk to get together afterwards and eat and talk.

It was sunny today, quite hot. Not a time to linger when one had a body that needed to go into the ground. They hadn't known the Pudseys all that well, but what with the bees, they had been invited. It was well known up and down the Esk valley that Benjamin Beecroft had a way with bees, and he always got the best honey out of a hive. There never seemed to be more hives than he could handle, and when folk needed to move on any, he was always the first port of call.

She watched as the people started into the church. Stark black sentinels in the bright summer's day, dwarfed by the ancient yew trees stood in permanent respect. Underneath their forms a scattering of headstones gathered, as if taking shelter from the elements. People waited about the trees and the jumble of headstones, keeping out of the way of the path to the church entrance.

Close to the door waited the widow with her only daughter – none of the other children had survived to adulthood. What would they be thinking now? The daughter looked as though she'd been slapped and hadn't quite woken up after the shock. Her mother carried herself in a stern manner. Resigned to the facts and what must be done. They'd probably have to move, Prudence reflected. They wouldn't be able to afford the rent, not with the master of the household gone. How much collapsed when one piece of the community was abruptly pulled out. One went on one's daily busy, assured of the steadfast nature of the ground under one's feet. That things cannot change. That we are safe from sadness, for the sad tales of folk songs are of history and we might live in better times now. Or at the very least oneself is immune from tragedy. Even having lost her mother, having watched Magdalene suffer with the death of her twins, Prudence still couldn't comprehend it all. It was almost as if being told a story, but something that did not really happen.

She followed the gathering into the church, walking just behind her Aunt and Uncle. Despite the summer heat the church was always cold inside, constructed of thick grey stone, heavy and with a sense of age. One was aware the building materials were older than the very ground. Inside the church was simple with hard, uncomfortable wooden pews, whitewashed walls and modest windows. An organ sat up on a balcony ahead, overseeing every congregation. Down through the rows of pews stone columns burst up, connected by their own masonry arches, but above this the grandeur switched to wooden rafters. This was a moorland country church, no great cathedral of the nation.

Prudence let her mind wander during the service. She knew of respect to the dead as much as the next woman, but she had hardly known the man, and was only here because she happened to be staying with the Beecrofts. Not that Danby Grange, where she had worked, or indeed Commondale where she grew up, were that far away, but in the indulgences of childhood or the long hard repetitive graft of service, there hadn't been time to become too acquainted with the gossip of characters up and down the Esk Valley. A woman got into all that when she was married and gained a foot in her community, buying and selling, running the house, talking to neighbours and minding her children. Scrubbing other people's grates morning noon and night didn't bring about a lot of company.

She felt a little lost after the funeral when the congregation had returned to the Pudsey's farm. The mourning food was to be shared as quickly and widely as the burning local gossip and current range of rumours. There were so many people wishing to pay their respects to the widow and daughter, and more importantly to reminisce on times past and gossip over times today, that had it been winter the good people of Eskdale would have been forced to attend in shifts. With it being summer a great many were able to sit outside and drink their mourning ale in the sunshine.

Prudence had helped her Aunt put a plate of food together, including the funeral biscuits which the human guests would have to wait for until the end to take with their wine. This plate was not meant for human consumption, and her uncle had quietly taken it and gone to the back garden. Pudsey's beehive, a woven thing of willow and straw, stood in the far corner. Her Uncle Benjamin needed to speak to the bees to let them know that their master was dead, and that if they'd allow he would be the new master. A little of everything from the table had been brought for them and he hoped they'd be content with these arrangements. Prudence strained forward a little so that she could see her uncle through the small window. He had his back to the farmhouse, and with all the chatter and clatter of plates, flagons and tableware it was impossible to know if he was speaking just now. Her uncle never had any trouble with bees, and after the correct length of time, Kenneth would help him load the hive onto the cart and they'd take it away. Probably not straight home, what with the time of year he'd want them away to the higher ground where the moorland stretched. Heather honey was especially delicious and sought after.

Loud laughter brought her attention back into the interior as someone was telling a tale of a cow long-since dead. Across the room she saw her brother, Jeremiah with his wife Christina over from Egton where he worked as a carpenter. The old woman Lythe was with them. Her husband, who had apprenticed Jeremiah, had passed on last winter, but Jeremiah and Christina kept her like a trusted old pet. She didn't walk too well, a hobble not just of age but also of some accident of youth that had severely maimed her ankle. From what Jeremiah said, the old woman still continued to help in the household, making bread and pies, albeit sitting down for the kneading most of the time these days. She was a substitute grandmother, Prudence supposed, for the Longbottom's maternal grandmother was away in West Yorkshire and their paternal one had died a few years ago. The help would be especially welcome now, for Christina was showing in her pregnancy, and in the new year when the baby came they would really feel the benefit of the old woman's help.

Prudence hoped it would go better than Magdalene's first birth. The birth itself had not been problematic, all told, but the twin girls had not survived long.

"That one's got a cheerier countenance of course."

She glanced round to see a couple of old women by the fire – despite the summer warmth some still flocked to the flames. They were nodding in that puritanical way of older women who had seen it all and suffered twice as much as the young folk of today. They were looking in Christina Longbottom's direction. "She was an Applecross before she married, and they've always been good hardy stock."

"Not like that other one, a Dixon wasn't she?"

"Of Glaisdale?"

"I believe so, but I'm not acquainted with the family."

"They say she won't let her husband near her now. Won't go through it again."

One of the women sniffed in scorn. "Best thing is to get back on the horse. I've seen her walking about. You'd think she was the first woman who had lost a child. We've all lost them."

"Aye, and it was her first."

"And twins at that."

"Bound to die early on. Wouldn't have known what to do with them."

Prudence had to slip away between groups of people. The old women were talking about Magdalene, but they couldn't have known the family that well for Prudence did not even recognise their faces. She had sobbed with her sister-in-law when those sweet little girls had expired, and it was a night she was cursed never to forget. She couldn't understand how so many batted the notion out of concern as though it was just one of those things that happened.

"The youngest is due to be married soon..." Prudence heard in the distance.

"That one looks like a stable horse; she'll manage all right."

The brightness of the full sun hit her and made her slow in speed as she tumbled out of the farmhouse. She could not listen to anymore of old women's gossip. So she was a stable horse now? Dumb, bulky and reliable. Compliant. How people sat and passed judgement without knowing a thing. They'd have seen her in passing, walking along the lane at some point, and that would have been enough for them to feel they knew everything worth knowing about her. As if she didn't have a thought in her head, or certainly not one worth knowing.

"Prudence." A bony hand grasped her forearm and held on tightly. "I've been looking for you." Magdalene Longbottom appeared in her periphery before filling her vision and drawing her away from leaving the farm property. Magdalene had lost a lot of weight these past couple of months and had become gaunt. Her face looked worse for the shadows her dark bonnet cast about the contours of her face, and had her head been free, the new strands of white would have shown starkly against the natural dark chestnut of her girlhood. "You've not got anything special planned for tomorrow, have you?"

"Well, I..."

"For I have been thinking, you're not ready for your wedding yet. There's so much yet to put together that you'll need."

"Don't worry, sister," Prudence assured her. "My aunt is helping me with that."

"But you'll not have gloves I wager," Magdalene continued. "You'll need a good pair of gloves. I want you to come to a good glover I know, in Glaisdale. We'll walk there tomorrow."

"It's always pleasant walking along the river at this time of year. I'll have to check that my aunt does not need me..."

"I'll call for you tomorrow, early," Magdalene said, not really listening to Prudence. "I must away now."

As Magdalene swept away, a flurry of grief and projects, the little cart and carthorse, led by Kenneth, appeared from the side of the house. The hive was in the back, her Uncle walking behind and watching it like a precious new baby.

Prudence hurried across to them as they started up the track out of the farmstead. "I might walk with you a little."

Her uncle heard her but did not look around for he did not dare to take his eyes from the closed hive. "You don't care to stay for the wine and biscuits?"

"No. I don't know the family particularly and I feel a little not myself." Prudence admitted, falling in to step with him. "People do say some awful things at funerals."

"Not about old Pudsey, surely?"

"No, not that. About other folk, still alive."

Her uncle smiled wryly. "Gossip's like blood to some, keeps them going. Learn not to mind it."

"I learnt that a long time ago. There was a time people were always trying to tell me something about my mother. Some of it sounded quite horrid, so I wouldn't listen."

Benjamin Beecroft dared to look away from the hive to examine his niece in profile for a moment or two. He was never sure how much Prudence really knew about her mother or her passing. Not that anyone really knew, what with rumours and mutterings, knowing glances as if one were supposed to know it all. But he hoped that she could block her mind to it. She needed to look forward, live her own life and start her own family. The two boys who had survived the fever were certainly trying, and although William was successful in his business of blacksmithing, his family life had already faltered with the deaths of his first daughters.

"That's the best thing, pay it no heed," he agreed on the subject of gossip in a general sense. "You know yourself what's what and how it is. That's all a woman need worry herself about. You've bigger things to think on. Not long before you're married."

"No, I suppose not," Prudence sighed wistfully. "It will be upon us before we know where we are."

Aunt Gilly pressed her lips together as Magdalene Longbottom's attention shifted to the open door and away from the farmer's wife. Gilly could not make up her mind about this young woman. She'd heard all the stories: how she was ruined by the grief, distraught after the death of her baby twin girls. It was so widely spoken of as to be accepted as fact that the woman had screamed for the first week after their death. The continuous death knell of a banshee. After that she hadn't spoken for a month for her voice was burnt by grief. They said she did not even speak to her husband, let alone allow him into her bed, for her heart would not permit the possibility of going through that trauma again. Indeed, to look at her, one might think she was starving or a poverty-stricken gin woman, for she was so skinny as to be skeletal. Yet this morning, in the sunshine, she looked positively excited about setting off on a jaunt with Prudence. Time enough had passed since the death of newborns for the black dress to disappear, yet here was Magdalene draped in her old dyed dress – mourning rules were all well and good, but most folk couldn't afford a new wardrobe every time someone died. A bottle of black dye and an old dress had to suffice for many round here. Gilly guessed that Magdalene was starting to wind things down, for she had a purple sash tied around her high waist, as if she was going to fade into the next colours for the final stage of mourning. What Gilly didn't know is that the seam and fabric had ripped, and in her hurry, Magdalene had decided a tied sash, tacked under the bust to be sure it wouldn't slip, was a quick fix to her problems. Eventually the black would go when the dress finally fell to bits, but she had no intention of being anything but a grieving mother.

"And what time will you be back?" Gilly asked as Prudence came traipsing down the stairs, one unlady-like thud after another, a patter of excited running. The two women were practically giddy. "I'll be making supper for you?"

"Oh no, there's no need," Magdalene answered on behalf of her young sister-in-law. "Egton is not far from Glaisdale, so I thought after we had been to the glover, we would go and see Jeremiah and Christina, and stay overnight. It will be nice for Prudence to spend some time with her brother before her marriage. She'll not have much time when she's setting up house across the way in Danby."

"She should go spend some time with William, then," Gilly muttered, but Magdalene had already turned her back and was stepping out onto the road.

"Goodbye, Aunt," Prudence said breathlessly, clutching her basket in one hand and her bonnet in the other. "I am quite looking forward to this. I haven't taken a good walk in ever so long."

"Oh Aye?" Gilly raised an eyebrow as the two women set off up the hill towards the village. "You've been managing to get yourself over to St Hilda's most days. That's hardly a tumble down to the bottom of the yard."

Prudence didn't hear her, although if she had, she would have been quite sure her mother would not have minded her skipping a couple of visits to the graveyard. She would have been pleased that the surviving siblings still spoke and visited one another. It would have made her proud to see them moving on with their lives and looking forward. William and Magdalene were not in a happy place now, but it had not yet been a year, and Prudence in her simple good faith of mankind, was sure that they would make their peace with the tragedy and there would be more children.

Neither woman thought of children today. They were as two giddy young maids, walking brusquely and chattering. Young maids in behaviour, but hardly against what local statistics considered youthful and virginal for women, what with Prudence at twenty-five and Magdalene already in her early thirties.

Even children only just mastering walking and laughing at the very sunlight shimmering on the stream of water coming from the pail couldn't match their elation. Prudence was excited about ordering gloves and then seeing her brother. Magdalene was happy to be returning to her home village of Glaisdale and to show off its features to her sister-in-law. And even if there hadn't been that attraction, a couple of days away from the marital home felt like a religious experience of ecstatic wonder.

They skirted around the green in the village of Ainthorpe, then headed down hill towards the River Esk. Up in the hills the river was a relatively narrow and none too deep rushing highland stream that worked its way down the steep-sided moorland valley, broadening and twisting its cutting deep path through the upper lands of Yorkshire before bursting forth at the cliffs and jumbled streets of Whitby and the sea. In the summer when the ground was not too boggy and waterlogged it was a pleasure to follow the tracks and paths along by the river, moving through villages, woodland and farmland.

Leaving Ainthorpe the two women walked through the countryside, through the stone-housed Lealholm and onwards to Glaisdale. The river ran with an unseen speed, despite its size, and supported a number of mills along the way. On the woodland approach to Glaisdale, they passed by two corn mills, before turning away from the water and puffing their way up the steep hillside to the village.

"Stephen Tyreman is his name," Magdalene spoke as she led the way to the glover's cottage. "He makes such fine gloves, and charges very reasonable. Well, he cannot go overboard, working out here, but he still has his reputation to build up. He is only about your age, Prudence."

A young woman with a giggling baby, three or four months old, appeared out of the door.

"Why, Magdalene Longbottom," she greeted the woman. "It's been a time seen we've seen you about here. And look at the changes, isn't my little Mary Ann a treasure. Just look at those chubby cheeks."

The baby was thrust at Magdalene, a glowing, smiling warm bundle of health. Not a baby to wither and die, indeed for this beginning of a women would last into her eightieth year. It was a sadness that the local wise woman had foretold no one that the mother, Mary, would only have another four years or so before her own early death.

Magdalene's giddy confidence faltered as she found her hands taking the sturdy weight of a healthy, happy baby. She felt something catch in her throat, and wasn't sure if she was to throw the babe to the ground, run away with it, or merely break down.

Mary Tyreman's colour dropped as she remembered that Magdalene was grieving for her dead babies. She'd heard that the woman had been quite destroyed. A primeval panic swelled up, somehow sensing that those were not safe arms for her child, but her manners held her nerves awkwardly at the starting line. Prudence solved her dilemma by tactfully taking the baby from Magdalene to take a turn to coo at the little chubby face.

"Your husband is in?" Magdalene asked.

"Yes, of course, he's in his workshop."

"How marvellous."

"You'll not get better gloves this side of Whitby. You'll excuse me, I was just on my way out with little Mary Ann." She took the baby back from Prudence, the fist around her heart lightening as she had her daughter back and no disaster had occurred.

"Yes, of course."

Stephen Tyreman looked like a tired man who could never get his eyes to focus enough, but then he would have to sew awfully neat and small, Prudence thought, to get the gloves set just so that the seam wouldn't be felt in the curl of a finger in the joint between each digit. He was quite happy for another customer, and certain he could have the gloves ready before the wedding. Prudence's hands, rough and used to work, were measured, and Stephen wondered at these farm girls with their men's' hands and broad knuckles.

With colours and fabrics selected the women were back out into the sunshine and through the village. Magdalene pointed out almost every house and accounted for Prudence a potted history of each resident, her girlhood memories and joy of the village. The two women meandered down to the river. The broadleaf woodland, with dappled summer light breaking through to the ground here and there, loomed overhead. Lush foliage and undergrowth swamped the land that was free of farming. Countless butterflies, bees and other insects swarmed over the blossoms closer to the river where the land opened up to sunlight. The buzzing flurry of activity made the very air hum. There was a narrow, high-arched stone pack horse bridge at this point on the river. Prudence walked brusquely up one side of the bridge, pulling her bonnet off as she went, to then stop at the peak of the crossing and gaze downstream.

"Prudence Longbottom, you look positively scandalous without a head covering!" Magdalene laughed.

Prudence glanced back. It had been a while since she had heard her sister-in-law really laugh. "I am positively overheating, that's what I can tell you." She said as her arms slumped to her side. Why had God blessed her with such a dense thatch of hair on her scalp? In winter it was a blessing but it summer it could be torture.

"You ought to at least pin it back better. That way it wouldn't be on the back of your neck."

"That's true." Prudence agreed, as though she had prepared her hair so loosely on purpose. Her hair would never yield to brushes and pins and Prudence didn't have a lot of patience for fussing about with it. Men were lucky they could just keep their hair cropped.

"Let me sort this out." Magdalene stood behind her and started to pull some pins out and pull tightly on the hair as if it were a bell rope. She'd get it all up out of the way.

Prudence ran a hand along the rough stone wall on the side of the bridge. "I've heard this one called Beggars' Bridge. This where you come for poor relief in Glaisdale?"

"Hardly," Magdalene muttered through a mouthful of pins. She was silent for a moment as she finished with Prudence's hair. "But I have to say; even here I've noticed more beggars passing through this year. Either heading down to Hull or heading north for the mines and work. There's the alum mining roundabout, but there's enough local folk needing the work."

"Aunt Gilly always grumbles about it. There barely being enough to cover all the rents."

"Aye, well," Magdalene sighed and started down into the water. "You know there's a story about this bridge."

"About the beggar who built it?"

"Well, I suppose but he wasn't a beggar. At least not at the end when he built it. It was a couple of hundred years ago. I remember my mother telling me the story. It was before there was a bridge here. A lad called Thomas Ferries had a sweetheart, and they lived on either side of the valley. When he wanted to go see her, he would wade across the river and run up the hill. Well, you know yourself at these times the Esk isn't all that deep. Anyway, Thomas was poor and the lass's family were well off, so they weren't best pleased about the two being in love. Thomas decided he would take to the seas and seek his fortune. The night before he was to go, he went to see the girl, but there'd been flooding and he couldn't get across the river. He swore if he ever got back, he would build a bridge here so that no lovers would be kept apart again."

Prudence clapped her hands together. "How romantic. And he returned a rich man and built the bridge?"

Magdalene rolled her eyes. "Yes, it all ended happily, and he married his lady love."

"It's how it should be with marriage. There are so many sad stories in the past. But we won't make the same mistakes..."

"Oh Prudence, how naive you sound."

Prudence gave her a silly grin. "I believe in true love."

"Really?"

Magdalene regarded the woman quizzically. "I still can't quite believe that you're to be married soon. Or rather not that you are to be married, but that you will be marrying Curnow Pengelly. I hope you don't think I'm speaking out of turn, but the man is so severe and so much older than you. I really don't understand why."

Prudence was blind to Magdalene's obvious worry. "Oh, he does make me laugh."

"Laugh? I've never met anyone so humourless."

"He is funny with it. And he sings such beautiful songs."

It was not the first time that Magdalene worried for Prudence's girl-like naiveté, and wondered that she was so trusting and simple in the face of the world. One could not even blame it on an easy and spoilt life, for she had lost her mother at a young age, and had already worked in service. She had first hand experience of hard work and the cruel way of nature and life. Yet she greeted every day as if skipping into another childhood fairytale, meeting folk with a ridiculous trust in their honesty and goodness. The comprehension of bad folk didn't seem to exist in Prudence's sphere of understanding.

"That strange nonsense he sings."

"It's Cornish. It's so wild and beautiful."

"Meaningless up here. I've heard the men talk that he turns to it when he's had a few at the Fox and Hounds. I suppose there's no harm to it although there's no beggar nor bugger that understands him, as my father would say."

Prudence tittered at the expression.

If the riddle of why on earth Prudence would be drawn to a man like Curnow Pengelly was impossible enough, an even greater mystery was why someone like Curnow would wish to marry someone like Prudence. Magdalene had come to the conclusion it was a way of getting a cheap housekeeper and respectability. Everyone knew Curnow had saved up his money, bought his joinery tools and had a lease on a property over at Danby where he would start the carpentry business. From what she had picked up from local gossip, Curnow had found himself on the north east coast of England, far from home after a storm had wrecked the ship on which he worked as ship's carpenter. A lot of the crew had drowned, but he was one of the few who had been rescued. When the storm had abated, they had managed to salvage some of the cargo, along with Curnow's tools. The other men had eventually made their way back to Cornwall, but at that point due to circumstances she hadn't really grasped, Curnow had lost all of his tools and money, and there had been some upset in Whitby. He'd left and worked his way up the Esk valley, labouring on the land often as a daytal man and lodging wherever he could. Whatever had happened, he had decided to better himself, save money so that he might get back to his trade. Yet there was no inclination to get back to his homeland where folk might understand what he was warbling about, and instead he seemed inclined to remain in Yorkshire. Magdalene wondered what there was back in Cornwall that kept him away. Whilst she had still been talking to her husband, before the twins had been born and died, she had discussed this at length with William, who had told her pregnancy addled her brain and she was looking for stories where none existed. Curnow was a humourless and hardworking, dull sort of a man who had taken a little too keenly to the drink in Whitby after the shipwreck, but was bettering himself afterwards. There was no drama. Although even William had been at a loss to attempt to explain what had brought Curnow and his little sister together.

Magdalene felt unease that Prudence was making a mistake. But it was enough to struggle under one's own woes through this life; one couldn't worry too far on another's behalf. People had to make their own mistakes. Pushed away from a false path without the understanding experience gave, they would only fight to return. "Come along," Magdalene sighed. "Let's get moving. We want to arrive in good time for supper."

They did not cross the river, instead walking along the southern side, following meandering, never-settling tracks through woodland. Sometimes the paths were rutted, dried dirt, at other times there were pannier ways, laid out with stone stabs, now with middle grooves created by hundreds of feet walking the way for years long since past counting. As they reached a height in the woods of Arncliffe, the river below in the valley just a distant glimpsed glitter now and then, Magdalene pointed out a large, cracked boulder with a yew tree growing out of the top.

"That's the wishing stone of Glaisdale."

"It's a big thing for a stone," Prudence mused, approaching the rock and placing her hands upon the cool surface. She gazed up at the yew tree, with its dense foliage of small needles, and twisted chestnut bark. These were trees that felt older than time. Protection against evil.

"They say if you run around it nine times you can make a wish."

"And will it come true?" she asked, looking back at her sister-in-law.

Magdalene merely shrugged and looked sadly away, as if it were only a nuance of childhood foolishness. Prudence wondered what Magdalene had wished for around this rock, what she might wish for now. Folk stories were good and well, but even wishes couldn't pull back time and make things be that were never meant to be so.

"We should get going," Magdalene spoke quietly.

Prudence felt suddenly impulsive. "I'll just run round," she said, bursting with energy as she bounded off the woodland track and pushed her way through the undergrowth to round the boulder. As the circuits increased, so her legs felt a little unsteady, and her breathing quickened. She held out her right hand to brush against the rough surface of the rock to steady her, fingertips moved over summer-dried mosses and crusted lichens as she went. She felt Magdalene's waiting, watching impatience, but as she counted past seven she could not stop the charade and felt that she must complete it or else bad luck would fall to her. As she finished her ninth lap, she stumbled to the end and the beginning, leaning against the boulder and pressing her forehead to the stone as she caught her breath. She had earned a wish by right now. She closed her eyes and saw Magdalene's troubled face. I wish for children, she thought, thinking of her own future situation. And please let at least one of them survive.

The track joined a better road on the approach to the village of Egton Bridge in the low undulations around the river. The women wandered past the Horseshoe Inn, then across the bridge to the north side of the valley and the start of a steep climb up to Egton at the top. Prudence puffed her way up, thinking she was sure this incline grew steeper every time she walked it. It was not as though she was unaccustomed to walking every day, and she'd been raised around hills, but this was quite ridiculous. She would not care to live here in deepest midwinter when ice would coat these slopes. Getting down may well be easy enough, albeit dangerous, but getting to the top would be impossible.

Christina Longbottom was brushing sawdust and curls of planed wood out of the doorway when Magdalene and Prudence arrived. She waved to them before breaking out into an excitable grin. "How marvellous you have come to pay us a visit. I don't feel like many folk come this way unless they are customers. And soon enough you'll be busy with your own home to manage, and you'll have forgotten all about your dear old sister-in-law, growing fatter by the day."

"Don't talk all daft," Prudence giggled, giving the woman a hug.

Magdalene loitered awkwardly at the side, feeling a little nauseous from the sun and the climb, and truth be told the sight of Christina's belly. She still had a few months to go, at least if her own reckonings were to be believed but she already looked larger than one might expect. Perhaps she was having twins. Magdalene felt her stomach knot. Christina still carried life and potential. She was just the failed after-image. Hollowed out by death. She thought of those tiny hands curling around her little finger and felt her knees buckle. She could force herself through conversation and the day at times now, but when the wilderness of grief swept back around her, she was lost.

"I shall go sit out in the garden for some quiet," She told Christina without bothering to wait for an invitation to be issued. "I fear the swift climb has unsettled me somewhat."

"Yes, of course," Christina started, turning as if to speak to Magdalene, but already the older woman was gone. "Ellen's out the back tending her gooseberries. And you know the way... quite obviously," she added under her breath.

Prudence held Christina's hands. "She still suffers, you know."

"Oh don't we know it; her husband more than any." Christina broke into a wide grin. "But we shall not let it spoil our fun. Come in and say hello to Jeremiah."

Jeremiah set his mallet down as the woman entered the workshop. There was a delicious smell of freshly cut wood in the room, background notes of bread and something cooking on the range. The ground floor consisted entirely of the workshop at the front, the kitchen to the rear, and a little garden area outside. A patch of land dedicated to the local village obsession with gooseberries. Upstairs were their living quarters. The entirety, with their two apprentices and housekeeper Ellen Lythe, made for compact living, but the property was a good one, warm and clean and a good thing to have inherited from the previous carpenter, Caleb Lythe.

"Pru, it is good to see you. Getting your last preparations ready?"

"Yes. We went to Glaisdale to order gloves today."

"Everything ready for the wedding," Christina gushed. "And Jem's almost finished your present!"

"Christina, do keep your tongue. It's meant to be a surprise."

"Of course," Christina tittered. "I am such a scatterbrain these days."

Magdalene gave a little shudder at Christina's inane laughter, shrilling its way out of the open back door and into the garden. She sat down on a little stool and leaned against the wall, closing her eyes. She had thought this a good idea to get away from Commondale, her husband and her neighbours, the setting where what ought to have been didn't work out. Just to take herself out of that scenery, and to be somewhere else, talk to other people. Yet life bloomed in other places, and she sunk back into sorrow, thinking that still she would prefer to be alone. She slumped against the wall and regarded her slack belly formed under the long skirts of her mourning dress and the horizontal creases of the lavender sash. All this fabric to conceal and hold it all in.

"Mrs Longbottom, I didn't hear you come out." Ellen Lythe, widow of Caleb, came clumping down between her rows of gooseberry bushes, a trug hooked in the crook of one arm, the other hand gripping a well-smoothed knobbled old walking stick. It thumped along as a third leg. As the years went by, the stick and her leg seemed to resemble each other more and more in lack of flexibility and general unattractiveness. Ellen had damaged her ankle a lot of years ago, and age and cold winters had crept in along lines of damaged bone healed awkwardly, scar tissue on sinew and weaknesses of aging flesh. The entire ankle had inflamed and swelled, and eventually lost all mobility. Ellen didn't care to go down the hill to Egton these days, for any steep slope made for awkward passage and left her traversing it sideways. Village children thought her very funny. She told Jeremiah he ought to fashion her a set of wheels on the lathe that they might strap onto her shoes, then she could just roll down the hill. Christina had been horrified, as if Jeremiah and Ellen had not spoken in jest, and told Ellen it was impossible for there would be no way of breaking. She would be killed. As if death was a worry, Ellen had scoffed, with her white hair and wrinkled face. Besides, the river would catch her, and that would save her a bath as well, wouldn't it?

"Are you still worrying over those gooseberries?" Magdalene sighed.

"Whilst there's strength in me to get out of my bed."

"And is that satisfaction enough in the face of what you have lost?"

Ellen raised her eyebrows. Magdalene had sounded rather bitter.

Magdalene looked at Ellen for the first time. "Tending your dead husband's fruit garden."

"It was our garden, not his, and I was always the better of the two of us. I could really get a gooseberry. I tell you, I remember the best one. It was so good I had it packed it a box and I had to ride over here directly to show him, Caleb I mean. Mind, this was before we were wed and I was living over at Commondale. I got our Eleanor to drive us across in the cart. Caleb could not believe his eyes."

Magdalene grimaced. "So I've heard." She'd lost count of how many times she'd heard this story.

"Of course, when he first died, I didn't look to the fruit. I didn't do anything. I say a body needs time to acknowledge the dead before it can get on with living." Ellen's eyes twinkled through the sags of creased skin, folded and crumpled through age, hard work and summer-squinting. "But things keep moving on. And next we have a wedding to look forward to. I hear it's a Curnow Pengelly she's to marry? I've not come across him. What kind of a man is he?"

Magdalene shrugged almost capitulating to the inevitable. "At least ten years older than her. Humourless. Short."

"Sounds delightful when you tell it so. Is he right for her?"

"I don't think so, but I'm hardly an authority." She caught Ellen's eye. It might be odd that Ellen was taking such an interest, but then Magdalene remembered that before she had married the old carpenter, she had worked as a housekeeper on the farm where Prudence's mother had grown up. Perhaps she viewed herself as a kind of surrogate grandmother. "Prudence says he makes her laugh. I don't understand it."

"Aye, well, Prudence has a simpler way of looking at things. And what is she to him?"

"That I couldn't say. Not that I've asked, and I doubt Curnow would confide in me."

"Well, all sorts of people enter into all sorts of marriages and make a go of it. All will surely be well."

No life nor marriage was constant smooth sailing without trouble or sadness, but on the day itself spirits were high and the future did look promising. Ellen Lythe had come across in a wagon from Egton. The wedding was to be held at St Hilda's. It was a fine church, oddly positioned a distance outside of the village of Ainthorpe and nestled at a corner edge where the hills loomed up out of the earth like a curving protective arm. They had arrived before the ceremony started, and Jeremiah had helped Ellen down before passing her the walking stick.

Ellen had cried out when she'd seen Prudence's Aunt, Eleanor MacCaskill. The two women had hurried to one another to embrace. Eleanor had been Gillian's twin, so Prudence supposed that was what her mother had looked like. Although Eleanor seemed too healthy and well dressed to be a credible future projection of what Gillian might have been. Not that she was ostentatious or showy in her wealth, but she and her daughter Muriel were most certainly the best dressed people at the gathering, and some of the few who weren't directly connected in agriculture. They lived in West Yorkshire these days and Eleanor, a widow, made her money from trading – Prudence didn't claim to understand. After the ceremony and festivities she'd had chance to speak a little to her cousin, Muriel who had told her she'd started an apprenticeship with a jewellers and was working on mourning jewellery.

"Not a suitable gift for a bride," Eleanor had smiled wryly. "However, I have brought you this for luck in your marriage."

Prudence might have been expecting linens or home wares, or some item that would help set up life in the new marital home. Instead Eleanor presented her with a beautiful pendant amber necklace, the sort that Prudence would never have occasion for wearing. It had its own little velvet bag to keep it in, although Eleanor said it should be worn, for the heat of the skin would make the amber glow. As Prudence had replaced it into the bag, Eleanor had clutched her hand around the gift and Prudence's own youthful fingers. Sadness and hardship seemed impossible on this day, when all were so happy and youthful bliss glowed from their very flesh. Prudence was illuminated by the early autumn sunlight brightening her hair, giving her face a warm flush of health. She could have been ten years younger, a young maid starting out on life. At an age when one could not comprehend the enormity of life, of all the potential ahead, but also the failures, the tragedies and sadness that would be jumbled in with the good moments. Every generation thought things would be better on this attempt and it would all be well.

"Understand that we are only women," Eleanor had said quietly. "When we are married we own nothing and are at our husband's liberty. A woman's jewellery is her wealth and her insurance. It always goes with the woman. If you ever find yourself in dire circumstance, it can be sold."

Prudence was a little bemused, but had smiled politely at her Aunt and thanked her for the gift. Her Aunt was an oddity as much as her cousin Muriel. She lingered in the background, not really belonging to this community of her girlhood anymore, and yet wherever she was, people were drawn. Prudence's own father and step mother bumped into Eleanor, and looked a little shocked and uncomfortable, perhaps more for the reminder of Gillian than of Eleanor herself. Then in the evening, when there was to be dancing and merriment, it was Eleanor who took out a fiddle and surprised the crowd by her ability and mental library of jigs, reels and dancing tunes. A few of the older congregation nodded and muttered that Eleanor had been known for this as a girl. One woman mentioned she'd been a maid over at an upland farm called Chequers and remembered Eleanor playing for the drovers as they stopped off on their way from Scotland to London. All days long since gone.

There was a loud hoot from her cousin Neil as the younger people gathered in the field by the church ready for the races. Prudence glanced after Curnow, but he had disappeared. Married and already alone. Part of her still couldn't quite believe it had happened. That Prudence Longbottom had walked into the church and Prudence Pengelly had strolled out, briefly on her husband's arm, but it seemed he was off talking to someone now. All this time planning and anticipating, an hour or so in church then it was all over. So much fun, so much ease at speaking the vows then in the vestry for registration, and something that was beyond her comprehension had happened. It was a holy union before God, a lifelong partnership but it was also a legally binding contract. Till death do us part. It all was a little surreal. Yet joyous and giddy as though life was finally to be happy, after years of work, after generations of misery, now the people of the valley had come to happy times. They had come out of the church to roars of congratulation. Curnow had scattered some coppers across the ground for the children to pick up, and had passed a bag of money to the minister. Even joy had to be paid for. There had been more cheering, then most of the party had headed off to the field for the racing, and everyone had dispersed. As if there was nothing more to be said.

"Mrs Pengelly?"

Prudence didn't react until a hand touched her forearm. She turned to find the minister beside her. "Oh my goodness, I shall have to get used to that," she laughed. "I wondered for a moment if someone was after Curnow's mother." As she said it, she realised she didn't even know if Curnow's people were still alive. As far as she was aware he had never tried to contact anyone in Cornwall since settling here in Yorkshire.

"This is for you," he said, offering the bag Curnow had given him.

"I thought there were costs to be paid?"

"There were. I've take out the parson and clerk's fees, it's all paid for. The rest goes to you, to get your household started."

"Well, thank you," Prudence took the purse, feeling a little uncertain about it. She always felt awkward when given something, in truth, even taking her pay when in service had made her feel a little undeserving. But if this was the way the wife got started with the housekeeping, then so be it. And she would receive more during the day, more to make her feel baffled and by the evening her pockets would be full of coin, ribbons, corn dollies and an amber pendant that looked far too fancy for a lass like her.

"Good luck to you and a blessing upon your union," the minister said. "May yours be a long and happy marriage."

Eleanor sat down beside Ellen Lythe near the gate as the young people started the races to win ribbons that Prudence had bought for the occasion. It was a wedding tradition that worked well on a sunny day, with plenty of healthy folk ready for some fun. It wasn't something Eleanor had experienced. Her own marriage had been a quick and necessary formality down in London. Her eyes drifted over the gathering. The older faces were familiar, but so many of the younger ones were strangers. It was a community she had ceased belonging to a long time ago. There was Prudence, a grown woman but still with something of the trusting girl about her, as if she would never quite grow up. She wouldn't have had much schooling, Eleanor supposed, and when she looked across at Muriel, who had studied and read more than most women in Yorkshire put together had, one sometimes worried what the point was. Muriel was a clever and curious woman, but she had developed beyond where a woman was allowed to tread. She'd taken on an apprenticeship, offered as a favour by one of Eleanor's clients, to try and keep her mind engaged, but she was already growing restless. Even here, as the young people laughed and ran about, Muriel didn't fit in at all. She laughed and chatted to people, but looked bemused as to why people would rush about in giddiness over a ribbon.

"I wonder if you'll know this joy," Ellen said. She shifted a little side to side on her seat and nudged Eleanor's shoulder. "Mother of the bride."

"I don't know. Muriel's never shown any interest in courting, and certainly never any angst that she's the only girl in town not getting married."

"A woman with two daughters and no weddings..." Ellen faltered as she realised she'd gone on to uncomfortable ground. "I mean..."

"I haven't heard from Elizabeth for years. I don't know where she is." Eleanor closed up. "Besides, none of us know what life will bring. And Prudence is married but her own mother never got to see it."

"Aye, that was a shame. And it's true, we don't know what's coming. I always thought I'd be Ellen Withers till my dying day."

"And then you discovered gooseberries."

Ellen let out a chortle. "And they led me to Caleb, I know. As you say, none of us know where this path is leading. Oh, will you look at that lad of Gilly's. He always was a silly beggar."

A couple of the lasses were sulking as Neil won a particularly gaudy red ribbon in the race. He scrambled up onto his feet, holding the ribbon aloft in the air and out of the reach of most of his competitors, as if he had just pulled the sword from the stone. Prudence had scampered down into the melle by this point and was laughing so hard she couldn't speak. Some of the flowers had fallen out from her hair, and her unruly long straw thatch was coming lose from the pins Magdalene had worried over that morning.

Prudence wiped her eyes with the back of her hand, then linked arms with her young cousin, Neil. "Come, we must go back to the village for the festivities."

Eleanor wondered where the strange little Cornish man was, as Prudence trotted off in husband-and-wife manner with her cousin. A lad almost ten years younger than herself, whilst her true husband was over ten years her senior. She spotted Curnow standing with a group of the farmers near the road. He had an expressionless look about his face, squinting a little as if gazing out to sea and trying to gauge if a storm was coming their way. His hands were propped in his waistcoat pockets, his elbows stuck out at angles as if trying to make himself look bigger than he actually was. He was a little shorter than Prudence, and indeed they had seemed like an odd match. Nothing was stranger than love, she supposed.

"Come along, Ellen," Eleanor sighed, standing up again. "Let's get you back to the cart and away to Ainthorpe. You don't want to miss out on the bride ale."

"That I do not. Especially as the Beecrofts are involved. You know how they have a way with the honey."

Prudence eyed the jar of honey Neil Beecroft had dropped off yesterday. It was a gift from her aunt and uncle. Honey to extend the honeymoon. Sweetness in a jar. It would certainly be sweeter than she had expected marriage to be. She turned the jar around and watched the sunlight cut through the glass, illuminating the amber tones inside. What had she been expecting from marriage? It wasn't as though she'd had time for reading silly novels, or had been in the vicinity of idealised, romantic partnerships as were depicted on some of the china and the figurines she'd been tasked with keeping clean when she had worked at Danby Grange. The marriages she had seen had been partnerships of hard work, children, and the pressure of keeping the money coming in. Marriages were made of families and farmers rather than romantic couplings.

Curnow was away at Danby Mill on a commission for the new looms and structural joinery. It was a project that would keep him busy for weeks if not months. Prudence ought to be starting on the laundry, but she was hypnotised by the honey. She removed the cloth top and dipped her hand straight in. The sticky gold surrounded her fingers, and she drippingly raised them to her mouth, closing her eyes as she felt the nectar on her tongue. Bliss.

Three weeks into her marriage and she was lonely. Certainly running the household on her own kept her busy, but there was still spare time – what with Prudence used to rising early and hard work – which left her lingering with her thoughts for company.

With marriage, she had moved in society, and even geographically, now living in the little village of Danby. It sat on the north side of the valley, south facing, and even in autumn the change in warmth was noticeable going from shadow to sun. Ainthorpe, where she had lived with the Beecrofts, was on the opposite side of the valley.

Danby was a small hamlet of cottages, an inn: the Red Briar which doubled as a recruiting post whilst the wars raged distant away in France; a mill down at the river, pump, general store and the usual surrounding farms. Across the way was her old place of employment, Danby Grange which held a mixture of memories.

Married life, the life with Curnow was not quite what had been anticipated. She knew Curnow well enough to know what to expect of his voice and his opinions, and she knew enough of his preferences of food and living to keep him happy. Yet the married life, the life of a man and a woman bound together had been a disappointment. Worryingly woman told her to enjoy these months, for the beginning was the best time. Curnow had such passion in him, she heard it when he sang his strange songs, or spoke of his homeland. At night he was perfunctory and to the point, then tired and snoring as Prudence lay in solitude wondering if it was all over, for she had hardly noticed it starting. The cows in the field got more. Perhaps. And maybe she would have thought nothing more of it, and assumed the lusts of humans were no more than animals, had it not been for prior experience at her old work. The eldest son with his eager hands and his clever tongue. Of course that had never been set to go anywhere, for what would such a well-to-do young man do with a poor housemaid, but Prudence hadn't appreciated that at the time. And now that she was with Curnow, she thought back to those days and wondered how there could be so much want in someone to whom she meant nothing, and so much apathy in one who had declared eternity in the face of God. She rolled on to her side as Curnow started to snore, and smiled to herself as she wondered if it was just that Curnow was lacking in practice.

They had a little terrace cottage in the second short row going up the lane from the Red Briar. Their plot neared the brow of the hill. One up, one down, with a little garden at the front, a yard at the back. From the upstairs' window there was a view out across the fields and ambulating hills that rolled across the valley before lurching up to the heights of the moors in the distance. It was positive luxury to share such a cosy abode with only one other person and Prudence was glad of it every morning when she woke.

Someone was knocking at the door and Prudence considered that reason enough to let the water heat up a little longer before she started on the laundry. She opened the door to a dirty, skinny woman dressed in rags, accompanied by an equally filthy and emaciated child who looked about three or four but could be older and stunted from malnourishment. The clothes they wore were patched in places and threadbare in others, and were probably crawling with lice. Prudence and her peers were far from rich, but they had just enough to keep the roof over their heads and food in their stomachs. Cleanliness was next to godliness, but a penny in the pocket and a roof to call one's own helped with personal upkeep. People who tripped down from that level were left to the mercy of the parish, or begging and vagrancy.

"Morning M'am," the woman started, curtseying, which set Prudence off in a titter. As if she were royalty. The reaction warmed the woman and boosted her confidence. "I am so sorry to trouble you in your busy day, and normally I wouldn't even think of asking good folk such as yourself for anything, only it is my poor little girl here. She has not eaten for two days and you can see for yourself that she is nothing but skin and bone..." she wrenched up her daughter's arm to demonstrate, the child scowling, tired of its misery being paraded for strangers.

"Oh you poor dear. I have a little bread here." Prudence went to the table where there was the end of a loaf, perhaps three or four slices. She saw the open jar of honey and hesitated, wondering if she ought to add some for the child. Guiltily, she let the honey be, and returned to the door, passing across the bread. "Have you not been to the parish for help?"

"We are but passing through. And God bless your sweet heart for your kindness." The woman pushed the bread on the girl who began to eat in something of an unreserved frenzy. Only the fact that she remained on two feet showed that she was human and not animal. "I do feel dreadful to ask on anything else, given what a good Christian woman you have shown yourself to be, but we have a long journey ahead of us. If you did have any coin that you might..."

"Where are you going to?"

"Newcastle."

"Newcastle!" Prudence breathed. "Why, that is a long way from here. That will take days and days if you are travelling by foot. Is that home for you?"

"It is, madam. Ours is a terrible tale. We were down at Portsmouth and have been abandoned by the military now that the war is over for my husband."

"The war isn't over. Why, they're still recruiting here to fight the French."

"Oh, we know this, but my husband was terribly wounded. He lost a leg. We have travelled north to get home, and money to pay for transport or food has long since run out."

"You must be lost to be travelling over the moors. This is not a good route to take from the south to Newcastle..."

"My husband was determined to get to Whitby..."

"And is he here now?" Prudence gazed out onto the lane, looking for a one-legged man.

"No, we have been separated," the woman muttered, looking to the ground. "We must get back to home and we will find him there, I know in my heart. Oh, dear lady," she clutched her thin, moth-eaten shawls to the base of her throat. "Do you not have any coin you might spare a couple of desperate souls, in the name of charity?"

Her voice was growing loud in a beseeching desperation. Prudence noticed a couple of her neighbours out, in their gardens or standing in the doorway, looking disapproving. Beggars were nothing new, for with the war and rising prices a lot of people were struggling and many were falling onto hard times. But most of the folks round here didn't have much, and it was hard to be charitable when one was barely managing to provide one filling meal a day. Jobs were scarce, and as the walking wounded, no good for the military but too good for death, started to flood the country again, there wasn't enough to go around. Some grumbled about the beggars, although this remote part of the moors didn't get anywhere near as many as some places en route between the major cities witnessed. Many folk said that these charity cases were victim of their own failings, sins and situations. Prudence wondered if it wasn't simply more luck as to where one found oneself in life, but people scoffed at her, and she learned to keep her silly opinions to herself more often.

"Look, here," She passed the woman a couple of coppers, for she couldn't shake the look of that starving child. She certainly had done nothing in life to deserve this. "I'm sorry that's all I can give..."

"Oh, bless you madam!" the woman glowed with the sense of metal in her hands and clutched at Prudence's hand. "You have a truly good soul."

"People can be funny, not understanding," Prudence lowered her voice. "I wouldn't loiter..."

"I understand. Come now, Martha."

The woman and child scurried down through the gate and out to the lane, the movement of their bodies like rags caught on twigs blowing in the wind. From the top of the hill came a hunting party from the Grange, smart gentlemen in overcoats and top hats, ladies riding side saddle in warm, well-tailored jackets, long, layered petticoats and skirts. Well sewn-gloves that kept fingers warm. Hair that had been curled that morning with hot curling irons. Worried over by maids whilst all they needed to do was contemplate the mirror. And after all that work, stylish, expensive hats pinned to their hair, covering most of the fine work.

Prudence stepped out of the doorway to watch the party pass. The beggarwoman and her girl halted at the edge of the road, bowing in the grass to their social betters. One of the women on horseback made a sneering comment about these blasted beggars blotting the fine scenery everywhere one looked these days. Prudence lifted her hand to her chest as she saw the eldest son from the Grange. He had broadened out fully into a man. They said he was engaged and would be married soon. She was a suitable lady with a fine pedigree and an annual income of two thousand pounds. Perhaps that was she who rode beside him, as he turned and touched his gloved hand to hers. His idle gaze looked across the span of cottages they were passing and he saw Prudence and looked right through her. She could not say if it was a purposeful denial, or he truly neither remembered nor recognised her. Maids come and go. The staff is there to do their jobs but not to be noticed.

"You mustn't listen to those sob stories."

Her brow creased, and she turned away from the doorway. Her neighbour was at the low, adjoining wall.

"These beggars, my love, they're always passing through. Not as much as other parts, I'll grant you. My sister lives over in the Lakes and they see nothing but. Folks like us, we can't afford to solve the troubles of humanity. You'll have nothing left before you know it and then your husband will be wondering what's for supper."

"I don't..."

The woman smiled patronisingly. "I know you're just newly wed. It's your first time running a house. They know who to pick on."

"I'd better get in. I've a lot of laundry to do."

"Aye, well, if you say it is so." the woman laughed. "Give it a year or two and you'll know the meaning of a lot of laundry."

Sob stories they'd all heard before, yet gossip was gossip and a new variant was always a welcome distraction. What might have been a hunk of bread and a couple of coppers could soon grow on wagging tongues, and whatever the version had been by the time Curnow came to hear of it, the tale was different to reality. In some respects it did not matter, even if it had been actual fact, his displeasure would have remained the same. By the time he returned home that evening he was not best pleased.

Other wives might have realised the moment they gave out the money that there would be trouble, for some the realisation would come when they saw the expression on their husband's face. Curnow was always dowr, and Prudence was always oblivious, so between the two miscommunication was frequent.

Prudence was hot and merry when he returned. The supper was ready, the laundry was done for the day, and she was high on honey, the jar now down to the half marker and put away out of sight. "How was your day, husband dear?" Prudence innocently laughed as Curnow came in through the door. "All went well?"

"Don't titter at me, woman," Curnow muttered. "I've listened to talk of beggars all day."

"It is very sad to think on; the hard lives some have. It reminds one of all one has to be grateful for."

"Don't preach at me." Curnow roared, the sudden intensity flickering up out of nothing and surprising them both for a moment. "I was destitute and I worked hard to get myself back here. It is not for you to go handing out my money to people who are the makers of their misfortune."

"But it was from the housekeeping, my money..."

"You do not have money."

"Of course I do. I got it when we married, and..." Prudence's well-meant, mild mannered contradiction was slapped out of her. Her cheek stung, an embarrassed flush raced up from her chest and into her face. "Why, Curnow, why..."

"It's all my money. It's my house. My rent. My work. And you are my wife here to mind my house."

"But the little girl..."

"You will do as you're told."

"But Curnow," Prudence smiled stupidly. "Surely this is all in jest?"

All the fury from every time someone didn't take the little man seriously, and there were decades' worth of such moments, tingled up into his fingers and balled around a fist. It made contact with Prudence's face and sent her to the kitchen floor. She cried out and clutched her face, still confused that she had been hit, and how this could have been committed by a little man, shorter than herself. He who had only ever been droll and amusing in her eyes. How couldn't anyone understand about that howling desperation she had seen in the little girl's eyes? It gnawed at a person's soul. She had given what she had, she had thought what she had brought to the house had been hers. She had not thought that anyone could object.

Curnow now towered over her. "Let that be a lesson to you. Wife."

Prudence lowered her face, keeping her hand to her eyes so that she didn't have to look at him. What was this woman's life? She felt her eyes watering. "Yes," she whispered. There didn't seem to be much else she could say.

Prudence overheard Curnow talking to one of the locals. It was about a week since he'd hit her, and the bruises had subsided enough so that she could be seen out of the house again, although she did not feel inclined. It was not that she was frightened, or even that Curnow had forbade it, in fact he never mentioned the matter in any capacity. Rather Prudence felt hollowed out and a little nauseous. It was not a feeling of sickness that led to actual vomiting - other than on one occasion - but a constant feeling almost like a strange motion in her body. In her mind there was a dampening. She had made her lot and where was the point in getting upset? She couldn't get out of this now. Perhaps people had seen she had made a bad choice. Some things had been said, or at least hinted at, she couldn't quite remember now, for she had probably not been paying all that much attention.

"Just a mild dose of the flu."

Prudence heard the lie on Curnow's tongue and assumed it was to explain why she lingered in the house.

"Aye, I chose wisely when I married. Not too old, but not too young either. Not accustomed to fancy living or needy. She was in service at The Grange as well. She knows how to run a house well. I've no complaints."

Prudence sat down on a little stool by the fire and put her hand to her mouth. No complaints? It had not felt that way last week. But he spoke truthfully, the house was run well. As a housekeeper she had been an excellent choice. Anything else didn't really matter, for it was he who owned everything and decided all. His needs were fulfilled, and Prudence, the unpaid servant got a roof over her head. She gazed out of the window. She supposed feelings and romance were the stuff of books and their social betters. The rich who could afford luxuries and more importantly time to reflect, experience and think on their lives and their options. Those at the bottom took what they could get if it meant keeping away from a life of begging.

Her mind wandered back to the amber pendant, a token more fitting to the neck of the next lady of Danby Grange than a lowly housewife like herself. She had slipped it into the pocket on her wedding dress and had never shown or mentioned it to Curnow. Her aunt's words and earnest look meant more now. That was the one thing she owned and she would not share its existence with anyone.

Someone started hammering at the front door. "Mrs Pengelly?" a voice trilled.

Aunt Gilly. Prudence slumped off the stool and answered the door.

"Prudence my dear, I'm here to call on the newly weds. I did not wish to intrude the first weeks, and then I know Danby's not far from Ainthorpe, but Mr Hammond offered me a ride in his cart so I decided an unexpected visit was in order." Aunt Gilly was particularly giddy this morning. Prudence peered outside. The remnants of the night frost still clung to the grass. A horse and cart were parked on the lane in front of the cottages, and the driver, Mr Hammond as her aunt had oh so cordially referred to him as, although most used the more common title Rodger the Bodger, was loitering at the garden gate. He doffed his cap to Prudence. "Morning the new Mrs Pengelly as was Miss Longbottom," he greeted her. "Your aunt's just sold me a fine crate of honey jars and a good slab of cheese. As a newly married woman, you'll be new on my rounds. You thinking of selling any home wares?"

"Why, I..." Prudence was surprised. It was odd to be spoken to as the female head of a household, but of course, that was what she was. "We're not farmers, I mean, my husband's a joiner. I don't keep bees or cows or chickens."

"Aye, well, most of my clients do like the farm produce, that's what I'm selling. But if you ever want to sell something, I'm your man. Earn a little extra money, perhaps a little for yourself. Some husbands round these parts are tight with what they let their good wives have, am I not right, Mrs Beecroft?"

"Mr Bodger!" Gilly screeched, forgetting herself for a moment. "Why, I mean Mr Hammond. I have no complaints in Mr Beecroft. But just you mind folks round here don't have much money. Rents are high for little accommodation, and then there are the tithes and the poor money..."

"I know it too well, it's a story I hear at every farm. That's why I come weekly to buy your good food to take back to Stockton for the town folk who are missing out on this godly nourishment."

"Don't make yourself out to be a saint. You're here for the profit as any merchant is."

"Well, a man's got to make a living. You find yourself knitting too much, I'll take stockings and gloves," he added to Prudence. "Get you a little pin money for yourself. You ladies will be excusing me. I've got a lot of house calls to make before I can head back to the market."

Aunt Gilly rolled her eyes at Prudence as Mr Rodger Hammond returned to his horse, patting the beast on the head and muttering something before the two of them continued up the hill. "He speaks close to the line, but he does give us a good price. Town folks do like your uncle's honey."

Prudence couldn't agree more, thinking on the empty jar in the pantry. "Aunt," she said, as the two women embraced. "Will you be coming in? I'll get the tea on." She didn't drink the tea they brought in from India, like the rich folk did. She didn't have the money for that. Prudence was in the habit of collecting and drying nettles in the spring time, which she crushed up and stored as an alternative. It had a bitter taste which wasn't to everyone's liking but as Gilly had taught her this habit, she doubted she would object.

"You do that, my girl," Gilly bustled into the kitchen. She looked around, nodding in approval. Prudence was a scatterbrain with too much goodness, but she was also a worker and knew the meaning of cleanliness. "I've brought a batch of scones. You always liked my scones the best. I remember you said they were a lot better than your step mother's."

Prudence caught a waft of fresh baking as the cloth was opened to reveal its cargo, and felt her stomach turn. "You'll not take offence if I say no this time. I am struggling to get over an ailment."

"Oh, what ailment is that, then?"

"Flu, I think." Prudence busied herself with cups. "I don't know its title. I still feel ill all the time."

"Sickness like?"

"I'm not bringing my food up."

"But you feel like you will?"

"Quite often."

"Well then," Gilly settled her rump into her chair. "You're quick off the mark, my lass, but this is how it is when one is married."

"Really?" Prudence looked miserable. "I can't say I like it."

"It does take a little getting used to." Gilly grew a little concerned. It wasn't like Prudence to be low. It was strange, given how much she'd been through and had to compromise. Even when her mother had died she had battled through better than many other children would have managed. It was her positive countenance, it wasn't to say that Prudence hadn't loved her mother or wasn't devastated, rather that Prudence had a child-like eternal optimism. As if she knew life was too short to waste a moment on being sad.

Gilly leaned forward and patted Prudence's hand. "It can get a lot better with a little time. Women can get some pleasure..." she blushed as she realised what she was starting to say.

Prudence brow crinkled, she couldn't see how anyone could enjoy feeling ill. Perhaps they were talking about something else.

"Just don't..." Gilly shuffled awkwardly, poking at a scone. "Don't be like Magdalene, my lass. Although I doubt you would be. Life's given you plenty of hard knocks already and look at you. I always say, no matter what, Prudence always dusts herself down and keeps going." Gilly put her cup down. "It's very common you understand, to lose babies and children. It's hard to find a woman who hasn't lost any. My first three died before they were full grown. I sometimes wonder what they would have been like, for I'd had girls, but it wasn't to be. And then there are the ones that never make it that far. The bloods come too early, and..." she fussed with her hands on her lap, making herself increasingly uncomfortable with the topic of the conversation, although it was really a monologue for Prudence merely sat and dumbly stared at her, not listening but trying to focus on not throwing up all over the kitchen table.

Gilly patted her niece's hand. "I tell you these things for you don't have a mother to tell you. You mustn't lose heart if such things happen, because they happen to all women. It's just nature's way. Anyhow, before we know where we are, it'll be time for Christina's confinement. I don't suppose you'll be away to help now that you might be..."

"Why ever not?"

"Well, a woman who's not had her first baby might not wish to see..."

"I was there with Magdalene," Prudence pointed out.

"Aye, that you were. And in other circumstances I might say it would be more fitting for someone in Magdalene's position to go and support her sister-in-law, but Magdalene..." Gilly shook her head. "She can still have some funny turns around babies and the like. Probably best not to have her there. And there's that silly midwife, muttering it's bad luck to have Magdalene at a birth." Gilly gave a long sniff. "By, if it were bad luck to have a woman who'd lost a baby at a birth then there'd be no attendants other than girls and maids and all them who know nothing about it."

As things transpired, Prudence's being in the early months of pregnancy was not to be an issue for the blood came and whatever it had been was lost. It had been something, she was sure, for it was so late and the aches grew past their usual intensity. One night whilst Curnow snored, she could not rest for the aches, and went downstairs. She sat hunched forward groaning by the low fire, felt her legs shake and grow weak as they might drop from their sockets. A chill slunk upon her as the pain grew and Prudence could not say if she were about to vomit or pass out. Something heavy slunk out of her, then calmness settled upon her body again. Prudence shivered and felt weary. She tidied herself up before creeping back up to the bed. The following morning, once Curnow had left for work, she neglected her chores and crept back up to bed. No matter how many coverings she put about herself, she could not get warm.

The lad from Egton arrived earlier than they had been expecting to say it had started for Christina and she had been asking for Prudence. He arrived in a flurry of snow, as if spat out of a storm and into their kitchen. Snowflakes perched in his eyebrows. With his errand complete, he asked if he might not sleep down in the kitchen that night, for the storm had blown up something terrible and he did not fancy trying to make it back to Egton tonight. Prudence had gazed longingly at the window. "But I must go to her now."

Curnow sniffed and took up another spoon of stew. "Only a fool would go out there now."

"It's coming down so tight you can't see the end of your nose," the lad added.

"But Christina needs me."

"People have died out in storms of the like," Curnow continued as if they were having a pleasant hypothetical conversation about the upkeep of meadows. "And it can be months till they're found. All depending on how long it takes the snow to melt."

The lad wrinkled his nose at the thought.

Prudence sighed and turned away from the window. She was letting Christina down. "I hope she will be all right. We must set off at first light in the morning."

"It will be right, old Ellen Lythe's with them, and I'd been and fetched the midwife before I came over to see you."

Perhaps all would be well. She knew that it took a long time from the first twinges to the baby being born. If Christina had both Ellen and the midwife, she would be well looked after and Prudence really was surplus. But after the experience with Magdalene, she needed to see that the process of birth could be a successful one, and she was so looking forward to the happiness in that little carpenter's family. She did not sleep that night, and well before first light she was up and back into the kitchen, getting ready with breakfast and disturbing the Egton lad who was asleep under a quilt on the bench. Ki, Curnow's little terrier, had taken it upon himself to sleep on top of the lad, and with Prudence's clattering the two of them grumbled and rustled for some time before admitting they were awake. Curnow was down shortly, grumbling about this nonsense, as if no woman had ever had a baby before, and went out briefly. It was no longer snowing, although the snow was mid-shin deep and bright and crisp. He returned with news that Farmer Purdey of Hollin Farm, a close neighbour, was heading over to Egton with his cart today and said they could travel with him. Prudence and the lad hurried down their porridge, then wrapped up warm as best they could, the lad muttering that he was keen to be back to his mother. Ki yipped them goodbye before breaking his solidarity and curling up by a warm fire whilst his master took his breakfast.

Their breath showed up as dense puffs of steam as they walked down the rise towards the Red Briar where Mr Purdey was already waiting with his horse and cart sled. Prudence led the way, following Curnow's tracks, but the snow still dragged back at her skirts and walking was hard. She had a basket over one arm full of food that she said was for her brother Jeremiah and Christina, but she suspected may be shared along the journey to Egton. Behind her she could hear the lad chattering, glad to think he'd be able to sit up in a cart and not have to tramp back home through all this snow.

"Mrs Pengelly," Mr Purdey nodded to her with a warming smile. The horse glanced at them and whinnied before sticking its nose back into the sack of oats. "I understand there's a sister-in-law to see to."

"Thank you for taking us."

"I am having to head to Egton regardless," he said, taking her basket and slinging it in a cavalier fashion a little too much for Prudence into the back of the horse sled. "And it will be better travelling knowing that I have company. It'll be slow going, but a quicker fix with the three of us."

Prudence noted the shovels laid in the back of the cart as Mr Purdey helped her up.

"And the energy of young lads knows no end so you'll be welcome."

"Which way will we go?"

"We'll cut across the top of the moors and down via Stonegate," Mr Purdey said, shaking the reigns and getting the horse started. They plodded up the lane Prudence and the lad had just come down. "It's the quickest and most direct route. I know the moors will have taken more of the snow than down in the valley, but it's a straighter, flatter lane and I don't want getting bogged down or stuck by the river. Besides, it's not snowing the now, and it's well frozen and still. If it gets too deep we'll have to turn back and go another way, but I don't think the snow has been too deep. Not for my old nag. She's long legs has this lass."

With songs and snacks from Prudence's basket, they managed the journey without too much trouble. The going was slow, for although it was no longer snowing, and thankfully the lay had not drifted, it was still a depth to cause irritation to a horse now having to lift up its hooves more than usual. The horse sled, a common feature for many of the farmers when the snows fell heavy, was willing and glided easily, in compensation for the higher steps the horse had to take. They followed the track up to the edge of the moors, at times a purple expanse but today a glittering whiteness, virginal and untouched by transport, languidly flowing out for miles in all directions. Up here, with the air frozen and crisp, they had a long clear view right across the moorlands, with the land dipping sharply down into the winding, twisting river valley. They passed by the snow-capped little knoll where Danby beacon stood, and had stood for a good two hundred years. Always ready in times of war and threat of invasion for lighting to send the emergency messages inland. They continued across the moors before heading down gentle slopes to the little village of Stonegate. There were rolling undulations across the hills this way, but they avoided the steep valley sides and twisting lanes, and were able to come into Egton, itself situated higher up away from the river from the top around noon, with red noses and cold hands but cheery countenances.

Mr Purdey dropped Prudence off at Jeremiah's home. He only had a short distance left to go to his own destination, and the lad could run on from there. Prudence stood outside the cottage in apprehension, trying to gauge at what stage the childbearing was at from the signs of the building. Smoke rose steadily from the chimney. It looked as though there had been some activity, for the snow was trampled just outside the front door and there was pink snow where used water had been thrown out. Other than that, all was quiet, and Prudence wondered if the labour pains had lessened and Christina was able to get some sleep. Or perhaps the baby had been eager and had shifted quicker than a lot of first babies were inclined to.

Prudence lifted her hand to knock on the door just as it was wrenched open, and a rather surprised woman staggered back in the doorway. She had a bowl of water covered with a cloth that she quickly put out of the way. She regarded Prudence, her ruddy face glowing like a fire against the stark whiteness of the snow. She had a mop cap set on her head, barely clinging on after a restless night and hardly helped by the springy, wiry nature of her hair.

"Oh please, is the baby come?"

"Baby?" the midwife almost shrieked, her voice a little hoarse. "Why, I think you'd mean babies for there were two of them that I counted." She paused and leant out of the doorway, taking in Prudence's face. "And who might you be? I know your face."

"Prudence Pengelly, was Longbottom. I..."

"Oh yes, now I know you. Jeremiah's younger sister." She took Prudence's wrist and smiled awkwardly. "You must be brave now, my girl."

"Brave? What has happened? Oh no, oh..." Prudence hurried into the house and ran to Ellen Lythe who was hunched by the fire, alone in the kitchen. Prudence knelt down by her side. She could see that Ellen was crying, and judging from the redness around her eyes had been crying for a time now. "Oh Ellen, please don't tell me..."

Ellen raised her eyes and felt a relief that Prudence was here. She was too old for this. She could not take the lead and manage things. She'd gone through too much sadness over her years and her old bones were no longer up to carrying the burden of life. It did not seem right anymore that she still lingered and others continued to die. "Prudence, my girl, I am glad to see you," she said, her voice unsteady. "I'm so sorry..."

"The midwife told me twins."

"Aye, but..."

Prudence clung to Ellen's arm. "They did not make it?"

"No, they did not make it. Born still and angelic. Prudence, you must go and talk to your brother, get him out of there. Annie says she'll stay and help us prepare the bodies, but that's not a man's place now and I can not face it on my own. I will have to ask you to lead."

"Yes, of course," Prudence murmured, standing up with a heaviness pulling at her. It would not take long to get two poor little dead twins ready for their graves, really she didn't know why the midwife felt they needed her help. It was the family history that turned it to a great strain. Too soon after Magdalene's tragedy, that the family lose another set of twins. Prudence had watched one sister-in-law destroyed by it, and now she would have to witness the demise of Christina's happy countenance. The Longbottoms did not deserve this ill luck.

As Prudence went for the stairs, Ellen started forward on her stool, thinking that Prudence had not understood her. Prudence was deaf to her warnings, and with a creak of wood ascended to the next floor. It was so still and chilled upstairs, as if the very breath of life was on pause. Prudence lingered at the top of the stairs, holding off the moment when she would have to see those little dead babies and remember it all of last year when it had happened to Magdalene's girls. She felt a little sick and put her hand to her forehead, realising her shawls were still over her head. She'd been in such a rush to get inside; and here she was still dressed for a snow storm. She slipped off her extra shawls and stepped out of her outdoor boots so she would not track anymore snow about the house.

Her brother was on a chair by the only window, back lighted by a bright, frozen white light. He was all cried out and looked like death, drawn, grey-ashened and aged by decades compared to when she had last seen him. At the foot of the bed, already washed, wrapped in white linens and nestled together were the twin babies, asleep like little angles. They had blue lips and intensely white skin. They would be ice to the touch, Prudence knew, remembering how quickly it went with little ones. She sniffed to clear her nose and realised the tears were dripping from her very face.

"Oh Jeremiah, I do not know what to say. How is Christina?" Her eyes went to the bed where Christina lay. Her pale skin glowed with sweat and her heavily stained nightgown clung to her lower form. Her eyes were closed, arms by her side but no breath left her body. "Oh no," she whispered. This is what the midwife was to help with. "Jeremiah," she hurried across to her brother and held his hands. The contact, rushing him back up into the movement of time, the reality of what had happened and what could not be got back proved too much, and he collapsed sobbing onto Prudence.

The siblings remained enmeshed together. They would have remained so if Annie had not appeared at the top of the stairs. She needed to be getting on, the day would soon be over and they couldn't leave things as they were. It was a tragedy, she'd be the first to agree on that point, but she'd been helping out at births since she was fifteen and she'd seen too many dead babies and too many mothers bleed out to think this was anything other than nature's cruel way. Twins were often trouble, both to the mother and each other, for there was not enough for either baby to get big and strong, so both were weak and small and often didn't make it.

Annie coughed gently, then roughly when she didn't get the desired response. "Begging your pardon, but we need to look after Mrs Longbottom now."

Prudence looked up and saw Annie with a dish of clean water. Linens were over her shoulder.

"I've already sent message to the rector. The lad's to tell Seth Knaggs afterwards. And we must get her washed. I know it grieves you so, but time waits not for anyone's grief."

Prudence lent back from her brother. "You go down now, Jeremiah. Ellen's wanting to see you and she's been waiting awful long. Me and Annie will get sorted up here."

Jeremiah forced himself to go downstairs, and with that, his marriage had come to an end. As Annie got the water and linens set up, Prudence looked back at Christina's wan body and felt a hollow wilderness of grief sweep through her. How could it be that a body was full of memories and thoughts and smiles, then the next moment it was a shell and all had disappeared as though it had never mattered or existed even? How could this be right at all?

Christina and her babies were buried two days later. They were interred at St Hilda's church, Egton. It lay a short walk west from the village, along a narrow little track that wove between fields, before arriving at a Norman church. The surrounding graveyard was encircled by a grey, drystone wall with views across undulations of farmland. That day everything was covered in white crisp snow as if to emphasise the purity of the eternal sleep. Only a few established broadleaf trees stood bare and leafless, protruding from the snow as sentinels to the locality's dead.

It was bitterly cold. The snow had frozen on top of previously trampled and now unlevel ice. Where no one had walked there were clusters of frozen ice crystals, delicately harsh memorials to the biting chill of winter. It was not the time to lay the dead in the earth, and the ground was unrelenting. The gravediggers had needed a full day and a fire on the grave site in order to break through and dig the final resting place.

The mourners looked like a gathering of silent, dumpy black crows, for so well wrapped up they were against the winter that they lost most human shape. Breath steamed out and hung as clouds in the still, frozen air. Teardrops threatened to freeze on eyelashes. Relatives and friends made the journey across the bitter moors from Danby, Ainthorpe, Castleton and even as far up the valley as Commondale. After what had already happened to the surviving Longbottom children this felt like a double tragedy.

The service in the church was cold, grey and empty, rather like the interior of the building. There was a certain eternal chill in these old places, even in summer. It was an indescribable sensation of the endlessness of death against the fleeting moment of human life, and even briefer moments of joy. When all that had to be said had been spoken, the men went to inter the coffin to the sanctity of hallowed ground, the women lingering in the background amongst the old markers of lives since past. It was all over, the final chapter on a life, and the survivors were to move on. Prudence held down a gasp in her throat, suddenly overwhelmed by the fact that she would never see happy, joyful Christina again. And that those little boys – for the twins had been two lads – would never grow up and delight everyone with their chortling playfulness.

Prudence felt a steady arm link with hers and for a moment she thought it was Curnow. When she looked around she remembered that he was walking with the other men. Magdalene, lavender sash put away in favour of full black again, gripped Prudence's arm to her and stared straight ahead.

As they turned to head down the little, block-stoned path away from the church and out of the graveyard Prudence's eye met with that of her father. He gave a little sad smile, as awkward as ever with his children. He and his second wife, clinging on his arm started out of the churchyard. Out at the lane there was quite the gathering of carts and ponies, all waiting to take their masters back home across the moors. At one a man was helping Ellen Lythe up into the cart, where they would wait until Jeremiah was ready to return home. Ellen had developed a shake since the death of Christina. Close to the gate gathered Christina's family, the Applecrosses. Amongst the faces Prudence recognised Christina's parents, her uncle Albert Applecross, a broad man in his forties, and one of Albert's sons, Richmond.

Magdalene and Prudence waited just inside the graveyard until Curnow, William and Jeremiah had caught up with them, then departed through the church gate, out onto the lane and the continuation of everyday life.

As they walked past the Applecrosses, Albert spat into the snow. His face curled into a sneer. "Fucking Hursts," he snarled. "You lot always were poison to good honest folk."

The three Longbottom children, William, Jeremiah and Prudence slowed to stare at Albert in consternation. Magdalene did not immediately realise that their group was being spoken to until she recalled that the deceased mother, Gillian Longbottom had been born a Hurst. Curnow, who had not grown up in the area, was oblivious as to what was being referred to, but could tell from the body language that some old grudge was being aired. This story he did not know, but grudges and grievances between families was an old tale repeated endlessly wherever people could be found.

Christiana's cousin Richmond stared at the group with equal disgust. Christina's mother looked distraught, unaware that there really was any problem, and looked in desperation at Albert, as if to plead with him, before turning to her own husband for support.

"Quiet your mouth, Albert," Christina's father said gruffly.

"I will not," Albert said, his attention moving specifically to Jeremiah. "It's your devil seed that has done this. You put it in her, and it has killed her."

Jeremiah appeared to visibly crumple from within at the charge he had killed his own dear Christina.

William, ignored and generally treated with scorn by his own wife since the death of their children, went for the older man. "You take that back now."

"Albert!" Christina's father shouted. "I never knew where this nonsense of yours came from, but you give it up now."

"The Hursts are unnatural."

"You will apologise."

"I will not."

"You have no respect," William grabbed Albert by his coat and flung him against the stone wall. Christina's father and Richmond went in to join the fray, one to break up, the other to join the fight. Jeremiah stood numbly and stared at the scrum, unable to encourage his body in to action. Curnow huffed inwardly, irritated that he should have married into such a jumble of nonsense that he knew nothing of. He had given all this up and was not inclined to get involved in feuds, grudges and fisticuffs of any strata, but it seemed it would be his duty for today.

Some thought a little man would be of no use, but Curnow had long learned to use his size to his advantage and knew the weak spots of men. A swift kick up between Richmond's legs from behind soon brought the young man gasping to his knees. Christina's father was trying to restrain Albert, and now that the third was out of the fight, Curnow was able to pull William away, but not before William had swung out with his arm and punched Albert squarely in the face.

Albert yowled and clutched at his face, staggering back onto the wall. He turned away, as if shamed by what had happened. Leaning forward, the blood seeped through the gaps between his fingers and spattered onto the white snow. He glared at the Longbottom cluster. William was breathing heavily, his breath hot furious puffs of cloud, fight-hungry arms held back by his brother-in-law, Curnow. Magdalene and Prudence were behind, as white as the snow and terrified. Beyond them stood Jeremiah, a walking, hopeless corpse.

"May you all live to be punished, unnatural Hursts," Albert spat to the ground again, spittle mingling with blood before he stalked away in fury.

Christina's parents, at a loss even now to understand what Albert's problem was, hurried to Jeremiah to apologise for their brother's behaviour and to assure him that no one in their right mind could blame him for what had happened to Christina. William Longbottom, senior, father of the family, walked up to his children, wife Megan still on his arm and shook his head at his eldest son. "That was not the behaviour of a thinking, dignified Christian."

William, or Little Will as he had been known in childhood scowled at his father. He shook himself free of Curnow. "Away with you. At least I stand for us children, which is more than you ever did." Stuffing his hands into his pockets, he stomped away in his fury, leaving the crowds, the people and the mourners. When it came down to it, parents who died young, parents who had other distractions, wives who could not stand to look at you, everyone was alone in this misery. There was no one to rely on.

Other than Ellen Lythe, who lived in the same house, no one saw Jeremiah Longbottom the following week. His disappearance was accepted as natural. Christina had just died and there was a certain etiquette to follow when grieving for a loved one. The building remained locked up and silent for the second week. The third week a couple of customers arrived at the workshop at the front of the house. Ellen answered, looking embarrassed and said that Jeremiah was indisposed but she would talk to him as soon as she could. Ellen, who had not mounted those stairs for a good two years forced herself up to speak to Jeremiah. He had been down now and then like a disjointed ghost, and eaten something, but he hardly spoke. One never knew when he would next appear, but as the world was asking after him, Ellen couldn't wait. He was going to have to return to the land of the living.

Jeremiah was lying fully dressed on the bed. He responded to her prattle in so much as sitting up. Ellen's heart was breaking for him, he looked so lost, and truly she didn't quite know how things were to go from here, only that they had to go somewhere. He had work already booked, pieces downstairs that needed to be delivered, and the rents to pay in a month or so.

She said her piece and assuming that he was mulling over what she had said, she hobbled downstairs again to return to the fireside. There was some movement upstairs, then an hour or so later Jeremiah appeared downstairs. He rustled through the kitchen and the workshop, gathering coin as he went, and slipping into his great overcoat, which was now too big for his grief stricken body, he went outside into the chill night air.

He never set foot through that doorway again.

Ellen was in a panic the following morning, but incapacitated as she was, she was unable to start out on a search herself. She sent the same lad, always happy for a little payment, off to send word to the elder brother, William, that Jeremiah had disappeared. She half hoped that Jeremiah had headed to one of his siblings, unable to face the home he had once shared with Christina, but that soon proved not to be the case. Ellen sat and cried by the fire, thinking of those occasions when people went out onto the moors in winter and perished, their bodies under the snow for weeks before eventually being discovered.

William had downed tools on news of Jeremiah's disappearance. He had slowly made his way towards Egton, stopping off at different households, inns, farms and the like in the hope that Jeremiah was there or at least that they had heard something of him. Most hadn't realised he was missing, but word soon got around. When he reached Egton, he had no good news for Ellen. It was late in the day so he stayed overnight, and it was the following morning that they got their first sighting.

A fish merchant from Whitby, coming up with his little cart of goods had stopped at the house and nodded to Ellen, commenting that he could see the master of the house wasn't back yet. William got up from the kitchen table and out into the snow upon hearing that comment, demanding to know if the man had seen Jeremiah.

"Oh, I've seen him all right," the man nodded. "He was alive and well two days ago at least, last time I saw him, but I couldn't vouch for that still being the case given the state he was in."

"Where is he?"

"Whitby."

"And you say he's ill?"

The man laughed like a donkey. "If self infliction is an illness, perhaps. The man's drunk and has lost his senses. The rate he's going, I would not like to wager whether it will be his coin or his body that gives up first."

William felt sick to his stomach. They were a god-fearing family, raised by their father's good Christian views and work ethic. Although not teetotallers, they had never turned to drink like this. His father had never fallen to pieces in this way when their mother had died. Jeremiah would bring great shame upon the family. He would need sense talking in to him. "Where did you see him?"

"One of the alehouses near the steps," the man smiled in an unpleasant manner. "You know Whitby, more alehouses than a man can count numbers. He'll move on when they get fed up and throw him out, but a few steps and he'll find his new abode."

William left for Whitby that very morning. The snow was not too bad for walking, and he made the little seaport town in just over two hours. Whitby, that whaling and fisherman port of ancient houses, streets and yards all tumbling upon one another on the steep slopes down to the Esk River mouth and the sea bottom. William looked a little overwhelmed, for he was unaccustomed to so much activity and people all at once, but he paid his toll and crossed over the bridge to the old side of the town, where the abbey ruins and St Marys overlooked the town from their vantage point on crumbling sea cliffs. A sea fret had loomed into the town during the day, and voices and bells, detached from physical substance, were heard at a distance. William pulled his collar tight, wondering at himself that a tall blacksmith would be nervous at coming to such a place, and headed in the general direction of the 199 steps in the hopes that he would soon find his brother in one of the nearby alehouses.

His search was not long and he found Jeremiah slumped at a back table in the third alehouse he entered. William walked up to the table and had to close his eyes for a moment, in some vain and futile hope that he would look again and see something more promising. It was not to be. Jeremiah had visibly lost weight, and somehow the very colour had left his flesh as if all hope had been buried with Christina. He wore a beard now, his hair was greasy and lank and his clothes were stained with drink, vomit and other things William cared not to think about. When he reached out to shake his brother by the shoulder he was shocked by just how little flesh there was on his brother's body.

Jeremiah groaned, rolled bloodshot eyes at William then dropped his head onto the sticky table top.

"Jeremiah, I am come to take you home."

"Go to the dogs with you," Jeremiah mumbled.

Some of the old sea dogs sitting close by took the pipes from their mouths and started to laugh. "Now there's a fellow that doesn't know when to stop."

William felt increasingly uncomfortable. His father had raised him god fearing and intolerant of drink and these were not the types of places he went to. Although he considered himself the moral superior of any man in the building that night, he also found himself under confident and awkward, as if someone was about to whip away his mask and show him to be inferior. A weakling. In reality a tall, sober blacksmith had little to worry about, in physicality at least, but he was keen to escape. He could not wait any longer. Taking his brother by the scruff of the neck, he manhandled him onto his feet and took him tottering out onto the street.

The cold wet creeping air slapped Jeremiah awake as they left the alehouse and moved away towards the steps. Jeremiah pushed William off, suddenly aware of his body, his very nerve endings, the state of his stomach and staggered to the side of a building. Planting his hands onto the wall, he leaned into his misery and threw up the contents of his stomach onto the cobbles.

"Jeremiah Longbottom, you are a disgrace to our family name," William scolded, standing erect and at a distance.

Jeremiah spat into the pool of vomit, then wiped his mouth on his sleeve. "You can go to hell."

"I am come to take you home."

"I have no home."

"There is building in Egton..."

"To hell with it; it means nothing to me now."

William was at a loss as to how to deal with this. He started to quote something from the bible in the hope that it would offer some solace, but it only made Jeremiah all the more angry, and he came swinging a weak punch at his brother. "Don't spout that shit at me. It's all lies. She's dead, do you hear me, she's dead."

He listened to his own breathing. What was he supposed to say to make Jeremiah see sense? "I know," he started feebly. "Christina would not wish you to be like this..."

"Don't you mention her name."

"She will not be forgotten."

Jeremiah seemed to deflate, and sat down on the bottom steps. "She is dead and I killed her. Albert was right..."

"Albert Applecross is nothing but a malicious fool with uncalled for bitterness in his heart. It is a great tragedy that she died, but life is cruel. Do I not know it, who lost two little girls last year?"

"Your wife didn't die."

William shrugged grimly. "To me that may be debatable."

Jeremiah made no comment, once he might have wondered about Magdalene keeping up this accusatory coldness for her husband, but he no longer cared. His eyes glistened with tears and he looked away. "She is dead and there is nothing worth living for now. There is no point to it."

"Suicide is a sin."

He looked at his elder brother with contempt. He always had been too godly and literal, just like their father. Their pathetic father who had abandoned their mother long before she died and made out he was the example of Christian duty and feeling. "Then the drink take me. I'll not be long for this world."

"You must come back with me. Get away from Whitby and this devil's drink. You stay with us for while, get your mind straight..."

Jeremiah stood up, unwavering as if suddenly sobered. "I'm not coming back."

"You will. I'll not have you sully our family name any..."

The lecture was broken as Jeremiah swung a steady and well-aimed punch straight for his brother's face. William staggered back, clutching his face as he felt a trickle of warm blood burst from his nose. His brother was broken, utterly lost.

"I am gone now and I'll not be back. You are no master over me. I am done with family and life."

"Jeremiah..."

"You go to hell if you wish, for I am already there." And with those parting words, Jeremiah Longbottom ran off into the night.

Everyone from Jeremiah's old life lost track of him. As time drew on, those who were able to go search him out were less than inclined. The few that still hoped he could be saved were unable either by physical incapacity or duties and responsibilities keeping them elsewhere. Death was a brutal tragedy, with the final insult that life continued. The figures in his life had their own worlds to manage. Weeks passed by, word got around and customers started to make arrangements for work to be completed elsewhere. Ellen Lythe, like the faithful old dog with nowhere else to go, lingered in the little house that had been her marital home whilst Jeremiah had been an apprentice, and later her little sanctuary after her husband's death. She took payment for items that had been completed and were waiting collection, dealt with other customers, apologising and muttering in confusion that Jeremiah would surely be back soon, if they'd just wait with the contracts. Men shook their heads. Work could not wait. If Jeremiah returned, they'd think on the matter then. Ellen rattled about the house that ought to have been full of the burble of newborn twins and wet flannelling drying by the range, but instead was a cold, empty shell. Everyone had either died or walked out of her life and she was left alone and forgotten, crippled by her damaged ankle and old age and unable to walk far.

A month after Jeremiah had abandoned his old life, worse was to come for it was rent time and the estate's agent was about collecting rents. Ellen felt sickened when she opened the door to him. He was a decent man, but she knew the cost of the rents, and what little had been made from the sale of a couple of small items wouldn't go anywhere to covering it. She knew that Jeremiah had cleared the property of all cash and she was left in an awkward position. She was certain that he needed the time to grieve and would come to his senses. If only she could get herself to Whitby and talk to him. Damn that leg.

The workshop needed to be ready for him so she made a decision and told the agent about the little money that her husband had left to her. It would cover the rents due and leave her a little over to keep her going until Jeremiah returned. The agent tightened his lips and lent back in the chair. His employers, the landed gentry of this region, had a living to make and did not worry that much about the state of their tenants – so much was clear from the living conditions they were prepared to actually charge a rent on. He had made some comment on it early in his career and learned swiftly how it was foolish to question one's social betters. He had been curtly lectured that the common workman who lived in such cottages was quite content with such conditions. It was akin to hard work and natural suffering, anything better would make their heads soft and lead to laziness and ruin. His employers would happily take Mrs Lythe's money this time, likewise when it was time again to collect the rents, they would happily tip her out of her home when she couldn't make a second payment. Jeremiah wasn't coming back and this workshop was his responsibility, not Mrs Lythe's.

He had always respected Caleb Lythe and gotten on well with him. He could not cheat his widow out of what money she had, knowing that she was only postponing the inevitable and in turn leaving herself in a very vulnerable position.

"You'd best let that money work better for you. Take a lodging in one of the villages, see if you can get a little light work to tide you over. A room is what you need to rent, not a property like this."

"But if Jeremiah..."

"My dear Mrs Lythe," he interrupted. "If Jeremiah was concerned, he would be back now. I fear he is lost. If you hang on here you will fall into debt, and then who knows where this will end. Caleb Lythe was a good man, and in good conscience I can not leave you to a future that would see you ruined. Better to adapt to a new life whilst you are still able."

Ellen wound her apron around her hands and looked about the workshop tearfully. "But what am I to do? There's all his tools here..." Everything that Caleb had worked hard to build up, and had looked after so carefully. Things that had been passed on to Jeremiah, and would be needed when he returned. Then outside there were her gooseberry bushes, which were too old to be uprooted. A garden she had tended with her husband. Prize winning fruit.

"Write to the brother, William Longbottom. He is a blacksmith; surely he will have some space for storage, or better, write to the father. Get everything crated off to be stored and then the family has it ready should he return, or if not for whatever reason, well... they will know what best to do. This is not your responsibility. I will have to start looking for new tenants, for my employers need their rents, but you may stay here in the interim."

Ellen couldn't stop herself from crying. "How long?"

"Regretfully I can not say, other than I would start looking now because it will not be long."

This was her married home, her one true home that had been hers, where she had not been employed. In truth, whilst she had lived at the Hurst farmhouse over at Commondale, she had felt as one of the family and it had been truly devastating when she had been evicted from both her home and her employment. Here she was again, to be booted out with little warning and no plan of where she might go next. She supposed she could write to Eleanor MacCaskill and beg her charity again, for Ellen had gone to her on the previous occasion and lived in Whitby for some time. Yet it had been many years since Eleanor had lived in Whitby, and Ellen wanted to think that perhaps she could arrange something under her own initiative. She was alone in the world and she ought to be able to manage herself thus.

With a local love of gossip and speculation that flooded up and down the farming villages of the valley, it did not take long for Ellen to find new lodgings. Anyone who might possibly have employment for her: those who hoped for a cheap bargain; those with more generous terms; and those looking for a tenant, wrote to the widow with their offers and suggestions. It was not the best time of year to take cuttings, but she did so never the less, determined to have new gooseberries with her, and with confirmation of her choice, was taken by William Longbottom senior in a cart also loaded with the carpentry tools, across the moorland road and down to Danby where she was now to reside.

She took a room as a lodger in a cottage close to the river in Danby, further down the hill from Prudence Pengelly, Danby Grange, the Red Briar and other establishments, on a little track around the back of the newly built Wesleyan Methodist Chapel – something her new landlady grumbled about in a rather joyous manner when they saw locals trudging up for their weekly celebrations. Margaret Harbottle, the said elderly widow and landlady, took great delight in pointing out to Ellen on her day of arrival that she was quite safe, for she crossed running water in the form of a small bridge over an even smaller beck, and need not worry about that miserable house of God.

"There is nothing wrong with a little merriment in life, where we can get it," she informed Ellen as she invited her into her small yet comfortable home, "And I for one shall not listen to a word they preach. Sinner this, sinner that. Repent and be miserable and draw a long face. Bah," she shook as if an arctic wind had just blown through her house. "There is nothing wrong with the good church we have had for hundreds of years. It is a walk, but we are all the better for it. Now my dear, let me show you your room."

Mr Harbottle, in his living days, had been very insightful and had invested some savings so that when he died, his widow might have an income to cover her rent and modest living expenses. It showed consideration to the highest degree, especially as he had only been a wheelwright in his working days. A man who made such plans carefully for a day he may not be there, was also a man who was careful with his money, and assumed others could live just as frugally. So it was that Mrs Harbottle decided it was best to take a little extra income and when she heard of the predicament that decent wife of Caleb Lythe's had found herself in, had taken the liberty of writing to her immediately with the suggestion that they could help one another in this way. Her own daughter, a Jemima Twycross as was Harbottle, was blessed with six young children and a successful husband who ran the general store in

Danby. Jemima was finding child rearing, husband helping and housekeeping collectively too much. If a good woman could be employed to come and cook two good meals a day, she would be very glad of it, and in turn Ellen had enough work to keep her in a healthy state of finances. Jemima had not moved far from her mother, in fact her fine house was opposite where the chapel had been erected. Mother and daughter still liked a good grumble about the poor architecture, placement and general lack of consideration, dumping such a site between the residences of two women who had no interest or support for such a movement.

And so it was that Ellen settled into life in Danby. Sometimes she would slowly make her way up the hill to visit Prudence in her little cottage, but more often Prudence would take an energetic stroll down to the Harbottle residence, followed by a more puffing exercise to return home, much to the amusement of locals. Occasionally she would pass by the local gamekeeper, Mr Hart, who would smile without warmth at her, in greeting only to save his own face, and make a comment that it was nice to see her so well occupied these days. The first time Prudence smiled dumbly at him and the man he was stood conversing with. As she passed by, she heard Hart snort at the other man and comment how marriage had at least silenced her brainless tongue. There was nothing worse than a woman who tried to tell a man his business, especially one who was merely lumbering stock. Prudence remembered meeting him in the lane and telling him he had been wrong about the kestrels he had shot. She supposed he still felt embarrassed about it, but it didn't do to insult her to better his wrong. She could tell from the way the men chortled together that no one was much bothered about what she thought.

It was in the summer that the old nausea, which, had Prudence been on the waters, she would have likened to sea sickness, crept back upon her. The energy drained from her limbs and it became a dreadful chore to get up the hill. Other maritime connections were exciting the locals, for there was a cluster of people near the Red Briar, a miasma of excitement about them. There was much talk and hand shaking and the slapping of backs. Prudence wondered if someone had received a lucrative contract, or perhaps a better tenancy agreement had come from the squire at Danby Grange, and there would be improvements made upon the cottages on the estate.

Farmer Purdey of Hollin Farm saw Prudence puffing up the hill and ran down like an eager little school boy, which was an odd image on his pin legs and rounded ale stomach, to carry her basket till she had reached the Red Briar and the junction where her own lane ascended. "It is a great day, Mrs Pengelly," he declared, shaking her hand and passing her the basket at the same time. "A great day for us all."

Prudence didn't know what to do with herself, trying to not tipple over the basket whilst the farmer pumped her arm up and down as if he was trying to fill a bucket with water.

Another man in the mêlée shook a newspaper at them. "We've done it!" he said, as if Farmer Purdey didn't already know.

"We've shown him."

"Rule Britannia is the best."

"That'll be the end of old Bony now."

"Bony?" Prudence breathed.

"We've only done it, sent Napoleon packing!" the man cried enthusiastically as if he personally had ensured the victory.

The news was a few days old, but news took time to come from the continent and following that, papers had to be dispatched across the county. Prudence hadn't been one for following world affairs and the goings on of the ruling world, but Curnow had known what she was talking about when she mentioned the men had been happy they'd beaten a bony man. Or rather Napoleon, Curnow had corrected her with a smile touched with condensation. Napoleon Bonaparte had been causing a lot of trouble on the continent; indeed there had been wars going on for years. She knew the militia had been recruiting from the Red Briar. Of course she knew that, but it had been going on for so long that she had stopped giving it a thought. Curnow had been in a more talkative mood and had decided to illuminate her that evening, explaining how the Duke of Wellington had won a great victory at the battle of Waterloo over in Belgium, and Napoleon, that little dictator of France, was finally beaten and sent packing. It was a great moment for their country. Prudence had nodded, finished her supper then gone out in the yard to throw it back up.

Others continued better with their exuberance. The landlord of the Red Briar was so pleased that he decided to rename his premises the Duke of Wellington to honour their great British hero. A sign painter was hired and a new pub sign erected with a rather wooden portrait of the great man peering down his sculpted nose, all resplendent in his red military jacket with golden braiding and buttons. Villagers shook hands and said life would be better now that the French had been shown what's what.

Prudence didn't feel that the French had any bearing on her life. Issues much closer to home, nausea and general lethargy made it more than a chore to get through the basics of her day to day living. The French could do what they liked, she had enough to do with trying not to throw up all the time.

As the weeks built up, her nausea did eventually wear off. And she would have felt better about it, if it were not for the fact that her abdomen started to swell at a rapid pace and people began to notice. She tried to ignore it all, for she did not wish to think on what it would mean for her, but nature it seemed, would go the full course this time. People smiled and nodded knowingly to one another. Some women, having been through the process many times, wrinkled their brows and shook their heads, stating that Prudence was getting too big too quickly and that something must be wrong. Others were polite in passing, but as soon as they thought she was out of earshot, commented that she must be brave, considering what had happened to both of her sister-in-laws. Probably just stupid, another retorted. He'd had it on good authority that Prudence was like a heifer. Good natured and hard working, but earthly simple minded. Perhaps that will get her through it. He'd always thought Magdalene Dixon thought too much.

Prudence returned to her cottage, sat down at the table and sobbed. She had tried not to think about what was happening inside her, but now that she admitted that she was indeed with child, she realised that she was going to die. The village gossips were correct. She had been very stupid.

When Curnow arrived home expecting his supper, nothing was ready and Prudence looked drained and haggard as if she had already taken her journey over the river of the dead. The lack of culinary scents in the building, coupled with a dying fire and a shaking rotund wife did not bode well. Even Ki loitered back on the threshold, sensing the unhappy atmosphere.

Curnow set his tool bag on the ground and considered his home. It did not look as though shouting or a slap would have any desired effect here. He mulled it over for a few minutes, a shadow in the open doorway. Prudence did not speak, which was noteworthy in itself, for she was always the one to fill a silence. Finally he entered the cottage, closing the door behind him. "What ails thee, wife?"

Prudence stared at him as if he were the last thing to grasp before she went under. "I am going to die."

"Very true."

She felt her chest contract into itself in horror. The easy way he responded sounded as though he had known about this far longer than she realised, and furthermore that he was quite comfortable with the state of affairs.

"Judging by your face, you have a date in mind."

"Don't you?"

He shrugged. "Only that not one of us is immortal. Our deaths are the thing we can rely upon."

"I am with child."

Curnow nodded. Even he, who was neither in tune with the ways of women nor massively interested, had realised this fact some time ago. This was the first instance Prudence had spoken of it, and it was not in anything resembling a joyful manner.

"Longbottom babies destroy their mothers."

"Magdalene is still alive."

"She is dead inside. I will be next. They're all saying it."

Curnow sniffed. Most of the idiots around here couldn't predict what side of the bed they'd wake up on, let alone anything more substantial. Her highly superstitious husband – for Curnow's head was more filled with folklore, sayings and ancient tales that even the oldest farmer's wife of the moors knew – surprised her with the following words: "Just a coincidence."

Prudence's eyes widened ever slightly more.

"You know how it is with babies. A lot die. A lot of women die. I saw it in my own family, I..." he stopped himself there, realising he was wandering into a subject he never spoke of in these parts. "Magdalene and Christina were never Longbottom women of blood. They only took the name by marriage."

Prudence let her shoulders drop. That was a fair point. Her own mother had survived the birthing chamber many times. Perhaps other people could be wrong when they said things. "So you don't think I'm going to die."

"I never said that," Curnow muttered, going to the pantry cupboard to look for something to eat. "Only that it'll be chance of circumstance and not family tradition if you do die."

She wasn't sure if she was supposed to find comfort in that.

"As long as it's not born on the day of the beast, all will be well."

And there was her superstitious Cornishman back again. "The day of the beast, I don't know when..."

He turned and stood up, half a loaf wrapped in a cloth in his hand. "When do you think it will happen?"

"I couldn't say exactly. Next year, but the winter still. Maybe February?"

"A long way off the day then." Curnow nodded, satisfied with this. "Then I say all will be well."

Curnow may well have been certain that no curse or superstition would have a say over Prudence's chances of survival, but Prudence remained convinced for the remainder of her pregnancy that it would kill her. Visits from family did little to quell her uneasiness. William and Magdalene visited one weekend, and when Prudence dared to utter a word, Magdalene could barely look her in the eye. At this stage

Prudence looked like a barrel in a dress, so large was her abdomen, and the maternity signal triggered something in Magdalene's brain that sent her back into her dark pit. It was not to be a happy Christmas at the Longbottom smithy.

Her father and stepmother came by in their pony and trap, with congratulations and a new garden gate that her father had made in the workshop. Her father was awkward, as was his way, and as a man who kept himself quite separate from the woes of women, did not worry over any potential complications. This would be what he hoped would be the first surviving grandchild. For a man who had sired so many offspring, it was a strange state of affairs to say he was now in his sixties and did not have one single grandchild to his list of achievements. The four dead babies did not count. Megan Longbottom, her step mother, was gushing and excitable, and repeated what she had heard other women say over the years. Megan had never birthed any of her own children, living through her child bearing years an old maid. There was some story that she had suffered an accident as a young maid which had rendered her infertile, but whatever the reason, the fact remained that she had no direct experience and was safely distanced from what was inevitable.

The only person who sat and held her hands, taking her worries seriously but soothing her with words of truth, was Ellen Lythe. She was there when Ada Robinson had been passing. Ada was known as the local midwife, through sheer volume of experience of helping with other deliveries over twenty years. Prudence had impressed upon her that she wished for as much help as she could offer. Ada had smiled kindly and patted her hand in a distracted manner, saying all first mothers were like this and she wasn't to worry. Of course, judging by the size of her, there were twins on the way, and they'd have a busy time of it.

Prudence had grown wan, taking the word of a professional now as gospel. She was following Magdalene and Christina. Ellen had clutched her hand and reminded her that both her own mother, Gillian Longbottom, and her grandmother Maud Hurst had delivered twins safely, both women surviving and both sets of twins at least surviving infancy. Maud's first pregnancy had been the twins Eleanor and Gillian. Ellen had been there when they were born.

"I know you go by Mrs Pengelly now, and you were a Longbottom before that, but underneath it all you're a Hurst woman, and the Hurst women always get through these things."

Ellen had taken to coming up to the cottage when her work at Jemima's kitchen was complete and she could get a lift up the hill in a passing cart. Some evenings she might stay over and sleep in the kitchen rather than brave a snowstorm that had blown up. She'd sit by the fire, contentedly wrapped up in layers of shawls and woollens, and click away with her knitting needles. Prudence wondered if this was such a good idea, to have her kitchen so reminiscent of Christina's, but she was so tired that she did not have the energy to protest. Waddling about the house took it out of her, as if there was a quarry rock in her hips trying to push her legs apart.

It was one such early morning when Ellen had slept over and Curnow had already set off to Danby mill to attend to repair work, that Prudence paused by the range and put her hand to the post to lean in to the steady weight of the roof prop. She closed her eyes as she felt a deep groaning ache below. It rumbled on for a minute and then wore off. She went to fetch the pail, then noticed that Ellen was staring at her.

"You all right, girl?"

"I'm fine. Just an ache. It's these winter chills. They go right through you."

"Had it before?"

"No, it's fine, really. Forget it."

Prudence felt another ache before Ellen left to head down into Danby village to start work on the Twycross family's meals. Ellen said she'd pop back up after she'd finished, but Prudence told her not to worry and not to bother trying to get herself back up the hill. It felt as though there might be snow coming. For the rest of the day Prudence busied herself in her chores, getting used to the aches as they came and went. By the evening the severity of the ache had increased and she had to stop eating and close her eyes as the wave came upon her. The nature of the pain was changing as well, as if her body was trying to pull the very flesh between her legs up into her abdomen.

Curnow watched his wife in silent observation as she dropped her spoon into her bowl of stew. She closed her eyes as if she was trying to summon the very lord above them. Her breathing grew measured and audible through her nostrils as she kept her lips firmly set together. As if something was greatly trying her patience and she was waiting for her fury to subside.

"Do you need me to fetch someone?"

Prudence opened her eyes and met Curnow's gaze. He knew. Even the man knew. And of course she knew herself what was happening. She may not have children herself just yet, but she was no innocent fool, she knew the process and had assisted others. She knew it would have to happen, only not yet, she pleaded with nature, she wasn't quite ready to die and would just like a few more days.

"Perhaps," she eventually spoke. "We might mention to Ada Robinson that I'm not quite myself."

Prudence was in labour for two days. She silently prayed that she might not die, then fell into a panic that if she was to live, did it mean the babies would be born dead? She alternated between roaring and crying and Ada told her more than once that she needed to stop holding back. Curnow gave up and left the building to spend the duration safely in the warmth of the Duke of Wellington. After the first day the undulations and contractions of her flesh grew so intense that she no longer had the focus to pray, only to plead that the damn things might be plucked from her so this infernal torment would stop.

And then suddenly they were out, two little baby girls with a shock of red hair crying at the indignity of it all. Ellen was washing their angry red faces down and swaddling them in warm blankets. Ada helped Prudence deliver the afterbirth. She gave Prudence's hand a tight squeeze and assured her she'd done very well and everything was looking very promising. At some point Prudence fell asleep. When she awoke she was surprised to discover than not only was she still alive, but the two little girls were still quite warm and breathing. They lay nestled together in their basket, half opening a begrudging eye when Curnow returned to inspect his offspring.

They will die in the next few days, Prudence worried, thinking on how joyful it had been when Magdalene's girls had been born, only for them to fail in the first week.

A week later they were contented and putting on weight and Prudence conceded perhaps they ought to have names. Three weeks after the birth, mother and girls were all doing exceedingly well and Prudence was ready that Sunday to be churched and to get the girls to the font to be christened. And so the family made the trek to St Hilda's, walking there and accepting a ride in Farmer Purdey's cart on the return. In those cold-stone hallowed walls of old Danby church, the arrival of Kerenza Hurst Pengelly and Derwa Gillian Pengelly was announced to the community and blessed under the sanctity of God.

The snows finally melted away and the greenness of spring burst across the valley like a rushed seeping of ink spilt upon a cloth. The world bloomed. Primroses and cowslips were out in the hedgerows like little pads of floral butteries, birds were busy back and forth to nests of chicks and the first lambs were being born to the moorland herds. It was an afternoon in late May, and Prudence was sitting in the garden peeling potatoes and thinking about precious little. Derwa and Kerenza, now three and a half months old, were napping on a blanket in the grass, shaded from the sun by the drying laundry.

A figure walked up the lane that skirted the front of the cottage gardens, a mere fleeting image in a background until he stopped at the garden gate. He set his tool bag on the grass verge by the wall and set his hands upon the top of the drystone wall. As the light breeze rippled through the sheets he caught glimpses of the two little children napping in the garden. Twins yet again. The mother was oblivious, humming to herself as she worked at her potatoes.

"I'd heard you were with child," he called over the wall. "It gladdens me to see all three of you doing so well."

Prudence jumped as the unexpected voice interrupted her idyll, and dropped her knife in the bowl of water. She gazed across the garden to the stranger at the wall, a gaunt man with grey at the temples. Well dressed for an artisan or craftsman, certainly someone of that status. A travelling craftsman? A beggar? He wore a flat cap on his head and a red neckerchief around his throat. The accent in his words was very local. Her eyes widened as her brain caught up with what she was seeing and she ran across to embrace the man.

"Oh, Jeremiah!" she exclaimed gleefully. "They told me to forget you; that you were done for."

He smiled, a little tired by the experiences of the past year. "Aye, it did feel that way for a time."

"And you are back? You have come back to Egton?"

"No, no I will not return there. The house has been rented out to others a long time. Not that I complain," he added when he caught a vein of worry in Prudence's face. "Even if it had been kept back for me I would not go back there. Too much sadness resides in those walls."

"Oh, Jeremiah..."

"Don't fret little sister. I am well. I have started a new chapter one might say. I've been over to Commondale to fetch my tools from father."

"Everyone knows you are well?"

"They do now."

"And what has happened to you? Where are you to go? You've been lost a year."

"I was a drunken wretch and things happened, I..." Jeremiah grew a hand over his thin face. "Let us not worry about the past. It is done and I have moved on. I have honest employment now as a carpenter in the shipyards at Whitby. I've worked with wood all I can remember, yet I have been learning new things. It's an art to create a vessel sea worthy. I am busy and occupied and content with myself. I have lodgings in a smart boarding house in Whitby where a number of the men working at the yard live, so I keep good honest company."

"I am very glad to hear it," Prudence said. "Now, would you like to come and meet your nieces?"

Jeremiah looked uncertain. "I wouldn't want to wake them."

If Prudence had stopped to think, she may have wondered if his hesitancy was lack of confidence around babies, or perhaps a pain from all that he had lost. Prudence was full of joy, giddy from lack of sleep and couldn't see beyond herself. She pulled her brother through the gate and hurried him across to the sleeping babes. Kerenza half opened an eye to give them a disinterested look before snuffling back into sleep. Prudence went to pick them up, but Jeremiah stopped her. "Let them be. They look very happy where they are." He watched Prudence's blissful face and wished Christina could have had this.

"Oh Jeremiah," she suddenly burst out. "I did not think. I did not mean to upset you."

"I keep myself busy with hard work now. I realised hard drink wouldn't undo what had happened. Spending time in alehouses puts one in the way of unpleasant company. I... no..." he shook his head, considering his younger sister's blissful ignorance and happiness. "And how is Curnow? Is he about?"

"He's at work!" Prudence laughed. "It's the middle of the day and the week. Where else would he be?"

"Aye, I just thought I should say hello before I head back down to the coast. Whereabouts is he working?"

"He's back at the mill just now."

"I'll just nip down and say hello. I never know when I'll next get chance to come back up." He kissed his sister on the cheek. "Take good care of yourself and the little ones."

Fetching his bag from the grass, Jeremiah walked down the hill to the river and the direction of the water mill. A weight slunk around his mind. He had meant to mention it to Prudence, for Curnow was not the easiest of men to speak to, but she had been so happy he could not darken her joy. But he could not return to Whitby without speaking of what he had heard. Unintentionally he feared he had caused some trouble. A drunken tongue wags too easily, although in his defence, even sober he would not have thought it would have been a problem to speak of his family.

Curnow did not seem to be particularly surprised to see him, although he was not a man taken to great words or emotion. He nodded to Jeremiah, noting the bag of tools he carried. "Looking for work?"

"I've been back to fetch my own tools. I have good employment on the shipyards in Whitby. But a man works easier with his own tools in his hands, and I had a feeling father might have taken them for storage."

"Aye, they hoped in the beginning you'd come around."

"It took a little longer than that, but I have seen the error."

Jeremiah wasn't sure how to broach the subject. One couldn't start a casual thread of conversation with Curnow and gently bring it around to the point, as if one accidentally arrived there. As if to save him from a quick shock. "I spent a lot of time drinking in the beginning."

"I heard."

"You worked in Whitby quite a few years back."

Curnow stopped with the plane, a corkscrew of wood shavings dangling.

"I talked about my family, I still do. I mean to say I had mentioned your name on account of you having worked in Whitby. A few remembered you..."

"People remember things."

"What I mean to say is some of these people are less than reputable. They were surprised that you might still be in the area."

Curnow had turned his back to Jeremiah. He had set the plane against the wood but not restarted his work. "I would not think on it anymore," he said.

"Aye, well, I thought I would just mention it."

"I would be obliged if you did not give out my location."

"Of course not." Jeremiah wanted to ask if there was any need to worry. Especially on his sister's account. What had Curnow done in Whitby, what had happened that had sent him up into the Esk Valley? He could have played the over protective older brother and demanded the truth, but he doubted Curnow would tell him a thing. Besides which it was a bit late now. They were married and had two daughters. He wanted to say something, or offer some help, if only for Prudence but he could not think what to say that Curnow might take seriously. It felt as though their talk was at a close. "I'd best be off," he finally managed. "I need to be back in Whitby before dusk."

"Aye," was all Curnow had to say.

'Aye' may well have been all Curnow had to say, but Jeremiah's warning came to proof in the late summer when Curnow's Whitby history started to catch up with him.

The workshop he had set up at the cottage was aglow with early autumnal sunlight that afternoon. Curnow was at work on a new kitchen dresser destined for Danby Grange, at a pre arranged design and price. The housekeeper had been keen to leave the price until the article was finished, and perhaps her mistress could have a look at it, but Curnow had insisted. He had too much experience of their social betters than to haggle for a price when the work was done. He'd made that error in his youth, and been offered an insult of a price to the craftsmanship, barbed with elocution and mutterings of daylight robbery, inferior woods, and by God, man, I could get something of better quality for half the price. He knew that his work was good and he no longer cared for games.

Prudence was away over the other side of the valley in Ainthorpe, visiting her Aunt Gilly and family. The girls were with her, already losing their babylike looks and becoming children more with every day. Derwa and Kerenza were like a pair of small red headed ducks, sat straight, eyes alert and heads up, looking about at everything with that blank yet inquisitive stare that little children got away with. An elder child would be reprimanded to mind its manners.

He was focused on cutting out the dovetail joint for a drawer and did not hear the approach of a visitor. When he stood up to straighten out his back, he realised he was not alone, and judging by the way the man was looking about, he had been here for some time.

The man, a little grizzled having not shaved in a couple of days, wore a nice enough suit except that it was worn around the edges. He had rough hands, but not from an honest day's work. He had a calculating look that at first glance could have been mistaken for friendliness, but this man did not have friends. He had aged since Curnow had last seen him, for there was an abundance of grey in his beard and what hair that was showing from beneath the cap. There was also a new slashed scar on the face.

Neither spoke nor nodded an acknowledgement, but merely looked at one another, almost as if to wonder what the other was doing here. Curnow remained standing, his hand lowering onto the main body of the dresser in front of him. It was with coincidence that his fingers found a flat file resting there, the long metal body of the tool with the work-warmed wooden handle.

The stranger broke the silence. "We'd thought you'd left the county years ago."

Curnow's eyebrows may have risen slightly, if at all, but he gave no response. Ki, who had been stretched out asleep in the sunshine, had woken and was immediately on edge, reading the tension in the air, but also sensing a smell he had not been close to for a lot of years. He moved to the edge of the space, by a pile of cut off pieces of wood, and stayed in a pensive state of readiness.

"Can't say we liked you. Can't say we missed you," the man ambled on, picking up a wooden mallet from the workbench and weighting it in his hand. "But we thought you had sense in your head. Thought you'd left the area a long time ago."

Perhaps Jeremiah hadn't been completely honest with him as to just how much he'd been talking and with whom. Curnow had always been a little surprised he'd gotten away from Whitby so easily. He had to travel a few miles to disappear from that sea port underworld. Perhaps it was so that things not looked for were easily hidden in plain sight.

The man let out a sigh. "What with you being a Cornishman, we'd thought you would have headed on home, where you belonged. Makes a man think, that you didn't. After what you did in Whitby, you'd be sensible to leave the county. Makes a man wonder what devilry keeps you from your home. Must be something really bad. Makes a man think you'd be a dead man if you ever went back to Cornwall."

As if to add emphasis to his point, he slammed the mallet down on the workbench. He smiled, noting the way Curnow did not so much as flinch. For a little fellow, he'd always been a cocky bugger. He supposed that was what had first attracted his employer's attention. Curnow Pengelly could get himself noticed without wanting to. Turned out he could disappear rather competently too. Not forever though.

He spread his hands over the workbench and leaned forward. He was almost six foot in height and towered over Curnow. With the longer shadows of autumn, he appeared as a magisterial might facing off the Cornishman. "It's all got my employer thinking he was perhaps too lenient in that little matter you were involved in. Forgetting about it when you left. When we heard you'd had the cheek to hang around, it got him thinking."

"You're just the scouting party."

The man shrugged. "That is true. Rumour's one thing, but we wanted to know where you were, what your situation was. I've heard you have two babies now. Girls as well. That's nice." His eye glinted.

Ki hopped up onto all fours in ready support as Curnow suddenly moved. His hand grasped the handle of the file and with a dull slam he had stabbed down into the workbench with the flat metal end. She showed no hesitation to the flesh and bone he would have to hammer through to find his place.

The man let out a roar as the file was stabbed through the back of his hand, pinning him to the workbench. He arched backwards like a cat stretching out, and his eyes widened as he saw the thick dark flood of blood come out across the bench. It swallowed up specks of sawdust, following the groves and lines of cuts in the heavy durability of the wood.

With the man lowered towards his own hand in agony, Curnow stepped up to the bench, so they were now at an even level. He looked the man in the eye. "You get gone," he told him. "And don't you be coming back."

The man gagged on his pain, tensing for Curnow to pull out the file. Instead the man walked away and returned to his work. He always had been a hard bastard. The man breathed heavily through his nose, focussing his energy and preparing himself for a second jolt of pain. Gripping the file handle with his good hand, he wavered for a moment before roaring with the wrench as he freed his hand, letting forth a gushing of fresh blood that went spattering to the ground. Tossing the file to the floor, making the dog jump, he took a grubby handkerchief from his pocket and wrapped it around his hand. Already it was wet and red with his blood. He clutched it tightly. He'd have to walk back up onto the moors and get some moss to pack it with on his way home.

"We're not disappearing, Pengelly," he told the carpenter as he backed out of the workspace. "This will be brought to a conclusion. You mark my words."

Curnow gave him a disdainful look, but said nothing. He would not be intimidated. By the time Prudence got home, the blood had been soaked up in sawdust before being tossed into the fire. The file and the floor were mopped up and the general ambience suggested that nothing of note had happened there all day.

An old solider from the wars, now one-legged and unfit for a lot of work, was sitting at Whitby harbour. The man had a fine voice, a positive disposition despite what life threw at him, and a well used but tuneful fiddle. He leaned back, his mind fully involved in the music as he sang, accompanying himself on the fiddle. His voice boomed out across the seagulls and bobbing boats, the chatter of the fish market and the distant singing of the herring girls who were gutting and processing fish with sharp knives and lightening speed. The smell of salt, seaweed and fish guts were thick in the air, sending the screeching seagulls into a frenzy as they dive bombed the inky greasy waves of the harbour for the discarded offal.

Jeremiah had finished his shift and was taking a stroll along the harbour front before he would return to his lodgings and supper. Their landlady, an opinionated and older woman with a domineering need for exactness, but a kind heart underneath it all, always made sure her lodgers had a good warm supper waiting for them. The house was warm, a talent for a chilly sea port lurching towards winter, but between the fires, her constant talk and walk and the knitted goods she was constantly at, it was a surprise they were not sweating in fevers. Mrs Linskill, widow, was a great knitter, and her paying guests were quite convinced she knitted in bed whilst asleep, although none were bold enough to creep into her room to check. The woman was prolific and always had a ball of wool in her apron. Her hands clicked away at the needles with no need to watch what she was doing. She was in the kitchen instructing the maid on the correct consistency of stew – click click – greeting people in the morning click- click – away to the shops and down the alley click – click. They were no mere squares of basic stitch she produced either, but socks and blankets, ganseys and hats, plain coloured and patterned. When she learned of Jeremiah's tragic history – he was not sure how, but Mrs Linskill always got what she wanted – she took a particular care of him. Out of concern for his scrawny, grief-ridden frame and the chills he might suffer, she took to knitting him a gansey, collating the patterns of the Whitby fishermen, a family emblem of her own design and good luck knots. At a point she had to give up knitting and walking with that particular construction for it grew too cumbersome, and the project kept her more in her rocking chair by the fire. A gansey, a fisherman's best friend, that closely knitted jumper, a creation made all at once, as one piece, in one colour and with patterns interwoven into its flesh.

The gansey was long since finished and Jeremiah sported it that evening as he wandered through the business of trade and commerce. The fishing was done for the day, the last of the salt barrels filled with gutted herrings being shifted for transportation. Jeremiah could not claim happiness, but he had found some level of peace and acceptance in his new life. Work kept him busy, then walking among the crowds in town, ignored and just a piece of the background, was reassuring to him.

He paused to stare out at the bobbing water, and gradually became aware that he was being observed, and not from a great distance either. He turned to find two herring girls, busy with their knitting and finished with their own day's work, walking along behind him. They were close to one another, their heads together and eyebrows lowered in some consternation as they examined him – not his face or his being but rather his back.

They were put out when he stopped and turned. One of the girls straightened. "Away back with ye, we hadn't finished looking." She had a bold, broad accent, almost hard to understand. Jeremiah was growing accustomed to tuning his ear to different accents. Where he had grown up there had been little else but his own, yet here in the port they got people from all over the country, and even further away as the continent, men from Holland, the Baltic States, Russia and Norway. This girl sounded Scottish.

"Collar looks like da's old gansey," the second girl spoke to her compatriot. Her eyes glittered, flitting all the time as she knitted as if blustering on the wind, before she met Jeremiah's eye.

The two girls were dressed similarly, the dresses covered over in many layers and shawls criss-crossed over their chests to keep them proof against the sea elements. They had dark shaded bonnets on, hair coming loose. The one who had told Jeremiah to turn back was blonde, the other girl a dark haired creature. All the time their hands were busy with their knitting needles, fish-gut stained aprons with pockets for sharp knives, balls of wool and needles. They did not know the meaning of being still, always doing and moving. Either their hands were a blur as they gutted the fish, or their feet were pattering as they marched up and down the harbour in little knitting clusters. These girls came from all over the country, following the herring work and staying together in boarding houses considered suitable for young women away from home.

Jeremiah tipped his cap to them. "Evening, ladies."

This sent up a titter of giggles, the girls leaning their heads together to share in their amusement as he started to walk away. The blonde girl was a little bolder, stepping forward as if he might catch her arm or ask her name, but he only wandered by. The other girl watched him go, quickly trying to retain the detail of his gansey pattern to memory.

If Jeremiah came into contact with the blonde girl again, he never noticed her, and she eventually gave up trying to attract his attention, turning to a more susceptible young fisherman hailing from Flamborough. He did not think of the other girl either, but when he came upon her knitting whilst perched on a pile of wooden crating, he recognised her and remembered the laughter from a couple of weeks ago.

He paused to give her a second glance, and when their eyes met and he realised she had also recognised him, he smiled and tipped her cap to her. "It is a fine evening for the time of year."

The girl smiled and shook her head as if it were a ridiculous thing to say. "Aye, well, the light holds better down here for longer."

"I doubt you'd need it for your knitting."

"Aye," she sighed. "That be the truth of it." She'd been knitting since she was a young girl, sitting in the dark cottage by the sea, learning the craft from her old granny who was virtually blind by that point but could turn out the most perfect ganseys quicker than any other woman in the village.

"You sound like you're a long way from home."

"Do I?"

"Scottish. I had an Uncle once who came from Scotland. But he didn't talk like you. He came from Falkirk."

"Falkirk!" the young woman chortled. "Why, that's away down south. Inland as well."

"You come from the ports to the north?" Jeremiah asked, desperately wishing his Scottish geography was better, for he did not wish to lose her conversation just yet.

"I come from the islands; the northern islands. The Orkneys."

"The Orkneys..."

"Off the north coast of Scotland. It's a long hard journey from here. You don't sound like you've travelled such a distance."

"No, I come from the moors inland," he waved his hand vaguely. "But a day's walk."

"One could say you're still at home..." she paused, expecting him to fill a gap, but it was obviously too subtle for him. She smiled, noting his expression and full attention. "That is if I knew what to call you."

"Oh forgive me, Jeremiah, Jeremiah Longbottom."

"Longbottom! What a curious name. Well Mr Longbottom, they'd probably say it isn't decent, me out talking to you like this, but never the mind."

Jeremiah stepped up to her. In her lap she had a mass of ready knitted article, all in the same deep, dark brown. The wool looked strong, comforting and proof to the elements. "What are you knitting here, er... I don't know your name."

"You might call me Miss Leask," she informed him. "And as to what I'm knitting, if you don't know then I shall not tell you yet."

"That would suggest you might tell me another day?"

Miss Leask slipped down from her perch with a nimble hop, keeping her creation cradled in her arm. She tilted her head and considered him directly. She didn't suppose she ought to be so bold, a working girl she was, no fancy lady but even so there was always talk of morals and good behaviour. Not letting those sailors get their way for once they had, a girl's life was ruined. "That remains to be seen," she told him. "But for now I'm away for my supper. Good night to you."

"And a good evening to you, Miss Leask," he called after her retreating figure.

Miss Leask smiled to herself, tentatively and not wishing to be too hopeful, but knowing that she had not started her knitting in vain.

"Sonneta, are you still knitting away at that thing?"

Maggie sat up in the bed, shivering as she felt the cold air of the room creep down her back. It was a hard cold night and one wanted to be in bed and under the blankets. The girls had piled all their spare clothes upon the bed to add warmth, and had managed to sneak a hot water pot from the kitchen. It was already rapidly losing its heat in the bed. It was virtually dark, only light from the moon touching upon the edge of things. It was a watered light that cut through the threadbare attic curtain. After a few moments Maggie's eyes adjusted. She could see the breath from her mouth; the air was getting that cold. She pulled the sides of her cap down over her ears and was grateful again for the thick long tresses of blonde hair that were loose for bed and kept her head and neck warm.

Sonneta, her bed fellow, was sitting up and clicking away with her needles. The light was poor but she didn't need to see what she was doing. The bulk of her creation lay on her lap atop of the blankets.

"Sonneta, do you not hear me?" Maggie pushed at her shoulder. "We'll have to be up in a few hours. You don't want to go without your sleep. You know what happens to the hands of tired girls."

She shuddered, with the cold or the memory it was hard to say. They all had cuts and nicks on their hands from the high speed gutting of herring – it was impossible not to. The knives were so sharp and they were going so fast that they often didn't notice until the salt got to the wound and it started to hurt. Slices and cuts soon healed and hands remained as intended. She remembered a girl who had been out chasing the lads several nights in a row. She had been a little distracted in her work even when well-slept, but at the end of that week she was positively sloppy and heavy handed. Her knives were particularly sharp. Everyone heard the screams, and before Sonneta had looked to the girl, her eye line had automatically gone to the salt barrel where the gutted fish went and she saw the top inch of a finger lying there. Human blood mixed with fish guts. They'd used the girl's hand rags to tie up the finger to try and stop the bleeding, then taken her back to the boarding house to ask if the landlady couldn't stitch up her finger. The lassie was pale and shaking at this point, her arm slick with blood. The landlady, a staunch woman of few words, had ignored the state of the girl and held up her hand as if it were a slab of meat up for consideration of purchase. She'd pursed her lips and everyone had thought she would sew the wound up. The landlady was actually thinking there wasn't enough skin to pull across to stitch it, and she doubted these young girls could afford a doctor. Besides, it was a big wound, no time to delay, so she'd wrenched the girl across to the fire and rammed the stub of the finger against blisteringly hot irons. No one had thought it was possible to scream more than when the finger had been sliced off, but it seemed there were even higher pains. The girl had passed out to the bubbling of boiling blood and steam mixed with the thick scent of cooked, scorched meat.

She had lived, and although an ugly sight, the finger had healed up. The girl had adapted to the shortened digit and continued in her career. She'd switched to another gang of herring girls and Sonneta had lost track of her. She wasn't even sure of the girl's name any more. It felt like a lifetime ago. What an age for a lassie of twenty one to feel. But Sonneta had joined this travelling band when she was sixteen. It was a long time since she'd just been allowed the innocent carefree days of a child.

She put the needles down. "Aye, best get some sleep." There was only the bottom waist band and then she'd be finished. It would be completed tomorrow.

It had been some weeks since she'd last spoken to Mr Jeremiah Longbottom. It had been a fleeting and odd conversation whilst knitting on the harbour. Sonneta had seen the Yorkshireman about since then, but only at a distance. Early in the morning when they were already hard at work, he'd walk by, looking at the faces of the girls. Searching. She told herself it was foolish pride to think he might be looking for her, but when she felt his eyes upon her, he seemed to settle as if a task were complete and he headed off to work. So she had started her new knitting project, and asked around a little now and then as to who this Longbottom was. He was a carpenter working at the shipyards. Not a local, by the minute standards of locality being within a one mile radius, but to Sonneta he was a Yorkshireman and very much the local. He had only been in Whitby a year or so. He came from the moors, they said, up on the hills above Whitby. And he was almost ten years her senior. Beyond that folk didn't know that much. Some said he'd been drinking for a while but that had all stopped and he had become respectable since he'd taken on his work. A carpenter, she thought to herself. Creating with his hands, just like her with her knitting.

A few days after the temperatures dropped again the narrow streets and alleyways were lethal with ice. Whispy flakes of snow blew in from the sea, obliterating the view of the coast. Bells ringing were disembodied, hovering in the frost. Sonneta had been up to the cliffs, taking in the full galling blast of winter at the abbey before scuttling down the steps and into the shelter of the old town. Here clusters of buildings leaned towards one another over lanes, their heads almost meeting. Her fingers were numb and her cheeks bright red as proof against the cold. The chill pricked at the flesh of her face, but she felt invigorated and alive. She moved through the shadowed hulks of locals, nestled down into their collars, shawls pulled up tight, hurrying from bright fire to fire. She was looking forward to getting back under cover with a warm bowl of soup in her hands.

In her eagerness to get home, she ran into a cluster of men, begging their pardon and staggering away only to steep out onto sheet ice. Her feet lost their purchase and she skittered about, wobbling dangerously and certain she would fall until she bumped into a man heading in the opposite direction. He slithered on the ice and they grabbed at one another's arms for balance, laughing in embarrassment as they tried to get off the ice and to the side. Staggering away, they made land on tilted cobbles and tumbled against the side of a building at the start of a narrow alley.

"Begging your pardon, that ice caught me completely unawares!" Sonneta laughed. She looked up and felt a rush of hot surprise as she recognised the face smiling back at her. "Why, Mr Jeremiah Longbottom, fancy bumping into you."

"Miss Leask."

She was very conscious of the fact that he had a hold of both her arms and was clasping her tightly to his own chest as if she might blow away in the wind. She also knew how girls ought to behave and that she ought to have said less than she had and hurried away. A girl's honour and good name was all she had in the world. Talk of manners and good breeding suggested that she ought not to even feel these emotions and longings that tumbled about inside her, although the rougher cackling talk of the fishwives told her that the realities of human nature and society's expectations were not one and the same.

Jeremiah's smile bloomed. "How very fortunate."

I am tired of my life, Sonneta thought. Tired of the herring, the impermanence, nothing solid to hold on to. Tired of always behaving and repressing and never feeling as though I live for a moment for myself. Afterwards when she was winding her way back home, she realised he might think she was experienced and had done this many times. A girl who seduced a man like that, was hardly the shy blushing virgin that Sonneta actually was. A better suggestion was a strumpet with low morals at best or a fee-taking tart at worst. She was sure he understood her entirely, with that naiveté of a girl in a first proper love. Despite her gasping innocence, there was a niggling of doubt of the woman that she could have made a terrible mistake.

Worries and regrets were for afterwards. In the moment she had pressed herself up against him, straining on her tiptoes that she might touch his face with her cold fingers then press her lips to his. It unlocked something that once released was uncontrollable. They moved deeper into the alley, suddenly her skirts hitched up and she was gasping as they were joined. Hot twists of steam glided upwards from every pant, dispersing into the darkening atmosphere. Then it was over with a shuddering end and her feet slipped back to earth. They embraced again, clung to each other as if washed upon storm battered rocks. The chatter of people passing on the lane close by finished the moment, and in awkwardness they parted, continuing on their separate journeys and wondering desperately if they had made a terrible mistake. What was that other person, almost a stranger, actually thinking?

The underlying worry lingered during the following weeks, but did not ignite for they met again. These meetings were held under more chaste circumstances, talking a walk by the sea front together, strolling up to the abbey ruins above the town and generally padding every street and alley of Whitby without ever seeing anything. Sonneta gabbled away without reserve or thought, and Jeremiah knew everything there was to know about her history, her family and her background. He was more reserved on his own past with only vague mention of parents. Whenever the subject arose, he was quick to switch to tales of what had recently happened at the ship yard. Sonneta was simply too happy to be in his company to think anything of it. All this time she carried around the gansey she had made purposefully for him, symbols and patterns of Whitby interwoven with some of her personal favourites from Orkney. Every time she was about to offer him the jumper, she lost her nerve and the bundle made its way back to the lodging house with her. Impulse eventually got the better of her one early evening when they stood on the sea cliffs looking out to sea as the wind blew back into their faces. Jeremiah made a comment about the maritime chill of the wind and how it went through a man's bones, to which she responded by shaking out the gansey and offering it to him. There was a delighted surprise on his face, which only made her blush with embarrassment. On her walk home she scolded herself, worrying that he would think her a silly fawning girl, like a dumb puppy desperate for attention. Not an adult and his equal.

Sonneta was very much an adult, a woman in her early twenties, with a body that biology was pushing to full womanhood. Shortly after she had handed over the gansey, she was at work in the morning gutting herrings, singing with her friends as they worked when a dreadful sensation overwhelmed her. The smell of the sea, of the dead fish and the guts, which had always been there and which her nose had become a little blind to, suddenly intensified as if the sense of smell had just been born to her. The awareness of the smell bloomed throughout her mind and turned her stomach.

Sonneta dropped her knife. For a short while no one noticed, until her friend Maggie grew aware something was not as it should. Alerted either by the lack of gutting or the silence where Sonneta's should be singing, it was enough for Maggie to stop in her own work. She saw Sonneta's knife on the little table, with her friend staring at it with a bizarre concentration.

"Sonneta, are you quite well?"

"Come on girls," the overseer roared, soon picking up on a pause in activity. "Those fish won't gut themselves."

"I'm going to be sick," Sonneta muttered. She picked up her knife and hurried away from work, much to the annoyance of the overseer. Darting up the alleys into the town to escape the eyes of her fellow girls, she found a little corner to hunker down into as waves of nausea battered her. She closed her eyes and hugged herself, almost wishing the vomit to come so that she might feel better and return to her work. After ten minutes or so the feeling had subsided and she felt better, but at a loss as to what had happened. It had been the smell, she was sure of it. A smell that had never bothered her before. What would the girls be saying about her now? She did not dare go back to work, and scurried away to the boarding house, sneaking in and hiding in her bed for the rest of the day.

Much later Maggie found her, accompanied by the overseer. Oh lord, she thought, they will not give me work and I will be shamed, for I ducked out of a day's labour. I don't know if I have the money to get back home.

The overseer didn't tolerate fools and gave Sonneta a stern, knowing look. "You're a good worker, lass, so a little patience I have for you. And I don't suppose you'll be the first."

"I'm awful sorry I ran away. I don't know what I was thinking..."

"Nevermind, I doubt you'll be with us much longer."

"What?" Panic pricked in her eyes. She was going to cry and embarrass herself further.

"You need to go tell him, and get yourself wed."

Maggie looked aghast as the older woman came out with her blunt advice. "You don't think..."

"I've seen it too many times before. Oldest story in the world." She looked back to Sonneta. "You mind he treats you right. You were a good worker and you deserve a good end."

The overseer had lived long enough to see the same youthful dramas played over and over. Every girl sure no one had ever felt love that way before. The truth of it all was etched in her weather-worn creased face and her hard, unforgiving work ethic. Years went and the girls came and went. Sonneta wasn't the first and she wouldn't be the last. With that final wish, she departed, leaving Sonneta in confusion and tears and Maggie goggling with what might have been going on. Oh what gossip she'd have for the other lasses when Sonneta had calmed down. In truth she was a little jealous. She was yet to get such devoted attentions from a man the way Sonneta obviously had. It was not just, for she was much prettier. She would never admit to such frustrations, either to others or herself. She hugged her friend for the first few minutes until the sobs slowed and she thought she might get a word of sense out of her. She leaned back so she could look upon Sonneta's tear-stained face. She clutched Sonneta's hands in hers. "You must realise what she is talking about."

"I don't know," Sonneta moaned. "It's never bothered me before, the stench of it all, you know me, Maggie. But today I thought I was going to die."

"She thinks you're with child."

"What?" The idea clearly hadn't crossed Sonneta's mind, and the sudden unexpected suggestion stopped her tears and distracted her from her woes.

Maggie felt like the older sister, the wise one, the woman who understands how things worked. "When did you last bleed?"

"Well, I..." She had no idea. Her mind had been so giddy thinking of Jeremiah these past weeks that time had rolled into a blur thinking only of when she might next see him. Some days even remembering to eat was a chore. She certainly hadn't been paying attention to the bodily routines and reflecting it had been lucky she had skipped on the chores of washing out her monthly rags.

"Since the Christmas service at church?"

Sonneta slowly shook her head. Definitely not since then. She couldn't remember when the last time had been. She was not this naive. She knew how women had children and she had known it had been a risk when she had been with him in the alley, but since that day she had buried any worries away and thought no more on it.

A touch of jealous horror ran through Maggie's face as something else occurred to her. Sonneta was now ahead of her in life experience. "You've not gone with him? What? Already? With your carpenter man? Or was it someone else?"

"Maggie!" Sonneta scolded. "He's the only one for me."

Maggie sniffed and went back on her haunches. She had been the first one to see Jeremiah. She remembered giggling about him, and that piercing dark look of a troubled man. How romantic, she'd simpered, then she and Sonneta had giggled and followed him down the road to try and make out the patterns in the sweater he wore. "Well, if he's that wonderful then you've nothing to worry about have you?"

Sonneta gave her a questioning look, before realising the full implications. She sunk back into herself. If he wouldn't take her, she would be ruined. She would have to try to get rid of it, or just throw herself in the sea. She was completely at his mercy.

She and Jeremiah had not known one another long enough. They could not be confident in their long term feelings for one another. She was concerned that he might think she had behaved the way she had in order to trap him, or that she had been looking for a way out of her work and he had been the willing man to turn up at the right time. She wanted to explain that it wasn't like that at all, but simply didn't know how to compose all these confused thoughts and worries into a coherent speech that he might understand and empathise with. In short Sonneta was terrified.

They were sitting together on a low wall near the sea front, and she was very conscious of him staring at her. She hadn't spoken much this evening, and she knew her behaviour strange, distracted and distant as if she might not even wish to be here anymore.

"Something is bothering you."

"I am with child," she blurted out. It was hardly the great speech she had been formulating, or even a line that would gradually lead up to the essence of her worries. Sonneta closed her eyes.

The blood drained from Jeremiah's face. "Not again."

"Not again?" Sonneta's eyes snapped open. "Why, I have never before. You were the only one." She stopped when she realised he wasn't talking about her.

He shook his head and stepped away from the wall. He had sworn he would not go down that road again, for he could not take the pain. He was a curse on women. What on earth had he been thinking, walking out with this young woman? "You see..." How to explain? He never talked of his family, of the deaths. Of his prior life in Egton. He got up from the wall. "My wife..."

"Your wife?" Sonneta shrieked. She had not imagined this possibility, that he had treated her wrong from the very start.

"Yes, my wife," He turned back to her and she darted away.

"Sonneta, please. I am a widower. My wife died before I came to Whitby. I... I don't want to frighten you, but my wife died giving birth to twins."

She nodded solemnly. "I see. And the babies?"

"Born dead."

She did not know what to say, so she stared out to sea instead.

Jeremiah looked at her in anguish. He was going to have to relive it all. Both in memory with Christina and experience with Sonneta. It would kill him. He could not survive it twice. What had he been thinking? He ought to have blotted her from his mind the moment he heard Sonneta and her friend giggling behind him.

"And you're sure of it?"

"Yes."

Why did life have to be so very hard, she wondered. She had tried her best to be good, faltered now and then but she always tried to make the right decision. This all felt very hopeless. She could sense what he was thinking. She was going to die.

"What are we going to do now?"

Jeremiah ran a hand over his face. "First thing's first. Tomorrow we'll go see the reverend about getting the banns read."

She looked surprised by the ease with which he said it.

"Come along, Sonneta," he said, taking her arm. "I won't leave you." No, he thought, he wouldn't leave her. But it would not be all that long before she was leaving him.

Jeremiah was riddled with an impending sense of doom. He tried to keep his worry hidden from Sonneta. They were married as soon as they could in Whitby. He found a small cottage to rent further up the river valley where the air felt clear of the blubberhouse fumes and smog of industry. The walk to the shipyards was not too far, and the sweeter air aided in keeping down Sonneta's nausea. She suffered particularly badly it seemed, Jeremiah could not remember Christina suffering like this. Was it a good sign? He did not know.

Whilst Sonneta was so incapacitated, she was unable to process the herring, and as she grew and became ever clumsier, she doubted they would have her back. She learned to keep home and attempted to cook, missing her own mother more and more every time she wondered how to do something. She had not seen her mother for four long years. Neither mother nor daughter could write and did not have the money for hiring a letter writer so they had not kept in touch. They just assumed all was well, and the worst had not occurred, for then someone would try to get word out of a death. Jeremiah wrote her a letter which they sent up to Orkney but she never received a reply. She did not know what to make of it: was her mother dead; could she not find someone to write; had the letter been mislaid in transit; was she angry that her daughter had married down south and would not be returning to her people? Or perhaps it was a benign and sorry reason that after four years of no contact, she no longer cared. As time went on the pain lessened – absence is the greatest healer – but it was a wound that would never completely heal.

When the labour pains started, as they inevitably would, Jeremiah ran for the midwife whilst his neighbour's wife sat with Sonneta. The old fisherman's wife had given birth to eighteen babies, fourteen of them live, and she smiled with the memory of birthing every time Sonneta groaned, for pain is the first thing to lessen when we look back. Her needles clicked in a steady motion whilst she chattered of her own experiences, laughing at some incidences that could only be laughable when one was healed and the child was safely full grown, the rest a simple memory. She stayed with Sonneta through the entire process, saying a girl needed extra support the first time, and tutting that Sonneta's own mother wasn't there. She didn't understand that Orkney was a long distance and kept muttering that it was only but a day's cart ride.

When Jeremiah had delivered the midwife safely to the cottage, he found a dark cold corner outside and threw up. Sonneta was going to die. He could sense it that there was a birth and death mix coming for the family. Prudence had taken the only family luck when she had safely delivered her twins, Kerenza and Derwa, who were thriving. There had been no more children for William and Magdalena.

Before the year was out Sonneta gave birth to a baby girl, who was promptly named Ewat Leask Longbottom before the father had even chance to come and look upon his daughter for the first time. Jeremiah sent notes to his brother and sister announcing the arrival, and asked them to pass on the news to their father. Prudence, now five months pregnant herself, cried with delight when she read the good news for her brother, and hoped they would be able to meet little Ewat soon. She told her daughters, who were only one and a half and did not really understand what mother spoke of, but ran about the kitchen holding hands and babbling about babies. Prudence sat on the stool and had a little cry as she remembered poor Christina and her dead little twins.

The snows were almost gone as April arrived, bar the tiny drifts still caught in the shadows of dry stone walls, and between the woody stems of heather on the hilltops. Transport ran easily up and down the Esk Valley. The bodgers were back negotiating for produce to sell in the towns. Prudence had returned to her late pregnancy waddle. Some less than sympathetic villagers laughed at her gait, but she did not mind it too much. Although she was huge and people sneered at her, she was much smaller than last time, and felt that she was only carrying one child. Even with one child, her abdomen still swelled to impractical levels, and chores were harder now that she had such a bump to negotiate around. When that did not disable her, she had two little ones to contend with. Prudence smiled through most of it like the dumb, good-natured heifer people said she was.

One morning she was slowly plodding up the rise towards their cottage, the girls running figures of eights around her ankles, and her basket feeling heavy on her arm. She had just been to the village store. A sweat was thick on her forehead and she was looking forward to having five minutes in the cool, shadowy kitchen corner to catch her breath and composure. Her brow creased as she saw a man loitering at the front door. He was too well dressed to be a travelling beggar, but no one local either. He was most definitely a stranger. He did not even resemble any of the local families. He was peering in through the window with an air of confident mischief.

"Can I help you, sir?" Prudence spoke loudly, as she unlatched the front gate and unleashed her children upon the garden. She was not settled by the way he did not jump at the suddenness of her speech. His confidence felt too great, as if there was nothing in this world that might hurt him, but a great many things he might hurt.

The man turned around and smiled. It did not reach his eyes. "Looking for Pengelly. Curnow Pengelly."

"He's not here at such a late hour. He's away at his work. Are you looking to order a commission?"

The man looked at her.

"Carpentry?" Prudence wondered if she'd misread him and she was talking to a fool. "Is there some work you need doing?"

"It's words I'm wanting. You let him know I've been by."

"If you'd let me know your name I'll certainly pass on any message. Heaven knows we're always in need of money, so any work is gratefully received."

He walked past her and paused at the gate to look back at the young family. "Always in need of money, aye, that could be said for all of us. You mind those girls, mind no harm comes to them."

When she told Curnow of the stranger's visit that evening, he barely glanced at her and said it was nothing to think on. The next day the gossip in the shop was of the stranger who had been seen wandering in Danby.

When Prudence's time came, Ellen took Derwa and Kerenza down to the little cottage to entertain Margaret Harbottle for a day or two. Ada Robinson arrived promptly in her role as midwife, nodding to Prudence and telling her that this ought to be quick, given it wasn't her first, and she'd already had twins and all of that. By the time Curnow arrived home from work, Prudence was coated in sweat, her senses almost overwhelmed by the intensity and frequency of the contractions. She had not been able to settle, and her hair, straw like and awkward at the best of times, stuck up in every direction.

"Mr Pengelly!" Ada shrieked as he hurried into the kitchen and over to Prudence, who had refused to go to the bed, wishing instead to pace or crawl about the place as a distraction to the pain.

Curnow dropped to his knees in front of her face. "You must hold on," he told her.

"Mr Pengelly, you ought to go to the alehouse for a little while." Prudence merely puffed at him.

"Don't let it happen today," he continued. "Any day but today. You must keep it in. It is the day of the beast..."

"Right, out with you," Ada manhandled Curnow back to the front door. "Your opinions and help are not required at the moment."

"Prudence!" Curnow called out over the determined midwife's shoulder. "You must hold on!"

But when a baby wanted to be born, it would come, regardless of what anyone on the outside thought. And was there ever a woman who wanted the process to go on any longer than it really had to? A good hour before midnight the baby, another girl, entered the world with a scrunched up red face and a cry in her mouth. When Curnow arrived in the early cold dawn light of mid spring, the girl was tidied up and wrapped in blankets, sleeping contentedly. Prudence was sat up with her, her hair having gone limp, she looked as though she were steadily deflating.

Curnow stood over them without joy. "When was it born?"

"Last night..."

"It was the day of the devil..."

"Oh Curnow," Prudence wailed, bursting into tears. "Don't say things like that. She's a dear little heart. And look, I have named her Rosen, like you said you wanted to use the name if it were a girl. And Maud after my own grandmother. Rosen Maud Pengelly."

He did not come any closer. Prudence wiped her eyes with the back of her sweat-greased hand, although the tears continued to flow. "It is all very well you putting commands out like that, but a woman doesn't have any control when a baby is coming."

Curnow sank into a chair, suddenly feeling very weary with his life. "The devil will out," he sighed, "The devil will out."

The following morning, only just morning as the greying light started to appear over the tops of the moorland. The movement of day radiated across the valley and onto the slope of Danby village. One of Farmer Purdey's farm labourers did not go directly to Hollin Farm, but instead was found banging on the Pengellys' door. The twins were still down with Ellen Lythe. Prudence had been dozing in a chair by the dwindling fire, Rosen sleeping again in her little crib after an early morning feed. Sleep-confused, Prudence got to her feet and slumped to the door, opening it and looking at the young man in consternation. "What hour is this to be banging? You'll wake my husband, and never mind the baby..."

The young man looked distressed. "Oh Mrs Pengelly, there's been an awful accident. You'd better come quick, down to the river."

She suddenly felt as though she were about to be sick. "My girls? Say it isn't so?"

"I don't know anything about girls, but you'd best come now." The man was skittish like a young hare, desperate to get away again.

What was she supposed to do? Prudence flung some clothes and shawls into her basket, making a little nest, and settled Rosen into the new carrier. Flinging a couple of shawls about herself, for she had never undressed for bed last night, Prudence followed the man outside, with her daughter's basket suspended in the crook of her arm. She still felt weak from the birthing, and did not move fast. She was grateful that they were heading down and not uphill. Down the road they went, past the Methodist church, past the lane where her girls stayed with Ellen, out of Danby and down to the River Esk. It twisted through the valley bottom as a boundary between Danby and Ainthorpe. Here a stone bridge crossed over a straight section of the river. Danby mill stood at the river edge a little further up, still in view just before the river curled up into the arms of Ainthorpe. There was a weir built in the river to help the waterwheel turn. Greenery was warming up on both sides, some trees with their spring budded leaves overhanging the river's edge. Two men stood thigh-deep in the river, a third awkwardly half-crouched on the river bank caught between peering down and almost looking as though he didn't quite dare to dive. A tree had collapsed into the river which still needed to be removed, and caught upon it, so that it might travel no more, was the face-down body of a man. He was quite cold, quite still and quite dead, yet the steady running and burbling of the river almost brought life to him.

Prudence stood in the mid point of the bridge and stared down. Farmer Purdey looked up, his eyes widening when he saw who his stupid lad had brought. With a baby in a basket no less.

"We need the doctor here, lad. Mrs Pengelly, you must step away," he went to take a step, wading in the deepest part of the river and knocking into the body. He looked to the man still hopelessly loitering on the bank and gestured to him to go do something useful. The man moved and hurried around onto the track and to Prudence to pull her away, but she shook him off with a look that said he had better not touch her again.

"We ought to get him out of the water," the man in the river said, and together, he and Purdey manhandled the body over to the river bank. In the effort they unintentionally turned him over, and Prudence saw Curnow's waterlogged face.

"There has been a terrible accident," the man who lingered just behind her spoke. "Your husband has drowned."

Prudence said nothing. She watched proceedings as the body of her husband was carried up into the field. She did not believe it, even when the doctor came and all were in agreement of accidental drowning. No, she thought, that is not so. He did not do this to himself. He has been killed and I do not understand why.

The baby in the basket started crying. Quite numb, Prudence picked up the basket, ignoring the men, and started back up the road to the cottage. She passed the doctor hurrying down towards the river. She did not even notice his questioning stare, a movement as if he were about to speak to her before remembering what he had been called to. She puffed her way up the steepest parts of the walk, feeling the dullness in her legs from the loss of blood and the lack of sleep. I have only just given birth, she thought, I should not have to deal with this.

She did not notice that the front door was open. Prudence sat down by the fire and looked in the basket for the first time. Rosen was furious now, that she had not been picked up and fussed, and worse still that her tiny stomach was empty. Her mother realised that she could not fall to bits, in fact she might not even be able to grieve for she had three small girls to look after. She picked up the baby and looked at her angry red little face. Why had Curnow thought she was the devil?

As Prudence sat and nursed the baby her tired eyes roamed the room. She settled on the small details, quiet changes that would normally be easily missed and tidied away. Something that had been moved slightly. Another object knocked to its side. A lid not quite replaced. Someone had been here. When Rosen was finished, Prudence burped her and settled her back into the crib, before going for the little tin in the pantry store where Curnow kept his savings. The tin was there, but shoved back into the shelf deep as if it was to be not seen for a long time. Prudence opened it and stared blankly for some minutes before she registered that it was empty. They must have come whilst she was down at the river. She put the lid back down and held it firmly in place with the palm of her hand. Was this what it had all been about? Money? But why? The underhand shadowed nature, things seen in the corner of her eye, but nothing openly spoken of. What had been so important that it gave them the right to take her money and her husband and leave her with three tiny girls to support on her own?

She sat down upon her stool and regarded Curnow's shirt, hung from the ceiling and almost dry. How could his stern mien be there one moment and vanished the next? There had been so much, an abundance of superstition ridiculous even for the most paranoid old woman in the valley; a humourless dryness; that depth and wealth of life experience he never let anyone near. He never spoke of his days before he had followed the River Esk out of Whitby, but she felt he had lived through a lot. He even spoke another language. How could so much be there, so much that had taken decades to amass and develop, then suddenly it was all gone as if it had never mattered? She had stood on that bridge and looked down upon the sodden body, but she had known Curnow was no longer there. She thought of the strange songs he sang. Who would teach the girls the songs of their forefathers now?

The awful thought struck her that none of the girls would remember their father.

Prudence had lived through grief and bereavement before. In childhood she'd lost her own mother and many of her siblings in the same day. It was not although she had been hidden away from the cruel reality of life. Yet the finality of it all had never really struck her before. The utter tragedy and waste, the very fact that life itself was cruel to set up so much in a person only to wipe it away as if it were a mere smudge on a window. When her siblings had died she hadn't really understood what was happening, and had been more distracted by all the attention she received from her two grandmothers and Aunt Gilly. That had only increased with the disappearance and subsequent death of her mother. What kind of a woman had her mother actually been? What had she thought in the quiet moments when the children were asleep? What did she worry about? Did she have hopes?

"Prudence!"

She could not say how long she had sat there becoming weighted down by ever more dreadful thoughts. Rosen was still asleep and the bright sun spoke of the morning. Her Aunt Gilly stood in the doorway, a solid, real reassuring shape on the horizon. Her face was ashen.

"Prudence, my child. They said you were on the bridge. They said that you saw." She stepped tentatively into the cottage. Prudence looked stunned, as if all sense had been slapped out of her. "Oh, my poor girl." She hurried across and hugged her niece tightly. She looked down and saw the baby snuffling in her cot. Not even a week old. What had that idiot been doing at the river? The doctor had confirmed it as drowning – as if they had needed a trained man to deduce it – and some of the men said he had probably been drinking, celebrating the safe delivery of a daughter. It didn't seem like the Curnow Gilly remembered, but what else could it be? Unless he had stumbled into the river at night by accident. It must have been so.

"I am here to help you in any way that I can. For this is not going to be an easy time for you. Ellen has said she will look after the girls for you a couple more days. Your uncle has gone to find the reverend. There is much we must do. Mourning clothes. We must not buy too much for you will have to be careful with the money..."

"There is no money," Prudence said flatly. "It has been taken. Someone came in whilst I was at the river."

Gilly's eyes widened at the affront. "Stealing from a young widow with three young babes!" She shrieked. "What has become of the world? Do people know no shame?" Her voice faltered and she remembered herself. Rosen started to whine. But Lord, how would they manage with the rents? Gilly couldn't have them, not with Kenneth and his new wife and own baby son living with the rest of them in the farm. There wasn't enough room as it was. She didn't know if the local poor relief would stretch to carry them, certainly not for the long term. They would have to work something out. Prudence would have to marry again, but decency meant she couldn't do anything for the first year.

Gilly shook herself out of her thoughts. Before the rest of their lives, they had to get through this first week. "We'll take a couple of your dresses and dye them black," she decided. That would be the most economical course to take.

Prudence looked up at her Aunt in utter consternation. "But where is Ki?"

Ki had actually been found the same day Curnow's body was discovered floating face-down in the River Esk. It was over a week before anyone thought to tell Prudence. John Hart, one of the local gamekeepers had found the dog hung from his neck and quite dead in a Hawthorn bush close to Danby Mill. "Damned waste of a decent little dog," he had grumbled as he dug a hole and got the corpse buried in the field.

And so another life was extinguished.

Time held no meaning to Prudence. Between the preparations for burial and mourning, as well as the relentless schedule the baby brought, she had no moment to stop and think, and no energy to cry. Aunt Gilly had dyed her dresses for her, and her uncle had arranged everything for the funeral. Curnow had been brought home to be washed and made ready for his final journey for burial. Magdalene had appeared at the house that afternoon and helped Gilly to get him ready. Prudence had been in the room but had been too disjointed to gear herself up into any kind of action. It was so strange having him there in the house, yet he was already gone. There was just a body, water bloated and cold, and no Curnow. She was glad when the pall bearers arrived to carry him away to St Hildas, a good hours' walk from where they were. It would be better to have what was left planted in the ground. Prudence followed in a cart along with Ellen and the girls, the little toddlers unable to understand what had happened and why everyone was so dreadfully sad. Yet Prudence wanted all of her girls back around her and would not hear of them being sent away.

After the service the mourners headed back to Danby, a train of black silence, foot and hoof-driven. They gathered at the cottage and in the garden where Prudence and Curnow had once lived together. Ellen and Gilly had prepared the food and hosted the event as if Curnow had been their own shared husband. Prudence was in a daze, hauntingly sleep-deprived, and could not face the locals. It had been too much in a week. People wanted to offer their condolences and dole out trite phrases such as that it would all be all right in the end. As if that would provide food and raise the girls.

Her twin daughters, Derwa and Kerenza, played with Sonneta and her little girl Ewat in the corner of the garden. Satisfied they were safe enough, Prudence drifted through the gatherings, slipping out into the backyard to sit behind some lumber and keep out of sight. She was carrying Rosen with her, who blissfully slept through everything, oblivious to the awfulness of her first week on this earth.

"Prudence, I..."

She looked up to find her brother, Jeremiah, loitering close by.

"I am so very sorry."

She smiled weakly. When people apologised or tried to offer their condolences, she always felt as though she needed to pat them and assure them all was well. As if she needed to shoulder their woe and discomfort. It was exhausting, but she could not shake off that sense of expectation. To prove that good old reliable Prudence would keep trundling on.

"I am not the first to have lost a spouse."

Jeremiah lowered his eyes. It was a complicated business. He was happy. He had a little girl, a pretty young wife he loved, a good job and really, a man ought not to hope for anything more in life. But the joys of the day could not completely wipe out the sorrows of the past. Christina had been like a limb, and one he could not regrow. He loved both his wives, but the love of one would not negate the love of the other. It was not something he spoke of. It seemed that was all buried in the past now as far as the community was concerned. "Aye, well, the circumstances," he conceded. "Christina died with the babies. Whereas Curnow..."

"...was murdered." Prudence's eyes widened as she blurted it out, surprised by how bitter she sounded but more so that she had voiced her fear.

Jeremiah looked wary. "Why would you say that?"

"Oh, don't tell anyone, Jeremiah, please don't. They'll think I'm foolish."

"It'll stay between us."

She looked down at Rosen. "Curnow just wouldn't have drowned like that. I'm sure of it. It was that man who was hanging around, I'm sure it must have been. I don't know who he was, some stranger. But he must have been watching. When I went down to the river, someone went into the cottage. They took all the money..."

"Father mentioned that."

"Oh yes, Father." Prudence pursed her lips. Her father had been to the cottage to offer his condolences, but that was all. As he had stood in the doorway, awkwardly twisting his cap in his hands and not knowing quite what to do or say, Prudence felt like a child again. The magnitude had hit her. They would be paupers. She had no way to decently support her three girls. She had told him the money had been stolen and he said that was a terrible shame. Folks didn't know the word of sin anymore. She waited but nothing more was forthcoming. She started to suggest that perhaps she and the girls ought to move in with them, but he cut her down quickly, stating there was hardly any room in the cottage as it was, what with Megan and himself, and Megan suffered so badly in the cold and the damp with the aches in her hips and legs. Young children needed the patience of the young.

"He wasn't much help." She looked up at her brother. "But what I don't understand is why someone would do all this? Why would anyone do such a thing to Curnow?"

"You would do best to forget all about it; mention it to no one," Jeremiah advised. "Even the money, I would not contact the magistrate or make an issue. Just walk away from it all. These are bad people involved, but we can make an end of it here."

"You know what happened?"

"No," he shook his head, then crouched down beside her. "I only hear bits in town. But it makes me uncomfortable. I pretend I am dumb and I have not put some of it together, but I sometimes think it might be better for me and Sonneta to move to another place. I think it is at an end, with the money and reputations set to rights…"

"Reputations? Oh…" Prudence lowered her eyes. He meant Curnow's death.

"If we were to start talking about our suspicions or what had happened. Well, it might drag it all up again and then perhaps we might not be left in peace."

"I see." It would be a lie to live. Tell the girls their father had drowned in the river and to think no more of it. "But I don't see," she turned back to her brother. "I know there was a stranger about and he took our money but I don't see what grievance he had against Curnow."

"I don't know the details of it myself. I've heard odd comments here and there. I do know who is involved and they are not good people. There's an inn keeper, a rich man, I think he deals in smuggling as well. He has a couple of men working for him, not good men. It was probably one of them who had stolen your money. They will see it as recompense."

"But it's my Curnow who's dead."

"People like that don't think like decent folks, like you and me. I heard this innkeeper once got himself a slave."

"Slave? You mean he treats his servants bad?"

Jeremiah let out a sigh. "Prudence, you're not that naive. I know we don't see the black men up this way, but you've heard about it. We see them now and then in Whitby, the black men I mean. These criminals, I mean, the people who might have been involved in Curnow's death, well, they get slaves sometimes. Rumour has it. Most of the time by underhand means, there's stories that they get them over from Liverpool, the pregnant or the wounded that the Captains toss overboard for they take valuable space from another that has a better chance of surviving."

Prudence held a hand to her mouth. "They'd throw a human overboard to drown in the sea?"

"They're just cargo," Jeremiah said gently. "I don't think people in the business see them as fellow man. I don't know whether to say those thrown overboard near the port are lucky. Better chance of swimming ashore than in the middle of the ocean. But then if they make shore, they run into types like our fellows. And then there were stories that he'd stole some from Dentdale."

"Dentdale?"

"It's a valley a long way from here..."

"Yes, I know, I've heard of the knitters."

"Well, there's a plantation owner up that way who used to have them working on his farm in Dentdale."

"And this man stole some of the slaves?"

"So rumour has it."

"I don't see what this has to do with Curnow. You're not saying he was stealing slaves?"

Jeremiah shook his head. "Another rumour has it that some Captain who had been over the Caribbean had bought her from one of the plantations and brought her over here. They say she was very pretty. For whatever reason, she ended up in the possession of this inn keeper. She got away from him one night, and was found a couple of days later dashed upon the rocks at the bottom of the cliffs."

"You don't think Curnow..."

"What, killed her?"

"I will not believe such a thing of Curnow!"

"Neither would I. It was probably an accident. If she ran away in the night and wasn't familiar with the coast and the cliffs... It's a treacherous line. But knowing that man's reputation I think she took the better alternative."

"I don't see how Curnow fits in."

"This all happened before I went to Whitby. I think he knew this girl..."

"Knew?"

"I don't know how much." He caught her eye. "But he probably helped her to get away."

"Not well enough," Prudence sighed.

"They gossip about all sorts in town. Folk have long memories. You remember Aunt Eleanor used to live in Whitby?"

"Oh vaguely, but they've not been there for years and years."

"Uncle MacCaskill was already married."

"What?"

"That's why they left. His first wife turned up, all the way from Scotland, and the whole town knew he was a bigamist. No one would trade with Aunt Eleanor. She had to wind things down and move away. They went over to Haworth didn't they, where grandmother came from."

"I know they're in Haworth. I used to hear from Cousin Muriel now and then but... oh, we're different sorts of people."

"Do you remember Cousin Elizabeth?"

Prudence creased her brow. "Cousin Elizabeth? Why, they never talk of her. But yes, I remember a little girl. She must have died."

"They say she lives with rich men."

"What, like a mistress!" Prudence shrieked, then ducked down lest anyone from the funeral party might realise where they were, hunkered down behind the woodpile like a couple of children. "Jeremiah, you terrible gossip," she scolded.

"It's just what they say. Although I don't think they realise we are related to the MacCaskills." He dropped off, as if remembering for the first time why they were here. "But you'd be best leaving the facts of Curnow's death be, if you follow what I'm saying. It will be hard enough for you and the girls as it is, but if you stir the hornet's nest... It makes no difference somehow, what I mean to say is that it won't bring him back."

"But I need to know the truth of it."

"And I've told you it, or at least as much of it as can be found."

"It won't bring him back," Prudence's face was stony set. "I still can't believe he's gone. It's like someone just put out the candle. There's so much and then there's nothing. As if it were never there to begin with. I keep expecting him to come back here now. He'd be cross to see all these folks sitting about eating his food."

"I know. I couldn't stay in the house after Christina..." Jeremiah let the thought stop there. "But you are not alone. You have the girls and you must be strong for them. Where will you go?"

"I don't know. Father won't have me and... I don't know. But perhaps I am glad of it. I want us to be in our own home. It's just..."

"We'll have time before the next rent is due to figure it out."

"I know," Prudence wiped at her eyes with the back of her hands. "I'm just too dim, I feel it, to work all this out. I really don't know what I'm going to do without him."

"Carry on," Jeremiah told her. "That's what you'll have to do."

Just as Jeremiah had been unable to remain in Egton after the death of his first wife, as the weeks went by, Prudence realised that the cottage up high in Danby was no longer a home. People were home, not stone and masonry, and they would not be able to stay. The twins had moved back in with her, and despite the lack of sleep and the hard work, the little girls were a blessing.

The family remained in the cottage for the length of the rents already paid, and were given a little money in the form of poor relief from the parish. Prudence knew how hard this was gathered, from farming families crippled by rents for shabby housing, tithes to keep reverends and their many hobbies in motion, and the poor relief. With all of these taxes and dues, it felt as though one never had a farthing left for the comfort of oneself or one's own children. She must do something, only what could a woman do with so many small children?

In the short term she sold all of the lumber and the joinery tools that Curnow had left behind. The poor relief helped, although the kindness of locals and friends, when not demanded as a regular payment by the parish, was far greater. Aunt Gilly brought honey as treats for the little girls, and Farmer Purdey always had a few spare eggs to make sure the little lasses grew up well. When the time for the rents grew closer, Prudence knew she was ready to quit the cottage, only what could she afford to move to? Gilly had told her about a small cottage in Ainthorpe, which was much more suitable, for the family had no need of all the space for carpentry, and it would be a fresh start with no history within its walls. But how was she to fund it?

Magdalene suggested that Prudence and the girls move in with her and William. Prudence could then go off and work and Magdalene could look after the children. Neither sibling was keen. William looked about his home and the thought of four more bodies made it too cramped. Then there was the smithy, which would be dangerous with such little girls about. Prudence did not want to be away working every day and missing her children, and she saw the way Magdalene looked at them and knew that they would be a little less her own children if they went there.

It looked as though it would be their own viable option, for she was only a few months into her widowhood and no one else would approach. When her own father heard talk of her woes, he would shuffle off, muttering that Prudence was a grown woman and he had no more energy to carry others now. Megan, his second wife, was not best pleased with his response, for she had considered suggesting to him that Prudence and the girls come to live with them, but reading his countenance, she knew it would not be worth the time even making the suggestion. Brow-beaten second in command she was not however, for Megan had been a woman of a small income and independent means before William had married her in middle age. She had no children of her own, a few nieces and nephews now full grown whom she never saw due to distance and time on everyone's parts. Until Curnow had died, Megan hadn't known anyone in particular and dire need. From conversation with Gilly, she learned of the little property down in Ainthorpe village that would be perfect for the Pengellys. She went to the land agent and arranged the tenancy herself before telling anyone of what she had done. Prudence was the first to be told, in the form of an offer, that whilst she needed help, Megan would be willing to rent the little property for her. It would still leave enough out of her annual income to cover her own wants, and thus all Prudence would need to arrange was the food and clothing for herself and the girls, and any fuel and sundries for the property.

Prudence would always be grateful to Megan for coming to her at such a time in her life. The locals of the valley nodded their approval that the family had finally come true to the widow's aid. And so

Prudence, Kerenza, Derwa and Rosen left the carpenter's cottage in Danby and moved across the river to the village of Ainthorpe. Although it was another hamlet, it meant easier walking for Ellen Lythe as she did not have such steep hills to climb anymore. Ellen was growing frailer with every winter and could not keep up with the rigours of Jemima Twycross's kitchen. Prudence gradually took over some of those duties, and shared the work, and naturally the pay with Ellen. She also supplemented her income with a frenzy of knitting which she sold on to the travelling bodger, along with surpluses of dried nettles for teas and soups and elderberry wine when the hedgerows provided a glut. When old Mrs Harbottle died and the house could no longer be kept, Ellen Lythe moved in with the Pengellys and spent much of her time resting or sleeping in her dotage, and telling the young girls stories of the moors and their own ancestors as children; their own grandmothers and great aunts and uncles who would run screaming and shrieking across the upland heather.

When Prudence's socially acceptable period of mourning was over, the bachelors began to talk. Granted she was viewed as being a little dim, and was not the daintiest of women in the valley. Her hair resembled a wild thatch, and her way of walking like a loyal cow. Despite all those negatives, there were many attractions, and in fact a wife who was not too bright could be an attractive thing, for she would be more obedient and not question her man's wisdom. She kept a good house, and was canny with the money for she did not have a lot to live on but made it go far and the three girls were well looked after. Then there was the rental money from her stepmother, and a man might hope some of that continued should Prudence ever remarry. Prudence had proved herself as a solid, durable type of woman who dragged herself through any trial. There were three red-headed girls of another man, which were not an ideal load to take on – presuming they could not be offloaded on to any of the relatives – but time moved quickly and they would soon be old enough to be sent off into service and earn their own keep. The men viewed Prudence's hips in the way they considered the livestock and declared there was plenty more childbearing to be had.

Prudence heard more than most gave her credit for, and was well aware what the general consensus was regarding a man's prospects should he wed her. She was a little horrified by just how many came to her door when the appropriate number of months had passed, even the gamekeeper who had openly sneered at her in the past. He was now a widower with four boys to raise. The thought of her girls having to grow up with those rough lads brought her into a panic one night, and she brusquely turned down every man that came to try a'courting her. They were managing quite well, and the love of her little girls was all she needed. She couldn't stand the thought of another man raising them, and they in turn thinking he was their father.

In the spring after Derwa and Kerenza had turned four and Rosen was swiftly heading on towards two Ellen Lythe died. She had caught a fever and chills during the early spring, her breathing had grown ragged and the energy drained from her. She slipped away one night, aged somewhere in her seventies – no one was quite sure where – and was buried in the graveyard at St Hilda's.

Prudence managed, for she had the job at the Twycross's kitchen on her own now, although the money was tight. Food prices were constantly climbing and some days she felt that she was only coping because her employers ran the shop and discounted some things out of sympathy for her situation. Between that and the fact that her girls often ate at her place of work, they managed.

The year following Ellen's death started with birth as Jeremiah and Sonneta's third child, Agnes Sonneta Longbottom was born, bringing company to Ewat and Robert. The family had now left Whitby and were living at Runswick Bay. The old carpenter of the village had died and Jeremiah had taken over. He was no longer working on the large ships for whaling and transportation, but what he had learned in Whitby held him in good stead, for fishermen headed out in small craft from Runswick, and there were always repairs required. Whilst Jeremiah felt calmer for his family, being away from the criminal underbelly of Whitby with their dark connection to Curnow, it was impossible to escape the shadow of smuggling at the coast. Smuggling and evading the customs man was rife across the country, and with prices going up, making a little profit for oneself was ever more appealing.

Families all over the Esk Valley and the coastline watched the money and hoped they would scrape through. Those hardships would have been enough, but a series of three deaths, and one of a complete stranger at that, were the catalyst that ripped up what stability Prudence had managed to create for her girls. The first to pass was their stepmother, Megan Longbottom. No one knew the exact circumstances. It was assumed she had fallen or taken a funny turn in the home. She was found on the kitchen floor murmuring and unable to move much of her body. She did not seem to recognise anyone or be aware of where she was, and in under two days she had passed.

The family came together in Commondale: children, spouses and young offspring travelling from Runswick and Ainthorpe to gather and support their father. William was silent and uncommunicative. Other than his son Will, he felt estranged from his children. It had not mattered all that much before, for he had been with Megan and they had spent happy years together. Now she was gone and he lamented that he had lost so many potential years with her, being young and foolish and getting into an unfortunate marriage with Gillian Hurst. That union had been a mistake from the very beginning. He watched Prudence as she spoke to her children outside in the autumnal sun. She was quite different from her mother, who had been slight and dark haired, tired and worn out from continuous child bearing, but also bitter and uncommunicative. Here was Prudence, blonde with thick messy hair, a sturdy reliable build and incessant chatter of a cheery sort that seemed as though it continued to cover the fact that she was not particularly bright. Jeremiah's wife, Sonneta, the Scots' lass, was just as cheery, but in a calmer, more confident way. She worked hard as well, helping Jeremiah, and before they had wed, she had been a herring girl.

Magdalene watched Sonneta, and felt irritated by the woman's youth as well as her easy popularity. She had an irritating sunny disposition, as though she knew everyone would love her before they had even met, and that she could guarantee friendship with all. She carried little baby Agnes about, the baby's head peeping over her shoulder in unabashed curiosity at the entire family. Sonneta was only twenty-four and already she was married to a good man, with three healthy living children, and she had not suffered a single loss. What did she know of the true hardships of life?

The funeral came and passed. Prudence wondered if her father would expect her to move back to Commondale with her girls, to live in his house and play housekeeper to all his needs. She was the only daughter, and a widow at that, so perhaps it was expected. It would solve a lot of financial problems, but she never felt completely at ease with her father, and preferred to stay closer to Aunt Gilly. She did not say anything to her father nor her siblings, and perhaps someone else had made a comment, for just after the funeral William randomly announced that he would not be leaving his home and was quite content to live alone. He needed the peace and quiet to come to terms with his life.

And so that was that, and things may have rolled onwards easily enough, but for the visit of the land agent from Danby Grange. Rents were due on the cottages, and he appeared at Prudence's door, full of apologies. He did not usually even disturb Prudence on those days, instead going directly to Commondale to speak to that kind woman Megan Longbottom, who had always taken care of her stepdaughter's rents. He had walked up to Commondale as usual, passed on his condolences to the father, William Longbottom, then eventually gotten around to the purpose of his visit and the matter of the Ainthorpe rents being due. Everyone knew that Megan's fortune had gone in its entirety to William, and the agent had assumed the father would continue to look after the daughter. When the agent had brought up the matter, William had been surprised that he would even ask such a thing, and made it quite clear that he would not continue to support his daughter. Why, she was a grown woman in her thirties. The land agent didn't tell Prudence of all that had been said, such titbits were for the alehouse at the end of the day, but he had waited patiently whilst Prudence stood and deflated, ever weary, before working through her savings and managing to put together the rents.

Two weeks later, after church, she and the girls walked across to Commondale to visit grandfather, as was their habit. They would overnight with Magdalene and William, then walk home the next day. Prudence did not get anything positive from the visits, but felt duty bound by the laws of family. She wanted her children to know what family they could, for there was hardly anyone in the world to care for them. Curnow had never told her anything of his family in Cornwall, in fact she could not even say which village he was born in. There was a whole history to the girls that they would never know.

Whilst the girls played in the yard and William looked on, a little bored by it all, Prudence sat down and closed her eyes. She was weary with the work and the worry. She did not know how she was going to make the next rent payment.

"You look tired, daughter," William observed.

"That I am."

"You'll known by now that I have refused to pay your rents for you," he blurted out, assuming that she was about to pester him for money. "Megan should not have indulged you for so long, but my dear departed wife always had a kind and generous heart. She was a good Christian woman. But I can not be expected to support you now, Prudence. You are a grown woman and a mother, and you must cease expecting others to carry you. You must support yourself and do some work. You ought to be married. It's not right for those girls to go without a father."

Prudence opened her mouth to protest.

"You look at Jeremiah's wife," he continued. "She was a herring girl before she married. She works hard."

I am working, Prudence thought. I have worked. I have been in service. I have been used badly. And I am supporting myself and my family now, without attaching myself to a new man, purely for the reason of securing an income. She almost started to speak, angry at his off hand manner towards her, but she saw that it would do no good. He would not help her, and the tirade would only give him more fuel to call her an ungrateful daughter. He was grieving, she thought, trying to be charitable. She must not think too harshly of him.

"I am a widower," he continued. "I have lost two wives. You would not understand."

Prudence clapped her hands together. "Come girls," she called to her daughters as she quickly packed their things away into her basket. "We must go now, grandfather is tired."

As they walked up the hill out of Commondale – for Prudence was so furious she could not even stand to overnight with her brother and Magdalene – they passed by Bartholomew Tinder, a groom from Danby Grange whom she was vaguely aware of, whose people came from Commondale. He doffed his cap to them as they approached from opposite directions.

"Afternoon, Mrs Pengelly."

"Afternoon, Mr Tinder," Prudence nodded at him, with no intention of stopping.

"I hear you're still widowed," he commented, stopping on the side of the road to wait for them to come to him. "What I mean is that you did not remarry. It's hard for a woman to manage. If I could help with that..."

Prudence looked in horror at him. That was the worst marriage proposal she had received yet. And out of the blue, for the man had not seen or spoken to her since she had left Danby Grange all those years ago. She stared at him as if to ask him what he thought he was talking about, but he was not looking at her, rather the little girls who trotted along beside her. She felt uneasy. "Come along girls," she said, tugging on Kerenza's arm. "We must hurry if we are to get home before dark."

"Mamma," Rosen complained. "I am tired."

"Very well," Prudence huffed, picking up her youngest daughter. "I will carry you. Now come away, for we must home."

The second death to destabilise Prudence was of a man she had never met or heard of until he died. He had lived near the market town of Pickering and had worked as a tailor. In later years he had developed a penchant for drink, along with poor judgement coupled with a generous hand at the cockfights he liked to attend. Upon his death there was barely enough money to pay for his burial, and there were debts outstanding on his poor widow. The plight of this woman, now homeless and penniless, distressed Mr Twycross the shopkeeper greatly, for the woman was his own sister. He said they would take her in, for family ought to look out for one another, but she was too proud to accept charity. A compromise was reached and it was agreed she would run the kitchen in the Twycross family home. And just like that, Prudence lost her main source of income.

She still had her knitting and jams and jellies to sell to the bodger when he came by, and the honey, butter and eggs that came from her Aunt Gilly and Farmer Purdey for the girls to eat, but it was not enough to keep the home going. Prudence sold her wedding ring to get a little more money, but she knew it was only a temporary stop gap. She needed employment, but she needed something where she could look after the girls at the same time. It was possible that she could have pleaded something at Danby Grange, but the children would not have been welcome, and she did not think she could have endured being there again. She saw the young master trotting through the village on his fine horse, and thought of all those rents the family took in, for shoddy housing, driving their residents to near-poverty and not much caring. The mother worried over her china and porcelain, the daughters over fine dresses and the men over their shooting. They had never really known hunger.

Aunt Gilly was trying to impress on her the need for marriage. Not that there were many options these days, for Prudence had not put herself in an eligible position by turning down so many in the past. Gilly wrongly assumed Prudence was clinging on to some misfounded loyalty to Curnow and reminded her niece that it was almost four years since her husband had died and she ought to move on. Prudence countered that she could work, her keep didn't have to be so hard won. There was a job at Danby mill that she could take. Ah, said Gilly, but what would she do with her children? Prudence grew silent. Magdalene offered to take them, to let them live in Commondale. She could care for the girls, and Prudence could either walk to the mill every day, or perhaps stay with Gilly, and only see the girls on her days off. The thought of Magdalene taking over and raising her little girls drove Prudence into inactivity and she spoke little. Every option filled her with fear and heartache.

Gilly had already been to speak to her elder brother, Prudence's father, but no help had been forthcoming. William was adamant that Prudence ought to marry, and if she was so foolish as to ignore everyone's good advice, then she would have to solve her financial problems on her own. He would not help and he would not have them in his home. Gilly supposed he was still grieving for the death of his second wife, and allowed his bad temper for this, but was nevertheless chilled by his distinct apathy to his only living daughter. Not to mention three of his grandchildren.

The third and final death killed off any final hope Prudence had been clinging to for some kind of resolution.

Her eldest brother, William Longbottom, was reaping the great successes in his work as a blacksmith. He had trained under his father, and taken over the business as William weakened and wished to spend more time with Megan. Magdalene and William lived and worked in the cottage where William and Gillian had raised their own family. Without the hoards of children to feed and a healthy steady income from work, they had been able to improve and extend the cottage, so that they enjoyed a better standard of living. Many of these costs ought to have been born by the estate, but were not. It was only begrudgingly accepted that the tenants were so keen for better living that they would pay for the work themselves. Magdalene kept a fine little home, and had both the space and the means to support Prudence's three girls.

Will was busy with orders, in fact they were backing up, he had so much to do. He had taken on an apprentice, which brought in extra money but extra bother as he had someone to teach who worked slowly and did not have the physical strength yet to take on some of the tasks. They were working on new wrought iron gates for Danby Grange, an order that had been permitted to queue jump due to the status of the family. With rough-gloved hands, he and the apprentice manoeuvred one the gate frames out of the workshop, where they were running out of space and went to carry it around to the back of the house. William Longbottom senior was coming down the little track as they moved the heavy item, and made a comment on how busy his son was. He would need extra help. With half an eye on the apprentice, Will muttered something about how his father was not to worry. The workshop was a just little chaotic, before they continued on their lumbering route around the property.

It was as the lad was helping Will fix a bit of hessian over the gate frame to keep it clean outdoors that they heard the shrill scream of an animal in intense pain. They both froze for a moment, staring at one another in horror, before Will broke the stillness and ran back around to the smithy. Magdalene was already there, screaming her husband's name, and for a moment he feared that she was dying, until he saw that she had her arms under his father's armpits and was trying to drag the unconscious man outside. There was a sickening smell of cooked flesh, smoke rising from William's body, his arm bloodied and blackened, skin cracked open with the boiled redness underneath.

William had been alone in the smithy. Perhaps he had tripped and fallen, and somehow his arm had gone into the fire. Magdalene didn't know. Judging from the damage, it seemed he had remained far longer than anyone with sense or strength would have stayed in such a fire, for the flesh was burned right down to the bone. Magdalene had heard the screaming and reached the smithy first, to discover her father-in-law writhing in the fire, his face starting to catch fire. She had pulled him away and smothered out the flames. The lad was sent off for the doctor, but this being a sparsely populated place, there was no doctor in Commondale and the lad had a good few miles to run before he reached the nearest doctor's house. Evening was falling by the time the doctor arrived at the Longbottom's property. William was still alive, although feverish. His mind walked passages they could not see. Magdalene had cleaned him up as best she could, and although his eyebrows and hair was burned off, there would have been little more than scaring to the face. The arm was beyond saving, and the doctor said if they were to save him, it would have to come off. Will agonised over what he had been told, for it was impossible to communicate with his father, and the decision had been left to him. This was his father, that great physical presence, who had trained him in this art. A blacksmith was nothing without his arms.

It all came to naught, for his father died in the night. The doctor assured him that the amputation had been a last desperate attempt they could have tried, but for the old man, the trauma had been too much for his heart.

William Longbottom was buried in St Hilda's. Megan's grave was opened up so that his body could join hers. The engraver was commissioned to add his name to her headstone. Within the churchyard it was a long distance from the memorial to his first wife and many children, and had no one known of the family history, it would not have been obvious that there was any connection at all.

It transpired that the old man had left a will, in which he left all his worldly goods, and those of his second wife to his first born son, William Longbottom, in their entirety. There was a note directed to his son Jeremiah, assuring him that he was proud of what he had achieved, and that he had no need of his father's support for he was a competent man. And it was the natural order of things that the eldest son stood in priority of the family name. Of Prudence there was no mention.

Prudence returned to her home that evening and threw one of her dishes at the back wall in the kitchen, screaming in utter frustration.

The twins were outside playing with other children from the village, but Rosen was sitting on a little stool by the fire, and watched as her mother broke down to her knees, sobbing in despair.

"Mamma?"

She looked up, her vision blurred with salty tears. She could see sunlight glinting off golden redness from the child's locks, and knew the voice to be Rosen's. Prudence wiped off the worst of the tears and the snot from her face with the corner of her patched apron and looked at Rosen. "You remember this day, my girl," she told the four year old. "Family ought to stick together, to look after one another. Family... we are born with a duty to support one another and to share. You can't rely on anyone but you should always expect of your family..." Prudence shook her head sadly, wearily, and looked at the floor. "He should have given to us."

"Yes, Mamma."

Later in the evening, when the children were asleep in the bed they all shared, Prudence sat downstairs and gazed out of the window at the falling dusk. Calmer, the air now still and the light fading, she had the constitution to understand life as it really was. No one owed anyone anything. One was merely lucky if one had family that cared or helped, but truly there was no obligation on anyone. She had been wrong in her anger. She was an adult; her father had no obligation to her, and he had made that very clear in the past. She would support her family and her girls; she could neither rely on nor look to anyone for help. She would take the work at the mill and work out a way so that her girls would be safe. She would do all of this on her own. Ever since her mother had died, she had never really had anyone truly her own, instead relying on the kindness of relatives and friends who were not obligated. Her father should have helped, but he had never done anything for her, even back when her mother had died. If he had not helped her when she was a little girl, she had been foolish to expect anything as a grown woman.

It was just unfortunate that she neglected to mention these revelations to Rosen.

So it came to pass that Prudence starting working at Danby mill, training up on the looms. She was far too old to be learning a new trade, but she could not go back to Danby Grange to domestic chores, and the owner at the mill had been persuaded to let her try, on account of Curnow having provided such good work. The Pengelly family were forced to quit their cottage, and out of necessity had to separate. The girls, Derwa and Kerenza now six years old, bright-eyed little twins with tangling waves of red hair and innocent smiles; and their younger sister Rosen, went to live with their Uncle William and Aunt Magdalene over in Commondale. Prudence was welcome to go there and stay anytime, but it was a long walk back to the flax mill, and with long working days, it became too exhausting to see the girls every day. Several nights a week she slept in a corner of the attic at Aunt Gilly's, recalling those innocent days before she had married, staying with her Aunt and Uncle, laughing with her cousins, and Curnow and Ki ambling about the country lanes. So much had changed. She wondered what Curnow would have thought, had he known how little time he had left, or that his death would be marked with a lie, declared as a drowning and not questioned for fear of wakening the culprits. Dead is dead, he would have most likely said, and would not have cared what they had written at his grave. She had worried for a time that his eternal soul would find no peace for the lie they had allowed to settle, but in time she realised that wherever Curnow had gone, he would not mind.

Wherever he was, she sighed as she drifted off into an exhausted sleep. How strange it was that we did not know the hardships of life when we started off in marriage and work, leaving our childhood home and setting off into adulthood, thinking we would make a success of it, where generations before immemorial had somehow floundered and failed.

The winter was a bad one, and there were some weeks when she did not manage to get through to Commondale at all. Prudence felt the chills keenly, and the joints in her hands swelled red and inflamed. She had no gloves now, having sold that fine pair she had commissioned in Glaisdale all those years ago before her marriage. A fine little pair of gloves they had been, and they would have kept her hands warm when she was outside. Now, with her knuckles all swollen and overworked, the gloves would probably not have fit. She knitted herself mittens that would stretch over the growing knobbles of her fingers.

After years going through the motions, emotionless, doing one's duty and what ought to be done, Magdalene came to life. William had survived Magdalene's cold, stifling grief by growing ever more busy at work, and delighted now in the happy home he found himself in that winter. Magdalene suddenly had three little girls to look after, who in the novelty of a new place, actual toys and new faces to pour attention on them, adored living with their aunt and uncle. During the winter they helped their aunt with the bread and vegetables, and sat together, all snuggled by the fireside whilst she told them fairy stories of the moors. On warm, sunny days in early spring they would go down to the stream that ran through the hamlet, dabbling in the crystal clear water with sticks, laughing at the bubbling sounds of running water bounding over pebbles. Rosen cried when she dropped a rock in the water and it splashed her dress, but Magdalene hugged her until it didn't seem so important anymore.

At first the girls were overjoyed when they saw their mother returning from work, and would rush her, screaming with joy. Time affects any heart, and the screams grew fainter and slower to come, as they settled happily into life as part of the Longbottom family. The ragdolls Prudence made for them did not seem quite as good as the toys at their new home, although the twins kept their rag dollies in their apron pockets so they could take them out when they were missing their mother. Prudence never knew this, and found each parting all the more painful, seeing how much her children were growing and developing, and how little she had to do with them. She couldn't afford to support them and give them a good home on her own. If she tried that, the girls would never get any schooling and would soon have to follow her into work at the mill to keep the household going. Yet if she did not bring them back, she would lose them for good to the temptations of Magdalene's easier living. She would have to marry, purely for financial support, an idea she loathed, but it seemed to be her best option.

Prudence had always believed she had an eternal well of sympathy for Magdalene's life – the death of her own baby twins and the barren years afterwards. It was now too late for Magdalene to have children of her own, and she supposed she sat by the fireside in the long winter nights and regretted that she hadn't tried again. Fate and circumstance had come to her aid and brought her the family she had been denied, including the little twin girls she had thought she had lost. Prudence was no fool not to notice the expression of ownership and possession that was growing on Magdalene's face. She was more than happy to take over looking after and raising the girls, and probably would not have minded if their surviving parent met with an accident somehow.

One ought to take care when wishing for accident and misfortune, for it falls like rain and it is hard to control who it may strike.

The spring had come upon Commondale hot and early. The girls were taken to playing outside, picking spring flowers, throwing twigs into the little river and traipsing up to the moors. Magdalene took them out on longer walks when time allowed, but had her chores at the house which she would not neglect. Generally the girls were well behaved and stayed near the cottage when Magdalene had to work, but Rosen was the worst for ignoring instruction and wandering off. Now that they had been at the Longbottom's several months they were no longer in awe of Aunt Magda, and knowing that she was not mother, knew they would get away with more mischief here.

Magdalene was kneading bread – she refused to buy bread, just as her own mother had done, even when they could afford to. One of the twins, in actuality Derwa although she thought it was Kerenza, often getting them confused, was at the table helping by kneading a smaller lump of dough. She was not making a good job of the task, spending more time watching how her aunt pummelled the dough, than thinking of what force to put into her own work. Kerenza was sitting in the windowsill, swinging her legs and humming to herself. The twins were now seven years old, and Magdalene had started to teach them how to read. She had been a little disappointed that Prudence had not bothered. She realised that money was not ready, and she couldn't afford to send them to lessons, but Prudence could read and write to a certain level. Surely she would want her own girls to blossom.

She looked up from her work and gazed around the kitchen, noticing for the first time that Rosen was no longer with them. "Derwa," she said, whilst looking at Kerenza. "Is your little sister just outside?"

Kerenza shared a knowing smile with her sister, hopping down from the windowsill and sauntering outside. She returned in a few moments, shaking her head. "She must have wandered off."

"That child," Magdalene muttered. "Go out and fetch her for me. She'll be late for her supper else."

Derwa returned to her kneading, lifting her hand to look at the sticky strings of uncooked bread that stretched upwards, as if refusing to release her.

"That bread will be like a brick, Kerenza."

"It's Derwa."

"Sorry?"

"I'm Derwa," she told her Aunt. Kerenza never cared when they were muddled, but it bothered Derwa. She was often mistaken for Kerenza, but the same didn't happen so much with her sister strangely enough. It made her think she was the one people didn't want to know.

They cleaned up and put the bread in the oven, Magdalene promising Derwa her little loaf would come out like a brick. She glanced out of the window, noting that Kerenza and Rosen still weren't back, and muttered to herself, wiping her hands on her apron. Derwa went and fetched the little book they were learning to read from and sat up in the sunny windowsill, vacated by her sister, to skim through the pages.

Derwa looked up from the book abruptly. Something awful clutched at her heart. She was swamped by terror. Tears started to roll down her cheeks. The book fell from her fingers and clattered onto the floor. She ran across the kitchen, pulled a pan from the cupboard and scrambled inside, already feeling her nose clog up with mucus as her crying increased. She pulled the cupboard door to, plunging herself into darkness, and buried her face into her pinafore, her little shoulders shaking violently.

Sometime after this Magdalene returned to the kitchen, noting the book absent mindedly tossed to the floor. She tutted to herself, picking the book up and setting it on the table. There was a cough, and she turned to find Rosen in the doorway.

"There you are, my little heart. And what a grubby face you have." She bent over the child, wiping furiously at the girl's face, much to Rosen's disgust. "And where is your sister?"

Rosen looked blankly at her.

"Oh, you are hopeless. Well, come along, up to table and we'll start getting supper out. At least Derwa ought to be somewhere, for she didn't go out to find you. Derwa? Where have you gone?"

They heard a snuffle and Rosen pointed at the cupboard.

Magdalene's brow crinkled. "Don't be daft." But when she opened the door and peered in, it proved Rosen was not daft at all. Derwa was curled up at the back like a frightened animal. "Derwa, what are you doing in there? Get out this instance."

Derwa made no response.

"It is suppertime and you must get out." Magdalene reached in to try and pull the girl out, but Derwa howled and wedged her body into all the angles so that she might remain fast.

Rosen giggled at table. "Silly Derwa."

William Longbottom appeared in the doorway. "Wife, what are you doing?" he asked, watching Magdalene grappling with something in the cupboard as if she were fighting a wild animal.

"It's Derwa, she's refusing to come out." Magdalene huffed, and gave up, stepping back. "Very well, your supper will be on the table. You can come out when you're ready."

"Where's Kerenza?"

"She's not back yet. I sent her out to find Rosen."

"Rosen's here."

"Yes, I know that, but..." she looked at the little girl. "Did you not see Kerenza?"

"Yes."

"She found you?"

"Yes. She said I had to come home."

"Why didn't she come with you?"

Rosen shrugged and looked meaningfully at the range.

"Rosen, where did your sister go?" William asked.

"Away up the hill. Can I have my supper now?"

The adults shared a look. Although the girls liked to wander off and play outside, they had a natural internal clock that always had them back in time for food. "I'll go look for her," William said, "You stay here with the girls."

William met Prudence quite by chance later in the evening. He had not expected to see her today, and was shocked as he saw his younger sister walking at a brisk pace by the river. Prudence couldn't quite explain it either, for she had not planned to make the walk. It took about an hour and half to get up to Commondale and she was tired, but had felt on a whim that she needed to see her girls this evening. It had been pleasant and warm walking, and dusk was only considering an approach as she saw her brother.

Prudence waved to him. William felt physically ill. He was not sure that he had ever felt quite as dreadful as he did in that moment, seeing her cheery face and realising he was about to crush her. The simple fact was that Kerenza was lost. He'd been out looking for her, stalking up the track he thought Rosen had meant. He went as far as he thought a seven year could go, calling the girl's name and wondering if the lass had taken a tumble. He got a reply from a local shepherd, who soon joined in the search. Word started to spread across the valley and local farmers, wives, workers and maids started out to check their own properties in case the girl had had an accident and was lying unseen. The landlord of the inn near the bridge set off with his staff and regulars to thoroughly check the river – a task William couldn't face doing – but no drowned child was found.

"Why, William," Prudence spoke as she grasped his hands. "You do look ill. I hope you don't need me to carry you home, for I'm awful tired after today."

"You should not have tired yourself out walking here after work. And you'll be away early tomorrow."

"I know but I miss my girls."

"Prudence, wait up. You don't understand."

Prudence stopped, not for her brother, but for the sight of the local landlord heaving up a log that was half submerged in the river to check what was underneath it. "What is he doing?"

How could he answer such a question? He gripped his sister's arm. "I have some bad news. It's Kerenza."

"Kerenza?" she turned, not making any connection with what she had seen. In the background the man let the log drop with a loud splash, straightening, then seeing Prudence for the first time and growing still. "What's the matter, is she ill? I knew there was something that made me come..."

"No. It's not that. She's wandered off."

"Wandered off?"

"We're looking for her now. The whole valley is..."

"Nonsense," Prudence waved it aside and continued onwards to the smithy, a little faster than before. "She knows when her supper time is, she'll be back now."

William hurried after her. "Magdalene sent her off to find Rosen. Rosen came home after a while but Kerenza never did."

A seed of nausea that she had first felt when William had so casually chosen the term "wandered off" was rapidly growing in her gut. Prudence stopped a few metres from the cottage door where her daughters were essentially being fostered. "You don't know where she is?"

"This is what I've been telling you."

"But she's a good girl, she always comes home for her supper." She burst into a run and came gasping through the doorway. Magdalene was hunched up by the fire as if suffering chills of the deepest winter, and was sobbing into a handkerchief. She jumped at the sudden noise, hoping for a moment that someone had found Kerenza. It was worse, it was the mother and she would have to face her. It was a horror to have to tell a woman that her child was lost, and that it was her fault. Prudence had entrusted her three daughters to her, and now there were only two.

The two women stared at one another. William peered over Prudence. "Has she returned?"

Magdalene shook her head miserably. "Have you...?"

"No. Everyone's out looking but dusk is starting to fall."

Prudence left the room and hurried to the little bed the girls shared together. Only Rosen was there, curled up fast asleep. She ran back to the kitchen. "Where are they, where are the twins? I don't understand what you've done to them."

"I haven't done anything," Magdalene sobbed.

"Derwa's in the cupboard," William sighed. "She won't come out."

Prudence crouched down at the open cupboard door. It was dreadfully quiet. There was a blanket pulled up to and clutched by a balled little figure. The head raised and a tearstained face looked at her. "Where is your sister? Derwa, where is Kerenza?"

"Mamma, mamma," the little girl sobbed.

"Derwa's been with me all day," Magdalene said. "She doesn't know."

"Derwa, get out of there," Prudence reached in to pull her out, but Derwa froze, filling the space and becoming immoveable. "Mamma, I can't. I daren't. I'm so frightened."

"She wouldn't come out for her supper," Magdalene spoke. "I tried..."

"You tried?" Prudence lurched up, not sure if she were about to be sick or scream. "You tried? Where is my little girl? Where is she? You were supposed to be keeping her safe."

"I was. She just went out..."

"You sent her out to fetch Rosen."

"And she did, she did," Magdalene's speech was a gasping cry now. Tears dripped onto her lap. "Rosen said she found her and sent her home. She just says she went away on the road and I..."

"Rosen is not in charge of her sisters!" Prudence shouted through her sister—in-law's distress. "You were supposed to be looking after them. You are not fit..."

"Prudence!" William pulled her back by her shoulders. "You are upset and you don't know what you say. We must focus our energies elsewhere. She will be somewhere and she will be found."

Prudence glared at Magdalene but said no more. "Give me a lamp," she asked, turning away from the wretched woman. "I must search. I must find my girl." She took an old miner's lamp from a hook on the wall. William lit it and the two set back outside to rejoin the hunt. Prudence crying her daughter's name, her feet pushed on by a blind terror of where the girl might be.

They searched until the darkness fell so tight that they could not see their outstretched arms. Prudence wanted to continue with the lamp, but William eventually persuaded her to come back to the cottage, under threat that she would only trip and injure herself, and really no one would be moving anywhere now. Perhaps Kerenza had returned. She had not, and Prudence spent the night in the kitchen, awake and distraught, waiting for dawn so that she could continue the search. At some point the sad little bundle that was Derwa cried herself to sleep in the cupboard.

The following day the community searched the farmland and moorland, covering a radius of eight miles or so from the smithy's cottage. Eight miles in any direction seemed enough to cover the distance a seven year could have walked. Rosen was taken back up the road where they thought she had been when Kerenza had collected her, and asked for details, but the four year old didn't understand, grew confused and started to cry. Farmers traversed the fields and poked around in becks and steams with their walking sticks. Shepherds roamed moorland. Farm lads helped farmer's wives to check the wells and go through the farm buildings. It was disconcerting enough that there was no reply to the cry of the little girl's name, but that no sign was found, not a body or a little scrap of clothing or anything, why, it was as if she had vanished into the very air. Older residents muttered about old tales of witches and shook their heads. A couple of wives raised their eyebrows and remembered old stories of changeling babes and children who wandered out onto fairylands and never were seen again. Wherever she was, Kerenza was not in Commondale.

In the evening mist from the coast started to creep across the moorland. William had lost track of his sister and was back at the cottage, where Magdalene was comforting an unsettled Rosen. Derwa was still in the cupboard. Prudence was dragging herself through heather on the moorland above Commondale. She had walked up to Pines Lodge, the farmstead where her mother had grown up. It was now the property of some distant and wealthy cousin who never came here, and rented out to sheep farmers. She had passed the property and gone up onto the moor. Oblivious to the chill in her hands, the dying light or the mists rolling on. She could not give up, and despite her throat being hoarse and parched, she continued to call her daughter's name, desperately searching for a sign.

Her heart leapt when suddenly she saw a child standing in the heather further up the hill, knee deep in heather and stock still. "Kerenza!" Prudence screamed as she started to run, the claws of heather fronds pulling at her skirts and slowing progress. She stumbled on to a sheep track and made better speed, but the child was running away from her, leaping across the bushes of heather like a deer. "Kerenza! It is Mamma. Please stop."

Prudence staggered to a halt and stared about her in desperation. The child had disappeared. "Oh no, no no no no no no..."

She started walking again, pulling herself up to the top of a hillock to gaze across the expanse of moorland. The distance was lost to the mist, and when she looked back she could not see the farm in miniature as one usually could from this height. A damp chill crept around her. She dropped to her knees, sobbing as though her heart would never cease to break.

It was some time, she could not say how long, before movement caught her attention. The shifting of feet. She looked up to find the child standing a mere couple of metres away from her. It was a young lad, and on reflection she did not know how she could have mistaken him for Kerenza. He had dark hair, certainly nothing like Kerenza's brilliant red, and was a little taller. He was dressed in old fashioned clothes, a little threadbare and patched with what looked like ribbons.

"My little girl," she managed to speak. "She's gone missing. Kerenza. She has beautiful red hair..."

The little boy regarded her. "I've not seen her."

"Are you sure? She's gone missing and we've searched all over but we can't find her."

He looked rather grave. "She's still in Commondale."

Prudence's tears stopped abruptly with surprise. He spoke with authority, yet he had said that he had not seen her. "Kerenza. Do you know where..."

He shook his head. "You'll never see her again."

"Is that a threat? What have you..."

"I've done nothing. I'm only saying so you can stop looking."

"You know something." Prudence tried to get back onto her feet so that she might get hold of the lad. "You have to tell me. Take me to her."

The boy darted back out of reach, then was away bounding across the moorland and disappeared into the mist.

"Come back!"

No reply came.

With sadness, the community of Commondale returned to their daily tasks. Every place had been searched. No child was found. The local consensus was that she must have been stolen away. By someone or something. It felt disrespectful how strongly the sun shone, how the birds sang with joy in the trees, how the clear water bubbled down from springs and into the beck. So much life and joy but Kerenza had simply disappeared as if she had never existed. After losing the boy in the mist, Prudence made her way back down to the village. At her brother's house she demanded pen and paper, and sat writing a letter, pained by every pen stroke for Prudence had not written anything for a long time. Once complete and folded, she gave the letter, addressed to her brother Jeremiah in Runswick Bay.

As soon as it was light, Prudence had left the cottage and was roaming the countryside. She had not eaten for over a day and felt weak and light headed, yet she could not stop. Kerenza had to be somewhere. Prudence headed south out of Commondale village and up on to the moors in the direction of Castleton. She dragged heavy, drained legs with her. She followed a track that started downhill into Castleton, but before entering the village, swung away onto the Blakey road to the high moors. A short way from the village she came to Gallow Howe, and slumping down beside a rock she gazed numbly out across the spread of moorland and dippings of valleys and villages. Gallow Howe. They had hung criminals here once upon a time, she thought, although that had ended a good hundred years ago or so. These days criminals were packed off for trial, and if death was to come, it was usually at York where they ended their days. Prudence squeezed her eyes shut and buried her face in her skirts. What if Kerenza had been stolen away? She may never find her again. Her dear little girl. She should have been there for her: that was what a mother was supposed to do. She should never have allowed Magdalene to talk her into letting the girls go to Commondale. She should never have let them out of her sight.

Eventually she wandered down to Castleton, asking anyone if they had seen Kerenza. Her head a blur. She continued down the little track, eventually leaving the village and heading through farmland towards the familiarity of Ainthorpe. Aunt Gilly found her and took her home, putting her straight to bed. Prudence could not sleep and was desperate to get up. Her cousin Neil kept her in place whilst his mother prepared a tincture, which she brewed up with hot milk and took to Prudence, forcing her to drink it. At some point, the herbs had their way with her mind and she drifted into a terrified sleep where Kerenza was running across the moorland and would not look back. Prudence screamed and screamed but with no effect. Her daughter would not return.

The following day Prudence woke as a saddened corpse. Gilly sat with her and told her that she had to get herself out of this. There were two little girls who needed her. She had to go fetch them. She and Neil accompanied Prudence back to Commondale where the family awaited her in apprehension. No more news had been heard of Kerenza, and it was now agreed that the girl was lost. There must be a curse on the family, for the father had gone in a strange way as well, hadn't he? He had drowned shortly after the birth of his daughter, Rosen.

In the afternoon two things happened. Firstly Jeremiah arrived, having received Prudence's letter late the day before. He had been up at first light and gotten a lift in a fishmonger's cart as far as Castleton. The man had been heading onwards to Blakey, but had dropped Jeremiah off, who had then walked the rest of the way to Commondale. He said that Prudence and the girls were very welcome to come and visit him and the family at Runswick, and they could come back with him if they wished, although it would be tomorrow they would set off, as it was a long journey for little ones. The words of condolence caught in the back of his throat. He did not know what to say. No one even knew what they were sorry for, as Kerenza was simply absent. People were starting to talk about her as if she were dead.

Prudence crouched down by the kitchen door and looked at her daughter. Derwa wiped her face and nodded, heart broken but feeling it was safe to come out now. She crawled into her mother's arms. "Mamma. Kerenza, I..."

Prudence put her hand gently on the back on Derwa's head and closed her eyes. "Don't," she whispered.

1823

Derwa

In the late autumn Prudence married a Mr Gilbert Medd of Glaisdale. He was a respectable tradesman; a cobbler and widower with a sickly eleven year old child, an exuberant sixteen year old lad and a need for a housekeeper and mother to his children. It was not a love match on either side, but a business arrangement of mutual benefit. The union gave Prudence, Derwa and Rosen a decent home, good shoes and a fresh start in a new village. Danby and Ainthorpe were impossibilities, for those were where dear Kerenza had lived, and Commondale was where she had disappeared. Everyone thought she was dead, either sunk in a bog and drowned or stolen away by gypsies or fairies, but the bottom line was no one could prove anything. Prudence never found out what had happened to her daughter. It was a draining heartache to live with. She never felt true joy again.

Part of the arrangement with Gilbert Medd was that the girls would keep their family name Pengelly, to remember their father. It was a desperate last effort, for there were no pictures and Rosen knew the man only as a name and a concept. Derwa had vague memories of a shorter man with a stern face but a kind soul, accompanied by a little dog. Both of whom had vanished from her life a long time ago, at the point at which children just accept whatever comes or goes as the normality of life, for they know no different. The other part of the Medd arrangement was that the fee was to be paid so that both Rosen and Derwa could attend the little school and learn reading, writing, arithmetic and a little needlework.

Many a marriage was that of a bargain struck to make life easier, and although the match between a tall woman with more hair than her scalp knew what to do with, and a balding man fifteen years her senior, with wire glasses and very neat and particular ways, didn't seem like an obvious match, both parties seemed relieved that they had found harbour and help after all their troubles. They looked forward to a time of tranquillity. They lived in a little house close to the graveyard of St Thomas' church up on the hill of Glaisdale village. Mr Medd enjoyed a steady stream of customers that kept the extended family solvent.

The Tyremans still lived in the village, but circumstance of life had not been kind. Prudence would see the three children playing outside the glover's workshop, and be halted by the vivid memories of walking here years ago with Magdalene. She had not yet married and had come to order gloves for her wedding trousseau. It felt like something she might have read in a book, an event that happened to someone else. Such sunny innocent times when she could not really even imagine having a child, let alone a husband. Now she had lost both. The glover, Stephen Tyreman had lost his own dear wife, Mary. She had passed away some years ago after giving him three children: two daughters, Mary Ann and Hannah, and a son John. Prudence could still recall Mary Tyreman holding the little baby, Mary Ann, all starting out in family life and so hopeful. Now that baby was a little girl.

Shortly after Kerenza disappeared, Prudence and the girls had stayed with Jeremiah and Sonneta in Runswick for two months before moving on to Aunt Gilly's in Ainthorpe. Prudence had needed to be away from everything, just to focus on her two girls and listen to the sea. Sonneta, that curious little thing from the northern isles that Jeremiah had found gutting fish, was quite the treasure, now with three children of her own, the patience of a saint and a sunny disposition that never felt patronising or disrespectful to Prudence's heartbreak. She helped with the girls when Prudence needed to sit and grieve, and taught Derwa how to knit. Derwa picked up the habit quickly, and her needles were soon tapping away with impressive speed as she prepared woollen clothing for all the family.

Magdalene and William had come to Runswick twice but Prudence had refused to see them. Perhaps it would have happened regardless who had been looking after Kerenza, for deep down Prudence knew she had let the girls play outside and hadn't always known where they were from one moment to the next. But Magdalene's carelessness with all that had been precious to her was unforgivable and she could not so much as look upon the woman without suffering from an incontrollable rage.

In the interim news had swiftly spread, as bad news always did, of the disappearance of little Kerenza Pengelly, and the understandable breakdown of her mother. Prudence lost her job at the mill, for she simply ceased coming and never sent word back to her employer. The mill owner was a decent type, and acknowledged what an awful situation it was for a mother. He did not let things sully Prudence's name on the work market. Although he doubted he would be prepared to employ her again if she returned. He had only taken her on as a favour to Curnow Pengelly's memory, and really she had come to weaving too late in life to become a fast and skilled worker.

The general consensus about the villages was that Prudence ought to marry again. She had been a good housekeeper, and there were always widowers popping up who needed someone to mind the house and the children. Perhaps now that she was completely broken, she would give up her pride of self sufficiency and any foolish notions of clinging on to Curnow's memory, and accept a good man and a domestic position. There was some talk that even Stephen Tyreman might approach her, but in the end she had encouraged the older cobbler. She did not wish for anymore children, which she was sure any wife of Tyreman would be expected to provide, as he was only in his mid thirties. And indeed, a few years later he did marry another woman and produced another brood of children.

So they lived for some years in relative peace and uneventfulness. Calm domesticity and the changing of the seasons was always followed by the vague shadow of loss, but they became adapt at pretending it was not there. About a year after their marriage, Gilbert's sickly younger son, Andersson, named after a grandfather of his dead mother, passed away with winter chills, and was buried close by the in the graveyard along with his dear mother. The eldest son, Matthew had been learning his father's trade, but was a giddy, excitable boy, easily distracted. For a change of scene and to be in a place where things happened he moved to Whitby in the spring to fill a position of draper's assistant as arranged via his father's contacts. He sent home letters with increasing time gaps, full of chatter of the characters he met, great larks in his free time and all the gossip of the railways. Had they heard of the great iron road way of Darlington? It was going to revolutionise the world, mark his words, he knew the future when he read about it.

Later in the year Prudence received a letter from her Aunt Eleanor. It had travelled through the twisting valley, for Eleanor had sent it to Mrs Pengelly of Danby, and after some deliberation on the postman's part at the Duke of Wellington, he had taken it down to Gilly Beecroft at Ainthorpe who had accepted the letter and paid the fee on her niece's behalf. From there Prudence's younger cousin, Neil had walked it across to Glaisdale one pleasant evening.

Prudence hadn't read it straight away, instead enjoying the company of her silly cousin, whom she still saw as a ridiculous young lad even though he was now a man of twenty-eight, jobbing here and there at the farms of the Esk Valley and still not settled with a wife of his own. He was a great entertainer full of tall tales and miraculous discoveries, and kept the girls up well past their bedtime, delighting them with stories of his exploits. Even Mr Medd chose to stay out of the workshop and remained in the kitchen to enjoy a pipe.

The next day, when chores were finished and Prudence had a moment to herself, she went and sat on her bed and took the letter from her apron pocket. Her reading was not as good as it had been and she knew it would take some time. She had not heard from her aunt in years, in fact she had neglected to tell her about her recent marriage, or anything beyond the birth of the twins. The first thing Eleanor wrote was to ask how Kerenza and Derwa were, and whether Prudence and Kurnow had been blessed with any further children. The sunlight streamed through the small window and illuminated Prudence's greying thatch as she squeezed her eyes tight shut and put her hand to her mouth. How much had been lost in a few precious years.

When she felt ready, she continued with the letter, for she guessed correctly Eleanor had some major news to pass on. Indeed it was, for her grandmother, Maud Cornforth, as had been Hurst and nee Feather, had passed away some weeks ago. She had lived to a great age of eighty, but had been a confused old lady in her twilight and Eleanor believed it had been the wasting of the mind that had finally brought her to the end. Eleanor apologised that it had taken her so many weeks to write and she begged Prudence's assistance that she might pass on this news to her two brothers. They had conducted the funeral very quickly after Maud's passing as it needed doing as soon as possible – Prudence didn't quite understand the need for this comment, as no one lingered for weeks when someone had died, and wondered if she was being stupid as she didn't know what Eleanor meant – and then there had been some family issues to sort out and of course, Eleanor had been distressed at the loss of her mother. Even though it had been expected for some time, the circumstances had been extremely upsetting. Since then things had settled back at the little house in Haworth, although Prudence could understand they were still in a period of mourning. Her cousin, Muriel had moved away to start an apprenticeship with an apothecary...

Prudence lowered the letter. Her reading must be very bad because women didn't generally start apprenticeships, and certainly not with apothecaries. And no one started up new trades at this stage in life; why Muriel was only a year younger than herself. She picked up the letter and started to read that section again. It was correct, Prudence was an apprentice. Eleanor noted that this would surprise Prudence, even though they all knew how fond Muriel had been of reading strange volumes. In fact, much had happened to Muriel in the interim, for she had married an eminent medical doctor, Kaarel Must, and had been living in Edinburgh with him until his recent death, when she had returned to Yorkshire. Her husband had been an encouraging and open minded man, who had taught her much and had even allowed her to help with a number of medical cases. It was something that had delighted Muriel's mind, and on all of this an apothecary in Pateley Bridge had agreed to take her on as a kind of assistant.

"Pateley Bridge." Prudence murmured to herself as she lowered the letter. How curious life could work out. And that Muriel had indeed married. She had wondered if such commonplace things would have ever happened for her odd cousin.

She took out her memory box, a treasure crafted by her first husband, where she stored all of her little trinkets and notes - worthless to others, yet priceless for her life. There was a jumble of all the letters Prudence had ever received, along with odd little lengths of old ribbons, a cone she had taken from one of the trees at Pines Lodge, and baby teeth from her girls that she had sewn a little cloth bag specifically for. There was also a rag doll that had belonged to Kerenza. It had been abandoned at the smithy's cottage on that fateful day. Prudence put Eleanor's letter on top, then for an unknown reason decided to flick through her other old letters. Her hands went into the box and found something hard and cold at the bottom. Digging through, she pulled out a necklace. It was an amber pendant of honey gold lit up beautifully by the sunlight. An intense memory of her wedding day swept through her as she held aloft the gift from Aunt Eleanor MacCaskill. It had been an insurance, an object of money that Prudence would own and could cash in if hardship struck. She had completely forgotten about it, buried under letters and worthless scraps of ribbons all these years. It wouldn't have solved any problems long term, but she could have sold it and put it towards the rent to keep her girls close by a little longer.

"Where is Pateley Bridge?"

Prudence jumped at the question. She had not realised she had an audience. Derwa stood in the doorway. She could not say for how long, but she must have been standing there with her inert knitting for some time whilst Prudence read the letter. Prudence put the necklace down on top of the letters in the box. "It's a long way from here, away over to the West. I'm not exactly sure."

"And you have a letter from Pateley Bridge?"

"No, this is from my Aunt," Prudence sighed. "You've never met her. She's a bit of a strange woman. She has written to me to say that my grandmother has died."

"She is dead?"

"You never met her either."

"Is the necklace from grandmother?"

Prudence shook her head. "She was your great grandmother; my grandmother. But no it wasn't. This was a wedding present I'd forgotten about. From long ago when I married your father. My grandmother was poor. She wouldn't have had any money or anything to leave anyone. She lived with her daughter, my aunt."

Derwa stood and mulled this over for a time. She was only nine, but had grown to be a slightly nervous and serious child. Knitting seemed to calm her, and she was so prolific that the entire household was well stocked with stockings, hats, scarves and jumpers. They could have seen out a hundred score winters. She could have supplied Runswick as well, only that Sonneta produced even quicker, and was raising her own daughters in the art. They didn't go and see Aunt Magdalene and Uncle William anymore and Derwa had stopped asking. She remembered everything that had happened when Kerenza had gone, but she also remembered happy times there and longed for more family. There wasn't an awful lot of relations, especially when she listened to her classmates account long lists of siblings, cousins, half cousins... Her mother's family circle was small, even discounting the two she no longer would speak to. It seemed a section had moved across to the west of the county and many of her mother's siblings had died when she was only a girl herself. Prudence had taken the girls to her mother's grave once, and they had read through the list of children's names together. Rosen had not been much interested, preferring to chatter with her two rag dollies, but Derwa had asked about the aunts and uncles who had never been and what they were like. What with her own father's family being a mystery lost in Cornwall, a place too far to travel to, they seemed to be rather adrift in the world. Sometimes she would day dream about Cornwall, the happy hoards of family living there. A land which was warm and in the south and had lots of sea. Derwa imagined the fields there were walled with thatching and the sun never sank behind the hills.

Of course, with her mother marrying again, they had gained a third family, the Medds. Gilbert Medd was not one for talking to little girls, and although he got along well with mother it seemed as though they both had a job to do and that was all. Mr Medd's parents had died a long time ago, as had his other wife, and he was very sad when Andersson died. Although Emily's mother (Emily went to the school) had said that the lad had been born wrong, carried his mother's sorrow, and had never been long for this world. And it was true, Emily had said, Andersson hadn't grown that tall. There was still Matthew Medd, but he lived in Whitby and Derwa had never really liked him. He was a very talkative, happy lad but it never seemed that it mattered who was listening, and he was certainly not interested in hearing what other people had to say. He enjoyed "great larks" and never understood when these pranks upset or hurt other people. It was the lark that mattered, and damnation to any of the consequences.

To hell with the consequences. It was easy enough with childhood games to guess how things would end up, but as one got older and fell into the routine and cycles of adult life, how could one know if everyday choices would have dire consequences for the rest of one's life?

Derwa finished with her schooling at fifteen. Unlike her younger sister she was still living at home. Despite remaining in the nest, she worked, and never had an idle day. From helping Mr Medd out in the workshop cutting leather, she had moved across to dressmaking and found she had a talent for visualising how a shape cut out in cloth could be stitched and worked to hang in the right way off a certain type of body. She earned her keep in dressmaking, with a little knitting on the side. Rosen had gone to work as a maid on a farm in Danby. The tenants were Applecrosses, the head of the household was called Richmond Applecross, a name which had made Prudence lower her brows, but when Derwa asked her about it, she only said there had been some fuss at a funeral a long time ago and she did not know anything more about it. Rosen said that Mr Applecross's old father, Albert lived on the farm with them, and he had been quite rude to Rosen in the beginning, saying he knew who she was. As if that was a reason to be rude to anyone, Rosen, who was quite brash for all her twelve and a half years, had muttered. One of Mr Applecross's nephews, Samuel Applecross, was also working at the farm, and had taken old Albert's line with Rosen until one day she had slapped him around the head with a cheesecloth, knocking the sense from him. He had stumbled off and fallen in the pig swill, much to the old man's delight. After that, both the old man and Samuel treated Rosen much better and said that her fiery red hair showed there was more of her father's people in her than anything else. Rosen would look in the little mirror at her own red hair and wondered what it signified for her.

Derwa had walked part of the way to Ainthorpe with her mother that morning for the air before turning back for Glaisdale. Her mother was off to visit her Aunt Gilly, but Derwa had a couple of dresses to get made up and didn't have the time for a day's visiting. Mr Medd was to be out all day delivering boots, so she hoped the peace and solitude of the house would add speed and zest to her work.

She paused in the little lane, to sit up in a wide verge and enjoy the early spring sunlight for a few minutes. A carriage came past, one from Danby Grange she guessed, judging from the family crest on the side. One of the farmers' wives had reached the same point in the lane and scrambled up onto the grass to stand beside Derwa and nod her head in deference as the carriage rushed by. On the back stood the groom, and as he travelled past he stared at Derwa in a most disturbing way. There was something quite dreadful about the way he stared at a person that Derwa wobbled and involuntarily grabbed at the farmer's wife's arm.

"Goodness above, girl, what is the matter?" the woman shrieked as Derwa unsettled her basket of eggs.

"I don't know," Derwa spoke, watching the carriage disappear off up the land. "That man on the back..."

"What, the groom?"

"He made me feel ill."

"I'm not surprised," snorted the farmer's wife. "There's always been something wrong with that Bartholomew Tinder. They say he does a very good job over at the Grange, well he must do or I'm sure they would have given him notice a long time ago. Only child, you know, inherited the lot when his parents both perished over at Commondale a few years ago. And he earns plenty well I'm sure, but no woman would have him. No woman in her right mind, or her wrong mind for that matter, ha!" She paused in her character evaluation and looked at Derwa, her pale face shaded by the bonnet, tendrils of red hair escaping. She'd heard Derwa had a twin once, but she'd run away or died or some such thing over at Commondale, around the time Tinder's parents died, and that no one had ever really found proof of what had happened to the girl. Not that it was something she would ever think to ask Derwa. She liked her gossip, but Derwa's worried little face stopped questions.

"Look at all the muck and dust they've riled up with their carriage, racing about like that. I don't know what," she muttered, hopping back down onto the lane in a very nimble way, not so much as cracking an egg. "I don't know what they've got to rush about for, for heaven knows they don't have to lift a finger, not one of them."

They parted with the usual greetings of a good day and Derwa returned to Glaisdale village. She followed the track that went up around the back of the church, intending to swing back down to the front where home stood. Coming up the track leading a donkey was Damon Eddon, a lad a few years older than her who she first met in her school days. Even then he was one of the older boys who came intermittently depending on what season it was and what needed doing on the farm. Damon's father farmed to the south of the village and the family did all right, for as well as all the usual farming of the area, they had quarried some sandstone on part of the land. Damon had always been a cheery lad, confident but not overbearing and something of a champion for the weaker or shyer children in the school. Derwa had always looked up to him as a great protective bear when she had been a little girl. These days she wasn't quite sure what she made of him. He had grown yet taller and broadened out, less the boy and much more the man, but still had that easy boyish smiling countenance. If one had been searching for a definition of kind, it would have been Damon Eddon.

His face brightened when he saw Derwa. "Good Morning Derwa!" They had always been on first name basis ever since the school, where Derwa, overwhelmed by the noise and sheer number of children, had sheltered in his shadow. "You out enjoying the sunshine? Skulking away from your work?" he joked.

"Only for a little while. I went part of the way with Mamma. She's away to see Aunt Gilly today."

"You not off visiting?"

"No, I have a stack of dresses to sew up, I'll be busy the rest of the day and perhaps the evening."

"I think you must do nothing but sewing for I don't see you out as often as I used to."

"It has been a cold winter."

"Aye, that's true enough," he paused, reflecting on something. "Perhaps you'll be wanting to take more walks out, now that spring is here. It's very pleasant on an evening. I always like to head off..."

"Damon Eddon!" a voice shrieked, interrupting his pastoral musings. His mother was rushing up the hill towards them. Derwa wondered that the woman got any work done at home for she frequently appeared whenever Derwa bumped into Damon, scolding and shouting that her son needed to get on with whatever he was supposed to be doing. In recent months an addition had joined the usual complaints, something in the form of: "Betty Boddy is down at the farm to see you. You'd best away back." She commanded, puffing away as she reached her son. The mother gave Derwa a look up and down, assessing her from the previous time and still finding her very lacking. And that dreadful red hair, like the sin of the devil itself upon her head. It was no wonder her father had thrown himself into the river.

"I'll be back soon enough, but I still have to get thiss'en to the paddock."

"Get on with it then. I'm sure Miss Derwa will have some chores to get on with at home, or some stitching she's behind on."

Derwa nodded to the woman. "Good Morning Mrs Eddon."

"Good Morning indeed, as if folks have nothing better to do than take the sunlight."

"Mother, don't be harsh so."

Derwa excused herself and hurried back to the cottage. She didn't know why Mrs Eddon had taken against her so, for she had never done anything to her or her family, or in fact anything of any note in the village. As long as Derwa could sit working with her needles she was quite happy, but she was hardly a bold or standout girl in the area. She thought herself bland and inoffensive, and couldn't understand why Mrs Eddon was so frustrated at her presence. She should try to be more like Betty Boddy, although she wasn't sure how she could do it. She could hardly grow taller or spout beautiful blonde hair. And one couldn't put on such a deep hearty laugh without it sounding forced. Betty loved to laugh. Derwa guessed that she loved Damon as well, for she always seemed to be over there visiting, and she'd heard a couple of her own clients gossiping that Mrs Eddon was very keen for a match between the Eddons and Boddys, to bring those two farming families together. Betty would be eighteen this year, which all the older ladies said was a good age to be married. Damon was twenty and such a man and a hard worker. They would make a handsome couple.

Derwa sat and sewed for the rest of the morning, her mind wandering. She was sixteen now, but in two years would she suddenly be a good age for marriage? She couldn't imagine her being of any use to anyone around here. She wasn't as tall as her mother; in fact Mamma said she took after her father in a lot of ways. She was strong but didn't look robust, which she supposed was what folk looked for in a farmer's wife. Perhaps that was why Mrs Eddon disapproved of her, with such slender hands and arms, she didn't have the strength to churn the milk to butter.

At noon it started to rain and the sky turned a dark grey. The rain thrashed against the windows in such a thunderous roar. Derwa shivered and went through to the room she and Rosen shared to fetch another shawl. Whilst she was there, she heard a louder crash, and when she returned to the kitchen was horrified to find three young men smashing open the back door and forcing their way in. They were laughing raucously, the backs of their coats pulled up in some vain attempt to keep the rain off. Their hair was plastered to their scalps, and for a few minutes Derwa didn't recognise Matthew Medd. A strong retching stink of alcohol followed the young men, mingled with a stumbling camaraderie, so that they hardly noticed that Derwa was in the room.

One of the men was carrying an over-filled leather satchel that made a chinking sound as it was swung about, before being hurled unceremoniously onto the kitchen table.

"Imagine the look on the old squire's face when he realises!" one of the strangers roared.

The other man snorted in his laughter. Matthew crept through the room as if making a pantomime of being as quiet as a mouse. "I think Pa has a bottle of brandy hidden away somewhere. Let me go search it out."

As Matthew left the room his two friends noticed Derwa.

"Well, Tobias, do you know who this red-haired little vixen is?"

"A spirit come to congratulate us on our great fortune no doubt."

Derwa, never the most forceful of girls, was struck dumb as the two approached, stepping around her. The wolves coming in for the kill, the quick nip to the throat, and the poor dumb little lamb too stupid to think to run or scream for help.

Tobias gripped Derwa by the back of the neck and buried his face into her hair. "She smells just grand."

"Better than them old salted cod you hang around with?"

"It seems our Matthew has brought us to a country house of wenches. What a treat for the afternoon. Come on girl, you going to entertain us two rich men?"

"No, I..."

The other man – she never heard his name – stepped up against her and pressed his hands against her breasts and laughed. "Come along then, we've had a good morning. Spin her over and we'll take a turn."

Rosen was pushed face down onto the table, crumpling against her cut out pieces of fabric, her tip toes barely touching the floor. She struggled now, something deep inside of her telling her she must fight for herself as no one else would. The nameless man grabbed her hands and pulled her arms outstretched across the table, laughing as he spilled his boozy breath across her. Tobias flung her skirts up over her head, and to the soundtrack of a young girl's screams, had his way with her.

When he was done, he wiped himself off on her skirts, then stepped back. "Must have been her first time, there's blood here."

"I thought Matthew had brought us to a wench house. Don't tell me you got to deflower her?" Tobias let go of her limp arms and hurried around, stumbling drunkenly over a stool. "Move aside, it's still fresh enough for me to claim a virgin this day."

Once both men had taken their fill, they slapped one another's backs, then picking up the satchel yelled to Matthew, who had not returned. "Matthew, my lad, we're away now. Come now or we're gone. We'll not linger for you."

Matthew did not appear, for he was passed out snoring in his father's workshop. Derwa remained on the table for a lot of the afternoon, terrified that now she had been violated she would soon die. As it grew dark, she dared to get up. She wiped her legs down from the blood and other viscous discharges that dribbled, before running away to her bed. So that was what a man did to a woman. Why did anyone ever want to be married? She buried herself under her quilts, and wept herself to sleep for she did not see that any good was to be hoped for now.

Shortly after Derwa had gone to bed, Mr Medd returned home. First he shook his head at the dressmaking mess Prudence's daughter had left in the kitchen. This was not like Derwa. He then went to his workshop and found his son sprawled on the floor, snoring loudly with what was left of the medicinal brandy bottle clasped in one hand.

What had happened transpired over the following days. It seemed that Matthew had fallen in with a bad crowd in Whitby, his appearance at the shop slackening off. The draper did not rush to fire him out of a duty to his acquaintance with Mr Medd. He later informed his friend in a letter that he had been very close to sacking the lad, and when he learned that Matthew had turned up drunk in Glaisdale, he regretfully had to confirm he would no longer be able to offer employment to the young man.

As it happened, Matthew got off lightly in punishment for his misdeeds. In boasting and chattering at the alehouses in Whitby, he had told his two friends of Glaisdale Manor, just outside of the village, and the rich squire who lived there. He was a fool and did not deserve his money, so the inebriated trio decided to travel inland and rob what they had convinced each other was theirs by rights. They entered the manor house in the morning, enjoying their good fortune to find a satchel of rents on the desk and a cabinet full of fine spirits in which they indulged. Satchel in hand they had dispersed, the butler thinking he saw two or three rogues racing away across the lawns. At this point the story to public knowledge and reality separated.

Tobias and friend were caught up at the inn on Blakey Ridge, where they had been staying and drinking for three days, whilst gambling wild sums on cockfighting behind the pub. The squire, who was also in charge of justice in the area, was reported to have turned a new shade of purple when he had found the two men and the incriminating satchel. He promptly had them arrested and sent off to York to await trial. Thieves' honour being prevalent, Matthew Medd's name was never mentioned, and his part in the drama never progressed. The two rogues were found guilty and sentenced to transportation in the end, but the jury of local gossips put two and two together and guessed that at the very least Matthew must have been talking to the men about Glaisdale manor, for hadn't he been working in Whitby at one time? Then he had appeared back at home, and his father had been furious with him. He had been at home for a short time before Mr Medd dragged his son off to enlist in the militia and he was away to who knew where.

Derwa had tried to talk to her mother a few days later and explain that she had been attacked, but Prudence was too weary and numbed from what life had dealt her. She didn't understand why Derwa thought she had met with these two men who had been sent to York for trial. Her daughter looked well enough, so if she had been pushed about a little, then she had recovered and there was nothing to worry about. Prudence's broken spirit could not face another lost daughter, and so chose to ignore what was coming.

Derwa started to have nightmares about Kerenza. She'd never forgotten the time her dear sister walked out of their lives, and what had happened to her, but time had numbed the pain and allowed her to try and move forward in her own life. After her own rape, the memories came rushing back as if Kerenza had only just disappeared. Derwa dissolved into a wan, nervous little creature who was constantly bursting into tears. She could not focus on her dressmaking and Prudence had to finish some of the half finished pieces on her behalf. Derwa's health started to fail. She lost her appetite and started to throw up most days. She lay in her bed and cried for a week. Mr Medd wondered that they shouldn't send for a doctor, but Prudence was sure the expense was unnecessary and it was just a nervous complaint.

Derwa had been an innocent maid, but she was not a polished rose of the upper classes who were kept sheltered from biological realities. She had grown up in the countryside and she understood the principles of rutting. Deep down she knew what the problem was, but she couldn't find the courage to face it and speak its name, so she retreated inside herself instead. It was only weeks later when Prudence started to agree that they might have to fetch the doctor that Derwa shot out of bed and got back to work, out of pure fear of being found out.

Ignoring a problem never made it go away. Derwa was young enough to hope otherwise. After a few months she felt better and thought perhaps she would get away with it, although her bloods had not returned. Eyebrows started to rise here and there as the weeks went by. There were wives in the village who had born far too many children not to know the signs. No wonder she had been sobbing for so long, had her silly little heart broken by a lad who had had his way with her and wandered off. Silly girl should have done something about it or spoken out and forced a marriage rather than scurrying about like a little flame coloured mouse. Didn't Prudence Medd say Derwa had been chattering about being attacked a time back? Probably but she'd never known much about who or when or how. Perhaps it had just been a fancy. Perhaps, but then there were those two lads caught over Blakey way who had broken in to the squire's house. What of it? They'd come from Whitby and Matthew Medd had been living there. He came back and his father soon had him bundled off into the militia and out of the way, hadn't he? You're not suggesting Matthew... ? Goodness no, but perhaps one of those lads? Well, if it had been one of those lads it would have barely been an in and out job for Derwa would never have known them. She must be quite a loose girl, lacking in morals if she'd let a man do that after just meeting him. Eyebrows reached higher. It always was those that pretended to be sweet and innocent. The good women of Glaisdale just had to be thankful that this had come about long before any of their boys could have become entangled with such a girl.

Derwa was pregnant. She had felt it move one night and had thrown up from sheer terror. When she went out she could tell from the way people looked at her that they knew, no matter how she tried to adjust her clothing to hide the fact. Her face burned in embarrassment, which was only taken as proof to the more sordid assumptions of her history. It was a fictional character and conduct discussed and created over the past weeks to the point it was accepted as fact. She overheard two women talking, saying that the reverend was going to speak to Mrs Medd about decency and the fact of the girl, for it seemed as though she were walking through a dream and had not seen what others had spotted weeks ago. Derwa fled into the churchyard of St Thomas' and hunkered down between a jumble of old gravestones, crying violently. Surely there should be no more tears, for she had cried all the water in the world, yet still it came. Derwa knew that it wouldn't help anything, in fact she ought to have faced up to the problem a long time ago and then maybe something could have been done about it. She wondered if there still was time for a wise woman to help her. She rustled through the clothes in her basket, keeping her fingers busy whilst trying to think on how much money she had saved from her work and if she could pay for help. And what if that wouldn't work? She would be an outcast. Perhaps there was nothing left to do but follow her father into the river.

"Derwa?"

Dramas of drowning were abruptly halted and her head snapped up, wide eyes staring. Damon Eddon was crouched in front of her.

"I thought it was you I saw running into the churchyard."

She felt an ache in her heart. This wasn't like the school yard chants, when she could run to her protector and he would tell the boys to be kind to little Derwa Pengelly. This wasn't a problem that could be easily swept away. Oh that any of them had to grow up.

"I'm sure you don't want to be seen associating with the likes of me."

He smiled gently. "I'm sure half of what I hear isn't true."

"The worst of it is."

"Aye," he sighed. It was a delicate subject.

"I think I've been very stupid," she started, suddenly everything bursting out. "I told Mamma that I had been attacked, but I should have been more adamant. We should have made a complaint for the squire to deal with or I should have gone to that woman over in Castleton who can deal with this sort of problem..."

"Such a thing is wicked."

That was easy for a man to say, Derwa thought. Of all the things that could happen, he would never find himself alone, unmarried and expecting a child. "I should have said more or fought more. Maybe I should have hit them more..."

"Them?"

"The two men who..." she stopped. She was going into too many intimacies. "Never matter."

"Look," Damon shuffled uncomfortably and clasped her hands in his big warm paws. "This wasn't how I'd thought it might be. But we can find a way through this. This isn't your fault and yet you've been left with a mark against your name, that your child will carry as well. I would say a new name and a ring could solve that."

Derwa was sobbing again and not really listening. "Mamma is going to send me away."

"I wouldn't mind, honest. I'd even think on it as my..."

"I can see your mother coming up the lane." Derwa pulled away. "She's never liked me and I don't think I could take what she might say just now." The churchyard sat a little higher than the rest of the village, over the centuries the number of mouldering bodies had brought up the ground level with the surrounding drystone wall. "I must be gone." And with that she fled, running to the edge and scrambling down for the safety of home.

Home had lost its sense of sanctuary. When Prudence opened the door and stepped inside, Derwa instinctively understood that she would no longer be living here. Prudence closed the door but remained at the threshold. She was boiling over with conflictions. Shame at herself that she had been blind to what was so obvious. Horror that the entire village already knew. Fury that Derwa had brought this notoriety down upon her family. She felt tired, an ancient ache as old as the hills. She might not be able to summon up the energy to even care, only that she could not go through any more tragedies. Too much had happened. It was enough.

"Mamma, I..."

Prudence waved off what she assumed were coming excuses. She sat down by the fire. "I have been told what has happened. I am a fool that I did not see it for myself."

"Mamma, I..."

"What do you propose to do?"

"Mamma, I am frightened."

Prudence glared at Derwa. The surviving twin. "Is he going to wed you and solve this problem?"

"Who?"

"Who?" Prudence had to hold herself back from leaping up to slap some sense into her girl. "Who might you suppose I am speaking of? The man who you let put you in this situation."

"I was attacked, I didn't want..." Derwa felt herself starting to cry. Tears would not help she knew, but she couldn't stop herself. Her mother was growing white with fury. She was losing the only person she had left in the world and she had not done anything wrong.

"So he will not take responsibility."

"I was attacked. They were arrested and taken to York. You must remember. They were friends of Matthew..."

"You are not suggesting Matthew..."

"No, he was asleep in the other room. It was his friends."

"And you mention this now?"

"I tried but no one would..."

"This is a convenient story now he won't stand by you."

"Mamma, I am not lying."

"You have brought shame on me. On your father's name. After everything we have gone through as a family, I had hoped my girls still here would have the decency to..."

"Mamma, you have to believe me."

Prudence's chair scraped back as she swiftly moved out of Derwa's reach. The very horror that her daughter might reach out to her. She could still hear the comments and the laughter. There goes old trusty, dumb Prudence Medd. Always a loyal heifer. So stupid. She didn't see her daughter was heavy with child. Too thoughtless to teach the girls that a woman should be married first before she starts her life's work of rutting. It was to be expected that such a thing would happen. Derwa wouldn't have realised what would happen when the man asked her to part her legs. And another generation of idiots would come. Mind, Rosen's quite sharp, so they're not all bad. But Prudence, she had three girls, didn't she? She actually managed to lose a child, up round Commondale, didn't she? No one ever found the girl. Only Prudence Pengelly could manage such a thing. It's Prudence Medd now though. Aye, and it took her much longer than any other widow to realise she must marry again. Call her what you will, she's still a fool.

Prudence's hands shook as she backed away to the door. She was thinking of Kerenza again. "I cannot abide to look at you," she told Derwa. "You must be gone." In her confusion, it was she who left the house. She felt an urgency in her feet to move and keep moving.

Derwa burst into tears. She slumped down to the floor and cried until she was dry. Her mother would not know her. She wished her to leave the house. There was nowhere for Derwa to go. Perhaps she ought to go drown herself in the river, that would certainly solve the problem of the unborn baby, and drowning had been good enough for her father. Perhaps that was the fate of all Pengellys. Whilst it was a suitable melodramatic response that might make everyone think again, Derwa wouldn't be there to see the regret, and there was not enough resolve in her to end it all. Life still demanded things. She took her basket to her room and packed her second dress, her night linens, shawls and gloves and knitting, along with a couple of worn slim books she called her own. She looked through her savings. There wasn't enough to get her very far, and then what would she live on? She had nothing of real value.

Creeping through to her mother's bed, she pulled out the little box where she had seen her mother keeping her treasures. Derwa quickly found the amber pendant, which she held up, transfixed for a moment by the sunlight coming through the honey rock. Perhaps this could help her get started, for her mother would give her nothing else. As she was setting the lid back down, her eye settled on the top letters. Impulsively she snatched a couple and stuffed them into the basket between her linens, then scurried down to the kitchen to take a few supplies for a journey before she left the house. She did not think she would ever be here again.

She followed the river tracks heading east all of the time, her face ducked and shadowed into her bonnet as she hurried. Passing through Egton Bridge, she continued until she reached Grosmont in utter exhaustion. Derwa was a sturdy, enduring walker who had continued in her daily routines and habits as normal despite her growing condition, stubbornly refusing to acknowledge it, but she had to admit it tried against her pelvis these days. She found a hedgerow outside the village to nestle down in, swaddled in all her clothes, and took to looking through the contents of her basket before sleep overcame her. She recalled the most recent letter, for her mother had talked of the grandmother over in Haworth and how she had recently died. There it was in words, with the name of Prudence's aunt, still in Haworth. Could she help Derwa? Perhaps an older woman would be even more shocked by Derwa's shame. She ran her fingertip along the line of words, for she did not read so well, and stopped at the name of a cousin. Mention of doctors and apothecaries. Derwa had a timeless fear of what was coming to her. That was where she needed to be.

In the morning, cold and damp, she ate a little bread then headed up out of Goathland and onto the open moorland. She'd heard that transportation went this way between the coast and the inland cities. It was not long before a line of fifteen packhorses, slung on either side with baskets of salt from the salt pans, came up on the horizon. Prudence supposed that she might have walked alone, only that she was getting beyond the geography of her own knowledge. She did not know how to reach her destination. She needed to speak to someone.

As the train of horses approached, Derwa watched the lead driver, a man with a long stick and a dog about his heels. Derwa darted forward and joined him in step, calling out, "Sir, sir, might I have a word with you?" whilst trying to keep up and talk at the same time, swiftly losing her breath for the team were making fast progress over the dry, peaty earth of the moorland.

The man glanced at her, taking in the basket, the extended belly, the dirt around her skirts, and did not slow. "I have nothing for beggars."

"I'm not a beggar," Derwa gasped. "I ask only that I might walk with you. I need to go to Pateley Bridge."

"Pateley Bridge!" The man burst out. "Do you hear that, Arthur?" he called back to one of the other men. "Yon lass is off to Pateley Bridge." He looked back to Derwa. "You're a long way off. What's a lass like you got to do at Pateley Bridge?"

"My husband is there." Derwa surprised herself by how easily the lie came. "He has gone there for work and now he has sent for me. I must get there before..." They both looked to her belly. "Well, before I am not fit to travel."

"Aye," the man sighed, committing to nothing. Derwa could not tell if he believed her. He scratched his head, fingers slipping under the brim of his hat. They continued in silence. He realised she just wanted to walk with them, a little validity and protection to her journey. Whether she really was going to Pateley Bridge he didn't know. She seemed awfully young to be married, and what kind of man would send his wife off like this all on her own? But if he was just as young as she was, he would be lacking in sense. He thought of his own daughters at home, and how he would not care to think of them out in the world with no support at such a young age. He hoped to have them married with a few more years to their sense, and to reliable men. "We can't take you to Pateley Bridge," he finally spoke up. "But you could walk with us till Pickering."

"Pickering. And that, er..."

"I'd be thinking a woman like yourself would be better off travelling with the post. I reckon from Pickering you'd take the post to Thirsk or York, and maybe on from there to Harrogate. From Harrogate I'd reckon there'd be the post up to Pateley. But you're best off checking at every stop. Drivers'll tell you the best route to take."

Another half mile and they took pity on the girl. There was a pony at the back who was now only carrying half a pannier's worth of salt, so they helped Derwa up onto the creature's back and she rode the rest of the way down into Pickering town.

It was dark when a slender, rather stately woman with a slightly mannish face and red hair answered the door. The colour was the first thing Derwa registered when she stared up at the woman's hair. It was uncovered and it was quite red. She was not the only one with such vibrant hues. They must be related. The second thing she took in was the woman's dress. It was well made, and cost had not been scrimped on the fabric, yet it was kept plain and free of frills and fussing. It had practicalities in mind, so that a woman might easily move her arms about and complete her chores. Yet this woman carried an air of a higher class. This wasn't someone who would have to take in laundry to complete her income. There was a sense of intelligence that overwhelmed Derwa and her pitiful schooling. Now she was here she did not quite know how to begin, and after two days of travel and little sleep, she could barely think. She was so tired, that holding on to her basket felt like task enough.

"Please, I'm looking for Mrs Must, and the surgeon's housekeeper told me to come here."

"I am Mrs Must."

"Mrs Muriel Must?"

"Yes, I am the only Must in Pateley Bridge," Muriel sounded a little exasperated. "Are you in pain? Has she sent you here for a tonic?"

"No, I am here for I am Derwa Pengelly."

Muriel knit her brows together. "That is a very interesting name but I'm at a loss as to what that means."

"I am your cousin."

"I'm sure you are not," Muriel laughed. "I have never heard of you. And if you are thinking to claim kinship through my departed husband, I can assure you that I know you for a liar."

"I'm not a liar!" Derwa almost shrieked. Would no one take her word for the truth? This introduction was going quite wrong and the door would soon be slammed in her face. If Muriel Must did not take her in, the only place to go would be the nearest river. "My mother is Prudence Medd."

"I don't know any Medds."

"Her mother was Gillian Longbottom. I think she and your mother were sisters."

"Good Lord," Muriel gasped, finally making the connection. "Cousin Prudence. It's been such a long time since I heard of her. It can't be since her wedding. Yes, it was a man called Pengelly, a Cornishman. But come in; don't linger out there in the cold and dark."

Muriel ushered the young woman into her house, then locked the front door again and sent the girl through to the parlour where a warm fire was crackling. Derwa hung on the threshold for a moment, never having seen such a fine room. It was not big, but had three comfortable looking chairs, with stuffing and fabric covering even, walls lined with bookcases and framed prints. Curtains hung at the window. There was a proper fireplace, with its own poker in a stand. Beside the main chair, draped with a large shawl, was a round table that carried a glass lamp and an open book. This was quite another world from the farming folk she had known of the Esk Valley.

"You must be a very rich woman," Derwa breathed, feeling she ought to go sit in the kitchen. She was not wearing anything suitable enough for such a parlour.

"You've clearly not been told about cousin Emmerline," Muriel muttered to herself, pushing the girl into the room. "I'm not as rich as all that," she continued a little more loudly. "I only have a day woman, so I shall have to go fetch us tea and bread and butter myself. Do sit down there, then we can talk and you can tell me why you are here."

Derwa set her basket on the floor beside the chair and sank into the winged armchair opposite what was so obviously Muriel Must's favourite haunt. Her legs and back succumbed to the softness, her skin soaked up the heat from the fire and she felt her eyelids lowering. The baby wriggled and stretched its legs, as if thankful the constant motion had finally come to a halt. It had been an intense couple of days, from post coach to coaching inn, asking for advice, often finding she had just missed the next coach, and always trying to remain ignorant to the knowing looks people gave her. They stared at her abdomen and made their assumptions about her as a girl and what had happened. Or rather what she had allowed. As stupid as women were considered to be, a woman's fate was always her own fault. She had repressed her terror and tried not to think about her mother and how much she wished she could just be held and helped. She focused on two words: Pateley Bridge, and how she was going to get herself to the town. Beyond that she did not dare to think. Then suddenly she had reached her goal, was being helped down by the driver outside of The Crown Coaching Inn on the high street. It was growing dark and she had no idea where to go. She remembered from the letter there had been something about an apothecary. She'd asked the innkeeper's wife, who had told her she must want Mr Warburton, the surgeon, and sent her off up the sloping high street and up a narrow little side street. She'd found the premises, both his home and his surgery, and explained her errand to the housekeeper who answered the door. She had sent Derwa onwards a short distance to the house of Mrs Must and her final destination.

It was light when Derwa opened her eyes. She was horizontal, in a little wrought iron bed in a small room with a sloped ceiling. There were quilts heaped upon her, and she felt the most comfortable she had ever been in her life. She had no idea where she was.

She sat up in bed and surveyed the room. The sunlight drifted through a small window, sheltered only by a thin white curtain. Close by stood a small table with a ceramic bowl and jug. There was a chair by the side of the bed upon which stood her basket. Her shoes were by the door, looking quite clean. A rag rug on the floor boards. She looked down at herself and realised she was in her nightclothes. "How did I..." she staggered out of bed as if something had nipped at her behind. Her hair flapped around her shoulders, brushed and unpinned. She crept to the door and opened it a crack to peer outside. She saw a small corridor with a worn carpet running down the centre. Shabby perhaps, but there was something down on the floorboards. Derwa was in a bed in an actual room, not a partitioned attic space for the entire household. This is Pateley Bridge, she realised, as she grew aware of the sound of voices and movement downstairs. I arrived at Pateley Bridge last night, she remembered, in some sense of awe at herself that she had actually achieved such a feat. I found Muriel Must.

Quickly dressing in her second dress – the first being nowhere in the room – she brushed and tied back her hair, put a shawl around her shoulders, then dared to go downstairs. She did not know what time it was, only that the light looked like the afternoon. At the bottom of the stairs she paused in a corridor she remembered from last night. To her right was the parlour Muriel had taken her through to. To her left there was a closed door and the sound of voices, of discussion. Oh lord, Derwa thought, suddenly petrified, what if her cousin had sent for someone to take her away? What if her mother had come, although for that to have happened she must have slept for days.

"My poor dear."

Derwa jumped and clutched the banister as the voice came at her from behind. The corridor continued past the staircase, and went through to a kitchen. An older woman, certainly older than Muriel, who looked to be in her late fifties, was approaching. There was flour in her hair and a scent of baking. This must be the housekeeper.

"My name is Mrs Halliwell," the woman smiled warmly, clutching Derwa's cold, thin hands between her own. "It is a pleasure. I must say it broke my heart to hear your story. Such tragedy, and to one so young."

Derwa opened her mouth to speak. She wasn't quite sure what to say because she wasn't sure she'd told Muriel anything of her story.

The closed door opened abruptly and Muriel's head appeared. "Ah, you're up. Cousin Derwa, do go through to the parlour. I'm just with a patient but I will be with you shortly."

"Is that the..." a voice from inside the room started, but Muriel had shut the door again.

"It's just through here," Mrs Halliwell gestured to the door, and led Derwa through as if she was an invalid. "I'll go fetch you some tea. I'll wager you've an appetite on you as well. You've missed lunch but I'll go fetch a bit of bread and cheese to tempt you. Put you on till supper."

She returned to the chair she had settled in yesterday evening. In contrast to her memories, the room was now in full daylight. There was a book abandoned in the chair before her, with part of an embroidered bookmark sticking out of the top. Derwa's reading was not as good as it might be, but folk told her as a girl she ought to be glad she could read anything at all. Not that she got much opportunity to read, but it sparked her curiosity, being in a room like this and wondering what knowledge might be contained in all the pages that surrounded her. Leaning forward she picked up the volume off the chair, and took a few minutes to work her way through the wordy title on the front page: *Journal of a Third Voyage for the Discovery of a North-West Passage from the Atlantic to the Pacific; Performed in the Years 1824-25 in His Majesty's Ships Hecla and Fury, Under the Orders of Captain William Edward Parry.*

Mrs Halliwell bustled in with tea and sustenance, whilst Muriel and another woman moved to the hallway as Muriel bid her farewell. She then hurried into the parlour, and carefully shut the door when her housekeeper had headed back to the kitchen. Derwa stared up at her in bewilderment. "I feel lost."

"Perhaps not as much as I do, for I had no idea you existed until you appeared upon my doorstep yesterday," Muriel spoke. "But I have made assumptions and told quite a few lies on your behalf, so I think it prudent I inform you of your own fiction so that we will not raise any suspicion."

Derwa remained in ignorance and watched blankly as Muriel put the book on her side table and poured the tea.

"Your cover story," Muriel summarised. "I don't know the truth, but I saw that you weren't married. Well, you didn't have a ring yesterday."

"No, I'm not, I..." Derwa looked down at her hands, for the first time seeing the ring on her finger.

"It's a cheap brass thing, which I thought would fit well. I put it on last night. Best to have all the props. People are as narrow minded here as I'm sure they are wherever you have come from, so I think the truth ought to stay between you and me. I saw the need for a cover story. You are what, seven months gone?"

"Gone where?"

Muriel smiled gently. The last time she had heard of Prudence had been the wedding. Simple country folk. This girl was just a child. Too young to be in such a predicament. "The baby you carry. I think you have a couple more months before it will be born."

Derwa pursed her lips together. She did not want to cry and be deemed helpless or feeble. This cousin seemed so confident, intelligent and capable. Not the kind of woman to find herself with child and out of wedlock. Not the kind of woman to let anyone take advantage of her. Certainly she was older, in her forties, and age and experience did a lot for a body, but Derwa couldn't imagine Muriel being idiotic at any age.

"I will tell you your story. You are my cousin's girl, for we must keep to the truth as much as possible. It makes it easier with the lies. You were young and foolish and got married to a sweetheart on a mad impulse, even though you were both young and could have waited, and he should have waited and built up a little money. You married Robert

Pengelly..." she caught Derwa's surprised eye. "Better to keep it the same name, less chance of slip ups. And he was a fisherman's son tragically drowned this last month. His family have shunned you and your mother is too poor to take you in so I agreed that you could come and stay with me. We thought a complete change of environment would do your soul a world of good. Do you think you can remember all of that?"

"Robert Pengelly..."

"Yes."

"My father was Curnow Pengelly."

"I know, I met him many years ago," Muriel said. "I was at the wedding. I think it was the last time I saw your mother, or in fact heard about her. I didn't know whether she'd had any children, although one would assume there would have been offspring. But something must have happened, because you gave another name."

"Medd."

"Yes, that was it."

"My father died."

"I'm very sorry to hear that. My own father has passed as well. It is not an easy thing..."

"I was only a little child when it happened," Derwa said. "I don't remember him all that well. I have vague memories that might be him or perhaps I just think them up in hopefulness that I have kin. My sister Rosen had only been born when he died. Mamma doesn't like to talk about it much. He drowned in the river."

"How tragic. It was an accident?"

"I don't really know."

Derwa looked near to tears. Muriel thought she might lead her mind on to safer ground. "So there are the two of you, children, you and Rosen?"

"No. Yes. Oh..." Derwa wiped her eyes then reached out for a piece of bread. "I was a twin," she explained, suddenly feeling ravenous. "We were the first born, myself and Kerenza. But she was lost when we were just girls."

"She died?"

Derwa shook her head. "She just disappeared."

"My God, how terrible."

"Mamma couldn't afford to keep us. It was just us and Mamma for a long time after Father died. So we went to stay with Uncle William whilst Mamma worked. Looking back I don't know why she didn't make it easier on herself and marry. She did eventually, to Mr Medd. He's a cobbler. I..."

"For such a family summary I should offer my own. Or perhaps your mother told you about our side of the family? She must have done for you to come here."

"Not really. I just couldn't think of anywhere else to go. I only heard of you when she was looking at a letter from her Aunt a year or two back. It said Mamma's grandmother had died..."

Muriel's eyes went to the fire and would not look at Derwa.

"Mamma said Aunt Eleanor had written it, your mother. And she had said something about you moving to Pateley Bridge to work with an apothecary. It was such a strange name, Pateley Bridge, so I remembered it. And when Mamma said I had to go I thought I would come here for help for I couldn't think of anything else to do. Mamma doesn't believe me. She thinks I have done this on purpose, that I wanted them to..."

Muriel looked back to the young girl. "Your pregnancy is not the result of young love."

"No. Two men attacked me. They did things..." she paused to take a deep draught of tea. "I suppose this is what goes on between men and women, but I was awful frightened and I didn't want to. But they pushed me face down on a table."

Muriel shook her head sadly. If only she had come upon Derwa a lot earlier in the story, she could have done something to make this problem go away. At seven months it was far too late for anything like that. "You have been badly treat," she finally said. Perhaps she ought to have been indignant, but she had born witness to this kind of story too many times before to be shocked by the behaviour of her fellow man. "Did you not report them?"

"No one seemed much bothered. They just wanted to catch them because they'd stolen from the Squire. They caught them on Blakey and sent them down to York."

"And now you must live with the consequences."

"I must, but I don't know how to live with this shame or where I shall go. I must throw myself on your mercy because if you throw me out... I will work and do anything, only don't throw me out."

"Of course I will not throw you out, my dear girl!" Muriel looked horrified. "You will stay here, and I will get you through this. We'll think on what to do afterwards..." she stopped. "I see you don't know all that much about me. I am... rather, I was married to Kaarel Must. He was an eminent anatomist in Edinburgh." She paused. "You don't follow medicine?"

"I just sew dresses."

"He was very well respected in medical circles. He taught me a lot. I have always had a great interest, and he did not believe that women were incapable... anyway, he passed away some five or six years ago, and I have been in Pateley Bridge. Because of my connection and my training, Mr Warburton, the surgeon and apothecary here, agreed to an experience in taking on a woman as an apprentice."

"So you are a doctor?"

"I don't think Mr Warburton would approve of us saying that," Muriel smiled. "But I shall be more than adequate for your care for the rest of your term, and when the birthing comes..." she reached out and held Derwa's hand as her face blanched. "I've delivered plenty of babies up in these parts. I do understand that the first time is to be met with a great apprehension, but the body will get you through it."

At the corner where Muriel Must's lane joined the high street in Pateley Bridge, there was a little sweet shop that had opened a couple of years prior. Mainly frequented by children, elderly ladies and gentlemen who assured all there was a little boy they were shopping for, Muriel had developed quite a fancy to barley sugars. She had just purchased a twist, along with some ginger sweets for Derwa, when she saw the postman approaching her door.

"I hope that bundle is for me!" she called out, picking up her step to catch the man before he started hammering on the door. Mrs Halliwell could be a little funny about paying the letter fees. She was certain the man was trying to diddle a shilling out of them for no good reason, and had been known to turn away post from Edinburgh. Letters and periodicals were Muriel's lifeline with her intellectual world, and the fees were worth every farthing. The Edinburgh and London letters always set Mrs Halliwell's lips on a disapproving line, for the fees were calculated on distance as well as volume. Although that was reliant on the sender noting the number of sheets used, and although Elizabeth's letters were often extortionate for they came from abroad, she always lied about the number of sheets. A well padded bundle was always oh so innocently annotated as one sheet, as if a poor wretch like herself couldn't be expected to count. Muriel never quite understood why she worried so, for it wasn't her who had to pay for the delivery of her letters.

"Got yourself a bundle here: the usual cities, and one for your poor relation, Mrs Derwa Pengelly. That's only come from the other side of Yorkshire, so that'll only be six pence. Will you be paying for that one?"

Muriel rolled her eyes. "My cousin is my guest, of course I will. It's not as if the girl gets any communication." She quickly paid the man, popped a barley sugar in her mouth, then strode into her home.

Derwa was hunched over the table in the parlour, her belly so rotund that she had to sit a distance away from her work station. It wasn't ideal to practice writing, but Muriel insisted she worked at her reading and writing every day. In the first few days she had told Derwa that she ought to write to her mother and let her know that she was safe. Derwa had protested that her mother wished to have no more to do with her. Muriel was not convinced, despite everything that had been accounted for, and insisted she write. She was horrified what spidery and misspelt fumblings Derwa showed her at the end of an hour's hard work. It was what everyone would expect of her hand, and the letter was duly sent, but Muriel insisted that something was to be done about Derwa's education whilst she was here. She did not agree with popular attitudes that it didn't matter so much for women, and had taken it upon herself to set Derwa exercises to be copied out every day until her writing became neat and fluid. She also planned a stack of reading to bring Derwa's mind up to date, replanned when she realised how little the girl read. They would begin with some simple novels and poetry to begin with.

It had been almost a month now and the girl's handwriting had much improved, but they had not heard a word in reply from the moors.

"There is a letter for you."

Derwa dropped her pen and looked horrified. She had not expected a response. She took the letter and looked upon it, feeling a tremble grow in her hands. She was not sure that she wanted to know what was happening in Glaisdale, or what her mother thought now that she had taken the time to calm and fully reflect.

"I have a patient arriving shortly," Muriel said. "That letter will not bite, but I understand it may take a moment or two to open it. I'll give you some peace."

Derwa laid the letter flat upon her writing exercises and stared at it. She had honestly not expected her mother to open up communication. In her dreams her mother had thrown her letter to the fire, stating her eldest daughter was dead to her. She turned away and would not look at her. Derwa cried out for her mother's love. She was still a child. A frightened little girl.

The letter was swiftly ripped open and she looked to the end to see what sentiments her mother would end on. She did not, for it was Rosen who had penned the letter. Her sister. She returned to the beginning. Rosen said that her mother had asked her to write, for she did not quite know what to say to Derwa yet, and was still disappointed at what she had done to the family. Rosen took a more practical stance, and called her sister a silly fool. Why hadn't she tried to deal with the situation earlier on? Rosen knew someone who could help a lass who had gotten herself into trouble. She should have come to her little sister for help. Mother and Mr Medd were well enough, and the gossip of Derwa's shameful situation and disappearance had been the talk of the valley for a week until Mr Glossop had been caught with a farmer's wife, not his own, and as the saying went, out of sight, out of mind, and Derwa was forgotten. Almost, Damon Eddon had asked Rosen about Derwa once when he had seen her in the lane. Did Derwa remember Damon? He was that farmer's son that went about with Betty Boddy. In fact, they were engaged to be married and the wedding was going to be in two weeks' time. Betty had asked Rosen to be a bridesmaid, and she'd gotten the day off for the wedding. The entire day, would you credit it? She'd be able to laze in bed a good couple of hours before she needed to be up....

Derwa put the letter back down on the table and watched three teardrops fall into the writing and blur the ink. Why was she weeping over a wedding she had known was bound to happen? The whole village knew how it was inevitable between Damon and Betty. His mother wouldn't have any other daughter-in-law. What a thing to experience: a wedding, and to be a married woman. Derwa folded up the letter and thought back to that last day in Glaisdale. Her mother spurning her from the house. And before that she had been in the churchyard and Damon had come to speak to her. That must have been the last time she had seen him. Her fingers stopped mid crease as she was folding the letter and her memory focused on something he had said to her. She hadn't been listening at the time, bogged down by the magnitude of her situation. Were they hopeful false memories or had he... her little hands cupped in his hands, and he had said a ring and a new name would solve it all. Could she misunderstand now or had he tried to say he would take her? She had been too stupid to realise what he was saying, and had walked away. What would she say to such a proposal? Yes, oh yes. The moment was gone, and he was to marry Betty and they would have a fine, healthy brood of boys. Derwa was never destined to take the name Eddon. What a little fool.

She shut her exercise books, the school girl finished for the day, and slipped the letter into her pocket. Wiping her eyes and finding her sleeves were not enough, she dried her face on the corner of her apron, then heaved her ungainly form out of the chair and over to the armchair. She had her knitting to keep her hands busy. Muriel insisted she do nothing to earn her keep, so Derwa had taken to knitting all the essentials for the entire household, Mrs Halliwell included, and the unborn, who had a ready set of outfits waiting. She didn't even know how long she would keep it. She had wondered if there might be a foundling's hospital or orphanage, or perhaps Muriel would know a family that would take it, but she hadn't dared to ask. Maybe when the baby was born, Muriel would naturally present these options to her and the problem would be dealt with. Maybe then she could move on, take a job elsewhere and start again. Perhaps she might meet a farmer, she imagined, a man who looked remarkably like Damon...

Muriel fussing over tea things woke her up from her sundrenched dreams. Derwa blinked and looked about the room. It was dark outside. Muriel smiled at Derwa, then continued to pour the tea. Derwa got up and waddled to the table. It was a scene of quiet polite domesticity. Derwa was suddenly ravenously hungry, and tucked into a thick slice of bread with lashings of fresh butter.

"You heard from your mother?"

She glanced up. "Rosen wrote."

"Your mother doesn't write?"

Derwa knew in what sense Muriel asked. She'd been horrified by Derwa's penmanship when she'd seen her try to write a letter. "I think mother can but Rosen said she doesn't want to. I... I don't know what to say."

"Life is not easy. Give her time." She paused, noting that Derwa looked close to tears. "We shall finish our supper, then perhaps we could turn to Miss Austen. I for one am keen to find out what happens with Catherine. I have to admit I never had much time for novels and *Northanger Abbey* passed me by when it was first published."

"I'm sure it will all end well and she will be well married," Derwa muttered, sounding more bitter than she meant to be. "Everyone's lives work out so well. I suppose this Miss Austen is sitting in a palace today with fine children and a kind husband."

"Miss Austen died a good few years ago," Muriel corrected as she poured herself another cup of tea. "And there is a clue in her title. Real life is unkind and complicated, a fact overlooked by the religious and the pious and novelists alike for different reasons. At least the novelists are well intentioned, wishing to show us a way to behave and a hope for the future."

This was how their life puttered by for the remainder of Derwa's pregnancy. Muriel spent some time with Mr Warburton, the surgeon and apothecary, whom Derwa found rather strict and quiet, with an uneasy stare as if he could see through to her very soul. She was convinced he knew the truth of her situation, or rather the popular opinion, that she had been asking for this trouble. Muriel said it was just his manner, for being a Methodist teetotaller with strict ideas on life and enjoyment he tended to look as if he was judging you from the way you brushed your hair to how you held another person's gaze. In truth Muriel wondered if he was blind to a great many things, being so restricted in life and travel. But he was a competent surgeon and apothecary, and she had gained much experience working with him. And she was grateful for the progressive sides of his personality, for not many would have agreed to a female apprentice. Under his tutelage she had also developed in surgery. The technique and the knowledge she already had, for Muriel had taken part in many a dissection up in Edinburgh, but surgery on the living was a far more distressing affair, for more often than not, the patient was conscious and not subscribed any pain relief. The generally agreed theory was that pain was nature's way of helping, and an unconscious patient would more than likely succumb to their wounds. But the screams of torture were something born of nightmares, and hard to block out when one needed to attend to the work of healing. Muriel remembered running away and being sick in Edinburgh, after having only watched another perform surgery. As she grew older her confidence in the edict 'pain is good' grew fainter as she saw more, learned from cases and experienced life's pain herself. One could not really understand unless one had been the patient, and in the matters of childbirth she particularly struggled to agree with all that the eminent doctors and surgeons declared. Those learned men thought they knew best on all aspects of gynaecology, pregnancy and birthing. They could study and attend as many births as they wished, pompously telling women to stop complaining, the pain was there to help. Without the pain the birth would not go properly and they might die. But they would never have first hand experience, and that was crucial. The fact that they weren't even prepared to listen to the words of those with the experience was a mark against them in Muriel's eyes. Pain was passing, and easy to brush aside when it wasn't you suffering, but she had seen the terror and tension it could create in a body. Resistance. Quite often, it made the process worse.

Muriel had made her plans for Derwa, although she knew herself that birthing could throw up all kinds of unexpected scenarios. Plans sometimes had to be drastically changed at the last minute. She wished it were possible to offer decent pain relief, especially as the girl seemed so timid and fragile. There were herbs and tinctures that could help with relaxation but that was about all. She had read several articles from America, where they were working with ether, not specifically in birthing, but for pain relief, and they were having some successes, as well as some people who did not wake up afterwards. It hadn't taken on in this country, old traditions and learned dusty doctors who knew best shaking their heads at the folly of the New World. Besides which, they weren't going to take advice from people who studied medicine in institutions that weren't even a hundred years old. Sometimes their refusal to so much as seriously listen to new ideas drove Muriel to the point of having to leave the room to scream.

Derwa remained oblivious to what was coming. Under Muriel's encouragement, she would try to leave the house every day, even as winter set in, to get some air and take some exercise. She would follow their little road up away from the High Street, following the lane past St Mary's Church. Passing by the churchyard, it felt like a sunken lane, lower than the lie of graves, before heading out towards the full countryside. The landscape here on the hills was different to the world she had grown up with. At home the hill tops were open and covered in heather which bloomed purple for miles in high summer. Here the land was open and green, fields partitioned off with dry stone walling, and in places the earth became so thin that the rock of the very ground itself could be seen like a scar on the land. There were thousands of sheep, quarries for the rock for building material and a general busy productivity about the landscape. Other times she would walk down the hill towards the River Nidd, over the bridge then follow a footpath up the side of the river, past fields, giving glimpses of large fine houses situated in grand gardens tended by teams of gardeners.

On one such day, very close to Christmas, they received a visitor. Derwa, who would give birth in a week's time, was slowly clumping her way back up the high street. She passed by Mrs Warburton and the three children, a sweet girl and twin boys who always stared at her as if they had never seen such a large creature managing to walk about on two legs. Perhaps it didn't do for pregnant women to be seen, but Muriel was adamant the exercise would do her good.

Mrs Warburton nodded to her. She was a smart woman, about the same age as her cousin Muriel, and therefore about the same age as her own mother. Was it surreal for the woman to think she was seeing a girl who could have been her own child, and was said to be a widow already?

"Mrs Pengelly," she said. "You'll be away home?"

"Good Morning Mrs Warburton. Yes, I am that way."

"I saw you have a visitor. I can't say I care for some of her thoughts and ways, yet I've always liked Mrs MacCaskill. I'm sure you'll all have a very pleasant week."

Muriel hadn't said they were expecting visitors, and from Mrs Warburton had said, it sounded as though this one would be with them for some time. Derwa felt a little ill as she tried to increase her pace. She didn't want to speak to strangers, or to have to be polite and sit properly and behave for company. Another adult to stare into her soul and see all the badness that resided within. No wonder her mother had wished her gone. No surprise Damon had quickly married when she had left and he had seen the folly of his impulsive offer. Rosen had written again to tell her the pair were married, and Betty already thought she was with child. It made Derwa want to cry. She wondered if Betty had been forced to lay down on the table and endure the pain, or if there were more pleasant ways of going about it. No one would gossip about her and shake their heads, sighing over what a stupid and godless girl she was. She was a respectably married woman. She'd make an excellent farmer's wife.

She found Muriel in the hallway, fussing over baskets, when she returned. Muriel looked up, her face a little flushed and an excited glitter in her eyes as if she were back in her childhood. "We're going to collect holly tomorrow and decorate the house for Christmas Day."

"That will be nice." They had never done much at Christmas when Derwa had been growing up, although Prudence had always been sure to take the girls out to collect greenery that they might decorate their kitchen with. She'd sit and tell the girls stories of the fine balls and parlour games she had seen when she had been working at Danby Grange. It was another world, in which their social betters glided through in life.

"My mother is also come from Haworth to spend this time with us. I had thought of going there but we agreed it was better you did not have to travel at this stage."

"Your mother? I saw Mrs Warburton in town. She mentioned Mrs MacCaskill."

"Yes, that is my mother," Muriel beamed. "Come through into the parlour and meet her."

Eleanor MacCaskill was a fine, slender grey-haired woman not far from seventy when Derwa met her for the first time. She was seated in a chair by the fire, perusing a novel with a youthful joy at the words and plot. She was well dressed, in fine fabrics and a necklace made of the same material as the one Derwa had taken from her mother. Her hair was set up in a loose and unfashionable bun – age consented her to ignore fashions – and she had a red silk scarf tided about her head in a way like a giant ribbon rather than a headscarf meant by a working woman for practicalities. In Derwa's eyes she looked stately, intelligent, worldly and intensely intimidating.

"I must say, I am finding this *Northanger Abbey* quite delightful. That I never read it before..." Eleanor broke off as she saw the young, heavily pregnant girl before her, and lightened even more into a wide smile. "Why, this must be Derwa Pengelly. My daughter has written to me all about you." She stood up and approached the girl, her eyes dancing as she took in every detail. "I am sorry we have not met before, but I did not even know of you until my daughter wrote and told me of your rather dramatic arrival. Let me look at you." Eleanor took Derwa, who was stunned into silence and immobility, by the shoulders. "The hair must be from your father's side, and the statue. I met your father at your parents' wedding and remember him well. A Cornishman. I was sorry to hear he passed so long ago."

"She's not the only red head in the family," Muriel complained.

"Yes, but you get that from your father, who is of no blood connection to Derwa. My own late husband was a dear Scottish drover," she added to Derwa as an aside. "I do not know if I see any of Prudence in you, for I remember her as a tall, robust blonde girl with rather explosive hair. But I see my sister in your eyes."

Derwa stared up at her in awe. "My grandmother?"

"Yes, that is the one, Gillian Longbottom," Eleanor smiled. "She died when your mother was but a little girl I'm afraid. She and I were twins, as I'm told you are."

"My sister is dead."

"Muriel told me, and I'm very sorry for it. The loss of a twin is a very hard thing, and I'm not sure anyone other than another twin can completely understand it. My sister and I were estranged for several years, but I knew the moment when she left this world. I've never felt whole since."

Muriel shuddered. She remembered it as well, although neither her nor her mother had quite understood it at the time. She had been writing at her desk, then in a moment she had collapsed to the floor and was gasping for breath. She suffered along with Gillian, and as Gillian expired, Eleanor recovered and realised she was now alone.

"Come and sit with me by the fire," Eleanor invited. "You look very near your time. You must rest as much as you can."

"I felt it," Derwa blurted out.

The two older women looked at one another with a sense of unease. "The baby, you mean?" Eleanor asked, knowing that was not what she had meant.

"No." Derwa wasn't sure where the need to confess had come from. She had carried this within her ever since Kerenza had disappeared, a silent pact between the twins that she did not need to tell anyone. Now it was pressing against her. It had to come out.

"Sit down," Muriel guided Derwa to a chair.

"You knew when your sister Kerenza died?" Eleanor asked cautiously.

Derwa stared at her great aunt. "It took days."

Eleanor looked aghast at Muriel. She had received long letters from her daughter, updating her on all of the family history as accounted by Derwa. Kerenza had disappeared one summer afternoon in Commondale, having been sent out to fetch her younger sister, who did indeed come trotting home all alone. The popular opinion was that Kerenza had accidentally fallen and had sadly never been found. Perhaps she had been stolen away by passing gypsies. No one could think that she had run away of her own choice. "She must have met with an accident and become trapped. There are crevices and places on the moors where a search party could miss..."

"It wasn't an accident," Derwa spoke. "I felt it when her leg was broken, here," she indicated high up her thigh, close to her hip. "She was terrified and in pain for two days. I didn't understand some of it until many years later when it happened to me. She was locked in somewhere. He killed her in the end. I was so frightened. I hid in a cupboard until she was dead."

Muriel and her mother stared at one another in horror. In polite society, women, certainly of a particular class, would either pretend or genuinely not understand all of what Derwa referred to. The baseness and cruelty of man. Poverty gave experience of brutality, rape and incest. Eleanor had seen and heard of enough happening in the appalling living circumstances of the poor mill workers of Haworth. Large families packed in together in small damp quarters, overworked, underpaid and underfed, a drag through a miserable and thankless life, with no joy and relentless hard work until an early death. Cruelty and soullessness was a disease that multiplied in some veins, and no one cared. People died too frequently for anyone to really stop and consider one little ragged individual. They knew there were men, and a few women who did not think of the pain or terror when they inflicted such torture for their own warped moments of sickened pleasure.

Derwa started to cry.

Muriel threw up her hands. "The human race," she declared. "I sometimes wonder what I am trying to save."

Eleanor knelt down by Derwa's chair and got her arms around the girl as much as she could. She didn't say anything, for what was there to be said? She let the girl cry it out. It was something she would have to carry with her for the rest of her days. There was no way to make it better.

The next day Derwa slept late and when she came downstairs Muriel and Eleanor had already been out and returned with baskets of greenery. The three women decorated the parlour together, ate a fine lunch and then Eleanor decided to hand out presents she had brought. There were books and two broaches for Muriel which sent the women into more giddy laughter than Derwa had ever seen. Muriel eventually explained that many years ago she had briefly worked as a jewellery makers' apprentice in Halifax. The two dreadful, now unfashionable pieces were of her own hand. Eleanor said she had purchased them a long time ago and kept them for an appropriate moment.

For the coming baby there were some hand embroidered little dresses that Eleanor had worked on and books for Derwa – it seemed mother and daughter were determined to make her a reader. Mrs Radcliffe's *The Mysteries of Uldolpho* had Muriel in shrieks of exasperation, asking what she was giving such melodramatic nonsense to Derwa for. Eleanor, who had come to novels rather late in life, admitted that she had not read it, but had heard all the young women raving about it at one time, and thought it could prove an exciting distraction. To change the subject Eleanor said they would have some singing, and rather surprised Derwa when she took a violin from a bag and began to knock out tunes with a particular skill and speed that

Derwa had never seen or heard before. The sounds Eleanor could draw from the instrument were small miracles. Such sweet music from polished wood and cat gut. Derwa ardently wished she could create something quite as beautiful.

A few days later Derwa gave birth to a son. Eleanor remained in the parlour for the duration, listening to the groans and cries. Time was a marvel at erasing the sense of pain and although she had given birth four times, she wondered if it had been that bad? Perhaps there was a difference when you were the one experiencing the agony, and when you were only listening, left with the horrors of your own imagination. I am getting too old for all of this, she thought. Muriel appeared now and then, to fetch something or check on something else, and assured her mother that everything was in hand, and actually it was going very smoothly and straightforward. Derwa's young age and flexible body were playing in her favour.

And suddenly he was out and it was over and Derwa almost wondered what all the screaming had been about. Muriel washed off the red-faced screaming infant and passed him over to Derwa.

"He has all the fingers and toes I would like to see, and we are quite sure his lungs are functioning well."

Derwa received the parcel, topped with its angry face, and wondered in horror what she was supposed to do with the thing. Was she really to be left in sole charge of this tiny creature, not even knowing quite how to hold it or what would make it happy or furious, what would make it well and flourish and what would make it ill. The baby opened its eyes and seemed to look at her as if to confirm it would indeed be putting all of its trust and well being into her. It was a terrifying prospect. Derwa wished she could see her mother.

When mother and baby were settled and sleeping, Muriel came downstairs to the parlour to sit with her own mother.

"You have been up the whole night. I think you should sleep now yourself."

"Yes, yes," Muriel muttered, not bothering to explain a doctor's duty, or the fact this wasn't the first case that had seen her without sleep. She pulled her writing desk to her. "I am going to write to Prudence."

"Should Derwa not do that?"

"She can as well if she wishes, but I have one or two other things I wish to say to my cousin," Muriel paused as she wrote something on a sheet of paper. "She wrote to her mother when she got here, mostly because I made her. Her hand was dreadful, at least we have improved upon that. Her mother has never replied or sent any direct word by proxy. She's only had two letters from her younger sister, and that is all."

Eleanor waved her hand as if batting away a fly. "A lot of families are under the misconception that an unwed pregnancy brings shame upon them. She is not unique in that."

"She has already lost one daughter. She ought to hold the other two closer."

"Will you tell her what Derwa told us?"

"No. It's hardly my place, besides..." Muriel let out a long sigh and sat back in her chair. "What good would it do? It's been so long and everyone believes her to be dead. It's the truth, so it will not change the end result. It's only distressing to think of that little girl in her last days."

"That is true, but I was thinking more that she could support her surviving girl. All of this isn't the Prudence I remember." Eleanor drew a long breath. "Time and experience reshape us all."

In the evening Eleanor went up with Muriel to congratulate the new mother.

"I am very glad you have come through this safely," Eleanor told her. "And look at this fine little man. May I hold him?"

"Of course." Derwa watched with a mix of awe and envy how easily Eleanor handled the baby. She looked like she knew what she was doing, which was more than could be said of herself. "You are very fond of children?"

"No more than anyone else. This is something you'll understand when this one is a few years old. It's as much about the remembering of your own as anything else." Eleanor walked across the room to the little window, smiling as the baby shifted as if straining to look out on the world. "And what will we be calling him?"

"His name?"

Eleanor grinned. "That was what I was referring to."

"But that's not up to me."

"But you're his mother, I'd say you're the best placed."

"I thought perhaps the orphanage, or..."

"He's not an orphan."

"But I thought it would be better for him."

An awkward silence filled the space. Eleanor looked to her daughter and Muriel turned her back on the bed. "I don't think being a foundling would be better for anyone," Eleanor said gently. "Everyone here thinks you're a widow, so you've nothing to worry about on that account. Don't you want to keep him?"

"I don't know," Derwa faltered.

"What were you planning on doing with yourself instead?"

"I don't know. I supposed I would have to get out and work. Perhaps service. It wouldn't be so easy with a child."

"No, but he wouldn't be little for long."

"You should think carefully about this," Muriel muttered, her back still at the other women. "Once given away they can not be retrieved. But they will haunt you for the rest of your days." And with that, she left the room.

Derwa started to cry.

"Don't worry about Muriel," Eleanor told her, returning to the bed with the baby. "And don't fret over those tears. We all cry over a drop of rain in the first few days. You'll get over that. Now, you two have a snuggle," she passed the baby over into Derwa's awkwardly positioned arms. "And have a think on which names you've always liked. Given your family's not here, I think you can go with what you like best rather than worrying about what's gone on in the family."

And so it was that James Curnow Pengelly took his place in Muriel Must's household for the first year of his life. Eleanor MacCaskill left two weeks after the birth, stating she had business in Haworth, but Muriel told Derwa later that she could get itchy feet when she'd been a guest somewhere too long. Muriel's father had been a drover, and there had been a time when Eleanor had travelled about the country with him. It all sounded equally fascinating and terrifying to Derwa.

Travel was one level of horror. Babies were something far worse. For the first month Derwa was certain James would be given to an orphanage or a family in want of a baby. She was merely looking after him until that time. Each day she grew a little more competent in looking after him, and by the time he started to smile she decided that perhaps she wouldn't mention giving him away unless Muriel brought the subject up. Which, of course, she never did.

They may have continued quite happily in Pateley Bridge for years, if it were not for Muriel's growing discontent with Mr Warburton. He had been extremely generous and open minded in taking on a female apprentice, but whether it was the fact that the pupil was starting to outshine the master in the eyes of the locals, or she was simply too frustrated with his strict codes to living and inability to listen to her more outlandish ideas for the development of medicine, Muriel felt that she had reached the ceiling as a woman and a medic in this part of the world. She had learned his crafts, understood the nature and preparation of drugs and had progressed greatly in the field of surgery. He could teach her no more, and given her Edinburgh education and experience, she was now the more superior practitioner, although as a woman, that could never be acknowledged. Mr Warburton said that he wished to take on a new apprentice, and Muriel agreed that it was time for her to move on. Of course, being a woman it was hard to say what she could move on to. A new doctor in any town took some time to establish and gain the locals' trust, but an unknown woman wouldn't progress any further than a midwife. She could not return to Haworth, for she said she did not trust the doctor there not to spread rumours about her. It was a chance conversation whilst grumbling to her cousin, Emmerline Whitfield, that brought about a very satisfactory solution for everyone.

Emmerline was also a widow, but in stark contrast to Muriel, she was an incredibly wealthy woman. Her fortune came from her own family, as well as that of her late husband, who had been in the cotton trade and owned mills in West Yorkshire. Emmerline continued to run the family concerns herself and was training her son up to help in the business when he came of age. She did not fit in well with the mill owners' circles, for she worried too much about the people who worked in her mills, and seemed to be under the deluded misconception that the workers were people just like herself. She had been horrified at the living conditions, wept at the age of the children forced to go to work just to keep the family from starvation, and decided that tears were all well and good whilst sitting in a morning room ten times the size of what some families had to live in, but what was needed was positive change.

She built a village. There were terraces of fine stone cottages, with little gardens for vegetables. There was a water pump in every lane. She built a school that would provide free education for all the boys and girls up to twelve who lived in the village. There was a park for the residents to stroll in, a little cottage hospital, a home for unmarried mothers, a small row of tiny cottages that were to be provided rent free for elderly workers who now wished to retire, a library and evening class institution for those who wished to better their minds. A public bath to wash their earthly bodies. A small Methodist chapel was constructed and a more liberal Methodist preacher was installed to run it. The entirety was built uphill and up wind of the mills, so that people would have clean air to breathe. She then went to her tenants who were living in the slums rented out by her estate and told them she would be razing the buildings to the ground. If they would like to continue working for her family, they were very welcome to come and take a cottage in her new village. Emmerline never had trouble employing new staff.

She had been looking for a suitable doctor to man the cottage hospital, and whilst Muriel had been busy in Pateley Bridge, had not dared put the suggestion to her for fear of causing a disagreement with Mr Warburton. When Muriel started to write of her discontent, Emmerline put the offer to her and Muriel accepted, although wondered what was to become of Derwa. Naturally she could come with her, but would she want to? Emmerline mentioned that one of her teachers, a woman from Dentdale who had been teaching the young mothers all kinds of complex knitting so that they might better look after themselves in the future, wished to move back to her own valley. Perhaps Derwa could move across a little earlier, learn how to make these delightful little gloves, embellished with names into the stitching, and then she could continue with the work. Some of the girls that came to them had not enjoyed an easy start to life and knew nothing but mill work. They trained them in all the trends of knitting, and taught them some reading and writing. Perhaps Derwa would like to take a position as a teacher at the school and home, to help out with duties along with a full time, trained teacher?

At first Derwa was horrified, shrinking into herself at the suggestion that she should teach. She was just a girl, what did she know? She could write and read quite well now, Muriel pointed out, and all she needed was patience. Just follow the same technique Muriel had used with her when she had first arrived in Pateley Bridge. Her knitting was prolific and impressive, and with this Dentdale magic – Muriel waved her hands absently in the air, knitting being something she understood very little of – she would be a great master to help out other girls who had found themselves in difficult positions. She had told Emmerline that Derwa also was a widow, so no one at the village would know any different, and she need not fear of any stigma or ill treatment from the locals. Indeed, the entire concept of the village was revolutionary, and looking to bring better living to society as a whole.

So it came to pass in the autumn of James' first year, that the tenancy on the little house in Pateley Bridge was given up. The household was packed up and sent by several horses and carts across to Emmerline's little village of Whiteacre. They waved goodbye to Pateley Bridge, and Derwa wondered if she would ever return to her moors. She missed the intoxicating scent of purple heather in summer, of the fern speckled woodland slopes, even the winds and the fog blown across from the rugged coast. She missed her mother, who had still not written, but whom, Rosen assured her, had been told of James' birth. All she would say to Rosen was that she did not wish to see Derwa yet. Locking sadness inside of her, thinking that she would never abandon James in such a way, Derwa looked forward in her life, and for the first time in a long age, felt hopeful about what may be coming next.

1833

Ewat

Ewat, eldest of the Longbottom brood at Runswick, swung around to keep her back to the doorframe. She hoped that her father had not seen her. Jeremiah Longbottom was starting on one of his predictable grumbles about the state of living. They had all heard it so many times they could have given the speech word for word on his behalf. He'd found another of those posters, torn and ripped and brought it home like a dog with a sorry bone. It must have fallen from its place, and been trampled on the path, but enough text remained for the message to be read. Another ship setting sail from Whitby to Canada, where everything was better – according to her father – and a man could plan his own destiny. He could be in control of his own money, which was a subject that pressed closely on Jeremiah's mind these days. If it had just been one or two factors, he may have remained calm, but sometimes life's individual elements grew in number to be too heavy a burden. He had five children and a wife to support. There were rents to be paid, food to purchase, and on top of that there was always the tithes for the church and an amount to the poor relief. The Longbottom finances were not helped by a couple of Runswick sons returning to the fishing village of their birth with new skills. They had been away on carpentry apprenticeships and commissions, and with their return there were too many carpenters for such a small village. Jeremiah was the more experienced and had been there longest, and certainly no one held any question over the quality of his work, but he was not a Nagar, and so he would be last in the queue.

Realistically they needed to move away from this secluded little coastal village. They ought to have moved somewhere with more scope for work a while ago. But Jeremiah lingered, grumbling over the same old story, gradually eating into his savings and brewing bitterness. He had put aside enough for the family's passage to Canada, one way, but would not take the plunge and make a reservation on the next ship, as if he needed someone else to declare it an excellent idea and spur him to action. His wife, Sonneta, had suggested they move up to the moorlands, where he had come from, but Jeremiah paled at the thought. He did not wish to return to Egton to remember where he had served his own apprenticeship and his first wife had died. Neither did he wish to return to Commondale, much further up the valley, where his own childhood had been and where his successful, well-heeled elder brother now resided. Finances were very much boosted by a lack of children, for William and Magdalene had never had any more since the death of their twin girls. Jeremiah on the other hand had been blessed with five by his second wife.

Looking for options that did not entail crossing the earth, Sonneta had suggested the Orkneys, her home land, with a slightly joking lilt, knowing Jeremiah would never take her seriously. Canada was one thing, but the Orkneys? If a man struggled to make a living in Runswick because he was not born of the village, despite the fact that his own birthplace was but a day's walk away, he would not stand a chance at the far ends of the country. Sonneta knew he would not fit in there, and indeed, after all these years she was doubtful whether she would either. Even now she still wished she could go back and see her mother. The possibility of maybe, one day, was a flicker of hope. If they went to Canada, she knew there would be no coming back, and she would never see her homeland again. There was also the risk that the older children would not wish to come with them, and the loss of her own chicks was something she could not contemplate.

Ewat, with her dark curls peeping out around the edges of her cap, peered back around the doorway. Her father was in full flow now. The twins, Ayla and Hobart, were only nine and with youth were excused from having to pay attention to father. They squatted on the floor in a pool of sunlight and played a silent game, something with little sticks of driftwood that only the two of them understood. The twins had a silent affinity, as if they were all the other needed in this world for company. Ewat envied them that, for she sometimes felt alone. She did not have anyone to talk to who really would listen and understand. She occasionally saw her cousin Rosen Pengelly, when she was free from her work or seeing her unofficial betrothed, which meant not very often. Rosen was bright and chatty, confident and self-assured. Ewat couldn't imagine her having troubles. There was something closed about her manner and exuberance that stated she did not wish to hear the troubles of others either. Ewat had asked for her cousin Derwa's address, thinking she might be more understanding given her child out of wedlock (and Rosen said that she had kept it!). She imagined Derwa would be keen for any communication given that other members of the family now shunned her. She had the address in her little basket of treasures but had still not decided what she wished to say.

She wandered down to the shore to see if her brother and sister were working. Robert liked to help the fishermen bring in the catch, then he and Agnes, who, unlike Ewat, had no qualms about gutting a fish, would gut, pack and prepare the fish to be moved on for sale. Ewat worked as well, but she had inherited no talent for the handling of fish from her herring girl mother. She had no issue in eating a piece of fish, but she couldn't stand to have their glassy dumb eyes staring at her, the last moments of drowning in air imprinted in their gaze.

She had, on the other hand, inherited her mother's talent for knitting, and rattled off countless socks and ganseys, many of which were sold on for a small profit. With her fast work and little fingers, some of the fishermen whose arthritic fingers now struggled with the mending of nets would pay her for the work. She brought in some money, but probably could have done better going into service, however Sonneta was determined to keep her close. Now that Ewat was sixteen, everyone assumed she'd be marrying soon and then children and a home would become her main occupation. Ewat looked about her at village life, and although she loved the little village by the sea, she was not sure that she wanted it to be her forever after.

The village was so low lying that it was almost on the shore. In fact locals told her that the original village was now in the sea, so far out had the land stretched. The sea had reclaimed the land during a stormy period. The entire village had disappeared, just like that in the time it took for a man to be buried. Ironically it was only the dead man's cottage that had survived the onslaught. They said it happened a long time ago, which conveniently put it into the category of myths, and Ewat wasn't all that sure if she believed the story.

Whether it was true or not, the village of small stone cottages was clustered haphazardly in the space between the sea and the steep crumbling cliffs above. They were tall, sharp crags that hemmed Runswick in an almost suffocating embrace, somehow making the rest of the world feel very far away. Up on top of the cliffs there was rolling farmland, miles of wind-battered grasslands for grazing. Down by the sea, narrow path ways, alternating between stone and dirt to some hewn stones serving as steps, twisted between the haggle of little stone fishermen's' cottages. Their backdrop was the steep cliffs, punctuated by greenery, little trees and shrubs hanging on in precarious circumstances. Nets and baskets hung on the walls facing the sea, sun blasted dry.

As she neared the sea front, she passed by three women carrying baskets on their heads. Bait pickers. Then she was at the sand and the tide was out. She couldn't see her brother, but spotted her sister, Agnes, and waved to her. Agnes was busy gutting fish and gave her an off hand wave before continuing in her work. Hard, tidal-wet sand reflected the sky, rocks and hummocks of seaweed breaking up the long flat plain. The salt water far back gently lapped at the edges. The sand spread out in a great sweep to fill the edge of the wide, long running bay. At the southern end, away from the village, they mined alum. The land was busy with industry, whichever way one looked.

"I say, it's been a while since I last set eyes on you, Ewat Longbottom. Which is saying something for it is hard to hide from a local in Runswick."

Ewat grinned and turned to find Gerald Waterson stood closer to her than she had realised. "Gerry, I think it's you that's been hiding. I'm sure I haven't seen you for weeks."

"I've been hiding," he joked. "Easy done with incomers..."

She pushed at his shoulder. "Give over."

Gerry was two or three years older than Ewat, she could never remember which, but they had been playmates ever since her family had settled in Runswick. He was as a surrogate brother to her. They had moved into a cottage close by the Watersons, headed by a fisherman at the time. But old Mr Waterson was too canny a businessman to stay in the position of his father and his father's father, and had moved into the selling of fish, leaving the sea before it had chance to take his life as it did with so many of the fishermen. The Waterson's luck and standing had increased so it seemed as the Longbottoms began to struggle, although the two were quite unconnected.

She leaned back to take in his smart suit, the inkling of a beard upon his chin, hat and... "Gerald Waterson!" she shrieked as she saw the little clay pipe in his hand. "What are you doing pretending to be an old sea dog?"

He shrugged into his shoulders, almost glancing around to check that no one else was laughing at him, before he put the pipe to his mouth and took a drag which made him cough. "Not just old sea dogs who take a pipe, all the men do roundabout. And I'm becoming a well travelled man."

"You taken to fishing now?"

"No, but pa's letting me take a fish transport on my own now. I get all the way to the markets at York, in a day no less, and sell the fresh catch to the well-to-do land loving sorts who won't have seen any more water than that grimy up and down river of theirs."

"You've been to York?" Ewat looked suitably impressed. Despite her rather exotic roots – certainly much more than most of the folk in Runswick – she felt as though she'd seen nothing of the world, something which gnawed at her. At one point, when trying to encourage her to be a herring girl, her mother had told her of all the exciting places she'd been and seen. Ewat couldn't get over her phobia of the fishes' glassy eyes, and the idea of her being a herring girl soon fell flat.

"Aye, I'm away over there again tomorrow. Up early at the crack of dawn. Got a lot of country to get through." Gerry caught hold of the edges of his jacket, managing to balance the pipe stem between his teeth. It felt like an impressive manly stance, although it made him feel as though he was snarling at the girl now.

"All that way," Ewat sighed. "Maybe I could be a fish merchant."

Gerry laughed. "Bless your head. Far too much dealing for a woman to keep up with." Ewat's daydream smiled dropped, and he shuffled awkwardly, realising he was losing her. "Mind you, there's room at the front of the cart for a little one. You could always come with me tomorrow, take in the scenery, help out at market."

Ewat's eyes glowed. "Really? What time do I need to be ready?"

He looked like he might lose his balance. "You'll come?" He sounded just as excited. "As soon as the first light is appearing. Up at the top of the cliffs. Donkeys take the fish up, they've done that now, and the cart'll be packed and loaded and ready to go."

"I'll see you there then. Oh, I'm so excited." She grabbed hold of his elbows and jiggled them in joy before skipping off up the path to tell mother what she would be about tomorrow. Working at the fish market in York, she phrased it as when telling their parents. Agnes rolled her eyes later that night when they were in bed together chattering about the day's events. Agnes was convinced Gerry was after Ewat as a wife. Ewat wrinkled her nose and stuck out her tongue. "Gerry's our brother, you know that, and we are his sisters. I don't suppose I'll have feelings of that sort for anyone."

"Maybe not, but you'll have to get married sometime. Don't want to end up an old maid."

"I suppose not."

"Tell you what though, Margaret was only saying the other day that when you do get feelings of that sort..." Agnes broke off in a girlish giggle. "They hit you like a hammer. You forget how to speak properly and all sorts. Turn into a right fool."

Ewat laughed. "Agnes, if you think I'm letting anyone do a thing like that to me, you've another think coming."

Ewat never lost sense of what she was thinking or wanted to say when she was with Gerry. Excitement ruled her in other ways, and she was up at the top of the cliffs long before Gerry the next morning. The time had barely shifted into the next day, the light only just grimy and beginning to creep over the horizon. The sea could be heard but hardly seen, which was hard to believe standing on top of the cliffs with the great expanse of the North Sea before her.

A young lad got the two horses harnessed up to the cart whilst Gerry made a show of checking over his cargo. Ewat loitered awkwardly, holding her little basket of food and starting to have the first doubts as to whether this little jaunt was really such a good idea. Gerry offered a hand and helped her up onto the seat at the front, a simple plank with footplate for the cart, which was the only place to sit if one did not wish to linger in with all the fish in the back.

It was too late for doubts now. Steam rose in puffs from the horses' noses as the vehicle rattled and began to shift. They were off on their journey. The coastal line and the spray of salt was soon dispersing into the background as the cart climbed upwards and onto moorland. Ewat was familiar with this part for the family had travelled this way now and then to go up over the moors towards the Esk Valley at Danby or to travel up the river valley to Commondale to see old Uncle William, or down to Glaisdale to see Aunt Prudence. Reaching Danby, the cart followed the dirt road up to the village of Castleton, before swinging around gaining swiftly in height to start onto the Blakey Moors. The noise of the cart and the horses' hooves on the road filled her ears so conversation was difficult. Ewat was too exhilarated to idly chat about something and nothing, looking about her this way and that at familiar places that rushed by. The long shadows of morning were appearing as the sun rose, and the birds started to twitter. People were waking up and coming out of their houses, starting on the business of the day. Ewat waved at strangers, laughing and becoming unbalanced and grabbing at Gerry's arm to stop herself falling off.

The run across the Blakey Moors was a long one, but beautiful at this time of year with the heather blooming purple and the heady scent of blossom growing thicker as it was heated by the sun. The well-used road followed the high land, skirting around the top of the deep, steep dip of Rosedale to the east and Farndale to the west and cutting straight through like a sharp knife slicing straight through netting. They had been travelling for a couple of hours already as Gerry drew back on the reigns to get the beasts to slow down. He pointed out a lonely building ahead on the horizon.

"Blakey House."

"What?" Ewat twisted one way then the other in her seat, looking from Gerry to the building. "I know I am not well travelled, but this is not York."

"No, it is the Lion Inn. I change my horses here. You don't think these two would make it all the way to York in one stretch? I need to move fast, get these fish sold whilst they're still good and fresh."

"And they'll give you their horses?"

"No, they'll give me my horses," Gerry winked at her. "We've got quite the business planned out; you'll be surprised at our planning and connections, Ewat. I pay them to stable two of our horses here, always ready for when I'm coming to or from York so I can move quickly. They're desperate for the money so always happy to oblige. Not much money in keeping an inn in the middle of nowhere; only passing traders on the way to somewhere will sometimes stop by, but most don't linger. Up here you really are at the ends of the earth."

"I wonder why people would chose to live here," Ewat mused.

"Perhaps they're hiding from something, who can say. It's a place of lawlessness; and drunkenness and fighting. But it's all tolerated on account of a need for the money. Why, the innkeeper, Mr Iredale, has to take part in a little coal mining on the land, to supplement his income. Or at least he used to until his wife died some years ago. He's taken to the drink so I'm not sure quite what he does these days. His daughters did the sensible thing and got out to service. The son lingers; he's really the backbone of the place and you just hope it's only Callum Iredale we see this morning."

The horses looked relieved to see their stint of hard work was coming to an end. They knew where they were headed, pulling the cart off the road and onto the dusty track front of the inn. The sun blasted the building this morning, and with its backdrop of purple it looked stunning, but Ewat could imagine what a bleak place it might be in the deepest of midwinter. Yet there was life and commerce here. A gathering of ten little ponies, each laden with pannier sacks, were at a halt and taking their turn at drinking at a water trough. The head man was talking to a farmer's wife, before coming to some agreement and taking a great block of salt out of one of the panniers, to cut her off an agreed amount. A young man came out of the inn and waved to the pannierman, calling that they would take a pound as well, before sending a crouched farmer's lad away around the back of the inn. Ewat gazed about her in awe, literally feeling as though she was perched on the highest point in the entire kingdom.

"Mr Waterson," the man from the inn called out as he strode over to the fish merchant's cart. "Good to see you with us again so soon."

"And my horses?"

"Quite well. I've just sent the lad to fetch them." He went around to the horses, running a calming hand down the forehead of the first creature before starting to unbridle him from the cart. "Settle down lad, time for a rest."

"Will you be making any purchases yourself whilst we're here? Fresh catch from Runswick."

"Aye, I will. It's market day up here today, we may well sell a few suppers."

Ewat couldn't take her eyes off the man from the inn. She assumed this must be Callum Iredale. He would have been a little older than herself, perhaps twenty or so, and a tall figure busy and used to hard work and little idleness. That and the bleakness could make a man bitter, but he had something of the eternal optimist about him. He carried an easy smile, which he shared as he looked from the horse directly to her. The wind picked up and brushed through his longish sand auburn hair. It wasn't as clipped and tidy as Gerry's, but then he wasn't travelling to the city to impress city folk. He lived out in the wilds and was more as nature intended. He met her eye directly despite the fact that they had not been introduced, and more to the fact that he knew she had been staring at him, and looked amused in a kindly way. Ewat felt the embarrassment drench her to the soles of her feet.

"You don't usually come with a riding companion," Callum observed casually as he started to release the second horse from the cart. "Is this your sister?"

Gerry opened his mouth to contradict the assumption, perhaps be so bold as to make a guarded reference as to what his hopes for the future were, but Ewat was not in control of her tongue, and immediately agreed that this was the case.

"Well, it's very nice to make your acquaintance, Miss Waterson."

"It's Ewat."

"Ewat?" He said, then broke out into a wide smile, noting Gerry's look of horror out of the corner of his eye. "Well, we're not ones to stand on ceremony in these parts. I'm Callum Iredale. Ah, here we are," he changed the subject as the hired lad brought Gerry's other horses to the cart. "Are these not a well cared for pair of beasts, Mr Waterson? They have a fine time of it stopping up at the Lion Inn. William here has a way with the animals and has taken quite a fancy to all the horses and ponies we get passing through. You'll have no worries for these two you'll be leaving with us today."

"Aye well, don't pamper them too much," Gerry muttered gruffly as he hopped down from the cart. "They must remember they are working horses with long journeys to attend to. Now, let's see which fish I can be selling you."

Ewat didn't dare look at Callum again for fear of embarrassing herself. She watched the lad William lead away their first horses, then shuffled in her seat to gaze out across the fine view. To one side the heather-laden land rolled outwards for a distance before suddenly dipping down into the green depths of Rosedale, a long valley, like a giant's grove swept out of the heather uplands and gifted with good grazing land. A woman with a basket strapped to her back appeared on the skyline from Rosedale and started in the direction of the inn.

"We have something of a market up here," she heard Callum explain for her benefit. "Come up and sell all sorts, spare oats, bit of bacon, hand weaving. Times are hard and we must all do what we can. Is there anything you are in want of, Miss Waterson?"

"No, I..." Ewat shook her head, not sure what she was thinking, and looked around at the men. Gerry looked silently furious, but she was oblivious to him, catching only Callum's smile. "Ma keeps a chicken you see."

"Does she now? Well, that'll keep you well supplied with hand-woven goods."

She smiled, sharing the joke, but feeling very young. "Quite."

"Mr Iredale," Gerry started.

"Mr Waterson," Callum cut him off, grasping the two fish by their gills. "I'll keep you no longer, for I know you still have a long way ahead of you. Horses are all bridled up and ready to go. Good speed on your journey."

"Mr Iredale," Gerry spoke tersely as he swiftly pulled himself back into the driver's seat. Taking up the reigns, he shook the horses into action and turned them out of the inn's yard and back onto the road.

Ewat twisted around to watch the diminishing figure of Callum Iredale and the Lion Inn, wishing she was brave enough to wave back, but lacking in courage to raise her hand.

"What were you doing, telling him your mother has a chicken?" Gerry grumbled.

"I don't know," Ewat confessed, sitting back around in her place. "It just came out."

"Like you told him you were my sister. I'll have to set him straight on that another time."

"Oh, come on, Gerry," Ewat laughed. "We're as good as brother and sister, and it's not such a horrific thought to be related to me, now is it?"

Gerry looked over at his travelling companion, and her merry countenance cheered him and made him forget his earlier irritations. "Just as long as no one thinks those mad ramblings about chickens run in the family."

The horses enjoyed the good weather and the exhilaration of the exercise, continuing over Blakey Moor, then down through the village of Hutton le Hole and across the Howardian Hills, rushing by little villages filled with stone built cottages. Ewat drank in all the sights, a hundred little names on her tongue and quickly forgotten as they rattled on to the next village. On the brink of the hills, with the great vale before them and visibility being good that day, Ewat leaned forward in consternation, certain what she saw couldn't be right. She stretched out her hand as if she might pick the object from the background. "That looks like a tall house."

Gerry smirked. She could be quite clueless at times, but she was terribly sweet. "That's hardly a house. That's York Minister you're seeing."

"We're at York?"

"Not yet. It's just so big that you can see it from afar. Now come along," he shook the reigns, getting the horses moving again. "I've got fish to get to market."

Ewat couldn't get her mind from the notion of such a building being visible from such a distance. It must be awfully grand to tower over all of Yorkshire like that. She was so keen to see it close up that she almost ignored the city of York as the cart rattled through the city walls bar and into the city sanctum. Here there was a gathering of houses and people and fashions and business like nothing that Ewat had seen before. It was quite breathtaking, and to consider all the lives and folk and goings on that could be contained and concentrated in such one place was to bring one's imagination to its knees.

Gerry led the cart to the market, showing a confidence of familiarity as he negotiated his way down the narrow streets. They passed by butchers with bristling mutton chop whiskers and brawny forearms, bakers with loaves of comforting smelling bread, alehouses and inns, well to do families taking the air, flower sellers, dressmakers, shops with glassware and ceramics, post carriages arriving from other parts of the country. It was a conglomeration of all the arteries to the entire island. So much life moving through the narrow little streets and lanes, multi-storey buildings overhanging the thoroughfares and shadowing people that may have been in London or Edinburgh last week. Figures disappeared down little snickelways cutting their way through gaps between buildings and following near secret passageways, an inner maze that required a local's familiarity for navigation.

Ewat's guide tried to keep her attention by attempting to introduce her to the world of fish mongering. But between his need to get business completed and Ewat's distracted focus, she soon wandered away from the market, as if hypnotised by the sight of a great gothic tower peeking over the rooftops. Using that sight as a guide, she weaved her way through the city, growing ever closer, until stumbling around a corner, the lanes opened up and she found herself standing before the might of York Minster. She craned her neck back to stare at the gothic majesty in awe. She could never have imagined or described such a massive and beautiful building. And it was endless, heading off in every direction as if it were a city in its entirety. A living being perhaps, always in fluctuation and change. Stone masons were busy at work, and there was scaffolding in place to provide access to the central roof. It had been four years since the dreadful fires started by the lunatic Jonathan Martin, and still the cathedral had not been repaired fully to its former glory. She vaguely remembered the adults gossiping about it at the time, even in Runswick it had come out as big news. The great cathedral had been devastated, and all thanks to a mad man who thought he heard the voice of God.

One of the lads carrying timbers round to the front entrance, paused in his work to take in the lass gazing up at the Minster. Pretty thing, although a little naive looking and probably not from round here. Such a girl might be impressed that he was working at such a prestigious place. Ewat became aware of being watched and lowered her eye line to meet the grinning gaze of one of the workmen. She raised her eyebrows and stared disdainfully at him. What a nerve to think she was some silly trollop who would feint for the attention of a male. She ought to get back to Gerry, she thought, if they were to get home today they would need to head off soon. And really, she supposed, it didn't do for a single woman to be wandering about town on her own, but she couldn't help herself. What a sight the Minster was. She wondered if Callum had seen it. It could be something to speak of next time she saw him, let him know there was a little sense in her head, and more going on in her life than her mother's hen.

It was getting late when business was concluded and Gerry was ready to depart from York. Ewat had looked warily at him as she had climbed back up into the cart and he had encouraged the horses into a neat trot.

"We're not going to get back to Runswick today are we?"

He looked at her as if she were a fool. "I never manage there and back in a day. I usually manage to leave a bit earlier than we're doing now. Once I even got back to Blakey the same day..."

"Gerry Waterson!" Ewat shrieked in dismay, clutching her basket to her as if it contained all her virtue and worth. "You should have told me this before we set off. What are we to do now? Are we travelling through the night?"

"Well no, of course not. I sometimes sleep out, sometimes at an inn. Depends on the weather and the money."

"I hope you're not expecting me to sleep outdoors with you."

"Of course not. I was thinking of stopping at the Wellington in Sheriff Hutton."

"I'm to stay at an inn overnight? That's hardly decent. What will mother and father say?"

"Oh do calm yourself, Ewat. Do you not trust me? I'll pay for your room. You can tell the inn keeper we're siblings, as you seem so fond on doing. I thought it would be a good trip for you, to see a little of the world this way."

Ewat sunk back against the body of the cart and slumped her shoulders. Gerry seemed grumpy. She supposed she had overreacted a little, as if she hardly knew him. Her family had known Gerry all the time they'd lived in Runswick. He really was one of the family, so there was nothing to worry about. And he was as good as a brother. "Sorry, Gerry," she muttered. "It has been a long day and I think I got a little overexcited, what with all these new sights. Of course I am awfully grateful for you taking me along." She hooked arms with him as if to jolly him along a little. "I've known you as long as I've known myself, brother dear."

Gerry smiled a little. "I know it's a big thing to see, the city of York, the first time. And perhaps you'd like to come along again another time?"

"Oh yes," Ewat beamed. "I think I'm finding I'm very fond of this travelling."

The stay at the inn was comfortable, respectable and very uneventful. They set off early the following day to return to Runswick. Ewat felt high on adventure, as if the world had been opened up to her. Suddenly she was aware of the potential of inland Yorkshire. There was so much to see, although she still shuddered with horror at the thought of leaving her home county due to her father's musings on the blessed state of Canada. Notions of Canada left her mind as she felt her spirit soaring from the confines of both family and Runswick as the little cart pulled up the hills towards the moors. She felt on top of the world.

It was busy when they reached the Lion Inn at Blakey Ridge. There was a flurry of traders and farmer's wives selling goods; it was quite the little market out in the middle of nowhere. Ewat strained forward in the seat as they pulled off the moorland track and into the yard. So much to see. "Might I take a couple of minutes to look about whilst you change the horses?"

"Aye," Gerry was feeling generous. "We've got plenty of time to get back to Runswick."

Gerry brought the horses to a standstill and Ewat went to jump down from the side when Callum Iredale appeared from the busy yard, reaching up to take her arm and help her down. Ewat felt herself blush, embarrassed from the attention as if it were ridiculous that she might be treated as a lady.

"You enjoyed the sights of York, then, Miss Waterson?"

"Oh yes," Ewat gasped, daring to look at him again as she felt the blush start to subside. Her face was not so flushed, but she could feel a burning line along the underside of her arm where he had held onto her as he'd helped her down. "It's ever so big."

"I should introduce you properly," Gerry interrupted, staring darkly at the way Callum still held onto Ewat's arm despite the fact she was now safely on the ground. "This is Miss Longbottom."

"Longbottom?" Callum raised his eyebrows and looked to Ewat. "You've decided not to be brother and sister today?"

"We grew up together so it feels like it, but we're not of the same family."

"I see."

"Oh, Mr Iredale," Ewat burst out, suddenly remembering her snippet of intelligent conversation about York architecture she had been saving for next they met. "Have you seen the minister?"

"The minister?" Callum asked, his eyes twinkling. "Thank the Lord I've not seen him about today, that wandering sanctimonious fool."

"Oh, but I..."

"She means the Minster, I'll warrant," Gerry rolled his eyes. He hoped it was merely the altitude that was bringing on this silly behaviour. "The great cathedral of York."

"That I have seen, and a splendid sight it is." He worked on freeing the horses from the cart bridles. "You must both excuse me; we're very busy just the now and I'll have to fetch the horses myself today. So much to do a man doesn't have time to catch his thoughts. But I hope you'll be back through this way, Miss Longbottom."

"Oh yes, I do hope so." The gushing response was out before she could censor herself. Ewat coloured again in embarrassment. Gerry scowled. Why did the lasses never got so giddy over him, and Ewat in particular? She treated him as an old familiar sock.

Ewat wandered through the traders, not that she needed anything, but just to see how much life and trade went on up here. Talking to the farmer's wives in the hope her colour would settle again and she could leave a positive impression upon the locals rather than that of some silly girl grinning like an idiot at the innkeeper's son.

As she was approaching the cart to join Gerry on the final stretch back home, an older man came at the cart on a fast but slightly unsteady gait and glowered at Gerry as Callum finished fastening the bridles on the horses.

"Mac, I know what you're about, and you can get away with you!" he bellowed at Gerry.

Callum very smoothly finished his work and took the man by the shoulders to ease him away from the cart. "Father, that's Mr Waterson..."

"I'll be damned you're lying to me."

There were no words or twinkles for Ewat this time. Callum hurried the older man away, calling his greetings over his shoulder to Gerry. Ewat lingered by the horses for a moment, watching the two figures head towards the inn.

"And that is Mr Iredale the innkeeper," Gerry said curtly. He felt affronted, even though he knew the man shouted nonsense, and he had no idea who this Mac was or what Iredale thought he had done. "The drunkard that I mentioned to you. It won't be a good household to live in."

"I suppose not." Ewat watched their retreating figures as she pulled herself back up onto the cart.

"Let's head home." Gerry gave the reigns a firm jolt. "I feel the need of sea air in my lungs again."

Whilst Ewat Longbottom's giddy moments were generally restrained to the premises of the Red Lion Inn at Blakey, there was a decided change about her that summer. She carried a brightness in the eyes, an unexplained hopefulness and long sightedness, almost on par with her father when he spoke of Canada and the good living that was ready to be taken. On a night, when they were curled up in the bed but still far from sleep, Agnes would tease Ewat about her giddiness, and tell her that she was in love.

"Everybody can guess it," she giggled, delighting in Ewat sitting a little more primly and pretending to not know what Agnes was speaking about. "You're always off travelling with Gerry on his fish mongering adventures. Mother and Father only let you because they're sure an engagement will be announced soon. Although I don't know how that will work with Canada. Do you think Gerry will come with us, or will you have to call the wedding off?"

"Don't be ridiculous," Ewat scolded. "Besides, it's just talk with Father. We'll never leave Yorkshire."

As the weeks went by and the year fluttered into autumn, it became less the idle rantings of a disgruntled man and more a real idea. There was free virgin land to be taken, good farming, and no taxes or tithes or contributions to the poor relief of the land. A man could keep the money he made and prosper. Some families had made the journey three or four years ago and were now established. They wrote home, Jeremiah getting sight of letters from Mr Easton's brother and family, and they remarked upon the prices and the ease of finances if one was willing to work hard. There were also rather lyrical passages lamenting the loss of North Yorkshire and sight of the moors, but Jeremiah ignored those, thinking on how life could be made easier, and how he could achieve what he was owed after all these years of hard work. He was a competent and hard working carpenter, but in Runswick the work was constantly dropping. People were backward here, he decided, clinging to the ideas of local was best, outsiders weren't quite to be trusted. Canada, on the other hand, was progressive.

The afternoon when he returned to announce to wife and children that he had been to Whitby to talk at the harbour office about the emigration ships, Ewat realised this wasn't just an idle day dream. Father had gotten an exact price on one way travel for the whole family over to Canada. The seas would be rough in winter, but there were two ships pencilled in for departure from Whitby to Quebec in May next year. He intended the Longbottoms to be on one of them.

She sought out her mother in the early evening when Father had gone to the inn to discuss his plans further with the locals he was so keen to abandon, with hopeful laughter and back slapping, assuring everyone he was finally going to get somewhere. Sonneta sat in front of their little cottage, enjoying a burst of autumn warmth and sunshine that lit up her curls, catching hints of fire in the brown. She had left her cap inside, finding it an irritation on her head, and was living on the wild side with an uncovered head, knitting in public. She looked up and smiled as Ewat approached.

"There's my well-travelled daughter," she greeted her, the needles never slowing in their clicking. "Why, you'll have seen all of Yorkshire by now."

"Not quite." Ewat crouched down beside her mother. "Besides, I'm not as well travelled as you."

"Aye, well," Sonneta sighed. "I am a long way from my birthplace. But we never know where life will take us. And soon we'll all be extremely well travelled folk of the world."

Ewat felt her gut tighten. "Father's serious."

"Well of course he is," Sonneta looked at her daughter in consternation. "You've heard plenty of his Canada talk; this can't be a shock to you."

"No, but I thought it was just talk. Nothing more. I never thought he'd actually leave his country."

"He's going to book passage for us on a ship called the Hindoo."

Ewat bit her bottom lip and stared out to the sea. She felt sick. Wavering on a decision which had already been made months ago. She could feel her own life veering off from that of her parents and her siblings. There were things she needed to see out and she did not think she could leave the dry land of Yorkshire. "Mamma?" her voice sounded very weak.

Sonneta didn't look at her. "Yes?"

"I don't think, or rather I know that I can't. I can't come to Canada. Father would be best off not buying a ticket for me."

Sonneta put a hand to her mouth and looked away.

"There are plenty of girls who have left home younger than I am. Going into service, away for work. You were a herring girl when you were my age." Yet girls in service knew where their mothers were, and that they were often within walking distance. Sonneta had travelled much further, but if things had gotten bad she knew the way home.

"This is Gerry?"

Ewat looked up, surprised by the constriction in her mother's voice. "No. I wish people would stop joking about Gerry. There's nothing there of that sort. I want..." her voice drifted off. She did not dare to speak it yet, her girlish hopes that were only fancies of the mind. Nothing had been confirmed or spoken of, and although she thought constantly of every conversation and word spoken, thinking over each word, the intonation, the glances and what they all might mean in combination or separated out and laid out for judgement. It was a joyful feeling to sense potential. But she did not dare speak of it to anyone yet for fear the magic would break.

"Mamma," Ewat reached for her mother's arm impulsively and realised that she had ceased in her knitting. "I feel that my life is here. I have to follow that. I'm a grown woman, well, almost, and..."

Sonneta was crying.

"Mamma, you'd come back to visit. And I'd come and visit you."

Sonneta stared at the innocence in her daughter's face. She believed it in that moment, or at least pretended to so that she would feel the strength to go ahead with her convictions. "You are my first born little girl. There's something special about the first baby. I still remember you the first time I saw your dear little face. We were living in Whitby then."

"Mamma, I..."

Sonneta suddenly looked her straight in the eye. "It's you who has to live your life, Ewat, not me. For better or worse we all have to make our own decisions."

People of her parents' generation had all been tied down by duty and tradition and doing the right thing. They never thought that perhaps there was more to life, had never stood out on the tops of the moor in the crisp clear air with a bright atmosphere showing all the miles of the world. All the potential. They didn't understand the way a passion might burn one up from the inside. But to never see her mother again, surely it couldn't be that final? Ewat didn't know who to talk to, for none of her family could really understand. She thought of her cousin Derwa who had not denied what she wanted, even when it had meant disgrace and having to leave the area. Surely she would understand better than anyone these emotions Ewat was going through.

A letter was written, sent and received by a bewildered Derwa who only remembered Ewat as a bubbling little girl, all smiles and curls as frizzy as her mother's. The letter contained a prattling text, full of half formed thoughts and a lack of experience. She made assumptions just like everyone else that Derwa had allowed and wanted the violation of her body and the subsequent pregnancy. That it had not only been her choice, but her long term plan. In Ewat's befuddled mind, it was a great romance. And the undertones said that she would empathise and advise on Ewat's dilemmas, soothe her conscience and be grateful that some of the family were still willing to communicate with her. Derwa had rolled her eyes and crumpled the letter, stuffing it into her apron pocket before returning to her son. She didn't need stupid relatives like that. Her mother would still not communicate with her, and although Rosen would write letters and update her on all the gossip of the valleys, she showed little interest in Derwa's new life, and was even so bold as to advise Derwa it was best that she never returned to the Esk Valley.

When Derwa discussed Ewat's letter with Muriel, her cousin suggested she might reply. Although Ewat was clearly very naive about the world, it sounded as though she would soon also be quite alone. What a thing to face at such an age, that her family emigrated and she was left behind. She would be in need of a friend. And one didn't want to sever all contact with family. No one was perfect, and whilst some sins were unforgivable, being a foolish young girl was something most women had been at some point in their life. Derwa didn't feel so charitable. Ewat was part of "them over there", believing her to be a fallen woman, who had chosen her fate. If she was in need of family there was Rosen and their mother, and even their Aunt and Uncle over in Commondale. The Longbottoms had no history of lost children and were still in communication. Derwa had enough troubles of her own without worrying about a cousin she did not know in adulthood.

Callum Iredale did not provide any of the responses Ewat had imagined either. She brought up the subject of Canada one afternoon when they were returning to Runswick. The time of the year was well into autumn and the heather was bereft of its colour. Sheep were growing their fleeces again in readiness for winter. The sun cast long shadows, and although the light could be bright and warming, as soon as the clouds pulled over there was a chill in the air.

They were at the Red Lion at Blakey. Gerry had gone with the young lad to inspect the horse's quarters. Ewat had hopped down from the cart and was lingering, watching Callum as he held on to the horse's reigns.

"Clear day today," Callum spoke idly. "Can see a long way. Mind you, clearest is on winter, when the air is like ice. You could see to the ends of the earth from here."

"To Canada?"

"Canada?" Callum chuckled. "That's a long sea journey, doubt we could see quite that far. Happen we'll write to someone over there. Ask them to wave a flag, see if we notice it."

"I could ask my father. He's taking the family to Canada next year."

His eyes widened in surprise, traces of humour gone from his face as he stared straight at Ewat. Nothing was said, which made her uncomfortable, as if she'd said the wrong thing or assumed a confidence where there was none. In the face of awkwardness, Ewat's tactic was to prattle. "Of course I don't want to go. I don't think I could ever leave Yorkshire. I've already told mother I want to stay. I will have to find a position somewhere or something..."

"Aye, well," Callum ducked away, the sound of someone approaching breaking his silence. "A lot of folks are heading to Canada these days. Probably more Yorkshire over there than it is here."

Ewat felt as though she'd been slapped. He didn't seem concerned in the slightest that she might soon be gone.

Mr Iredale, Callum's father appeared at the other side of the horses. His hair was unbrushed, his shirt and waistcoat askew. He looked confused, as if someone had told him a puzzle and he could not make head nor tail or it. "I'm feeling a little weary," he said, looking at Ewat as if she were supposed to do something about it. "I think I may take a nap."

"Aye father," Callum muttered, patting the horse's neck and turning his back on both his father and Ewat. "I've got a handle on things in the yard, don't you worry. You go rest yourself."

Mr Iredale wavered as if there was something else he meant to say, but changed his mind. "My bed..." he started, staring at Ewat.

She shuffled awkwardly. Gerry had told her what a terrible drunk he was, and angry and beastly. She couldn't smell the alcohol on him today, and despite the fact he couldn't be all that old, he seemed rather frail. "Yes," she smiled at him, feeling stupid.

"I don't seem to quite recall." He looked about him. "If you could just show me the door?"

"The door? Why, the inn's just there." Ewat pointed. Had he grown blind now?

"Why, I'm not sure..."

"Ah, here they come with the horses," Callum sounded relieved. His father started to wander in the direction of the road and Rosedale valley. "Miss Longbottom, I couldn't ask you just to walk my father in the direction of the inn? The lad'll be here in a moment and then..."

"Yes, of course." Ewat darted away, hooking arms with the innkeeper and redirecting him towards his premises. "We'll just stroll back towards the inn, shall we?"

"Ah yes, thank you my dear. You always were good to have about the place."

Ewat laughed. "I don't live here."

He looked at her as if she was mad. "Of course you do."

"Thank you," Callum appeared at her side, taking over the leading of his father. "Thank you for your help. We won't keep you now. Looks like Mr Waterson wishes to be off."

Dismissed and hurt, Ewat stood for a moment watching the Iredales retreat into the inn. Pushed out and the door closed. She slowly turned around and trudged back to the cart. She felt like crying, but she would hold it in, for she did not want to hear Gerry's comments just now.

"You're a brave woman, dealing with that drunkard," Gerry said as she reached the cart. "You be careful. That man can turn on a sixpence in his humours."

"As you say," she sighed, pulling herself up onto the cart. She looked regretfully at the inn as they started to move. The building grew smaller as the two youngsters moved back down on to the road and away to Runswick.

Two weeks passed before Ewat found herself up on Blakey Ridge again. It was cold now. There was a frost on the ground that was struggling to thaw in the day light. The horses' breath puffed out in hot clouds as they picked up their legs and hurried along to keep warm. Soon it would be winter. It was a better time of the year for transporting fish, Gerry said, for the fish kept better with the lower temperatures. But travelling was harder on account of the shorter days.

It was quiet about the inn when they arrived. The horses pulled up in a prim halt in front of the Red Lion and Gerry looked about himself in irritation as if he had been expecting a formal welcoming committee to trumpet his arrival. He hopped down to a hiss of steam as the horses let out their breath. "I'll walk around back to the stables, see where they're at," he muttered.

Ewat looked about the place, wondering that any human had ever lived up here. The upland birds had departed for winter, flying away and dropping in altitude. The moorland sheep, tough creatures who knew this landscape twelve months of the year, hunkered down into their fleeces and took little interest in passing traffic. When the snows came, they could be harsh. Some of the shepherds would take their sheep down to the pastures in the valleys, some would let them rough it up here as long as possible.

A noise from the building broke her reflections on sheep. She looked to the inn and noticed for the first time that the main door was open. Gingerly she got herself down from the cart, telling the horses not to go anywhere, although the beasts were so tired they had no inclination to do anything. Wrapping her shawls more tightly about herself, and thankful she'd gotten her gloves finished last week, she walked across to the inn and for the first time stepped in through the threshold.

Inside the air had a scent of burnt peat, accompanied by a slight sound of crackling from a fire burning low in the grate. There was no other light source, save for the grey, unwilling daylight that slunk about the window panes. Coupled with the dark wood furniture and heavy flagstone floor, it felt dark and cold in the main public area. Hollow without patrons. Callum Iredale knelt on the floor near to the fire, picking up shards of pottery and swearing under his breath, lost in his own frustration.

"Why, Callum, we wondered if anyone was about."

He jumped at the suddenness of her voice and dropped his handful of ceramic pieces back on the floor. The sound was a shower of clinks and fragile tinkles. He looked around at her, realising Mr Waterson must have already arrived, but made neither apology nor move to get out and help with the horses. He gathered up the broken pottery again. "Bloody waste," he grumbled. "This place doesn't make enough to keep a rat and it's miserable even for the spiders."

Ewat's eyes widened, a little taken aback. Callum Iredale had always been so cheery; it was hard to contemplate he could be grumpy or irritable.

He stood up and unceremoniously dropped the pieces into the empty coal scuttle. "You still here then, Miss Longbottom? Not away to your Canada?"

"No, the ships don't sail till the spring, But I already told you, I don't want to go."

"Aye. By my reckoning this time next year you'll be Mrs Waterson."

"Gerry?!" Ewat felt her voice rising in irritation. "I am very tired of people making assumptions about me and..."

"He's a good catch for any young lady," Callum interrupted, stalking across to the bar to pick up his coat. It had been tossed aside onto one of the stools. "Good prospects, money. No reason for future worry. Why I'd marry him if he had half a mind to ask me."

Ewat stared at the floor. Why did he have to be so infuriating? "You have been breaking your crockery?"

"No, it was father."

"He was drunk again?" The comment, fuel-fed by Gerry's all-knowing commentary on the lives of others, popped out before she had chance to check herself. She blushed under Callum's scowl. "I'm sorry, it's none of my business, only that folk..."

"Folk talk, and like to think the worst." Callum concluded. "Father doesn't drink, not that most would believe it. He's sick. He's been like this a year or two. But it's getting worse. It's like parts of his mind disappear and he forgets things, people and the like. Or he can't understand what he sees even though it's as plain as the nose on his face. I made him a cup of tea this morning, as a treat, but he just sat and stared at it as if he'd never seen such a thing before." He gazed out of the window, his brow knitting. "It was as if he didn't know how to get it from the cup to his mouth. He couldn't make head nor tail of it all. He gets frustrated with things, lashes out, smashes things up."

"Have you not taken him to the doctor?"

"We don't have that much money, and the doctor can't do much about it. I asked one when he stayed over night here, what he thought about it all. He told me, had father been thirty years older he would have understood it as old age and a dying of the mind. Sees it now and then in the very old. But father's not old enough. It must be the drink, he says, his mind is ruined by too much drink."

"But you said he doesn't drink."

"Aye, but people don't want to believe me. Easier if we say he brought it on himself." Callum straightened, rousing his sense back out of rumination. He was there to do a job and not chatter with Gerry Waterson's lass about his confused father. "Mr Waterson waiting out with the horses?"

"No, he's gone round to the stables."

"No one round there. Our lad is sick with the fever, I've sent him home."

"The fever?"

He smiled wryly. "Not *the* fever. He's caught a chill. Nose running faster than a busy pump on wash day. I'd better head outside and deal with the horses."

They found Gerry in the stable, complaining at the lad who was curled up in the hay shivering and coughing.

"Laying about never got anyone anywhere."

"I thought the lad had headed home. He's been told to head home and rest up." Callum crouched down beside the lad and felt his forehead. He smiled as the lad looked up at him. "You'll get over this one, don't fret. But you're best off home with mother for a couple of days. I'll get Mr Waterson's horses sorted then take you home."

The atmosphere grew from mild displeasure to open, grinding tension, although Ewat wasn't quite sure who was at fault or why. No one said anything whilst the horses were changed over and Gerry didn't even bother to thank Callum when the fresh horses were bridled up to the cart. Ewat sat awkwardly up on the cart, feeling like a naughty child. She did not dare to take her eyes from her shoes. As the cart juddered into movement, she looked up, catching a strange look from Callum as they moved away from the inn. She looked over at Gerry whose lips were pressed together as if containing a scream.

"Are you quite well, Gerry?"

"Well enough," he muttered. "Could have done without the delay. But as there's nowhere else up top here to leave the horses..."

"It wasn't the lad's fault he was sick. You weren't very kind to him."

"Kind." Gerry sniffed. "I don't pay for kindness. Besides, what were you doing coming out of the inn with Callum Iredale? Hardly decent is it?"

"What? It's a public house. All sorts of folk go in there and we were looking for help."

"A public house, exactly," Gerry's eyes flashed at her, desperate to get the better on this one. "Not fitting for a young woman, an unmarried young woman to go wandering in there on her own. Decent young ladies..."

"Young ladies!" Ewat shrieked in amusement. "I'm a carpenter's daughter, hardly some lardy-de-da lady all prim and proper. I think you forget who you're travelling with."

Gerry set his expression back to stone and looked straight ahead. "Nothing wrong with wanting to better yourself."

Things, whatever they might have been, came to a head one freezing February. It was the first time Ewat had been out with Gerry in two months. Callum had sent messages and his regards via Gerry, who had never delivered them, and with a lack of response back, he'd eventually shrugged and told himself it was for the best. In Runswick Ewat fell into a malady, half expecting a concerned visitor who never showed, and wondering what was to become of her. Canada loomed ever closer and she had not arranged any means to stay in Yorkshire. She was not educated enough to work at the school to earn her keep, nor become a governess. Perhaps a nursery maid, Agnes suggested, but the thought of living in some big strange house raising other people's children made her cry. She supposed she ought to get herself to one of the hirings and find work, work with board so that she would have somewhere to live, but the nomadic future frightened her. Sonneta worried as she watched her daughter become a sad little drawing of herself, and Jeremiah told her all would be well when they sailed for a new life in Canada. Ewat had simply realised there was nothing for her here, that was all. But father would make everything right.

Gerry had not seen that much of Ewat over the darkest months, so he was glad he had managed to persuade her to come out with him today. Or at least he had been until they had stopped for a rest at the village of Nunnington on their way back from York and Ewat had given him such a horrified look in reaction to his proposal of marriage. She had refused him, which was the stupidest thing she could have done, for marrying him would solve all her problems. No one would ever love her as much as he did. She was a silly, ungrateful girl who would not get a better offer. And now they had to travel the rest of the way to Runswick, crammed together at the front of the little cart not talking and wishing the journey was already over.

Ewat didn't know what to do with herself. She huddled down in her shawls, pulling them up so they almost met the lip of her bonnet. She had a good shield to her face, especially if she looked out to her left and away from the presence of Gerry Waterson.

Over winter it had felt as though she couldn't think her way out of a black box she was stuck in. February was not the end of winter, but somehow the worst of it, and when Gerry had returned once again suggesting she get out of the house, her family had been so encouraging as to almost boot her out of the door. The snow was never so bad by the coast as it was inland, and inland and upland she could see from the drifts and lingering snow heaps that it had been a rough winter. The tracks had been trampled flat and clear, although Gerry had muttered that he perhaps ought to have brought the sleigh, judging from those skies, but they had managed on wheels never the less. Everything had seemed fine until he had brought the cart to a halt in that pretty little village and turned to her and uttered those devastating words.

Gerry was not a husband. He was a brother and a family friend, but certainly not a person she could go about referring to as 'my husband' or horrors upon horrors have to see in the bed. They had always been good friends, someone she could depend upon and now it was all ruined. How much could crumble off the back of one simple little question. Gerry loathed her; her family were going to Canada soon and she had nothing. No plan, no great work ethic. She was just a very hopeless case. So she sat on the bumpy cart ride, quietly crying to herself and wishing her life had worked out somewhat better.

It was snowing when they reached the Lion Inn on Blakey Ridge. The sky was a blank white, like a stretched, freshly-laundered cotton sheet. Flakes of snow silently fell, laying on the ground and creating a spongy earth for the horses' hooves to crunch through. Ewat's face had lost its feeling, her thoughts and skin numb from the crying. She looked about the world, all white and low visibility. It was as if nothing else existed, just this track, the snow and the stone building looming ahead.

A dark figure stood near to the inn, and as they approached they could see it was a man they did not know, or rather a fine looking gentleman. In his finery, riding boots crunching through the snow, long top coat swirling about his legs, scarves wrapped about his neck, and a top hat, of all the ridiculous things, sat on his head, the brim collecting its own small drift of snow.

"A-ha!" he cried, as if he had been expecting them. He watched in joyful fascination as Gerry pulled the cart up to the inn. "Other foolhardy travellers like myself. It's a fine reassurance to a fellow that he is not the only one. Come, come, my lady," he turned his attention directly to Ewat. "You look nithered as they say in these parts. Get you down and we shall visit the fire."

Gerry watched in disbelief as Ewat allowed herself to be helped down from the cart and led into the inn. Who was this idiot? He didn't sound as though he came from these parts, neither the geography nor any class, not even the local aristocracy, although he certainly had that privileged, educated note to his voice.

"Mr Waterson?" Callum appeared by his elbow like the very devil himself, making him jump. Gerry pointed off at the inn. "Who is that..." words failed him for a fitting description.

"Ah, I take it you've met Mr Cumberpound." Callum said. "Says he's a writer travelling about in search of inspiration. At this time of the year I have no understanding of it, but I suppose folks with money can indulge themselves in such whims. He's not familiar with these moors and the snow is setting in so he has taken the sensible approach and taken lodgings with us tonight. I did warn him that folks unfamiliar with the land who go wandering off, foot or horse, when the weather's bad, can get lost and not turn up again until the snow's all thawed off."

"He walked here?"

"No, rode in on a very tired horse."

"And he does this for no purpose?"

"He says he is a writer."

Gerry shook his head to himself. To have so much money one's days did not need to make any sense was a surreal luxury. It made a mockery of good honest hard work.

Callum unharnessed one of the horses from the cart. "Snow's pulling in. You'll be staying yourselves? It'll be dark soon."

"No." Gerry's volume made them both jump. He was adamant he would not remain. He wanted to be rid of Ewat as quickly as possible. "I'll set off forthwith. I want to be off these moor tops before the snow gets too deep. I'll take a couple of lamps if I may, and keep going. I want to reach Castleton at the very least."

It wasn't Callum's place to talk sense with a local, particularly judging by the determined look on Gerry's face. He nodded. "I'll get the horses ready."

Inside it was silent bar the crackling of the fire, and the pattering of flakes against the windows. The public room was better lit than the last time Ewat had been inside. Candle-lit lamps blazed on the walls, and across close to the fire where Daniel Iredale, Callum's father, sat, was a heavy wrought iron candlestick with a burning candle as round as Ewat's arm. Mr Iredale looked frailer than she remembered, somehow shrunken in on himself and bandaged up with knitwear so that he might fit properly into the chair. When Ewat and Mr Cumberpound entered, he shrank his grizzled face further into his scarves and muttered a curse on all rich devils. Ewat's eyebrows shot up, wondering that he could be so rude to a paying guest, but Mr Cumberpound appeared to not hear, instead going to the fire and admiring it with his hands on his hips, the snow on his hat melting and slowly dripping off the back.

"It's a fine fire," he declared, recalling how he himself had just added a couple of logs to the blaze, and thus was a part of the great survival of the moorland blizzard. "The type of fire to hold one proof against the weather. We ought to sit around it and exchange old ghost stories."

Ewat looked uncertainly at Mr Iredale. The light from the fire gave him a devilish glow.

Gerry entered the inn with much bluster, absolving Ewat and Mr Iredale of entertainment duties for a moment. "Ewat, ready yourself, I am setting off again now."

"But it will be dark soon and the snow's really coming in."

"Good God, man," Mr Cumberpound burst out as Ewat spoke. "You can't take the young lady and yourself out in this weather. A fellow could lose his bearings in weather like this."

Gerry scowled at the gentleman. "I happen to know my way. Ewat," he gestured to the doorway with a nod, to suggest a private conversation by the half open entrance to the swirling winter. Ewat clutched her shawls to the base of her neck as if he were taking her to the arctic where the whalers went, and peered out at the snow.

"I'm going now."

"But it's not safe..."

In the background Mr Cumberpound poked at the fire with the poker, setting off an eager burst of crackles and sparks.

Gerry looked from Ewat's earnest face, her red eyes, then the fine gentleman and the warm fire. The rejection started to smart again, like a frozen wound thawed out. Fish mongers were one thing but this idiot writer trotting about the moors at winter as if it were a playground was an entirely different league. "I suppose now you've turned me down you're setting your cap at this rich idiot."

"I am not..."

"He's only being polite to you because he thinks he's stuck here with you for the night," Gerry hissed at her. "Your problem is you think you're too good for everything but you don't know what you want. Now that Iredale's too poor to even think of asking you and you've knocked me back, you think you'll gain some advantage..."

"Gerry, what's gotten in to you? You're talking nonsense."

"You're the nonsense," Gerry snapped. "Turning me down was the stupidest thing you ever did. You're best off in Canada, good riddance. And if you think you're fetching a ride in our wagons again, you've another think coming."

Ewat's words failed her. She stared in horror as Gerry steamed out into the storm. He was good to his word, with the lamps on the cart, he shouted furiously at the fresh horses, whipping at the reigns and off they went. They heard Callum shouting something then it all went quiet. Ewat turned back to the inn. Mr Iredale was in a world of his own, but

Mr Cumberpound looked a little embarrassed. He had obviously heard more than intended.

"Mr, er... he has gone?"

"Mr Waterson. Yes, he has gone." She couldn't quite credit it. He had abandoned her, up here on Blakey Ridge, in winter, in a storm and miles from home. Her childhood friend, her brother, her rock. Turned down for marriage and suddenly all those years of friendship meant nothing.

Callum ran in through the door and shut out the winter. "He's gone without you, Miss Longbottom," he said, as if no one knew about it yet. "Did he think it safer for you to stay here? He'll fetch you when the snow's calmed?"

"No," Ewat moaned. "I don't think he'll be fetching me at all. I seem to be stranded."

Mr Cumberpound pulled a chair to the fire. "Perhaps a sit down and some warmth and it won't seem quite as bad?" He suggested in desperation.

Ewat took the chair, for it was the only option she had remaining, and looked miserably to the fire. She heard Mr Cumberpound muttering something to Callum about food for them all, and drink, to keep their spirits up. She looked around the room. The light from the windows was fading fast, a false brightness hanging on as the whiteness would not allow the night in so quick. But the shadows lengthened and deepened in the room, hiding corners and nooks, a blackness breathing and watching them. Snow pattered desperately against the windows before sliding down the glass in defeat.

"I am sorry Gerry was so rude," Ewat spoke, forgetting his proper name for polite conversation.

"This is Mr Waterson? He is your, er... Miss?"

"I'm Miss Longbottom," Ewat supplied. "And Gerry is a very old family friend. Or at least he was. I don't know where I stand now. He proposed marriage to me earlier today and I am afraid I turned him down."

"You turned him down?" Callum paused in his way to the kitchen.

"He seemed like a fine young fellow," Mr Cumberpound started. "A little volatile in temper perhaps."

"But I don't love him in that way. And it would be wrong to marry him, wouldn't it?" Ewat didn't sound completely convinced anymore. She'd been so certain in Nunnington.

"Quite right," Mr Cumberpound confirmed. "For love only." He stood up as if pretending to give a toast. "But even with a rejection, it does not seem like the gentlemanly thing to do, to leave you here on the moors like this."

"Quite right," Callum concurred.

Callum fetched in a supper of bread, cheese and some cold meats, along with weak ale and snow water that he melted in a pot by the fire. A table was shifted close to the fire, and despite the very clear difference in rank between Mr Cumberpound and the others, he was quite adamant they should all sit down to supper together. Ewat had little appetite for food, and looked miserably at the bread. She did not know how she was going to get home all on her own from Blakey Ridge, or what mother and father would say when Gerry returned without her. No doubt he'd have some story to tell, of how it was all Ewat's fault. She ought to be braver and have more confidence in herself. If she was more like cousin Derwa, apart from the illegitimate child of course, she wouldn't have anything to worry about. She remembered when it all blew up about the pregnancy. Derwa had just left the house and walked out of the village all on her own. The next anyone heard of her, she was away over in West Yorkshire. The girl had some gumption and sense if she could get herself right across the county. And here was Ewat worrying over how to get from Blakey to Runswick, and it wasn't as if she hadn't been making the journey regularly for the best part of a year.

"I propose an evening of storytelling," Mr Cumberpound suggested as he helped himself to another slice of cold boiled beef. "With the fire, the night and the storm that has stranded us, I do believe it is traditional."

Ewat looked from Callum, who appeared to be lost in his own thoughts, to old Mr Iredale who had fallen asleep. "I'm not sure I know of any stories," she said. "I don't read many novels and the like."

"Ah, but what about the folktales of the area?" Mr Cumberpound waggled his eyebrows. "I'm sure there's a wealth of stories about witches and magic, and souls lost out on the moors. And what about these little imps? What do you call them again up here? Hobgoblins..."

"Begging your pardon, but hobgoblins aren't stories. You've got to be careful lest you annoy them..."

"Marvellous!" cheered Mr Cumberpound, feeling he was getting to the root of what he sought. He noticed Callum smiling gently at Ewat, clearly touched by her earnest belief in the things. She would be the best for stories, just fresh from her mother's knee. "Do tell us of the hobs of the moors you know."

"I don't know I'd be the best for that. I grew up by the sea. I was born in Whitby, then we moved to Runswick when I was a child."

"Ah, Whitby," Mr Cumberpound nodded knowingly. "I have come from there. Fascinating place, tucked in a ravine but a hive of industry. Yet there is something about the place, a certain spirit or feeling. I believe there is an ancient force."

"I'm sure it's very safe now apart from the smugglers and fishermen when they've had a drop too much. Nothing of worry since St Hilda chased out all the serpents. Of course, there's caves and cliffs along the coast where the old hobs still hide. You'll have seen our coast? It's quite wild."

"Indeed it is. Walking in Whitby brought up the pulse," Mr Cumberpound chortled. "Although I did not yet get to Runswick. What sort of a place is it?"

"A village at the bottom of the cliffs by the sea. Father says there was another village, further out than where we are now, but it was washed away in a terrible storm. All but one house, and that was the house of a dead man, so he'd not have worried either way."

"How terrible. And were all the villagers drowned?"

"No, they were at the funeral."

"The funeral?"

"Of the dead man."

"Lord above!" Mr Cumberpound roared, slapping his knee and waking old Mr Iredale, who came to with a snort. "There is a twist of fate for you. And but for the hand of God, not a hob's mischief this time."

"I heard a story about a hob," Callum offered. "They used to talk about him in the inn, travellers and merchants and the like for they did not like him."

"He would steal their wares on the road?"

"Not quite. But they said he was a hob who had gotten ideas above his station, you might say. He'd decided to live as a man, and got himself a wife, from somewhere else, she wasn't a local lass, but they came to live on the moors, up over Commondale way. He had an uncanny ability for shifting across the moors at speed. Of course, this was a while ago, they don't talk about him so more now..."

"He died?"

"Just disappeared. Called back to the otherside I think they said. There's only so long such beings can live over in the realm of man before they have to go back. He had children as well, this Hob Hurst. One of them was hanged for murdering her husband, another was a witch who would fly over the fields down in the valley at night and curse the cows, make the milk turn sour."

As Callum prattled through the tale he had picked up in childhood from older farmers and merchants passing by, Ewat grew increasingly horrified. She knew that her people came from Commondale, and she was sure her father's grandfather had been a Hurst. She didn't know anything about murderers and witches, but hadn't her grandmother come from that line? And she had died when Ewat's father, Jeremiah, had only been young. Was this the gossip that went about her kin?

"But these are actual people you speak of?" Mr Cumberpound said. "One must be careful of such gossip. If it was spread by his competitors, it may be slander with the intention of destroying a business."

"It was all over long ago," Callum defended himself awkwardly. It was only stories he remembered from the chatter when he had been a child at the inn. His mother had still been alive, his younger brother as well, and his sisters were still at home. When the pack horse men stopped off, and the merchants and tinkers, not to mention the farmers' wives coming up to sell their wares, the gossip and storytelling made the very air dance with imagination. And there was more to be heard later on in the evening, listening in at the door to the public room, or from the window when there was a cock fight on. "Besides, the husband murderer was a recorded story. It happened a few years before I was born, but they were still talking about it ten years on. Father had a sheet about it, you know, the papers they sell at the execution. May even still be in the house somewhere for all I know."

"Your father went to the execution?"

"He must have done. He used to go down to York now and then. Hasn't been for a while now."

"Certainly not in this weather!"

Callum glanced across at his father, surprised to find him wide awake and seemingly taking it all in. He had not spoken a word all this time, but sat and watched Mr Cumberpound with such an intensity as if he was waiting for him to slip up.

"Isn't that so, father?"

Mr Iredale ignored his son.

"Well," Mr Cumberpound spoke, never one to miss a gap in the conversation as his cue. "I think one good story deserves another, and I shall now tell you one of mine. I am a writer, as I may have mentioned, and I write and record both stories I have heard, as well as others born of the creativity of my own mind."

"How exciting," Ewat gasped.

He smiled. "It's a better way for a man to make a living. Let me tell you the story of a young man far south in the country, perhaps as far south as a man can go without drenching his boots in the sea..."

And so the tall tale of Mr Cumberpound began. He was a theatrical story teller, his face full of animation and all the emotion of the characters as he worked his way through the plot. Ewat was entranced, never had she heard such a story so well told. The fishermen could spin a yarn when they had an idle afternoon sat fussing over nets and smoking a pipe, and there was some beautiful music of sad folk laments playing in the village, but nothing quite like this.

Mr Cumberland was reaching the climax of his story, two thirds of his audience on tenterhooks. "Desist, Sir!" he cried, leaping forth from his chair. "For your honour is a sham and the money is a lie."

This declaration brought Mr Iredale out of his thoughts rather suddenly. "I'm no liar," he spat at the gentleman. In one swift move, he too leapt forth from his chair, in fluid movement picking up the wrought iron candlestick close to him. He raised it high and without hesitation brought it down onto Mr Cumberpound's head with a nauseating crunch.

Ewat gasped and brought a hand to her mouth. There was a shocked silence, not even Mr Cumberpound had predicted this ending. He started to raise his hand, as if there was one final point to make, then stupefied raised his eyes as if he would examine his own head. Everything was still. Silently, a line like a snake began to twist a path out of his hair. It was thick and dark and viscous. His forehead started to break apart. With a shriek from Ewat, Mr Cumberpound dropped forward onto the table, slid back and collapsed to the floor. He breathed no more.

Silence in its calm state took over the room. The fire crackled on as if nothing had happened. Outside the wind picked up and started to howl at the windows as if it knew there had been a death. At the bottom of the window panes a drift was forming. The moment was on pause, and until anyone spoke, perhaps this thing had not really happened. Maybe Mr Cumberpound would jump up again and laugh. It had just been the dramatic, theatrical finish to the tale he had been telling. A pool of blood was oozing outwards across the flagstones.

"Mr Cumberpound?" Ewat almost whimpered the question. "Are you all right?"

Callum closed his eyes. "What have you done?"

Mr Iredale replaced the candlestick on the side, then with energy and strength that surprised everyone, hoisted the table out of the way so that there was only Mr Cumberpound's crumpled body infront of the fire. "Good riddance, I say," he declared. "I don't care how well-to-do a person is; he doesn't do that to my daughters and get away with it. Quick lad, we'll check his pockets."

Callum felt sick. He watched as his father bent over the body, rolled it onto its back, and went through the pockets. He eventually found a purse, quite heavy with coin and notes. He shook the purse in his son's direction. "This will be a saving. To help us through the lean times. You tell no one."

"Father, you are dreaming. My sisters have been gone from this place years. Mr Cumberpound had done nothing. And even if he had, you can't play executioner..."

Daniel Iredale spat at the ground.

Ewat crouched down beside the felled man. She gently nudged his shoulder. "Mr Cumberpound? Are you still with us?" she asked. His eyes were wide open, staring up at the darkened ceiling, flickering with shadows. Lost in that highpoint of telling a good story. He wouldn't respond now.

"We'll bury him, here," Mr Iredale decided. "Roll him away now, lad." He pushed the body away from the fireside, making Ewat stumble backwards out of the way with a moan. "Get them flagstones up in front of the fireplace. It's the earth under; we'll dig a good hole and plant the bugger."

"We can't cover this up!"

"Someone will hang for it if we don't." Mr Iredale stood up again and left the room.

Callum looked around for Ewat, who was standing some distance off crying. "Miss Longbottom," he started walking over to her. "I don't know what has come over my father. Please don't be afraid."

"I know it's not your fault. It's his diseased mind," Ewat whimpered. Her hands were beginning to shake. "But poor Mr Cumberpound. What will his mother think?"

"His mother?"

"Everyone has a mother and she will be heartbroken when she knows he is dead."

The repercussions of his father's hasty and warped mind were firing off one by one to Callum. This was a mess, a really big mess, growing ever more tangled by the moment. Callum wasn't sure he'd be able to fight his way out to end up in any position he wished to exist in. "It might happen that his mother will never know..." he started gently.

Ewat looked horrified. "So he'd just disappear? That happened to my aunt and she was never the same since. She turned awful harsh and cold. Hasn't spoken to her brother since. Abandoned one of her other daughters."

"I don't think there will be a happy end to this whatever we do."

"Oh God," Ewat burst out. Her hands were shaking so much, the cold from outside really creeping into the room and sticking daggers in her back. One of her shawls had dropped to the floor at some point and as she turned around to try and flee, her feet became tangled up and she went to fall. Callum caught her and she couldn't think anymore, sobbing on behalf of Mr Cumberpound and his poor mother, a woman she imagined with dainty lace collars and cuffs and an adoring collection of her son's books on her shelf. And here was her punishment for turning Gerry down, for refusing to do the sensible thing and leave on the cart with him. She might even have been home by now, with her own mother, safe in her home and oblivious to the fate of Mr Cumberpound.

Callum held her like a little child and was shocked to feel how much she was shaking. "I reckon we need a drop of brandy in you."

"Only bad girls drink brandy."

"You've had a shock, and need something to steady you." He led her across to the bar, and leaning over, pulled out a bottle of brandy. "Shock can cause mischief with a person. Why, I've seen it kill a man." He set Ewat down on a chair then looked about for a glass but could only find a tankard. He poured out a measure. "I remember years ago there was a cave in at father's mine. He has a little mine out the back, it supplemented our income. It were father and a lad working in there. Father was on the right side of things when the ceiling came down." He passed the drink to Ewat and encouraged her to take a sip, smiling gently when she screwed up her face as the liquid burned down her throat.

"So the lad died in the crush?"

"Oh no, he survived that. He was buried. Father had to dig him out, but he did it, got the lad out into the air. A prop had fallen over, lodged at an angle and saved the lad from being crushed from the big rocks. He was alive and well when father dragged him out. But he never made a sound. Like he couldn't believe what had happened; that he were still alive. He just shut down. He died that night."

Ewat took another swing of the brandy, certain she wasn't going to shut down this evening.

"There we are," Mr Iredale re entered the room with a couple of shovels in hand, along with a metal bar. "We'll get them there flagstones pried up, then we'll dig down and bury him."

"We can't bury him here!" Callum exclaimed. "A rotting body. It'll stink the place out. Besides, we can't lie about this. A man has died. His family need to know."

"Do they need to know what he did as well?" Mr Iredale glowered. "The law won't be interested in the like of truth and circumstance. They'll see a poor innkeeping family who struggle for money, and a dead rich man who is their social better. Someone will hang for it."

Callum's protest fell silent. He couldn't let them take his father, couldn't let the public make a spectacle of this ill old man. But Callum wasn't prepared to sacrifice his own life either. His father was right in that, the law wouldn't consider their case. He remembered a few years ago the magistrate and his men had turned up, chasing after a couple of thieves who had been robbing at one of the manor houses. Idiotic lads really, who didn't think beyond the day. They'd turned up at the Red Lion and started spending their ill gotten gains. They were drunk as lords when the magistrate arrived. They should have been miles gone by then. Miles they certainly gained in the end, for they had been tried at York and sentenced to transportation. Patrons and keepers of the Red Lion alike had seen the drama unfold before their very eyes as the squire who had been robbed turned up, roaring like a lion and looking like an over ripe plum. It had been the talk of the area for months.

Mr Iredale produced a knife. "We'll gut him."

"Oh no," Ewat moaned.

"Just as we do when we have to bury a sheep. Get them gutted and buried deep enough and they'll cause you no bother. You get started on the digging and I'll deal with him."

"No!" Callum burst out as his father stalked the corpse. "I.. look, it'll be messy," he started in inspiration. "Blood everywhere."

"That's how it is."

"Aye, but you don't want to be leaving any signs of this for folk to see. Wait till the hole's dug."

"And gut him down there," Mr Iredale concluded. "Good thinking, my lad." He looked over at Ewat. "Perhaps our lass needs to go for a lie down."

"Perhaps she does. Come, Miss Longbottom." Callum took her by the shoulders and led her down a corridor to the kitchen where a fire crackled brightly. There was an old wooden bench box that served as a maid's bed. There were blankets inside, which Callum took out. "You should rest here for a bit, take these to keep you warm. I'll go deal with father. Don't worry, we'll work it all out."

Back in the public area Mr Iredale was starting to lever up the flagstones with the metal pole he had brought. He looked gaunt and frail yet his physical strength had yet to desert him. Callum rolled Mr Cumberpound away to the far side of the room, for he could not have the body staring at him whilst he decided to settle on a course of action. For now he would help with the grave, if only to keep his father calm and distracted, but he was still not sure if anyone would be going in there. They soon had the flagstones cleared and worked on the hole, piles of earth mounding up at either end, shadows in the room growing longer, almost becoming mourners to this very secret of funerals. When Mr Iredale stood in the hole, found that his head was level with the floor, he decided they had dug enough. They had been at it for hours; father in the hole and Callum out on the top shifting the earth in the room so that it would not collapse back into the hole. Both men were overly warm and dripping with sweat.

"I reckon that'll be right," he said. "Give me a hand up out of here."

Callum helped his father out of the hole, and Mr Iredale went to fetch his knife. Callum happened to glance back into the grave and saw something lying in the bottom. "Father, you've dropped something." He sat down on the edge and dropped down into the hole to retrieve the item. Crouching down, he ran his hand along its edge, wondering what it was as he realised it was half buried in the hole. His father must have trampled it back down as he had finished the digging. Callum used his hands to loosen more of the earth, and finally managed to pull it out. He sat on his haunches, dumbfounded to find himself holding a long bone. It looked as though there were more down there. Putting it to one side he started to scrabble through the earth and pulled out several short, stubby little rocks, or rather bones, lots of them. Brushing aside a handful of earth, he uncovered a few of the little bones in situ and saw that they could resemble a man's foot.

He scrambled back in horror. There was already someone down here? All these years he'd lived and worked here and he never knew there had been a body buried in the inn. Had it been here long before his family came here? One couldn't really tell how old a bone was, but a man lay dead, concealed in the floor. Callum stood up, feeling a little queasy, and watched as his father started to drag Mr Cumberpound to his grave. His father's mind was warped, and he had been somewhere else when he had made the attack. He'd spoken of Callum's sisters. This wasn't the first time this had happened.

"Help me, lad," Mr Iredale grunted. "We'll get him in and gutted, then we'll go steady with the earth. Tamp it down regular. The ground'll still settle afterwards, but we'll keep an eye on the flagstones. Top them up as and when so they don't tell anything. We'll put the spare earth away in the cellar."

Callum pulled himself quickly out of the hole, saying nothing of the bones he had just unearthed. He watched as Mr Cumberpound rolled heavily into the hole. He did not know what to think. All these years, his father a killer? But why, who had it been and why had he never been missed? Was it really possible to get away with such things? It was beyond explanation or resolution. The dead creature down there; Mr Cumberpound. It was all lost within his father's crumbling mind.

There was nothing Callum could do. So he sat and watched as his father got on with the work he knew, then he helped to fill in the hole.

Ewat woke up to a cold hard surface and poor light. The fire had almost gone out and one of her blankets had dropped to the floor whilst she had slept. She sat up and looked about her, wondering where she was and why she came to be sleeping here. She ran her hand over the edge of the blanket and remembered Callum had brought her here. Oh God, she felt the gorge rise as she recalled Mr Cumberpound's face as Mr Iredale had attacked him with the candlestick. It could not have really happened, could it? Surely not? Here she was, stranded at the scene of a murder. She could not say which was worse, the unprovoked attack or that Gerry could leave her on the top of Blakey Ridge in the middle of a snow storm. He'd not even regretted himself after five minutes and returned. He'd just left her.

Swinging her legs around, she placed her feet on the floor and leaned forward, closing her eyes as she pressed her face into her skirts. Maybe it was all a strange dream and she would wake up soon, Agnes prodding her in the spine and telling her to get a move on. She sat up, stretched her arms to the ceiling then got up and went to the window. Dawn was creeping upon a white-cast world. Half the window pane was drifted with snow, and what she could see beyond was all the same hue. It appeared to have stopped snowing.

Ewat faltered in the doorway to the public rooms. Everything was as she remembered, the furniture back how it had been, the fire crackling away and the floor as it had always been. Any nonsense of burying the man had been discarded. Or perhaps he had not really been dead, only stunned, or she misremembered somehow and Mr Iredale hadn't attacked anyone.

There was a chill moving through the room, for the door was open and Callum stood on the threshold, his back to the interior. The snow was shin deep outside. The air very still, silence radiating from the snow crystals.

"Callum, are you well?"

He was slow to respond, looking over his shoulder to her. He looked exhausted, much older than his years. He hadn't slept and didn't know when peace would overcome him. There were too many details to be worked out before he could rest easy.

Ewat crept up to him, and stood at his side, almost touching his arm and barely daring to breathe. "I'm not sure if I've misremembered something. So many things happened last night. Gerry left me..."

"He hasn't come back."

"And then Mr Cumberpound..."

"He is dead."

"Oh." She put her hand to her mouth. "Poor Mr Cumberpound."

"I'm sorry to force this subject upon you, but we must make decisions whilst we have the peace of the place. I don't know how long it will be before folks come. There's some drifting, but it's not so bad, and I reckon your people will be coming for you."

Ewat nodded.

"Forgive me to distress you but I must be blunt. If what happened is discovered, someone will hang. I can't let my father go through that spectacle. His mind, it's... but they'd just as much say as I did it."

"Oh, but if you explained it to the squire, I'm sure he'd believe you."

"Rich folks don't believe the working man." Callum shook his head. "They'll say we killed him for his money, thinking we'd take advantage of the snow storm. Besides, it's already done now. Father had the energy of ten young men last night. We have dug the hole and buried him." He did not mention the gutting, nor what he had seen in the bottom of the pit. Some things needed to remain unknown, if they had been forgotten for this long.

"I think I want to forget it all."

"Thing is, I need to know where you stand."

"It doesn't matter about me."

"You saw it all. I have to ask you Ewat, will you keep this secret?"

"And his mother will never know?"

He shook his head. "Certainly not the truth. She'll know he disappeared. I am thinking of turning the horse out, sending it down the road. I'll say Mr Cumberpound set off last night in the storm. He's a southerner, doesn't know these parts. It's not unknown for folk to get lost on the moors and freeze to death."

She narrowed her eyes a little as the brightness of the snow gleamed. The rays from the sun, what they were, were starting to come over the horizon. "You can't do that."

"You won't stand by us?" Callum wasn't sure why he wasn't more disappointed; that she would not protect them from the noose, or that she wouldn't do it for him.

"I mean you can't say that was the way it was. There'll be searches and talk all over the moors. Gerry'll hear about it, and he saw Mr Cumberpound last night. He was very adamant we should stay at the inn, wasn't he? Gerry won't believe he then just wandered off."

Callum drew a hand over his weary face. "You're right. He can't have left in the storm. He needs to leave when there's been no one else about. I'll say he set off at first light. It stopped snowing a good couple of hours ago. That's the story, I'll get the horse saddled up and out now."

Ewat followed Callum to the stable for want of anything better to do. They got the horse saddled and bridled up, and walked around to the front of the inn. Callum walked the beast down to the road, the pair of them struggling through the depths of snow. They stopped, the horse facing inland and looking bewildered as if to ask, what now? Callum let go of the reigns and walked back a few yards.

"Away with you."

The horse just stared at him. A few wisps of snow started to fall. Callum smacked the horse on the rear quarters, which set off a steam of a snort and a few indignant steps forward, then it stopped.

"Get gone. I can't have you hanging around here, do you hear?" He walked back to Ewat, hoping the horse would realise it was not wanted. "Will you get going!" He threw a snowball at the creature. The horse snorted and took a few steps.

"If one of the farmers takes it on himself to get the sleigh out and come up here..."

"What are you doing?!" Mr Iredale roared from the doorway.

The horse looked skittish.

"Good butchering!" Mr Iredale started to run towards them, wading through the snow. He wasn't dressed for the weather. He wore only a threadbare shirt and trousers, but he was oblivious to what Ewat and Callum saw. His roar increased as he ran for the horse. The beast's eyes filled with panic, it whinnied and started its own clumsy run through the snow along the road.

"Father!" Callum started after his father to pull him back.

"I'll be back, my lad!" His father shouted, waving him off and running after the horse.

The horse was getting into a rhythm of this new kind of travel, kicking up snow as it went.

"I don't know what to do." Callum stared bleary eyed after them.

The snow fall was picking up. Ewat shivered and looked at her folded arms under her shawl. There was a layer of snow already forming on the wool. "We should go back in," she said. "Behave as if what you said is true. I'll be waiting for my father, and you'll be angry that no one has listened to your sense and gone out in the snow. Wondering how far Mr Cumberpound will get before he turns back."

"That may be, but I'll have to get my father. You wait back in the inn. I shouldn't be long." Callum started after the man and the horse, taking advantage of the tracks in the snow to move more easily. By the time he caught up with his father it was snowing heavily, the wind picking up and lashing the snow into their faces. Another storm was brewing and they needed to be indoors. Callum struggled with his father, who would not listen to sense. After shouting and pulling and pushing, Mr Iredale felt his rage boil and he swung around and punched his son square in the face before running off after the horse. Callum fell backwards in the snow, drops of blood spraying out from his nose. He swore angrily, struggling to get up onto his feet again and falling a couple of times before he was up. He yelled some obscenity at his father, a blurred figure in the distance before disappearing into the whiteout. Callum looked about him. He wasn't sure himself exactly now where he stood. He stepped down and found the tracks, horse and man in both directions, already starting to fill in. Guessing which direction held the Red Lion, he pulled his collar up, put his head down and leant into the storm. It was a slow walk, but he had picked rightly, and was relieved to find himself stepping into the yard and up to the familiar shape of the inn, snow capped and embraced by drifts, a lamp set in the window shining brightly. Inside the fire blazed and soup and hot drink waited, along with a terrified Ewat, fearing that in this winter-riddled misery, she would find herself as the last creature standing on the top of the world.

Mr Iredale was returned home the following day by one of the local farmers. The farmer had had his sleigh rigged up and had been travelling over the tops of the moors. On the snow-stilled journey he had noticed something up at one of the large moorland crosses. He'd stopped the horse and gone over to investigate, shocked when he'd recognised the old landlord of the Red Lion. Horrified when he saw the glassy open eyes, already misted over, and the blue skin. The man was quite dead. He must have perished in the night.

The farmer loaded the corpse into his sleigh, and continued on across Blakey Moor. There had been something wrong with Mr Iredale the last few years. Folk said it was the drink, but the farmer had spoken to him a couple of times as it was as if Mr Iredale didn't quite see him, or rather not as he was now, but as he had been. And another time it was as if he didn't even speak the language. It was a damned tragedy that he had wandered off in the storm and perished, but when a man lost his mind to that extent there was no saving him. Callum had done his best by his father, the farmer assured him, better than a lot of sons would have done, and he had nothing to feel guilt over. Perhaps it was a mercy that it was over, for it could not be a good way for a man to live, not such a hardworking, reliable sort as Daniel Iredale had been known to be.

Daniel Iredale's body was at rest in his room, carried there by the farmer and Callum. The three of them were in the public room by the fire, the farmer taking a draught of warm ale for his work and a rest by the fire. He watched the silent lassie and curiosity got the better of him. "You the new maid, then? You'll be in great need now that young Callum here has the running of the inn on his own."

Ewat's eyes were wide open in surprise at the assumption. Her mind immediately leapt upon the suggestion. It could be a good one.

"No," Callum, who still looked stunned from a sharp slapping, answered on her behalf. "Miss Longbottom is here sheltering from the snow storm. She was travelling over the tops the other night when the snow blew up. The driver decided to carry on but she did not feel it safe."

The farmer nodded slowly, drawing in the air between his teeth. "Aye, I can see the sense, especially for a young scrap of a thing as yourself. Does that leave you stranded here now? Where are you heading? Perhaps I can take you on?"

"Runswick Bay."

"Runswick? By, you've still a bit of travelling ahead of you. If the weather was better you could walk of course, but if you're not familiar with the moors in this weather."

"My father will be coming for me," Ewat spoke weakly, feeling a little miserable at the prospect. Then that would be that and she would have to go to Canada."

"He know his way?"

"He was raised in Commondale, and later Glaisdale."

"Commondale you say? He'd not be William Longbottom's lad?"

"That was my grandfather's name."

"Aye, and his son of the same name keeps up the same work. He's good, but not as good as his father was." The farmer shook his head to himself. "Now old William Longbottom, there was a hardworker. And he travelled all over to get the work done. He was hardly ever at home. It was a wonder he sired as many children as he did!" he chortled, rocking back on his chair. He looked at Ewat and settled down, remembering there were young lasses present who wouldn't understand such jests. "Aye, well. Good honest man, that William. And your father, he's a smithy as well?"

"Carpenter."

"Good honest craft there." He nodded to himself, then stretched out his limbs to wake them up. Back onto his feet, for there were still many chores to complete before the daylight faded. "I'll head down to Rosedale Abbey, shall I?" he asked, referring to the little village in the bottom of the valley across from the inn. "You'll be wanting father in at the priory church?"

Callum nodded dumbly. Already it was time to talk of planting his father.

"I'll get word sent to the reverend. We'll get it ready for the burial. I'll be back with my good wife. Help with the washing and the like?"

"Washing?"

"Aye, of the body. Get him ready." The famer patted Callum on the shoulder. "Don't you be worrying, we'll see you right. I know this is a lot when you're young and on your own. I'd best be off now."

"Oh, Mr Cumberpound." Ewat darted forward as he went for the door.

The farmer started laughing. "Begging your pardon, Miss, but I don't go by such a curious sound."

"I meant to say, did you see Mr Cumberpound?" Ewat explained. Mr Iredale may be dead, but they had to get their other stories straight and started regardless. "He sheltered here last night as well, but he was so adamant to be off, the moment the snow had stopped and there was a drop of light in the sky. He was off on his horse the moment he could. Then the snow blew up again."

He regarded the young woman. "There was another staying here?"

"Mr Cumberpound."

By this point Callum had sunk into a chair, as if the weight of everything was growing too much for him. He ran a hand over his face.

"He was a gentleman traveller, on his own horse. The Lord himself only knows what he was doing travelling about at this time of year. He'd come from Whitby, up onto the moors, and the snow had become too much."

"Nowt as queer as folk," the older man muttered. "And what way was he heading?"

"South, to York."

"I've not see any fool riding a horse in any direction today." He paused. "Mind you, old Dan was on about some horse that turned up. I thought he was just cracked, but perhaps there's something in it. But it were only a horse mind, no rider. You telling me there might be a man out there on the moors?"

"Could be."

He shook his head. "Another body to plant more than likely. I'll see if we can bring the bridles up later. Do you think you'd recognise them?"

Callum nodded. "It was expensive tack. Better than a lot of what I see passing through."

"I'll get word out that a man is missing. We'll be back soon." He nodded to Ewat. "Hope your father fetches you soon, Miss Longbottom."

"Thank you."

And with that the farmer was gone, the door banging shut after him. There were only two souls in the house. Silence and a crackling fire. Ewat lingered by the window, watching the farmer depart, before she returned to Callum's side. "I hope you don't mind me mentioning Mr Cumberpound, only I thought it best to get word out as soon as possible, else people might wonder."

"Aye," Callum sighed. "You're probably right. I find I can't think straight just the now."

Ewat sat down opposite him and fiddled awkwardly with the ends of her shawl. "He was right though, what the farmer was saying, about you needing help now that you're all on your own." She scraped her shoe around on the flagstone for a moment in idle awkwardness, before she remembered that deep below there lay the remains of poor

Mr Cumberpound. "You'll be in want of a housemaid, housekeeper or the like. What I mean to say is, I'm in search of a position. I'm not wanting to sail away to Canada..."

"Canada," Callum interrupted, deaf to her business proposition. "I ought to get away now. There's the money father took off him. It would easy pay for passage, then I'd be a long way from all this trouble. Start again. Set off as soon as father's buried."

Ewat stared miserably at the floor. "I don't know that would be such a good idea," she began, still working out the logic of it all as she spoke. "People might wonder about what happened to Mr Cumberpound. Why you're running."

"No one knows father killed him."

"But what I mean to say is, people love a good story. And they'll make up things if they don't know the truth."

"They won't call me a murderer."

"You called my grandmother a witch."

He looked genuinely shocked at the charge. "I've never said the sort."

"Not knowingly. But you were telling Mr Cumberpound about that hob and his daughters. One that flew about and was a witch killing cows and the other who killed her husband."

"That is true, father saw the execution."

"I don't know about that. But my grandmother didn't fly in the sky..."

"You're from that family?" Callum was surprised. "Aye, but you said about that old smithy being your grandfather. I think it was his wife, his first wife I mean..."

"Most of her children died all at once of some fever. Only my aunt, uncle and father survived. It broke her, the grief. She died very young." Ewat paused. "Oh Callum, I'm not angry at you, I know how these tales are. But this is my point, people love a story. Your father died, Mr Cumberpound disappears in the snow but his horse appears, and you run off to Canada. They'll never find Mr Cumberpound and they'll get to gossiping. What if someone thought to dig up the floor?"

"I'd not allow that."

"But you'd be away to Canada. Do you see? And if they ever found something, you couldn't say your father did it for who would believe you?"

He hung his head. "And I'd hang for it all." He thought again of the body he'd seen, whoever it might be. It would turn into a bigger, sorrier mess than even Ewat could imagine. "You're right of course. I can not think right from left just now."

"No, it's all been a terrible shock." Ewat said quietly.

And that was the moment that the inn door burst open and her father strode in, red-nosed and with a dusting of snow on his cap. "Ewat, lass!" he cried, striding across the room. "Thank God you're well."

He was followed into the building by her Uncle William. Jeremiah had walked over to Commondale, and the two of them had come up on William's sleigh. William would drive them all the way back to Runswick now, so that Sonneta would have her daughter back safe at home before the end of the day.

"I cursed that Gerry Waterson for leaving you up here on your own." Jeremiah said as he clasped his daughter to him. A tall young woman, but still a toddler girl in his eyes. "I don't know what he was thinking, but that's the end of your travels with him. He can not be trusted. I told him straight, I was mightily disappointed in his behaviour. And to think we had hopes you two might have been wed one day."

Ewat squeezed her eyes shut and buried her face into her father's coats.

Callum stood up. "Good Afternoon gentlemen, can I offer you anything? It must have been a cold journey."

"No thank you. We must be setting off forth with if we're to make Runswick by dark," William spoke. "We have to thank you for looking after Ewat in these circumstances."

"No need. The inn's here for stranded travellers. The weather was not good last night."

"Do we owe...?"

Callum shook his head at the offer. "It was my pleasure."

"I don't believe we've met before..."

"Callum Iredale," he spoke, offering his hand. "I run the inn."

"Ah, the landlord," Jeremiah nodded.

William looked questioning. "I thought the landlord was an older man."

"My father. He has passed..."

"Oh, my condolences." He looked abashed now. "We are indebted to you. Jeremiah," he said, the debt already forgotten as he turned to his brother, eager to be gone from the high moors. "We need to start off. The light will only hold so long and I do not like the look of that sky."

"Yes, of course. Many thanks again, Mr Iredale."

Ewat twisted under her father's arm as they headed for the door. Smiling sadly at Callum. Half hoping he would rush at them with desperate proposals of marriage or at the very least an offer of a job. Some helping hand after all they had been through together. Instead he nodded warmly at her, as if to say do not worry, it's finished for your part now. They left the building, the door closed firmly behind them. And that, Ewat supposed, was quite the end of that.

"Of course there was nothing to that. They were just old family friends."

Ewat was slouched in a pile of rope and netting as if she herself had been slung there as an obsolete tool. She was working on a piece of knitting, but couldn't settle in the house, or anywhere people watched her. She was lucky the spring was mild this year and already in April it was quite warm enough to sit outside and work sedentary for hours. She slunk about the village, trying to find a corner she could hide in, avoiding people's questions and looks as she went. Gossip was always the same. Some elements of misunderstood truth and a lot of imagination. People knew she had travelled a lot with Gerry Waterson. They also knew during one wintry storm he had returned without her. Jeremiah had been very angry with Gerry, and Ewat had been fetched back late the following day. The Longbottoms didn't talk so much about it, but then they were incomers and a strange lot. They'd be leaving in less than a month anyway. Gerry Waterson had said all kinds of things, although Ewat refusal of his offer had never popped up in any version she had heard.

Andrea Baker, a couple of years younger than Ewat, and one of her friends, were coming up the narrow track from the shore. They hadn't seen Ewat, who pushed herself back into the nets.

"They're going to Canada soon anyway."

She closed her eyes as she heard the young friend respond to Andrea's comment. Yet again. They wouldn't cease to be the topic of discussion until long after they'd left.

"I know, and thank goodness," Andrea agreed. "It still makes Gerry a little angry when he sees her. Especially after all he did, and then for them to behave like that."

"He was just being kind?"

"That's what he told me," Andrea said in a proprietal tone. "But they're not Nagars, so what could you expect. Anyway, it's all to the good because I am going to York now, and learning about the mongering trade."

"I suppose you'll need to understand it soon enough."

"You think I'll make a fine fish monger, do you?" Andrea giggled.

"No, but you might make a fine fish monger's wife!" The two girls giggled and linked arms, heads together in conspiracy as they sauntered up the track, passing Ewat without ever noticing her. Gerry had taken to flaunting Andrea Baker's company in a most painful way since he had taken up with her. Andrea didn't work as much at the shore helping with the day's catch anymore, for she was forever up on the carts with Gerry, travelling over to York or Kirkbymoorside. Locals nodded knowingly and said there's the future Mrs Waterson. Lucky lass, she'll be set for life. Occasionally someone said they'd wondered if he'd been after Ewat, but that idea was soon knocked back. The Longbottoms were off to Canada and besides, Ewat was a bit of an odd lass.

She looked down at her knitting, something she rarely did for Ewat was very competent, born and raised with the needles. She realised she'd dropped three stitches in the last two rows. Ewat huffed to herself and started to unravel the rows. She had to admit that she missed the trips to York desperately. The rush of the cart, travelling up over the moors and seeing all those little villages and valleys. Colours, hues and scents, a sense of the bigger world and all those people, all those lives. And now Andrea Baker was enjoying it all. Ewat supposed they'd still get to stop off at the Red Lion to change the horses. Only now Callum would smile at Andrea Baker and make easy conversation with her. She wondered how he was faring now that his father was buried, the snows were gone and he was running a busy inn all on his own. She only got the odd titbit of offhand discussion from people. She knew he was still there – thankfully he had taken her advice and not run off to Canada. But to say a man lived in a house said nothing of his mind or his day to day life, and there was no way to reach that information now. Father had read something in the paper about Mr Cumberpound missing on the moors. His family had even offered a reward for information. Nothing ever came up. The case as reported was that he had taken shelter that night in the storm, before setting off at break of dawn on his horse. The horse had trotted up to a local farm, riderless, and been taken in. A search had been made for the rider, but as the snow had picked up again, the horses' tracks were lost, and the area had a big, wide expanse of open moorland. Searches were made as the snows relented, but the papers reported that it happened that men were lost, especially those who were not familiar with the lie of the land. Whilst some unlucky travellers were found when the snows melted, others were simply absorbed into the landscape. There were boggy areas where a man could be consumed.

An investigator, hired by the family, had been by a week or so ago to speak to Ewat. She had recounted the story as agreed with Callum, and hoped he remained true to it as well. She knew the man had also spoken to Gerry, who had only a little to contribute, and had kept to the truth on that occasion. But she had heard him chattering drunkenly to his friends one evening when they were leaving the pub. He'd laughed that Ewat had probably set her cap at the rich traveller – such ideas had the girl, local lads wouldn't be good enough for her – and in his terror, Mr Cumberpound had ridden off in a blind panic onto the moors.

She wondered about Mr Cumberpound's mother, and that was the point on which she felt the worst. The woman would have been told that her son was probably dead. But there would never be a body or any definite explanation as to what had happened. And forth from that there would be a vague dull sense of hope coupled with exhausted desolation. Ewat could remember how her aunt had been when her cousin Kerenza vanished like that in Commondale. That had been on a summer's day, bright and hopeful. Time settled the gnawing urgency, and she supposed Aunt Prudence accepted that Kerenza was long dead, but there was always something missing in her eyes since it had happened. As if she had learned to live with it all, but would never really get over it. And so Ewat had helped to condemn Mr Cumberpound's mother to the same fate. But it was up against the alternative of Callum Iredale being hung for a murder he did not commit, and so ever would the old woman have to suffer.

An urgent pull on her shoulder brought her from her thoughts. Agnes leaned over her, her eyes in a bit of a panic.

"What are you doing hiding away here?"

Ewat huffed. "Trying to get a bit of peace so I might finish this."

"You've dropped a stitch there."

"Oh, for..." she slung the needles down into her lap. She'd just re knitted that section. What was wrong with her? Ewat never dropped stitches.

"Look, you've got to come back now," Agnes told her. "There's a man speaking to father. You're wanted."

Ewat felt a sickness ball up in her stomach. "A man? What about?"

"I don't know. I didn't hear that much before mother shooed me off to find you. Blakey Ridge I heard." Agnes paused. "That's where that man disappeared, isn't it?"

"Yes." She wondered if she was going to throw up. The investigator was back. He had said last time that she was one of the last people to see Mr Cumberpound alive and that made her important. Her and Callum and old Mr Iredale who had been found dead out on the moors. That was something the man had been very interested in, the state of mind of old Mr Iredale. What had been going on with him and Mr Cumberpound? Ewat couldn't say that she knew of anything.

"Do you think you're in trouble?" Agnes asked.

"I haven't done anything," Ewat mumbled. True, she was innocent of the murder and the burial, but she was embroiled in the lying. Lying before God.

"Come on then, best get it over with." Agnes pulled her sister out of her nest of nets, and the two of them trudged up to the Longbottom cottage as if heading for an execution. Their mother was sitting outside, nervously shuffling and crying. Her knitting was put away in her apron pocket, even that could not distract her, although her idle hands were skittish, and fussed with the creases of her apron as she sat. She wiped her eyes with the back of her hand when she saw Ewat and Agnes coming up the hill.

"Oh, Ewat."

"Now then, daughter." Jeremiah appeared in the open doorway of the cottage. "This is all sudden and shocking news to us, but I suppose you'll have known all about it for a good few months now..."

A voice from inside the cottage started a protest. "Oh no, I haven't yet..."

"And you won't be able to come to Canada with us."

Ewat paled. She heard her mother start crying again. Oh God, what if it was all worse than the truth. Perhaps the story had been told different, perhaps they'd heard Gerry's nonsense about her setting her cap at Mr Cumberpound, and now it was decided that she had killed him. Her hands started shaking, and she felt her sister take her hand and stand by her side. Their fingers gripped one another tightly.

"Mr Longbottom, I've not had chance to speak to your daughter yet." A figure appeared in the shadows of the doorway behind Jeremiah.

"Aye, well," Jeremiah gave the young man a sidelong glance then stepped out of the doorway so he may exit as well. Cap in hand, Callum Iredale stepped out into the light. He looked a little uncomfortable, which was not how she remembered his easy, confident manner. Likewise his dress was different, and he looked like he was in his Sunday best, all brushed and polished but desperate to break out and be back in his usual shirt and waistcoat, dealing with the horses or chatting broadly with the merchants and local farmers who passed by the moorland tops. His hands were worrying the brim of his hat.

"You do as you please," Jeremiah advised. "What you want. And don't be worrying about your mother and me."

Ewat didn't think one got a choice when it came to punishment for murder.

Callum stepped forward awkwardly, "Might I...?"

Agnes' eyes widened as she looked from the stranger to her sister, realising what was happening, furious that this had not been discussed already on a night. Then hit by an aching panic when she realised this would mean that Ewat wouldn't be coming with them.

"Ewat, could I; I mean Miss Longbottom, could I have a word?" Callum walked up to the girls and gestured further up the track with his head.

"Very well." Ewat started ahead of him, still clutching Agnes's hand. Her sister laughed and shook her off, saying she didn't think she needed to attend, before skipping off down back to her mother. Ewat looked back for her, feeling bereft. But it was better not to drag Agnes into all of this. She and Callum started up the track. She was conscious of the fishermen's wives glancing out of open doorways, ears aimed at windows left open. Callum was a stranger here and now the top of the list when it came to conversation. Everyone wanted to be the first to know. Ewat glanced over at Callum, then nodded to the buildings they were passing. "Perhaps we ought to walk a little higher."

"Aye."

They walked in a steady silence up out of the village. Normally Ewat would have been giddy to see Callum again, for she had missed him dreadfully. In truth the shock of his appearing at her home had sent her thoughts spinning, and the simple joy of seeing someone she held close had been forgotten.

It was as they came out onto the top of the cliffs that Callum started to speak. "I am sorry I've already spoke to your father. I did mean to speak to you first, but I didn't find you, and then when I found myself in front of your father at his door, it felt that an explanation was necessary."

Ewat nodded. "I understand, I suppose. But you shouldn't be feeling guilty. You didn't do it, and nothing you do now will change the fact that he's gone."

"He's gone?"

"Yes." Her eyes widened and her voice lowered. "Mr Cumberpound of course. Please tell me you haven't done a stupid thing and confessed, because I don't think I could bare the thought of you hanging. And I know it is a terrible thing for his mother, but he is gone and we can't bring him back."

"Oh no, Ewat, you..."

"I told that man how it was, how we'd talked it over that morning, just how we'd said."

"I'm not here about Mr Cumberpound. You don't need to worry about that. The magistrate has judged it as misadventure, and that the man is lost on the moors. The matter has been brought to a close. I know it will always hang over me in my mind, but I don't think anything good can come of telling the rest of the truth now."

The knotted tension broke and Ewat beamed. "I'm so glad to hear it. Really. I can't tell you how sick I felt when Agnes told me there was a man to see father, and I feared the worst."

Callum looked concerned. "I hadn't realised this had been troubling you so much. I'm very sorry for it."

"No, don't worry. It's all well now."

"Bloody Mr Cumberpound," he burst out suddenly. "I didn't even come here about him, and here we are worrying about dead men."

"Oh. Then why are you come?" Her face brightened as an idea came to her. "Have you come to offer me the position? Like I suggested? A maid, or maybe even a housekeeper, although I'd admit I don't have so much experience, but I'll learn quick.."

"No, Ewat, I'm not here about employment," Callum interrupted.

Ewat's smile dropped again. She looked at Callum, him worrying his hat again as if he would worry it into another shape. She'd never seen him so nervous. Perhaps he'd come to tell her that he was stealing Andrea Baker away from Gerry.

"I am come to ask if you'll have me?"

"Have you do what?"

"Do what? Look, I..." he followed her line of sight and saw she was staring at his hat. He tossed it onto the grass, feeling his hands sweat up now that he had nothing to fidget with. She was not making this easy, and he might have accused her of making it excruciating, only that she didn't look as though she had caught on yet and was still worrying about jobs as maids and men buried under fireplaces. He took her by the shoulders. "Ewat Longbottom, I have come all this way to ask if you will have me for your husband?"

Ewat stared at him. It was one thing to daydream about romantic proposals and to sit and go over every conversation in minute detail, thinking on every gesture and glance and give it a meaning that had probably never been there in the first place. Then here it was, placed in front of her and on offer. She did not know what to say, and deep down if she were honest, she did not feel quite old enough. So she said nothing.

Callum's ease lessened a little. He knew that she'd already turned down Gerry Waterson. Judging by the way Gerry flaunted the new lass he had travelling with him, there was only Gerry, Ewat and Callum who knew about the first proposal, and Gerry was clearly in denial about any feeling attached to that. Callum had jumped to conclusions, hoping that Ewat stating she felt no love of that sort for Gerry meant that she was in love with someone else. And in his own mind he had built that up to be him. But he could have been wrong, he now saw. Perhaps it had all been nothing more than kindness and good nature, for she was a happy, thoughtful young woman. She had been good with everyone he had seen her interact with.

"It's usually traditional for you to give an answer, even if you wish to think on it." He spoke, realising now he really did need to be prepared for a refusal.

Ewat looked a little confused. "But I'm just a silly girl."

"No more than the rest of us. I can't tell you how much I've missed your passing visits these past months. I always looked forward to your bright smile when Mr Waterson's cart was coming to the Lion. I felt terrible when you told us that evening that Mr Waterson had made you a proposal of marriage, then such joy when you said you'd turned him down for you didn't love him. And perhaps I have jumped to conclusions because I always thought we'd had a connection since you'd first started coming up to Blakey. But then I know as well I will never be rich like Mr Waterson, and it can be a hard and isolated life up there, so I don't know that I have all that much to offer you. Only that I know my heart brightens with the thought of you. I've not known anyone else to do such a thing."

"You want to marry me?"

He let his breath go in an easing of relief, slipping back towards the charming smile and away from the nerves.

"That was the purpose of my visit."

Ewat broke out into a grin. "Really?"

Callum laughed. "I've not walked all the way to Runswick in jest."

She took hold of his over warm hands. "Well, I'd love to marry you, so I'm guessing there's only one thing to be done then."

He picked her up and swung her around, whooping with delight, Ewat laughing, before her feet returned to the grassy cliff tops. Callum kissed her and Ewat felt elation as she could finally curl herself into her place she had been longing for all this time.

Prudence Medd sat at her mother's grave and gazed out over Danby churchyard. Her mother was at her back, a strong and silent solid support pressed against her spine. Just a vague memory of childhood, occasionally brought back in vividness by the scent caught on a breeze.

She wiped at her eyes for the people she had lost and the years that had already passed by before she was ready to let go. She was now forty-six years of age, and life had led her down a path she had not thought on when she had been a young woman only approaching marriage. As a youngster she had been unable to imagine what really having a child might mean. She held out her hands before her, browned off from the current summer and working outdoors. Her nails were kept short, but there was a line of grime under each, for she could not keep out of her vegetable garden. There was solace in tending the earth.

A blackbird flew across her vision and sat on the top of a headstone, warbling to the approach of evening. Prudence's eyes drifted across the yard. From here she could see Curnow Pengelly, and the memorial to her lost child Kerenza; "lost on the moors"; and the wooden marker for a grave only a month dug, where she had buried her second husband, Gilbert Medd. It had been a quick death, and although she was sad for him she did not find herself devastated. They had been an amicable couple, but there had never been any love. She would manage. The decisions of his estate, made after their marriage, had left her in a better position than she had expected. She had assumed everything would go to his son, still in the army, and she would have to move on to find a new way of living. Instead he had left her the house and a small annual income. The rest of the money had been left for his son. That was all. Prudence didn't think she deserved so much, thinking herself little more than glorified housekeeper, but her youngest, Rosen, had said it was the very least she should have gotten, whilst eying the house with a mind to her own future. She had just turned sixteen, and in the same breath announced her engagement to Samuel Applecross. Working as a maid at one of the farms would serve her well for starting out when she did become a farmer's wife. In Prudence's eyes she still seemed terribly young for all that life of marriage and children. Really she was still a child herself. But Rosen was determined and certain of herself and just how she wanted things to be. She would not make a mess of life the way her mother had.

Besides, Rosen had told her one evening whilst visiting, her cousin Ewat was only a year older and she had just been married. And Rosen was far wiser of the world than Ewat ever would be. Ewat had seemed like a grinning young girl at the wedding, Prudence reflected. They had come to Danby to be wed in the end, perhaps returning to Ewat's forebears, but certainly not wanting to make an event in Runswick. They'd just managed to get the wedding in at the start of May, then on the seventh the rest of the family had boarded the ship Hindoo in Whitby and set sail for Canada.

Prudence felt bereft. It wasn't as if she had seen her brothers every week, in fact she still had nothing to do with William and Magdalene, and found it strange to see them still living and existing when they had all attended the wedding. All much older now, wrinkled and weighted down by the sadness of the past. Magdalene had looked as though she would go and speak to Prudence, but then thought better of it and dissolved back into the crowds. William had tried, but Prudence had averted her gaze and pointedly slunk away. Rosen had linked arms with her and they had left the church, Rosen commenting that such people were not worth any energy. They did not need people like that in their family, in truth they were no longer family, and Rosen and Prudence had all they needed. As Prudence looked over Jeremiah's brood of children, the tears and the hugs, she was not so sure any more if there wasn't something to be said for forgiveness. Or perhaps it wasn't even forgiveness, only an acceptance that life dealt hard hands and people could only muddle on as best they could. Perhaps others needed to forgive Prudence for how hard she had been. She stood and watched a tearful Sonneta embrace her newly wedded daughter, and wondered on how Derwa was faring.

Derwa had been gone three years. Prudence had not seen her since that day she had declared she could no longer live with her daughter. She understood the bones of what had happened since, for Rosen had kept up a gentle trickle of a correspondence with her elder sister. Her son, James, was now two years old, and they were living in a newly built village over in West Yorkshire. Some scheme by a distant rich relative. Her own cousin, Muriel was living there too and according to Rosen working as a doctor, but Prudence thought something must have gotten lost in the telling, for women weren't doctors. Although Muriel always had been an odd and clever one. If a woman ever was to be a doctor, she supposed Muriel would be the one.

Perhaps she ought to make contact. She'd voiced the suggestion casually to Rosen, who had Derwa's address, and not received the response she'd expected. Rosen had been furious. Derwa had shamed the family, and she ought not to expect to come back and drag down the rest of them into the gutter. And now that she had a child and couldn't get herself a husband, she expected family to mind her. Now that Gilbert Medd was dead, she'd be expecting a share of mother's fortune, was that it? Prudence had been quite taken aback by Rosen's anger. If Rosen hadn't told Derwa about Gilbert's death, then she was probably still ignorant of the fact. And she had never asked for a penny from Prudence. She'd taken the necklace, something she'd never mentioned to Rosen, but Prudence had let that go. It had been some time before she'd realised it was gone, and eventually guessed that Derwa must have taken it with her at the time. Given how Prudence had refused all help and support, she could hardly deny her that material back up.

"I'll not have her spoiling the name of my family and chances of my marriage," Rosen had told her mother, angry red spots appearing on her cheeks. "And she'll not come here to be a drain on my family. We'll not support her, not a penny."

Prudence wasn't sure who the 'we' referred to exactly. "I have not yet contacted her."

"And best we have nothing to do with her."

"Rosen, you've been writing to her all these years," Prudence pointed out. "And Derwa will not usurp you in any way. You needn't worry."

"I'm not worried," Rosen said haughtily. "I know I'm the better woman. But I'll have nothing to do with her now."

Prudence closed her eyes and rested her head against her mother's grave, remembering Rosen's face as she had almost shouted those words. They had precious little family left now. Why shun Derwa? Jeremiah's brood were all gone to Canada. That only left little Ewat setting up home on that windswept height of Blakey Ridge. William and Magdalene were still here, but theirs was a dead line and they were not growing any younger. Even if Prudence did find it within herself to speak to them again, it had been such a long time, it felt as though such a rift could never be patched enough to make an attempt worthwhile.

But estranged people could form a friendship. Derwa and Muriel had never met before Derwa had rushed across to Pateley Bridge, and now look at them. They no longer lived in the same house, but they had both moved to the same village, and from accounts Rosen had passed on when she had been in a better mood, were thriving there. Could it work for a mother and daughter then? And there was a grandson she had never met. But all that took energy and Prudence didn't know if she had any left.

Prudence picked up her basket and said her goodbyes to the people buried in the churchyard. Those were the lucky ones. Some people only had memories sealed in stone in the churchyard. Their bones rested in other plots somewhere, in some cases who knew where. Place and cause of death unknown. All these mothers who may never know what happened to the child. Mothers like Prudence. Other mothers knew where their children were, but also that they would never see them again. Just think on poor Ewat who would more than likely never see her mother again. Or the sisters, Ewat and Agnes, separated across the ocean. That was perhaps too far a distance to bridge.

Bridging distances. Prudence thought back to Beggar's Bridge and smiled, thinking of that stone pack horse bridge in the valley bottom. How many times had she crossed it? Heard the stories of the separated lovers and how they had come back to one another with time. She'd run around that wishing stone again, make a wish and see what would come of it.

Historical Note

This is a work of historical fiction. Although I try to keep within the facts of the era, there will be a great many errors, all my own. A number of minor characters who appear in the book did actually exist, however they appear as highly fictionalised versions of reality.

I have a blog where I am gradually working through the historical and folkloric aspects that appear in the series. For the curious, more information is to be found here: https://yorkshiresaga.wordpress.com/

However, for immediacy, here are a few historical notes on the book:

There never was a farm called Strait Farm at Ainthorpe.

The song Curnow sings at the start of the story is a verse from the Cornish folk song, *Bre Gammbronn'* (Camborne Hill).

In Pateley Bridge Derwa walks past St Mary's Church. Today this is St Cuthbert's, however, on an 1850 map of the area it is marked down as St Mary's.

Joseph Warburton was the doctor-surgeon at Pateley Bridge at that time.

Today there is part of the village of Runswick at the top of the cliffs, but at the time the Longbottoms, the settlement was only at the bottom. Nagar was a name used for the locals of the bay. Stories do tell that the original village was washed away in the 1600s during a funeral, the result being that only the home of the dead man remained when the sea had done its work. The Yorkshire coastline is a crumbling one with the sea ever reclaiming land as the cliffs break down. Some villages such as Robin Hood's Bay have rather ugly concrete, but necessary sea defences up, for if they were not there the village would have long disappeared. As these sea defences rust and crumble and the question of what next comes up, the dilemma is whether we continue to protect against the sea, or accept the impermanence of things and the changeability of nature. Which is an easy thing to be philosophical about when your home is not under threat.

At Saltersgate Inn, now demolished, there was said to be a body buried under the fireplace. A customs and excise man, chasing unpaid salt taxes, got his head knocked in with a rock when trying to apprehend fishermen secretly salting their fish at the inn (a remote place), and was put to rest under the fire. As far as I am aware there are no legends of bodies being disposed of at the fireplace at the Red Lion on Blakey Ridge, but it's a good idea for a story and for this fiction, it made a good transplant.

Daniel Iredale is buried at the Rosedale Priory chapel church in the village of Rosedale Abbey. Today there is a church, but this was not built until the end of the 1830s in response to the population boom in the area thanks to ironstone mining. Before then the locals had used the chapel building from the dissolved priory for their religious needs.